Fantastic Defenders

ANTHOLOGIES FROM TANNHAUSER PRESS

Fantastic Defenders
The Forever Inn *
Silence of the Apoc
Whispers of the Apoc
The Witness Paradox

* *forthcoming*

WORLDS ENOUGH

Fantastic Defenders

EDITED BY

DONNA ROYSTON & DAVID KEENER

Tannhauser Press

Worlds Enough: Fantastic Defenders

v1.0hc

First Trade Paperback Printing: May 2017
First Hardcover Printing: March 2021

Published by Tannhauser Press
www.tannhauserpress.com
Fredericksburg, VA 22407

ISBN: 978-1-945994-40-1

Design, Layout & Packaging by Worlds Enough LLC
Cover Design by Don Anderson
Copyediting by Donna Royston

For the men and women of the United States armed services…defenders one and all.

Courage is found in unlikely places.

— J. R. R. Tolkien

CONTENTS

INTRODUCTION

ONE PLACE to begin, in talking about fantastic defenders, is the Japanese folk tale "Momotaro": a childless old woman finds a beautiful peach floating down a stream and she takes it home to her husband; the peach suddenly splits open and a miraculous baby boy is inside. When the boy has grown to fifteen years old, he hears of the people of northeast Japan being terrorized by demons who arrive by sea to pillage, kidnap, and murder. Momotaro determines that he will be their defender and fight the demons.

Or, if you prefer, look at Beowulf: the young man hears of a land being tormented by the man-eating monster Grendel and he sails from his home in Geatland to offer himself as defender to King Hrothgar.

In these two exemplar stories, we can discern the nature of the defender, who:

- is compassionate and feels intensely the distress of others;

- may defend an individual, but frequently is defending an entire people; and
- possesses an extraordinary firmness of will and clarity of purpose, and thus does not waver or give up—he is the enemy of despair.

As for the "fantastic" element, the defender may not have any special magical or supernatural powers—and still have to oppose supernatural creatures. Momotaro may be a gift from heaven to a deserving couple, but no special powers are given to him. Beowulf relies on his courage and his great physical strength.

Another example: Gandalf has magical powers—he is a wizard and also possesses one of the rings of power. Yet his actions with the greatest impact, for all his ability to bring down bolts of lightning on foes, are in discernment and hope. He counsels and persuades Theoden to resist and fight rather than surrender to hopelessness; he rallies scattered forces to return and fight; dread flees from his presence because his courage and unwavering commitment heartens people.

For a more (perhaps) unexpected example, we will direct your attention to Clarence the angel in *It's a Wonderful Life*. Clarence—in spite of his cherubic demeanor, tendency to giggle, and dithering over ordering a flaming rum punch or mulled wine "heavy on the cinnamon and light on the cloves"—proves to be a determined, indeed, a steely and almost cruel defender against an existential foe, despair. He allows George Bailey to see an alternate future in which he never existed: a brother dead in childhood; his mother old, embittered, poor; his uncle in an insane asylum; and most painfully, his never-wife Mary alone, childless, not recognizing him. This is tough love at the highest setting.

It's rather fun to put Clarence in the company of Gandalf, Beowulf, and Momotaro. But something even more unusual is under the surface of *It's a Wonderful Life*. In the process of saving George, Clarence doesn't just keep him from jumping off a bridge on Christmas Eve. He enables a revelation: it turns out that *George* is the defender of the town of Bedford Falls, and has been ever since he took over the family building and loan after the death of his father.

As the alternate-reality scenario later makes explicit, the fate of Bedford Falls hangs in the balance between the predator, Mr. Potter, and the defender, George Bailey. An unnoticed struggle is taking place in the day-to-day business of a bank and a building and loan, each shaped by the opposite purposes of the two men who own those institutions. And George wins the struggle. In daily increments, over years, George Bailey did not get rich and Bedford Falls moved away from the potential reality of Pottersville.

Readers may think we have stretched the definition of a fantastic defender too far by including George Bailey. Reject it if you dare. But look once more at Momotaro. He exists in a world where heaven can reward a childless couple with a son delivered via peach, and he defends a people from demons with the help of a few animal companions but no supernatural powers. George Bailey exists in our world, mostly, and defends his town against the man who sees people as cattle, and in one day of need he receives some heavenly counsel. There is not a fundamental difference here.

The real distinction between the two stories is in the nature of the monster and the hero's realization of his calling of defender. Momotaro knows what he's set out to do. George only knows what he articulated in his indignant speech to Mr. Potter (prompted by Potter's reference to the building and loan's borrowers as "a discontented, lazy rabble"). He runs his business, he makes loans, he celebrates the new houses of his friends. But his life is a disappointment to him. Distracted by his longing for the adventurous life he never achieved, he misses the big picture of his purpose in family and community, and is largely unconscious of his role as a defender. This makes him something less than heroic, and all the more interesting as a person, but without doubt he is still a defender.

So, step into the circle, George Bailey. Shake hands with Beowulf, but do be mindful of his powerful grip. I've enjoyed looking near and far for these defenders and, among the wizards, sorcerers, warriors, and questing youths, finding a guy in a business suit with a some petals from his daughter's flower tucked into his watch pocket.

One last thought. Why do we love stories of fantastic defenders? Here is a possible answer, first provided by G. K. Chesterton: "Fairy tales, then, are not responsible for producing in children fear, or any of the shapes of fear; fairy tales do not give the child the idea of the evil or the ugly; that is in the child already, because it is in the world already," he wrote. "The baby has known the dragon intimately ever since he had an imagination. What the fairy tale provides for him is a St. George to kill the dragon."

This idea was paraphrased more succinctly by Neil Gaiman as "Fairy tales are more than true: not because they tell us that dragons exist, but because they tell us that dragons can be beaten."

Chesterton and Gaiman are speaking not of fairy tales such as "Clever Gretel," but stories about fantastic defenders. These characters are the ones who see rapacious and violent enemies and refuse to flee, will not lay low. They run *toward* the terrors. We admire them and take heart from their courage. And when their stories are well told, we are entertained and thrilled; and then we treasure them and place them in the canon of undying literature.

DONNA ROYSTON
DAVID KEENER

THE IRON GARDEN

JEFF PATTERSON

0

This is zero. An unbroken loop signifying absence. A perfect ovum of non-being, unknowable and unobservable. Indeed, this mere act of identifying it is grievous sacrilege.

It is said the light of Ouranos touches all lost souls and forgotten localities. I can tell you from experience this was not always true. There were places vexed into a darkness no candle could vanquish, and souls so acclimated to the shadows that solace was inconceivable. I know. I was one of them. I envied zero, longed to be nothing, sought to feel my wings fall to ash. I was denied my goals, but granted something more: an epiphany.

Zero is never really zero. All sequences hatch from this nothingness, surging forward through the emptiness, inexorably turning unreckoned expanses into immensities of causality and consequence. Worlds are born. Prayers are sung. Blood is spilled. Worlds die. Gaze upon this vastness, forever denied the peace of oblivion, and weep. I know I did.

This sequence bursts from zero, and rides the light to a place called the City of Blasphemers. Its arrival perturbs the nature of things with discords far too small to notice.

At least to most eyes.

1

THERE was omen dust everywhere.

When Eigenea Mauer had incinerated the mad warlock Chornus, she'd taken pity on his ashes, and, in a rare act of sympathy, chosen to domesticate them. Now, as they swirled frantically across the parlor, she regretted that decision.

Dry rivulets flowed along the baseboards. Dark twists spun in the air like a cloud of starlings beneath the black lacquered arches. A rough-sketched whorl marked the center of the ceiling. Miniature whirlwinds writhed around the legs of her burgundy furniture.

Eigenea set down her tea cup and leaned over, knees creaking. "Better not soil my upholstery," she warned.

The ashes settled down. Eigenea took small pride that she could still calm them. The warlock's remains had proven useful as a warning system several times, but if they kept escaping from their urn she'd have to go down to the Tormentorium and have a chat with his soul. Still, they'd not been this agitated in quite a while. Something was clearly wrong.

She heard Aughan's lumbering footfalls near the front of the manor, heading to collect whatever dispatches had been left overnight. Ill tidings, no doubt. The city could at least let her wake up properly before dropping its problems in her lap.

She looked at the scrying glass hung between the sconces on the side wall. It showed the hawk nest on the western ledge of the steeple at the Jannanite monastery. She smiled as the mother bird dropped gobs of bloody meat to her rapidly growing young. This morning was to have been spent drinking tea and watching her favorite birds.

"Not today, my loves."

She tapped thumb to middle finger three times, and the glass showed views from crystalline occuli hidden throughout the besieged city of Orphicca. She waved through images of the main streets, where people somberly went about their morning business. Whatever was wrong, the populace was unaware. That ruled out another attack. At least she *hoped* it did. She did note a number of the City Guard's Elite on patrol. That was unusual. She spied on the six gates of the city, each guarded by angels, resplendent in blue and gold honorary City Guard robes with armored breastplates. But there were Elite on duty here as well.

She summoned the view from the northern wall, looking out at the Bahl-Maqrea siege encampment three miles away. It resembled a small settlement, complete with brick barracks. Magnifying the image, she saw troops undergoing inspection. They were not clad in their gray-green armor, and no other battle preparations were apparent.

Another wave, and the glass showed the Citadel. Eigenea noted the urgency of the people moving in and out of the building. Most were clerical, but a few were from the Elite.

Aughan's distant growl echoed into the room, that throaty thunder he emitted when scaring the foraging vermin from the yard.

It was then that she noticed the aroma.

The glass also communicated those smells she was attuned to, and most prominent was the unmistakable scent of the Gloss. The pungent essence was almost a musk, haunting the breeze just as the Gloss haunted Orphicca. Usually no more than a faint outgassing of contentment, this morning it downright reeked. Something had it aroused.

What she wouldn't do for some actual information.

For a moment, she thought of Sebastyn.

At the snap of her fingers the glass became a mirror again. Her scowling reflection emphasized the small sags beneath her cheeks and chin. She raked fingers up the wide streak of silver in her hair. With the other hand she tapped the mirror.

"A polite glass would be less accurate this early in the morning."

The image softened a bit, to the point where she could almost be mistaken for a younger woman.

The clock chimed seven bells. Where was Aughan with those dispatches? She listened, but could not hear him.

She looked down at the omen dust, still shifting across the floorboards. "Best be in your urn when I get back."

Stepping into the wide hallway, she saw the front entrance was open. Aughan stood outside, back to the door, hunched in a defensive position, affording Eigenea a view of his gray-furred buttocks.

"And good morning to *you*," she said drolly.

The silverback looked over his shoulder, his thick brow arched into his most formidable expression.

"Apologies, madam," he said in that impossibly deep voice Eigenea could feel in her clavicles, "but this soldier insists on seeing you and will *not* leave."

"What soldier?"

The ape stood aside. Eigenea looked down the path to the wrought-iron gate set into the black stone wall. Through the scrollwork she saw a young woman in a City Guard uniform. Officer's epaulets jutted from her shoulders. The blue feather arcing from left side of her cap marked her as an Elite.

Eigenea stepped past Aughan and looked up the facade of the manor. Above the second-level ledge, a pair of beaked gargoyles sat crouched, wings tucked, unperturbed by the soldier's presence.

"Well," she said softly, "*they* don't think she's a threat."

The silverback grunted. "They also let birds shit on them."

Eigenea smiled, then looked back to the gate. The guard's face was hidden by the slanting shadow cast by the brim of her cap.

"I'll handle this," she said.

"Madam," whispered Aughan, "do you smell the Gloss?"

"Yes. You'd best put some pants on. I suspect we're traveling today."

Aughan gave the soldier a defiant look, then turned, dropped to all fours, and went inside. Eigenea stepped into the doorway, tapping her left thumb to her hip. The gate swung open.

As the woman stepped through, she looked up at the facade, giving Eigenea a view of her face. She was olive-skinned, possibly Ynocean, with thin lips. Ringlets of dark orange hair hung from beneath her cap on either side of her face. Most unexpectedly, her eyes were the black of the Lastborn, those still ensconced in their mothers' wombs when the Gloss descended.

Ghosts of old, thought Eigenea, *this girl is sixteen and already an officer of the Elite.* All the Lastborn had matured far faster than expected, but the feat was no less impressive.

The soldier stopped short of the doorway, hand resting on the hilt of the saber slung from her belt.

"You've already interrupted my morning tea," Eigenea said in her best crone voice. "Let's have a look at you."

The soldier's face took on an apologetic expression. "I have been made aware, Archmage Mauer, that you keep a piss-pot, full to capacity, just inside the entrance, and that you are…quick to employ it when unexpected visitors disturb you."

Eigenea bristled at the honorarium. "What makes you think you are unexpected?"

The soldier's black eyes narrowed in puzzlement. "You were told of my visit?"

"No, but the Elite are on patrol, and there's Gloss stink everywhere. It was inevitable the mayor would fetch me."

The woman removed her cap, revealing orange hair pulled taut against her scalp. "Our blessed city has—"

Eigenea held up a hand. "First of all, Orphicca is not *blessed.* If it was we could launch weapons beyond the walls without them turning to dust. Our city is *forsaken*. Secondly, we should not speak out here. The breeze has a way of listening in." She stepped into the hallway and gestured for the soldier to enter. "What is your name?"

"Officer Karrid, Second Elite Battalion."

"Your accent is Ynochean."

Karrid stepped into the hallway. "My mother is Ynochean. My father is Tauran."

Eigenea cocked an eyebrow as she shut the door. "Those cities were at war when you were born. *That* must have been a scandal."

"Not nearly as much as them relocating here."

"Ah. Blasphemers, were they?"

"They thought of themselves as such. Is that the fabled piss-pot?"

She gestured to the squat wooden container perched atop a block of stone.

"Despite what you've heard, I've only used it three times," Eigenea said. "The first was when an Acromancer named Jayvist appeared on my stoop engulfed in purple curse-flame no water could extinguish. A ladleful from the pot left the flame flopping across this floor like a dying fish."

Eigenea led Karrid to the consultation room off the hallway. Two plush gray chairs faced each other with a small table between them. The walls were covered with framed maps and portraits of long-dead members of the Mauer clan.

"The second," Eigenea said, gesturing for Karrid to sit, "was when the mayor came to visit. He wore a hat so offensive that I snatched it from his head and dropped it into the pot, pushing it down with a walking stick to ensure every fiber was ruinously saturated."

Karrid smiled slightly. "His version is more…colorful."

"You *know* the mayor," Eigenea said, a statement more than a question.

"Yes, he dispatched me here."

Eigenea leaned back in her chair at that, scrutinizing the soldier. "The mayor has never made a decision in his life that didn't bear hidden significance," she said. "I'm sure he told you I'm not allowed out of the manor except to tend to the city's many sorcerous discords. But today he sends one of his Elite. Now, why would that be?"

"I am the lead officer in the investigation."

"What investigation?"

"An Unction has occurred."

The word hit Eigenea like a lightning strike.

"That's impossible," she said, standing. "It's only been four years. When did this happen?"

"During the night. In the Iquez district, near the Western Wall. The victim was…*is*… a City Guard."

"Damn." Almost reflexively, she looked up at the portrait of her great-great-grandfather. "Who knows about this?"

"The mayor, his staff, a small number of the Elite, and now you. It happened near the mill silos. The area is sealed. We've told nearby residents there's been an aqueduct accident."

Aughan appeared in the doorway, now wearing white pants and vest. He carried her field kit bag over one shoulder.

"We'll need the spindles out of storage as well," she said.

Aughan squinted at Karrid, then back at Eigenea. "What has happened?"

"Apparently the Shadowsaint has come back early."

2

"AND WHATEVER YOU DO," the mayor had said, "don't make her angry."

Karrid's briefing on the Mauer woman had contained other salient facts: She was a top-rated elementalist, specializing in lightning, waterworks, and, most notoriously, wind. She practiced other sorcerous disciplines through artifacts accumulated by her family. For the last four years she'd been under house restriction due to her actions at Rampart Square. The mayor clearly held great affection for the Archmage, based, Karrid deduced, on a common history of sacrifice, but he nonetheless portrayed her as a disruptive influence. His closing remark replayed in Karrid's mind now.

Decoding the Archmage's expression when she heard the word *Unction* was difficult. It could be interpreted as anger, fear, and remorse in equal measure, though who knew what complications brewed in the old woman's mind.

The ape, on the other hand, was easy to read. He was clearly protective of her. When Eigenea mentioned the spindles, the beast glowered at Karrid briefly, as if damning her for bringing such news to the manor. When the word *Shadowsaint* was uttered, his left hand reflexively gripped his right bicep.

Karrid had to tread carefully here. The ape was as personally involved in events regarding the Shadowsaint as Eigenea. So were the missing angel and the man imprisoned at the monastery. She was sworn to uphold the tenets of the Elite.

Consorting with an angry old sorceress and her retinue was not part of her training.

Eigenea hurried past the ape and down the hallway. The beast turned to Karrid with a mild scowl and commanded, “Stay here,” before following.

Karrid intended to. The mayor had warned her about wandering around the Mauer estate unescorted.

She looked up at the portrait Eigenea had glanced at. The largest on the wall, it showed a stern-expressioned white-haired man. The plaque embedded at the bottom of the frame read *Voskus Mauer, First Archmage.* Karrid knew of his exploits, of how he reportedly spoke to the city itself. Since his time, the Mauer line had defended Orphicca.

Beside the portrait hung a framed parchment map, dated nine hundred years ago, showing the peninsula that Orphicca dominated, jutting like a scimitar blade from the southern coastland. The calligraphy of the city’s name spoke to its importance. The fine blue lines representing the original walls formed a shape like a tilted shield. The city looked as if it had been stamped onto the land with fierce intent, and in a way, it was. Established far from the feuding kingdoms to the north, Orphicca was designed to be self-sufficient, prosperous, and beholden to none, a feat it had accomplished and maintained. At least, for a time.

She became aware of faint moans wafting from the floorboards, and stepped around the room to find their source. They were clearest near the door. She leaned into the hallway, looking towards the front entrance. They were not coming from outside. Turning to look down the hallway, she found the ape’s face nose to nose with hers.

"I am to ask," he said in a low rumble, "if you brought a conveyance."

"Yes," she replied, with all the respect she could muster. "It should accommodate both of you and your gear."

The ape grunted and turned away.

"Wait," sputtered Karrid. "What is that sound I hear?"

The ape raised his brow and tilted his head. "Those are the souls in the Tormentorium."

Karrid raised a hand to her throat. "Do they always sound like that?"

"I suppose they do. I barely notice anymore. It is impressive that you can hear them. Most among the living have little sensitivity to the damned."

"That's because she's a Lastborn." Eigenea appeared, now wearing a short, pale coat, and carrying another shoulder pack and a small satchel. "They tend to see and hear things they shouldn't."

Karrid watched Eigenea exit the manor, uncertain if the comment was meant as a slight.

The carriage was one of the Elite's largest, designed to accommodate several angels with their ungainly wings. Or, if needed, an ape.

The coach driver, garbed in an Elite longcoat, eyed the group as they emerged from the gate. The team of four black horses stood statue-still as Eigenea and the ape climbed in, the carriage's suspension barely sagging under their weight. As Karrid took the opposite seat, the ape stretched his legs out, pursing his lips in approval at the spaciousness.

The road from the gate wound through a glade of thick trees separating the manor from the city proper. The woods appeared far deeper than they could possibly be. In the obscured distances she thought she saw scurrying movement, and was about to dismiss it as a play of light when she remembered the arcane nature of this place.

Eigenea placed the satchel on the carriage floor. It contained a box inlaid with mother-of-pearl markings. She hefted it to her lap and opened it. It was filled with a gray powder.

"What is that?" Karrid asked.

"Soil blessed by a long-dead god. Makes an excellent desiccant."

Eigenea rummaged through the soil and pulled out a small rodent skull, followed by something wrapped in oilskin. She placed these on the seat, and extracted the last item: a small dagger, little more than a letter-opener, with a mirrored blade Karrid could see was exceedingly sharp.

"You seem prepared," she said.

"We knew the Shadowsaint would be back," Eigenea replied. "We've been preparing since our last encounter."

"But our preparations are far from finished," the ape added, looking out the window.

Karrid eyed the rodent skull. "What is that for?"

Eigenea picked it up. With the other hand she twisted her black and gray hair into a loose knot atop her head. She clipped the skull's small jaws to the base of the knot to keep it in place, winking at Karrid as she did.

The carriage emerged from the woods between two stone grain stores. Karrid had heard these hulking structures had fallen into disuse in the years before the Gloss. Now they stood without signs of neglect, though no hand tended to their upkeep. Karrid's life had been lived in a city under the Gloss's blessing. She wondered, once again, what it had been like when things occasionally fell apart.

As they turned onto an avenue, she saw Eigenea tuck the dagger into a small pouch on the side of her pack. It would be easy to consider the old woman a relic of the time before, but Karrid knew she was far too formidable for such unjust relegation.

"Who was the third?" she asked.

Eigenea looked up. "The third what?"

"Victim of your piss-pot."

"My ex-husband."

The answer surprised her. "I was unaware..."

"That I had an ex-husband? Did the mayor tell you I was an ancient curmudgeonly recluse?"

Karrid felt heat in her cheeks.

Eigenea leaned forward. "I've had four, who are easily segregated into the categories of 'the two the sea took from me,' and 'the two I got rid of.' The one who skulked from the manor drenched in warm, fragrant urine was of the latter group."

The ape grunted again. "It was an improvement to his scent."

Karrid smiled. "And what did he do to deserve such a fate?"

Eigenea smiled back. "He interrupted my morning tea."

The wide barricade sequestered the silos from the store-lined street. Several utility wagons sat on either side of the gate, giving weight to the story of the aqueduct collapse.

Karrid showed her badge of office to the City Guard. In moments, the carriage was allowed entrance.

Between two monolithic storehouses, six rows of silos stood like metal pillars, casting hard shadows across the packed dirt. The Elite troops on duty came to attention when Karrid climbed from the carriage, though she noted several of the older ones gave her what she had come to call *the look*, that hint of resentment at her presence. She didn't take it personally. The citizens of Orphicca had been granted unprecedented gifts from the Gloss, but had also been deprived of much. Any Lastborn was a reminder of that.

Eigenea and the ape exited the carriage with their baggage. Karrid noticed the Archmage scrutinizing some of the Elite. The ape turned and looked into the shadowed recesses of the silos.

"Do you smell it?" asked Eigenea.

The ape nodded, reaching for his bicep. "I had hoped never to smell it again."

Eigenea looked at Karrid. "Lead the way, officer."

She summoned two other Elite to escort them. They made their way down the third row. The morning wind made the top of the silos hum, reminding Karrid of the moans echoing through Eigenea's manor.

Another Elite stood guard beside the seventh silo on the left. Karrid paused before rounding the curved wall of the structure into a bright swath of sunlight slanting across the dirt.

Hanging impossibly in the air above that swath was the Unction.

Karrid heard reactions from both Eigenea and the ape. His was an explosive exhalation. Hers was a low hiss.

It looked as if someone had haphazardly draped and wrapped pink and red yarn around a sphere four meters wide, then somehow managed to remove the sphere. It was only upon closer inspection that the strands were identifiable as sinew and cartilage. In defiance of nature itself, this bubble of tangled, unmade flesh floated several inches off the ground. A few yards away lay a lantern on its side.

Eigenea stepped to the edge of the sphere. With a gentleness Karrid could see came from experience, she delicately pinched one of the strands between finger and thumb.

"Is there a pulse?" asked the ape.

Eigenea nodded gravely.

A shiver ran through Karrid.

Eigenea walked slowly around the form, eyes darting from point to point. She stopped, and leaned in towards a puckered knot of flesh bulging where several of the strands converged. Karrid watched the Archmage touch the knot. A crease in the skin opened, revealing an eyeball. It lolled to one side, pupil contracting.

"Who is this?" Eigenea asked.

"His name is Fenson," Karrid said, mouth dry around the words.

Eigenea closed her eyes. "I know him. A veteran of the last siege. Had a son who left Orphicca before the Gloss came." She released the knot, and the eye closed. Her hand made a gesture. "Sleep, now," she whispered.

Eigenea inspected all sides of the Unction, even dropping to hands and knees to examine the gap beneath it. Then, to Karrid's surprise, she slipped her hand between threads, spreading her fingers wide inside.

"What are you doing?" Karrid asked.

Eigenea withdrew her hand and made a fist. "Taking its temperature. The air is icy cold in there."

Karrid looked at the red nightmarish shape. "I have read the accounts of other Unctions. Now, seeing this, I don't understand how it's possible. Is this sorcery?"

Eigenea rubbed her hands together. "A great number of things are possible since the Gloss descended. The Shadowsaint isn't like any other manner of creature. Have you ever seen light pass through a prism?"

"Yes, to make a spectrum."

"This is similar. A prism refracts light into its component colors. The Shadowsaint does the same to bodies, inverting them into these forms. Fenson is still whole, just unraveled."

Eigenea withdrew a folded blue blanket from her pack, spreading it across the ground so the full shadow of sphere fell within the square of fabric.

"I take it he was on foot," Eigenea said, pointing to the fallen lantern.

"Yes, on standard patrol."

"Which direction did he come from?"

Karrid pointed back towards the barricade.

Eigenea dragged the blanket towards the silo. Where the strands had cast their shadow, the fabric was marked with dark lines. Eigenea examined the diagram, then refolded it.

"I am ready, madam," said the ape.

Eigenea nodded. The ape walked around the Unction, pouring a thin line of white powder from a pouch. When he'd made an unbroken circle, Eigenea reached above her, as if grabbing something from the air. Stepping to the edge of the circle, she said, "You might want to cover your ears."

Thin, jagged lightning snapped from her fingertips. The entire circle flashed with a crack that reverberated between the silos. A wreath of gray smoke rose and expanded.

"What was that?" Karrid asked, waving the foul smoke from her face.

"Ground *eidolacra* bones. Purportedly good at illuminating old presences."

"Madam," said the ape, pointing.

Karrid turned, and for a moment thought the flash had affected her eyes. There was a shape before her, like the afterimage of bright flame. The white-hot absence stood taller than her, wavering in the shadows.

The other three Elite stepped back. She felt the ape's hands on her shoulders gently moving her aside.

"It's not as big as it was last time," Eigenea said.

The ape walked behind it. "And it still appears to be missing its tail."

Karrid thought that sounded like pride in the beast's voice.

"Is that the Shadowsaint?" she asked.

"Just the imprint it made when it performed the Unction. This impression is like water filling a footprint."

Karrid took another step back to make sense of the shape. It had the rough outline of an upright form, flaring away at the bottom into monstrous spider legs. The edges of this strange anti-silhouette bristled with thin filaments.

Eigenea and the ape donned silver goggles with deep green lenses. They drew closer to the shape and examined it, poking it with tools and speaking in whispers.

Looking back at the Unction, another shiver struck Karrid as she remembered Fenson was still alive in this unnatural manner. She turned towards the glowing shape again, and behind it, the rows of silos receding back towards the gate.

"If the Shadowsaint was there when the Unction occurred," she said, looking back to the sphere, and the lantern on the ground, "how did Fenson not see it?"

Eigenea did not look up from her work. "It conceals itself."

"But if he came from that direction, and ended up here…"

Eigenea turned and raised her goggles. "Then he walked right through the Shadowsaint. That's what an Unction is. The victim passes through, like light through a prism."

Karrid imagined Fenson's meat splayed and twisted into the air. Nausea rose, but she closed her eyes and tamped it down with effort. When she opened them, Eigenea was standing before her.

"Did the mayor mention the name Patheus?"

"The missing angel?" Karrid asked.

Eigenea squinted. "Missing?"

"The Guard has been looking for him all morning."

"Where have they looked?" asked Eigenea.

"Taverns, mostly."

Eigenea gave a sad smile. "He won't be in a tavern. We have to find him. He needs to know about this."

The ape approached, holding a pair of wooden spindles a foot long and half that in diameter. Blunt studs protruded from the sides, and black tapered handles sprouted from each end. He handed one to Eigenea, and they both approached the Unction.

"If anyone has prayers for this soldier," said Eigenea, "say them now."

One of the Elite bowed his head. The other two looked away.

"Certainly."

"Thank you. I need to talk to the mayor."

3

IT HAD BEEN AWHILE since Eigenea had seen Defiance Avenue.

She looked out the carriage window at the line of humble riverstone dwellings of the East End. The sight comforted her for a few moments. She used to love walking here, back when the city was old. The mystique of the past captivated her: the misalignments of stone and beam, the cracks in the pavement, the faint warp of window glass.

Slate roofs gave way to the tiled parapets of Three Scholars Academy. Eigenea watched the clusters of small white simians making their way across the rooftop.

"There're so many of them," Karrid said.

"They're prodigious breeders, much like the population of this city used to be. At least if they get bored, they can leave."

The carriage passed beneath a raised aqueduct. Beyond it lay a small park, dominated by a black stone obelisk. Eigenea pointed to it.

"Do you know what that is?"

"The original boundary of the city, before it expanded across the peninsula."

"There's an inscription on the base, in the old language. 'As in Ouranos, so in Orphicca.' It was meant as a joke. Just as the grace of all the world's pantheons purported to shine on the world, so would this city light the way of all empires."

"I don't see the joke."

"Most empires claim singular favor of the gods. Orphicca was founded to be free from the artifice of scripture and prophecy. I'm sure your parents taught you that."

"They said old traditions were shackles."

"Exactly. Evoking the pantheons to commemorate the spread of the city was an insult to those traditions. Orphicca did not grow because of animal sacrifice and imperial edict, but because everything it needed lay within its walls. Farms, gardens, canals, all our needs provided for. That was something the city was proud of. Now, the Gloss has *assured* we survive, and that pride is but a memory."

"It could be argued," Karrid said, "that Orphicca is now the city of peace and plenty it set out to be."

Eigenea pointed to the side street they passed. "Look down there. The furnaces of Kiln Row sit cold and silent, for there is no need for new bricks. That textile mill stands dormant. The paint on that mural of the Founders hasn't required touch-up. There hasn't been a need for a healer in years."

"Nobody dies."

"And neither is anyone born."

"No one is in want."

Eigenea waved a hand. "Yes, yes. I know the argument. Old fruit doesn't rot. Bird shit evaporates from statues. Fallen leaves dissolve within a day. Suffer a wound, it heals by morning. We could all piss in the streets and they'd still be impeccably clean. We need not suffer the degradations of entropy, until we dare pass through the gates. Meanwhile, the rest of the world is dying a slow death."

"You seem...angry at the Gloss."

"I'm an Archmage. Anything outside my influence angers me. Since the Gloss, time has become a solid in which this city, and everyone in it, is suspended. It's an apocalypse of perfection. Look at those listless faces out there, so dead inside. Devoid of frailty and doubt, nobody considers the possibility that their life could be better. Such malaise was once reserved for the galleries and taverns of Aesthete Row. A decade and a half of perpetual sterility spread that feeling. Do you know there are people who slit their throats regularly, just to feel something?"

Karrid's hand went to her collar. The movement reminded Eigenea of a question she'd meant to ask.

"I noticed some of the Elite wearing 'S' pins on their lapels. I wasn't aware you allowed Sebastyn supporters within the ranks."

"It would cause an uproar not to."

"We could use a good uproar. Regardless, best to keep them away from the investigation."

Karrid tipped her head. "Why?"

"The Jannanites may have him well-secured at the monastery, but Sebastyn has ways of learning things. He's known as a pyromancer, but his real talent is communication. I can talk to the wind; he can talk to *anything*, and draw information from it. His supporters become his eyes. He doesn't have a following. It's a cult."

They passed through the gilded arch in the wall ringing the mayor's Citadel and the Magistrate House. The two splendid structures faced each other, their columned facades veined with deep green. As Eigenea stepped from the carriage, she immediately noticed the ward spells Voskus had cast on these buildings so many years ago. One Mauer could always sense the work of another.

They stood on either side of the sphere. Eigenea gently pinched some strands together and pulled them towards her, hooking them to a stud. She nodded to the ape, who replicated the action on the other side. A faint blue glow spread across the Unction, hissing as it rippled down the strands. When it ended the spherical shape began to deform, as if slowly deflating. Cold air flowed from the interior.

Eigenea and the ape turned their spindles in two-handed motion, like children pulling in kites, winding in the tangled strands as they slackened. Karrid watched the precision with which they performed their task, slowly moving around the form as they reeled it in, reducing its size with each turn.

It took nearly half an hour. When they finished, Eigenea handed her spindle to the ape, who wound up the last lengths of filament. Eigenea bound them with a thick leather strap before placing them in an unmarked black box, not unlike a miniature coffin.

"There is so… little of him," Karrid said.

"Most of the body is empty space," Eigenea replied. "Reduced to this state it becomes quite portable. Now, you are sure this is the first?"

Karrid nodded. "The mayor had the Elite combing the city as soon as this was reported. No others were found."

Eigenea looked to the space where the Unction had hung. "That means there will be three more."

"Can we be certain?" asked the ape. "If the Shadowsaint is early, can we depend upon the pattern playing out as before?"

"Let's hope so. If not, our preparations will be useless." She handed the box to the ape, and looked at Karrid. "This needs to be secured. I have a tabernacle at the manor that will keep it asleep. Can your guards return Aughan there?"

The scent of Gloss had always been strongest here in the heart of Orphicca, but today it was almost overwhelming.

Angel shadows slid across the ground.

Eigenea looked up to see a formation of three flying guard patrols around the city's center, blue and gold robes snapping with each wing beat.

Four Elite approached to escort them to the mayor. Eigenea noted none of them wore an 'S.' As she climbed the steps, she looked at the massive doors of the Citadel. For a moment, her mind went back to the last time she passed through them, to answer for the death of a citizen.

"Let's get this over with," she muttered.

Piter Oustus had been elected mayor seven years before the Gloss. After it came, nobody else wanted the job.

Watching him study the report on his desk, Eigenea had to admit, again, that he was perfect for the role. He was Nazoan. A pirate by trade. His southern island breeding showed in his skin, the color of strong tea, and the many ropey braids pulled into a black horse's tail. He wore what looked like a woolen shirt, opened at the front, revealing both the ceremonial tattoos on his chest and the slight paunch of his belly. A dark blue scarf hung limply from his throat.

"This is fine," he said in his elegant accent as he signed the report and handed it to the bailiff. With that, the bevy of staff and clerics crowding the office filed out, leaving only one bored-looking adjutant sitting against the wall, notepad in hand.

The mayor stared at the place the report had been and said, "I appreciate your making the time to participate in this investigation. If you don't mind my asking" – here he looked at her with his ice-blue eyes – "how in the name of Ouranos could you have been so wrong?"

"I am barely in the door and already this is my fault. Nice to see things haven't changed."

"This is no time for flippancy!" he shouted, bringing the palm of his hand down on his desk with a meaty slap. "You've spent thirty years telling me sorcery actually matters in the workings of this city. Now the damned Shadowsaint shows up early and you couldn't tell it was coming?"

"If you didn't restrict me to the manor all day…"

"By Jannan's bones, Eigenea. You couldn't have send Aughan to this meeting? He's the less stubborn of the two of you."

"Enough!" shouted Karrid, standing. "I'm sworn to act with due respect to both of you, but as long as I am lead investigator in this case you two will set aside this posturing. It's obvious you still have great respect for each other, so stop bickering and focus on the situation at hand. And I call attention to the fact that I am the only one in this room with a saber."

The mayor opened his mouth, but said nothing.

"Now," Karrid continued in a more measured tone, "I believe what the honorable mayor is saying is that times of crisis necessitate imperfect fellowships."

Eigenea looked at the mayor. "Is she exercising diplomacy? She didn't learn that from you."

The mayor flashed a smug grin, and waved a hand dismissively. "I grant assignments based on arrogance and sheer volume, but she had too much skill to ignore."

"I was curious about that," Eigenea said, squinting at Karrid. "You have many more experienced officers among the constabulary. Why her?"

"Didn't she tell you? Last month she figured out Bahl-Maqrea scouts were sneaking over the wall near Jade Heights. Caught two in the act, and uncovered their plan to dig into the city. I've got most of the senior Guard working on that."

The mayor stood, and Eigenea saw his woolen shirt was actually a robe, which fell open as he rose. He wore nothing underneath.

"You couldn't be bothered to dress?"

"I've been up since the Guard woke me with news of the Unction," he said, tying his sash. "My staff and I have been discussing our available resources ever since."

"What resources?"

"Well, *you*, mostly. I've convinced them that you're our best chance at stopping this thing. The question is, can you do it?"

"It's just another monster. But I need two things."

The mayor looked out the window. "When I was on the sea I saw horrible things. Islands populated by ghouls. Dead cities where everyone had turned to beasts because of sorcery gone bad. When I came here I swore I'd never let that happen to Orphicca. A lot of good that oath did. First the Gloss, then the siege" – he looked at Eigenea – "but I'll be damned if I let this thing stalk my streets anymore. What do you need?"

"Patheus. I can't calculate where the Shadowsaint will manifest. He can."

"That angel's crazy, Eigenea."

"You'd be too if you had numbers running through your head all the time."

The mayor leaned on his desk. "You think I don't? I've spent every waking moment tallying the figures on this siege for two years now. If he's as good as you say we could use his help here. Find him if you can. The Elite have been searching for him all morning."

"So Karrid told…" Eigenea paused, realization falling into place. "Oh, you sent the Guard to look for him *before* summoning me. I was your *second* choice."

The mayor sighed. "I thought he could bring a quick end to this. He almost did last time."

"He's probably somewhere in the Tumble, which leads to my second requirement. I need to practice my craft *openly*. Without city oversight."

The mayor's eyebrows rose. "The magistrates will have my hide if they find out."

"You haven't briefed them?"

"Of course not. We've kept the Unction quiet. When the citizenry learn the Shadowsaint is back, they'll panic. When the magistrates find out, they'll demand I release Sebastyn. He has supporters among them."

"And your soldiery."

"I know." He fell back into his chair, looking exhausted. "We go back a long way, Eigenea. I've watched you outrage your allies until I was the only one left. I owe you a lot. You saved my daughter from the Mother-of-Silence. You've defended this city more times than I can count." He turned to the adjutant, busily scribbling. "Make a note that I'm lifting the restrictions on Archmage Mauer, on one condition."

Eigenea tilted her head. "What?"

"If you can't stop it, do what you can to conceal it."

"I'll try, but I'll wager Sebastyn already knows. You should have let me cast that pyro from the city after Rampart Square."

"I *couldn't.*"

"Why not? I made a *lot* of people disappear for you in the years after the Gloss. Treasonous mages who started uprisings. Cartels who sought to take over."

"And if I had ordered Sebastyn sent outside, I would have found myself in the same predicament soon after. You, as well."

"They could have *tried.* Watch your back around the magistrates."

The mayor's jaw jutted out slightly. "I always do." He glanced at the clock. "They'll be out of session soon. You should go. "

"You've left out one bit of information. Sieges against us have always been short affairs. Our assailants came because their lands were dying, and they thought razing Orphicca would help matters. They left when they realized the futility of trying to bring down our walls. So, why are the Bahl-Maqrea trying to dig into the city?"

The mayor pointed to Karrid. "Ask her. She interrogated the prisoners."

Eigenea looked at her. "Is that a fact? What did you learn?"

The young woman returned her gaze. "They don't want to destroy the city. They want to infiltrate it, take it over, cast everyone out, and dwell in immortal splendor."

Eigenea turned to the mayor. "And you didn't think to inform me of this?"

"The Guard can handle the Bahl-Maqrea. I need you to focus on the Shadowsaint."

"Ever think they might be related?"

"If they are, I'm sure you'll find out. I want Karrid to work with you."

"Of course, she's long past due for a good influence."

4

KARRID knew of the borough called the Tumble through City Guard reports of street fights and petty theft. It had been one of the seedier districts before the Gloss came. Now, it almost looked quaint. Ornate shop awnings lined the narrow street, and strings of lanterns criss-crossed between balconies. The sidewalks were busy, but not crowded. Karrid smelled something frying, reminding her she had not eaten since yesterday.

"Patheus can be…difficult to deal with," Eigenea said. "The sound of his voice can make you fall in love with him. If you let him touch you, he might commune with you."

Karrid raised an eyebrow.

Eigenea smiled. "Nothing so vulgar. He can mingle thoughts. Ride emotions to their source. Communicate ideas. It's his favorite way of conversing, but if you're not expecting it, it can be disorienting."

Karrid found the idea intriguing. "So how do we find him? Do you have a spell?" she asked.

"Spells are very literal things, they only work when given very specific criteria. I never use them when a tool will suffice."

Eigenea pulled a thin stick from her pack and lit the end with a spark from her finger. Blue smoke curled up and gathered into a small cloud above them.

"Every living thing leaves a trail of dead skin," she said. "Especially angels."

The smoke elongated into a serpentine tendril snaking its way deeper into the neighborhood. Eigenea set off behind it at a brisk pace. Karrid hurried to follow, noting that the only breeze present was blowing against the flow of the smoke.

They followed it for a quarter mile, occasionally pressing against a wall to make way for tired-looking tradesmen pushing wheelbarrows. The smoke led them across a courtyard into a network of alleys, the last of which ended in short stairway down to street level. Karrid could see foot traffic crossing the mouth of the passage.

"Don't go left don't go left," Eigenea muttered.

The smoke trail reached the bottom of the stairs, and promptly went left.

"What's down there?" Karrid asked.

"They used to call it the Sinner's Quarter," Eigenea said, taking the dagger from her pocket and slipping it up her sleeve. "I'm not very popular down there."

Karrid rested her hand on the hilt of her saber. "I suspect I'll be hearing that a lot."

The stone storefront was etched with an apothecary's symbol. The smoke reformed into a cloud above the oaken door, outside a small window with its curtain drawn.

Within, an older woman sat behind a counter, with white hair piled high on her head and a thin pipe hanging from her lips. Karrid assessed the shop's racks and display cases, all filled with small bottles. To the right of the counter was a door covered by a long blue curtain. Her eyes returned to the woman, who was scrutinizing Eigenea.

"What do you want, witch?" the woman said venomously.

"Good morning, Miss Rayl. I am here to collect Patheus."

"He's occupied."

"I'm sure he is. I am collecting him anyway."

The woman traced a finger in a lazy circle across the counter, and the curtain stirred. An *eidolacra* stepped through. Broad, muscular, hairless, with a flesh tone close to purple, it wore only loose white trousers tied with a sash. Hanging from the sash was a very large sword.

The woman turned to the creature, and Karrid caught a glint of light reflecting from her neck. It was a small silver "S" hanging from a thin chain. So, this woman had trapped a ghost within a fungal body, *and* was an adherent of Sebastyn. Perhaps a show of civil authority was necessary.

Karrid stepped in front of Eigenea and placed her hands on the counter. "This is official city business."

Miss Rayl exhaled smoke. "I don't care if Ouranos itself sent you, filthy Lastborn. You and that heretic are not getting in."

The *eidolacra* drew its sword. It had not cleared the sash before the tip of Karrid's saber was at its throat.

Eigenea let out a sigh as she stepped beneath the blade and, with surprising swiftness, pushed a finger down onto the back of Miss Rayl's hand. The woman's eyes bulged as her shoulders began to tremble. The pipe slipped from her slack lips to the counter.

The *eidolacra* dropped its sword.

"What did you do?" Karrid asked.

Eigenea ignored her as she stepped to the *eidolacra*, knife in hand. She tapped the flat of the blade against the thing's chest. "I bet she's had you bound in there for a while."

The *eidolacra's* mouth moved, but Karrid heard nothing.

Eigenea shifted grip and touched the blade's tip against the breastbone, gently twisting it as if prying something out. "I'll make a deal with you. I unlock you," she jerked a thumb towards the old woman, "then you keep her occupied while we find my friend."

The *eidolacra* nodded.

"Good," Eigenea said, continuing to work the blade. "I'm almost—"

Thick smudge-pot vapor poured from the *eidolacra's* mouth, rising to the ceiling in violent gray undulations.

"A feisty one," Eigenea said. "That will make this all the more enjoyable."

She pinched Miss Rayl's lips open. The vapor pulled itself into a rapidly spinning column and flowed into the mouth. The sight of it almost made Karrid choke.

The woman writhed, eyes rolling back, limbs flailing. A moment later she fell limp over the counter, wheezing heavily.

"What's happening?" asked Karrid.

"She's got an angry ghost running through her head, rummaging through every memory of pain, loss, and failure, and making her relive them."

Eigenea grabbed the woman's hair and pulled her head up to see her face. The woman tried to spit, but only drooled down her chin.

"Did you enjoy that?" Eigenea said.

"Your t-time is c-c-c-coming, witch," she sputtered.

Eigenea smiled. "I wasn't talking to you. I know Sebastyn's watching. I wanted to thank him for the diversion. It's the most fun I've had in months."

She released the woman's head and went through the curtain.

The second story was one room, rising up to a web of beams. Thick drapes kept out the morning light. The only illumination came from a pair of candelabras.

Between them was a tall table with a mattress atop it. Beside it stood a drably garbed woman, but Karrid could not make out what she was doing. It was then she noticed a figure on the table, one with white wings hanging loosely off the sides to the floor.

The figure's head turned and looked their way, its face a rictus of something that might be construed as pleasure.

A moment later she realized what act woman was performing.

"Soooo…this is a brothel," she said.

"No, it's an apothecary," Eigenea said, "one that specializes in more esoteric substances."

The woman looked up at them with an expression of exhaustion. "Are you my relief?" she asked. "I've been at it since sunrise."

Eigenea let out a small laugh. "Go, we'll take it from here. Be aware Miss Rayl is feeling poorly. She said take whatever you're owed out of the till."

The woman quickly descended the stairs. Karrid walked to the table and looked at the angel. He was, like all angels, beautiful, with long hair as black as a starless sky. But his face bore an insensate quality, as if deeply inebriated.

"Ghosts of old," Eigenea muttered. "Is it too much to ask that the men in my life wear pants in my presence?"

The angel was, indeed, quite naked, and quite aroused.

"What was she doing to him?" Karrid asked.

"Milking him of his divinity."

Eigenea pointed to a tray at the foot of the table. Upon it was a wooden rack holding a row of vials. Most of them glowed with faint silver radiance.

"They dilute his ejaculate with tonic, then sell it to anyone desperate enough to try leaving Orphicca. They claim drinking it will let one pass the city boundaries unharmed."

"Does it work?"

"For a time. Any solution of divinity will suffice, but the effects weaken the farther from the angel you get."

The angel looked at them.

"Eigenea, love, is that you?"

The voice was like a thousand heartbreaking ballads all sung at once to Karrid's ears. She wanted nothing more than to hug this angel and never let go.

Eigenea clamped her hand over the angel's mouth. "Moderate your tone, Patheus. There's a Lastborn present."

Karrid felt the elation fade from her body. She looked down at Patheus, who stared at her.

"So there is," he said, his voice now thin in the empty room. "And an official one, no less."

"The Shadowsaint is back," Eigenea said.

"I know," he replied, sitting up on the mattress. "I felt it coming."

Eigenea glowered at him. "Why didn't you warn me?"

"Because you would have put me to work again, instead of helping me die."

Eigenea looked at the tray of vials, then back at Patheus. "You thought if enough of your divinity was depleted, you'd turn to ash like anything else that left the city."

Karrid noticed a tear running down the angel's cheek. "It might work," he said softly. "Ouranos knows I'm running out of ideas. I've let every mage in the city try their worst on me, committed every blasphemy in hopes of oblivion, but the Gloss won't let go of me. In Jannan's name, I'd hoped to be gone by the time the Shadowsaint returned. It's hard to believe it's been six years already."

"It hasn't," Eigenea said. "It's only been four."

The angel's eyes widened, and Karrid saw what looked like distant light shining through them.

Patheus grabbed Eigenea's shoulders and shouted, "What are you saying?"

"The damned thing's early."

Patheus leapt from the mattress and began pacing the wooden floor, limp wings dragging behind him. He whispered loudly, emitting a stream of babbling utterances Karrid could not comprehend. Eigenea leaned to her. "He's calculating."

"Calculating what?"

"Whatever significance the Shadowsaint's return carries. This is what he does. Give him a problem and he can't help but solve it. It's his nature."

Patheus turned to face them, straightening his posture and tipping his head back. Karrid saw a silver glow pulse beneath his flesh. Slowly, his wings spread, reaching out to a span of twelve feet, almost touching the walls of the room. He rose a full four feet above the floor, brightening as he did. Karrid shielded her eyes.

"He's having an epiphany," Eigenea said.

The Archmage crossed the distance to the angel and, quite unceremoniously, tugged on one of his feet. "Anything you'd like to share with the rest of us?"

Patheus looked down on her and smiled.

"The Shadowsaint has not returned," he said in a voice like a million lover's whispers. "It never went away."

The brightness flared and went out. Patheus fell to the floor.

Eigenea let out another sigh. "Fortunately angels don't weigh much."

She hoisted him over her shoulder like sack of flour.

As they passed through the manor gate, Karrid heard the gritty creak of shifting stone. She looked up at the pair of winged gargoyles perched on the ledge. They stirred, turning to look at the Archmage hauling the angel.

"That's right, boys," Eigenea called to them. "Patheus is back. Stay on the lookout for trouble."

The gargoyles leapt from their perch, spread their stone wings, and began circling the manor.

"Are they alive?" Karrid asked.

"As long as I tell them they are. It's an old Mauer trick."

Karrid studied the rest of the facade. There was a chip on a cornice, and cracks in the plaster. One of the higher eaves sagged a bit.

"Your Manor is immune to the Gloss," she said.

Eigenea turned, Patheus' wings dragging along the grass as she did. "Very observant, but it's more resistant than immune.

My great-great-grandfather's doing. Voskus cast a lot of protective hexes here, some I'm not even aware of."

"I'd heard he could speak to buildings."

"He did, but it was never much of a conversation. He *told* them what to do, ordered them to expand and rearrange themselves as needed."

A sparrow landed on Patheus' back. Eigenea waved it off with her free hand. Two more landed. Karrid looked up to see a small flock circling overhead.

There was a growl. The birds scattered.

Aughan stepped from the doorway, scowling in disapproval of Patheus' nakedness. He relieved Eigenea of the angel, carrying him into the manor.

Eigenea looked at Karrid as they followed. "Patheus has an affinity with the birds of the city. They're protective of him. He's often said they would die for him."

In the parlor, Aughan placed the angel on a burgundy couch. Karrid looked around the room, noting its tasteful decorations. She also recognized an ornate scrying glass on the wall.

"I have placed the Unction in the dream tabernacle," Aughan said. "Also, Abbess Zinthia sent a messenger. Apparently Sebastyn was in particularly good spirits this morning."

Eigenea puffed out her cheeks. "He knows. We'd best hurry."

She moved towards a side door. Aughan stepped in front of her.

"I have prepared lunch."

"We don't have time." She tried to step around him, but he extended an arm to block her.

"It is past midday and you have not eaten. I have no intention of going into battle with an famished old woman."

"You are a vile, mangy creature."

"And you, madam, are a petulant crone. We still have several hours before nightfall to prepare. If you do not partake of nourishment I will be forced to sit upon you and spoon feed you. Again. Besides, Karrid requires briefing."

Patheus sat upright from his slumber. "Someone's just insulted Eigenea. I can smell her fury. And dates. Do I smell dates? I love dates. I'm hungry."

There were, indeed, dates, along with cheeses, bread, succulent fruit, and lean strips of smoked meat. Karrid was still trying to size up the silverback, but one thing was incontrovertible: he served a sumptuous lunch.

"When the first Unction occurred," Eigenea said, "Sebastyn convinced the magistrates it was the work of a rogue warlock twisting the living into unnatural shapes."

"I've read the reports," Karrid said. "A stable worker returning home from drinking stumbled into it." She noted that the angel, now draped in a robe, stared at her as he stuffed his mouth with fruit, and guzzled from a bottle of ale.

"There's a lot left out of the official account," Eigenea said, "such as the fact that the City Guard who found him assumed he was tangled in a net. It wasn't until six hours later they realized it was living tissue. Every mage in Orphicca was summoned. Thanks to Sebastyn, I spent the next two nights looking for malign sorcery."

Karrid raised her brow. "You don't strike me as one who follows orders."

"I'm not, but you have to remember this was just six years after the Gloss came. We still hadn't realized the full impact of its descent. I elected to play nice for the mayor's sake. Meanwhile, a messenger and her horse were discovered interwoven together, and an ironmonger the following night. The mayor enacted a curfew. That didn't go over well."

"My father told me of the riots when I was a child."

"Your father is Tauran," Patheus said suddenly. "Your mother is Ynochean."

Karrid leaned back. "And how would you know that? Another epiphany?"

"I can see the characteristics they bred into you, etched on unfurling scrolls throughout your body. You have other traits as well, inherent with being a Lastborn, but they're not as easy to see."

"I've met many angels. None have claimed *that* talent."

"They are not me." He closed his eyes. "I can see the night of your conception. Your mother wore the long blue dress your father had a weakness for. I can feel their heat, the passion, the release."

"Manners!" Eigenea shouted, slapping the back of his hand.

Patheus looked at Karrid again. "Ynochea and Taur. Such lovely lands. But of course you'll never see them. Just as I will never behold Ouranos again."

"Is that why you want to die?"

She regretted the question even as it left her mouth, but the angel's words at the apothecary had replayed in her head for the last hour. The voracious creature now staring at her, lips wet with ale, bore little resemblance to the sad thing she had seen on the table. She was about to apologize when he picked up his bottle.

"Existence is like vigorously shaken ale," he said. "This world is the sediment that settles over time. Ouranos is the foam that forms at the top. But they're both made of the same stuff. Mortals think Ouranos is some shining realm in the sky. It is much more than that, yet far less. It folds around this world, stretching beyond the pinioned boundaries beneath, above, within and without. It exists in the reflection of sunlight on water, and between the ticks of the clock."

"I've been told you like to commune," Karrid said, placing her hand on the table, palm up. "Show me."

The angel looked to Eigenea for approval. The Archmage nodded. Patheus drained his bottle, then placed his fingertips on Karrid's palm. She felt mild dizziness, and a strange weightless sensation. The room warped and melted and spun and—

> *Can you see it? This is the domain of angels. Take the duration of a single heartbeat. Slice that length in half, and half again. Repeat until the resulting increments pass too swift to measure. Ouranos lies in the gaps between moments. From here, we watched your races grow, build nations, generate ideas. Those ideas had essences, wisps of intent that slipped between moments and pollinated Ouranos. They were the most beautiful part of you. You slept, and dreamscapes blossomed. You imagined something greater, and the gods rose. Every culture has a pantheon, and they all exist here. See? It's like a continent, with tribes of gods dotted across the landscape.*
>
> *Now, look down. That's Orphicca from above. It's what Jannan saw when he first visited. It's what we all saw when the Gloss arrived: a perfect reflection of the city hanging over*

us. The world used to call this the City of Blasphemers, and it wore that name with pride. Eigenea told you it was founded to be free from the artifice of scripture and prophecy. Between you and me, the gods smiled at that, happy to see you get on with progress without constantly pausing for litanies and sacrifices.

This must be disorienting. Here, focus on something you're familiar with. How about our dear Eigenea? There. That's better. Look at her. She was a damned handsome woman then. The ferocity with which she fulfilled her role as Archmage was extraordinary, No wonder she had so many husbands. Of course they were long gone by the time the Gloss came.

You're inquisitive about the Gloss. I can smell it. Why? You weren't even born yet...oh, I see. You want to know why the Lastborn came to be. You wonder what your role is in Orphicca. Quite frankly I don't know, but I was there when the Gloss came. I was the one that carried Eigenea up to greet them. Didn't you know that? Of course not, you weren't born. Eigenea's the reason the Gloss descended...

The room snapped back into place. Karrid saw Eigenea lift Patheus' hand from hers. "Best to start slowly," the Archmage said.

The sensations she'd felt were elusive impressions of unbound vistas and spaces that didn't exist. The angel's thoughts, so powerful yet undisciplined, echoed into memory.

Patheus frowned at his empty bottle, then gave Karrid a knowing grin. "I've never communed with a Lastborn. Your senses are quite robust. I should indulge myself more often."

Eigenea grabbed his chin. "Right now you need to find me the Shadowsaint."

Patheus' eyes lit up. "Yes! Ciphers to calculate!"

The angel rose and hurriedly left the room.

"I don't understand," Karrid said. "An hour ago he wanted to die, and now..."

Aughan grunted. "He's Patheus, what do you expect?"

Karrid looked at the ape. "I'm an Elite officer, charged with defending the city from invaders. Dealing with crazy angels is new to me. Please *tell* me what to expect."

Eigenea placed a hand on her arm. "He's the most supremely intelligent creature I know. Give him a riddle to solve, and his aspect changes. It consumes him, sets him down paths of thought even *I* can't follow. Take that riddle away from him, and he has nothing. I'm not talking about something as crude as boredom, I mean *nothing*. A despairing void we can't grasp. That's what he sought at the apothecary: Death by slow decay. Feeling himself emptied inch by agonizing inch. Angel bodies aren't like ours, they're just the forms we can see, like a flat reflection of something far larger. If I could take his pain away I'd do it in a second. I suppose, as an Elite, you disapprove."

Karrid was surprised by the statement. "It *is* disquieting."

"Why?"

"Killing angels. Releasing angry ghosts. You're the Archmage of Orphicca. You should be above such matters."

"Come," Eigenea said, rising from her seat. "I want to show you something."

***

Eigenea led the way down the narrow stairway with a lantern. Karrid followed close behind. The moans that rose from below grew louder with each step, but ceased when Eigenea slipped a key into the metal door at the bottom.

"Welcome to the Tormentorium," she said.

The stone-walled room was ten feet to a side, lit by a hanging lamp, and lined with shelves. Evenly spaced across these sat twenty or so teardrop shaped decanters.

Karrid looked around. "I expected…"

"A dungeon of pain? It is, in a sense. There's a soul in each bottle."

Karrid peered at the nearest decanter. Movement swirled within, like a miniature storm cloud.

Eigenea led her along the shelf. "Some of them, like Chornus here, were merely insane. Being freed of his body came as a relief to him. Others made the error of using malignant sorcery in *my* city. For them, separation from the body is agony. Like the Red Magus, here. That's Thran the Carnifex next to him. And this one is the Mother-of-Silence. Not so silent now, are you? Come, scream for our visitor."

A small snap of blue electricity leapt from Eigenea's hand to the decanter. The miasma within convulsed, making a sound like distant boars being slaughtered.

Karrid placed a hand to her mouth.

"Don't feel sorry for this old hag," Eigenea said. "She struck over a dozen children mute for mocking the old gods, then stripped a few of their skin for good measure. Burning her alive was a pleasure."

"Why are you showing me this?" Karrid asked.

"Because you're an Elite, sworn to take whatever steps needed to protect this city." She gestured to the decanters. "I want you to understand the lengths *I* will go to."

With that, she moved to the door. Karrid watched her, realizing just how formidable she was.

"Come on," Eigenea said, holding the door open. "You have much to learn, and little time."

Karrid climbed two steps, hesitated and looked back. She saw Eigenea lean towards the decanter containing the Mother-of-Silence. At the edge of hearing she heard the Archmage whisper, "Don't worry, old girl, I have plans for you very soon."

It took Karrid several moments to realize the room at the top of the stairs was *not* the one they had descended from. It was smaller, without windows, and dominated by a six-foot-square table. Bookshelves stood beneath a panoply of city maps, charts, and sketches. Wall sconces cast everything in stark light. Karrid had seen similar chambers in the Citadel. This was a war room.

There were sketches pinned to the wall. Some showed a shape like a mantis standing upright, others resembled a garden slug balancing on four crab legs. The only common elements were the numerous tendrils hanging from the midsection, and the large stinger tail reaching over the head.

The fabric Eigenea had spread beneath the Unction lay across the table, marked with its intricate shadow. Patheus bent over it, eyes wide, studying it intently. His aspect had changed again. He was now luminously pallid, as if sculpted from sunlit cloud.

"What do you see?" Eigenea asked.

"Sums and dividends. Dominant denominators. The functions of Unction." His finger traced along the curvatures so rapidly it became a blur. "Acute angularities. Recursive negations. Implied contours. The Shadowsaint has not fully manifested."

"How can you tell that?" Karrid asked.

Patheus straightened, eyes faintly aglow. "The world is written in numbers. They are the root structure of existence. Show me a rock and I can extrapolate what mountain it came from. Sign your name and I can tell by sweeps and angles of the script what you favorite color is" – he stepped closer – "or how many people you've killed."

Eigenea stepped between them. "You said it hadn't left."

"I thought it was like a ghost, returning to haunt a location. It isn't." He pointed to the diagram. "See these torsions? It's wedged in lower geometric latitudes, far below the complexity threshold it needs. These curls, here. That's where it fought to gain purchase. It's trying to unfold itself. A point becomes a line. A line becomes a square. A square becomes a cube. A cube becomes a form you cannot perceive. The spaces around you are rife with directions not found by any plumb or compass. That's where the Shadowsaint lay, pooled like rainwater, resting. Now it's pulling itself up, robbing victims of dimension, cladding itself in their breadth and depth. But each Unction depletes it of strength." His finger raced around the diagram again. "The vectors of each depletion dictate when and where it will appear next. The numbers tell me where to go."

"How long will that take?" Eigenea asked.

Patheus didn't answer. He hunched over the diagram, oblivious to all else save the convoluted pattern. Karrid could hear his constant muttering.

"And there he goes," Eigenea said, relieved. "We won't hear from him until he's got it solved."

"You were expecting something else?"

"Four years ago he showed up at the door stinking drunk, kissed Aughan on the lips, and proceeded to fly around the manor raving about 'configurations' and 'predictive schema' before collapsing. As Aughan threw him into the street he cried out 'it will appear in Kiln Row.'"

Karrid straightened. "The second set of Unctions began at Kiln Row."

"Yes. And he felt it coming ten days before it happened. We had no idea what he was speaking about until we heard about the Unction at the abandoned foundry. After that I spent two days scouring the city for him."

"You two have a history."

Eigenea turned and scrutinized her. "You could call it that."

"When we communed, he told me he carried you up to the Gloss when they arrived."

"That's true. Did he tell you anything else?"

Karrid considered how to answer when her eye caught something on the shelf behind Eigenea. It was a glass box, like a large terrarium. The black thing mounted within had two long segments, hinged and angled like a man showing off his bicep. It tapered to a curved point like a ceremonial dagger. Unfolded, it would be eight feet long.

"That's its stinger," she said

"Yes, Aughan's trophy."

"It looks like stone."

"It is. Solid, all the way through. I've studied it for four years and have no idea how or why. Best guess, it ossified after Aughan cut it off. The Shadowsaint has been a persistent mystery, defying all classification."

Patheus muttered something.

"Let's leave him to his work," Eigenea said, turning for the door.

Karrid followed her, glancing back at Patheus. For a moment she thought the angel glanced back.

5

THEY FOUND AUGHAN before the scrying glass.

"What is it?" Eigenea asked.

"The gargoyles have spotted an interloper."

The glass showed an aerial view of a figure in the glade, aiming a spyglass at the manor.

"Shall I have them *greet* our guest?" Aughan asked.

"Let our friends handle it."

There was movement around the edge of the image. A skunk emerged from under a bush, followed by another. The observer was oblivious as a total of nine formed a circle around the tree. As one they turned and lifted their tails.

"I could have interrogated him." Karrid said.

"All you'd learn is that Sebastyn has people watching us, and we already know that. The key is to be prepared for the worst."

Aughan looked at her, eyes conveying that he knew what she was planning.

"You are awakening the garden," he said.

"Yes, only as a precaution."

"That doesn't make it any less an act of madness."

"Well, you've called me a madwoman often enough." She placed a hand on his shoulder. He was tense as stone. "Go, prepare our infantry for tonight."

Aughan huffed as he left the parlor.

Eigenea waved at a wall panel. It slid aside, revealing a long corridor with a square of sunlight visible at the far end.

She gestured for Karrid to follow. "Have you read the testimony of the woman who first witnessed an Unction?"

"On the fourth night? Yes. There was a thunderstorm. The victim was a man running in the opposite direction. She described the creature that appeared just after it happened, and how it leapt away from her."

"I was there when she testified," Eigenea said. "She didn't actually see the Shadowsaint, just the rain cascading over its shape, but it was enough to sketch an outline. It was the first hint of what we were dealing with. I wanted to tap her memory with a Recollection Stone, but after her testimony she walked out the nearest city gate and turned to dust within twenty feet. Several people and angels watched as she did this. None tried to stop her."

"Poor woman. How horrible."

"All of Orphicca was terrified. After that fourth night it took months to accept that the Unctions had ended. The Guard scoured the streets every night and found nothing. A long time passed before the fear faded. Once it did, every mage in the city came to me with their theories. The Shadowsaint was a fallen god or vengeful ghost. Some thought it was an ancient dark force awoken by the Gloss. I dismissed them all, especially Sebastyn, who insisted it was punishment for

Orphicca's arrogance. He told people they needed to pray to old gods, renounce the founders' heresies, and, most importantly, follow him for salvation. I'd never paid charlatans much heed, and wasn't about to start with him."

The corridor ended at a round outdoor space a hundred feet wide. The encircling wall was featureless stone, save for four doors at the compass points. The ground looked like a blast crater.

Eigenea watched Karrid's reaction to the bleak concavity. The young woman peered at the packed dirt. "There's something under the ground here."

Impressive, thought Eigenea.

Two simple wooden chairs stood at the center. Eigenea stepped down the shallow incline, slipping slightly. Karrid came up behind and helped her to a chair.

"What is this place?" Karrid asked.

"A project. One I hope I never need." She pulled out her blade and pricked her thumb with the tip. A bead of blood welled up and dropped to the soil, vanishing instantly.

"Did you know," she said, "that the Kiln Row Unction was the daughter of a magistrate?"

"No," Karrid replied. "City Guard records don't identify the victim."

"More secrecy. Unsurprising. When I examined her I found a family brooch tangled in the sinew. The next day, the assembly declared emergency measures. Word of the Unction spread fast, and people panicked. Sebastyn wasted no time whipping his followers into a fervor. They performed rituals in the streets, chanted prayers to the sky, and demanded the mayor abdicate in favor of their leader. You can see why the mayor wants to keep this quiet."

"What did you do?"

"Nothing. I was looking for Patheus. Found him in a tavern on the third day. Aughan dragged him to the previous night's Unction and he sobered up fast, claiming to see strange mathematics in its pattern. He fell into a fugue. I thought he'd lost consciousness. An hour later he roused, shouting that the Shadowsaint would appear in the Rayamadra district. We raced there with an attachment of City Guard and found a shopkeeper closing up. Our arrival startled him, and he took a step backwards. His body contracted like a billowing blanket pulled through a hole in a fence."

Eigenea saw small glints flash across the ground.

"Of course," she continued, "we couldn't see the Shadowsaint, at least not until Aughan broke the shop window, grabbed a sack of spice, sliced it open, and threw it towards the Unction. It clung to something, forming an outline, and I thought to myself that Aughan was the wisest, most resourceful creature I knew. Then the damned fool lunged with his blade, receiving a sting in the arm for his troubles. But the strike made the Shadowsaint visible. Horrible-looking thing. Like a bent old man riding a scorpion. The guards moved in, but it dropped into the paving stones as if falling through a trap door."

Eigenea saw that Karrid had noticed the small spikes stabbing up from the soil, no more than an inch long. She looked down to make sure none were underfoot.

"Patheus studied the Unction, said the Shadowsaint needed time to gain shape, that it wasn't bound by the constraints of solidity. That got me thinking: we'd seen it take refuge in the structure of Orphicca, just like the Gloss. It could be some form of parasite the Gloss carried with it, like a tick on a horse.

The six-year duration between appearances might be its pattern of dormancies and feeding. It manifested after delivering Unction, but remained unseen until kinetic energy rendered it visible. Then, at least for a few moments, it might be vulnerable. Wait too long, and it slipped away like a specter."

Small skeletal bushes rose to all sides of them, along with jagged brambles and serrated stalks covered in barbs. Karrid studied the closest growth.

"Go ahead and touch it," Eigenea said. "Mind the sharp bits."

Karrid extended a finger. "This is wrought iron."

"I convinced the magma deep below the city to reach up and refine itself. I needed material that wasn't infused with Gloss."

Karrid looked around the garden. "You conjured these. For what purpose?"

"A contingency, in case our efforts fail."

Karrid looked at her with concern. "Do you think they might?"

"It's happened before. Rampart Square was a *disaster*, and my plan was foolproof. The Square was evacuated. A hundred head of livestock were brought in and set free to roam. City Guard ringed the vicinity, including thirty archers. Ten minutes later a boar blossomed into Unction. The archers let loose, and the Shadowsaint appeared. Aughan vaulted across the backs of animals with one arm in a sling. He was ready for the stinger, cut it off with a single backhanded swipe. The thing howled. The rest of the Guard closed in."

Black vines snaked up from the ground, sprouting spikes as they wound between the other growths. Some of the structures were over ten feet tall and still rising.

Eigenea waved a hand. "I think that's enough for now."

The growth slowed and halted. The space was now a garden of dark thorny shapes. Karrid rose to admire one of the iron trees.

"The records say you killed someone," she said.

"And if I had my way I would have killed more. Sebastyn's people came out of nowhere. Pyromantic fire rose along one side of the Square. The animals broke into a stampede, sweeping Aughan away and trampling many of the Guard. I was able to counter the fire, but it took a while to find the Shadowsaint. Sebastyn was kneeling before it, arms outstretched. Some witnesses claim he was merely praying to it, but I know him better. I ran, blade out, lightning churning in my fist. I was ten feet from them when one of his followers appeared in front of me and ran me through with a pike. I remember the woman's face grimacing at me, and my rage rising. The wind responded. It lifted the woman, dragged her through the air and sent her over the wall half a mile away. Meanwhile, the Shadowsaint sank into the stones again." She placed a hand at her side. "Four years and I still haven't fully recovered."

Karrid looked surprised. "The Gloss didn't heal you?"

She gestured around her. "The manor is resistant. So am I."

"My dear Eigenea!"

She turned to see Patheus in the doorway. He gazed at the shapes of the garden with wide-eyed wonderment. "You've conjured an immolation—"

Eigenea raised a hand, stilling the air carrying his voice. "The wind listens," she said.

Patheus's eyes widened. "I forgot. My apologies. I've finished. The Shadowsaint will appear in Cenotaph Circle just before tenth bell."

Eigenea looked at Karrid. "Tell the mayor to send as many Elite as possible. Only ones you *trust.* We're going to need a lot of feet on the ground for this."

Rippling banners of green and purple aurorae filled the sky.

The thirteen bronze spires of Cenotaph Circle sat on marble plinths, each casting three shadows from the ring of lamps around them. Eigenea looked to Voskus Mauer's memorial, imagining how disgruntled he'd be over being surrounded by something as mundane as bookkeeping centers, where the balance sheets of Orphicca were tabulated.

The Circle always reminded Eigenea of the standing stones in the eastern isles, and for a moment she could smell the rich green of that place instead of the tang of Gloss.

At twenty minutes to tenth bell, Karrid approached. "We've got Elite on each street, and archers on all the rooftops. This district is abandoned at night, but we've barricaded the streets just in case."

"Good. Aughan is on his way. Where's Patheus?"

Karrid pointed to a nearby corner. The angel was leaning against the building, arms wrapped around himself.

Eigenea looked up at the lights above. "I saw the northern aurora once, when I studied with the Cold Shamans. There are algae shoals under the ice that glow in response, turning everything a luminous green."

"How far have you traveled?"

"One cannot be an Archmage without knowing the world's sorceries. I visited most of the great empires, and several abysmal ones. How do you think I ended up with a silverback?"

Aughan emerged from the shadows, carrying a large barrel over his shoulder.

"What is that?" Karrid asked.

"Our infantry of the evening," Eigenea said. "We're going to pull the livestock trick again."

Aughan pried the top of the barrel open. The lid levered up with a faint hiss of stale-smelling air. Eigenea took a small bottle from her coat.

"It pains me to interrupt your dormancy, my friends," she said, holding the bottle over the barrel, "but I'm afraid Orphicca needs you tonight."

A single drop of pale liquid dripped into the dark interior of the barrel. Instantly, a red glow shone within. Eigenea noticed Karrid stepping back as the bloody light intensified. Suddenly, countless pinpoints of red rose up.

"They're star-flies," Karrid said, smiling at the lights around her.

"They'll avoid the lamplight," Eigenea said, "stay in the shadows of the cenotaphs. If one hits the Shadowsaint, it will Unction like anything else."

The star-flies swarmed into the space in great sweeps and twists. Eigenea took up position beside the nearest stone, and sent Aughan to wait three stones away. The silverback squatted on all fours, muscles tensed, blade clenched in his teeth. Karrid and four other Elite took positions around the perimeter of the cenotaphs, sabers out.

Eigenea took in the view, glancing occasionally back at Patheus leaning against the wall. The aurora overhead shifted to the east, vanishing over the building-tops. The star-flies continued their aerial dance. The Circle was dead quiet.

Tenth bell rang out.

Aughan straightened at the sound of it. The Elite looked at each other. Eigenea gestured for Karrid and Aughan to approach.

"Stay here and keep watching," she said to Karrid. "Call out if you see anything."

Aughan followed her over to Patheus.

"The Shadowsaint isn't here," she said.

The angel was shivering. "Yes it is. I can feel it."

Eigenea gripped his chin. "Patheus, you need to focus."

The angel closed his eyes and traced shapes in the air before him.

Eigenea looked over at Karrid, then at the star-flies. Damn, it was cold tonight.

Patheus snapped back his head, looking straight up the side of the building. "On the roof."

Aughan leapt upward, grabbing the second story ledge, swinging himself over to the drainpipe.

"Get me up there," Eigenea said.

Patheus grabbed her shoulders. Cenotaph Circle fell away beneath her. A moment later she was on a patchwork of tin tiles, next to a lightning rod sticking up like a black spear. The roof was dark, and Patheus brightened to compensate, revealing a brick chimney.

It was then Eigenea noticed the City Guard archer at the edge.

He turned at the sudden light.

"Stay where you are!" Eigenea shouted.

A confused look came over the Guard's face. He took a single step forward.

Eigenea thrust out a hand, willing him to stand still, knowing it was already too late. She saw distortion at his edges, as if she were looking at him through water. The Guard's limbs bowed unnaturally, his torso caved in, and his head collapsed. With sickening swiftness the entire body drew into itself, flesh and fabric contracting into a tight ball. The archer's quiver fell to the ground, arrows scattering. Eigenea muttered "no" as a lacy sphere of Unction snapped into being, lolling forward through the air on leftover momentum.

Fury ignited within Eigenea as she stepped forward, heat rising in her fingers.

Aughan vaulted from the edge of the roof. He grabbed the lightning rod, pulling himself into a feet-first swing and sailing over the top of the Unction. There was a loud crack, like shell breaking against rock. Eigenea looked through the Unction and saw the air ripple beyond. Aughan floated, posed as if riding an invisible horse. He raised his blade and brought it down hard.

Eigenea heard a piercing shriek and something clattering on the tin roof.

She ran around the Unction to see Aughan wrapped around a black thrashing shape. Thick crab legs splayed across the tiles. Something like a torso bent beneath Aughan's weight. Tendrils flailed to block another knife strike. The blunt stump of a severed stinger pivoted like a wagging finger.

The heat in her hands became arcs of lightning between her fingers. She held her hands before her.

The Shadowsaint twisted, throwing Aughan off, sending him against the chimney.

Eigenea planted her feet, and let loose a white hot bolt. The Shadowsaint writhed as a web of lightning sizzled around it. A tendril snapped out, striking her side and sending her sliding across the roof. She rolled over in time to see it looming over her.

The angular head looked like an unfinished sculpture, with flanges jutting from each side that reminded her of a carriage with its doors open. The corded texture of the wide torso resembled exposed muscle rendered in black oil. The tendrils reaching towards her were barbed. She could make out plated segments, overrun with rivulets of ichor that reflected the bright light.

Why is the light so bright?

Patheus' swift descent blinded her. She shielded her eyes and rolled away, hearing sounds she could not fathom. Rising to her knees, she squinted through her fingers.

Patheus hovered three feet above the roof, facing the Shadowsaint. His wings swept backward, shielding the Unction. The Shadowsaint stood still, head tilted back. Eigenea looked for any sign that it was about to strike, and found none.

Two feet of gleaming saber emerged from its middle.

The Shadowsaint blurred with motion. Eigenea caught sight of Karrid standing behind it, still gripping the hilt. Tendrils swept around, catching Karrid in the midsection and catapulting her towards the edge. Aughan leapt into the air and snagged her leg, pulling her to him. They both landed hard against the roof.

Patheus did not move.

Eigenea stood, pain raging through both legs, heart hammering in her ears. Afterimages of Patheus burned in her vision. All she could make out was a convulsing silhouette, and the glint of Karrid's blade still protruding. She stepped forward, wincing, hands sparking. She held them up, and as lightning snapped between her fingers, she saw its face before her.

There were nothing like eyes, but Eigenea knew it was looking at her.

There was nothing like a mouth, except perhaps the sliding serrated mandibles.

There was nothing like a nose, but she heard a distinct intake of breath, as if sniffing.

Ever so slightly, the Shadowsaint tilted its head.

It's studying me.

The face vanished in a burst of motion. She heard growling. Aughan was straddling the thing right beside her, plunging his dagger into it.

"Hang on to it!" she cried.

A tendril snapped to the edge of the roof. Before she could react, it contracted, and both figures went over the side.

Eigenea ran to the edge in time to see Aughan hit the paving stones on his side with a loud thud. Karrid's saber bounced off the street, twirling into the air.

The Shadowsaint sank into the road as if it were water.

"Damn!" Eigenea shouted.

Aughan rolled to his hands and knees, punching the pavement in anger. City Guards ran to assist him, but he waved them away.

Karrid appeared beside her, hands on knees, breathing heavy.

"That was a reckless move," Eigenea said.

"I know," Karrid replied.

"Eigenea," said Patheus, floating before the Unction. "Something's not right. This doesn't match what I saw before. I'm taking it back to the manor."

Before Eigenea could protest, Patheus took two of the strands and parted them aside like a curtain. Pulling his wings in close, he stepped inside the Unction.

"It's all right," he said softly, "I've got you."

He rose, the Unction around him like a bubble, and sped away over the rooftops.

"He's right," said Eigenea, "Something else is going on. The damned thing was studying us."

"What does that mean?"

"It means I need to go see Sebastyn."

6

THE MAYOR wasn't happy with Karrid's report, but was mollified by the fact that the Shadowsaint's return could be kept secret from the citizens for another day.

Karrid returned to the barracks just before twelfth bell. As she bathed she played the events on the rooftop over in her mind. It was true she had been reckless, but not without reason.

Standing in the Circle, she saw the ape scale the wall, and the angel carry Eigenea up to the roof. She broke into a sprint. She was halfway up the first flight of steps when she felt something like a weight landing on her back. She ignored it. When she'd reached the roof, and first beheld the Shadowsaint, she was terrified. Then she saw Eigenea, Aughan, and Patheus all engaging it, and discipline urged her to do something.

Then Patheus spread his wings and floated in front of the Unction. The Shadowsaint stood perfectly still. In that moment, she felt something similar to the communion she had shared with the angel. Impressions of confusion and anger surged in her. It lasted only an instant before she realized she had a clean shot. Her strike was true. So was the kick the Shadowsaint delivered to her stomach. She would have been broken on the street below if not for Aughan.

On the way from the baths to her bunk she rounded a corner and walked right into another Elite. He was young, perhaps a couple years older than her. His insignia marked him as a patrolman. He smelled of sweat and...

"Pardon me, Officer," he stammered as he stepped back.

"Just coming off patrol?" she asked.

"Yes."

She leaned forward and sniffed. "Had an encounter with a skunk, did you? Best wash yourself."

"Y-yes, Officer." He scurried down the hall towards the baths.

She watched him retreat and muttered, "Damned if I'm sleeping here tonight."

Papa sat on the stoop, puffing smoke from his pipe.

"You look like you've had a long day, dark eyes," he said, rubbing a hand through his black brushy hair.

The aurora-light brought out his Tauran handsomeness. She wondered how much of that was the Gloss' doing.

"Part of the job, Papa."

They went inside, where Mama fussed over her bruises. Papa uncorked a bottle of wine and they sat at the table.

"Now how did you get so banged up?" Mama asked.

"Mama," Papa said, "you know her assignments are classified."

"Ugh. It was too much to hope for a daughter with my taste for gossip."

"At least she inherited your looks."

Karrid remembered the angel's words. She looked to her parents, still so beautiful against the tide of years thanks to the Gloss.

"Papa, when you were young, what was your favorite dress of Mama's?"

His eyes widened. "Oh, that long blue one. She filled it out nicely."

Mama tossed her orange mane back. "I still do."

7

"YOU used to make that climb *much* faster."

Eigenea squinted up against the midday sun. Abbess Zinthia waited atop the wide stone steps. The robed albino woman gave a wry smile.

"The only feasible explanation," Eigenea huffed, "is that they are steeper than before."

Her knees protested as she mounted the last step and gave her old friend a hard embrace.

"You haven't been to service in a while," Zinthia said, straightening her hood.

"No, but I drink copious amounts of wine from your vineyards. That should count for something. Abbess Zinthia, this is Officer Karrid of the Second Elite Battalion."

Zinthia bowed. "An honor. We've had several Lastborn join the order these last few years. I fear adulthood has burdened them with the city's malaise, but I do find their presence enlightening."

"Thank you. This place…I've seen from down there countless times, but up close…."

Eigenea followed her gaze. Between the splayed buttresses and the gape of the absurdly large portico, the Jannanite monastery looked like a roaring predator prepared to strike. To one side lay the windmill and dormitories. To the other, vineyards spread across the slope of the hill. Many monks worked the field. Eigenea noted more angels among their number than last time.

Zinthia stepped between Eigenea and Karrid, linked arms with them, and led them towards the portico. "I take it from your labored gait that you had a rough night."

"We both did," Eigenea said. "Poor Aughan's covered in healing amulets."

"And I assume this involves the Shadowsaint?" Zinthia said to Eigenea with a gleam in her red eyes.

"That's classified," Karrid said.

Eigenea chuckled. "Very little city business eludes the Jannanites, Karrid. If you haven't noticed, there are angels among their number. They have their own methods of learning things."

"We *named* the Shadowsaint," Zinthia said, "after the mythical demon that anointed people into damnation."

They stepped through the portico, and Eigenea heard Karrid's gasp as she saw the towering vestibule. Light slanted through high windows onto a pair of squared columns bridged by a horseshoe arch of wine-red stone. Beyond it, filling the wall above the inner door was a mural of Jannan. He stood atop a hill, arms at his side, wings spread, long violet hair flowing over his shoulders.

"He came here eight hundred years ago," Zinthia said with reverence, "and declared Orphicca to be the perfect city."

"I've heard he is interred here," Karrid said.

"Quite the opposite."

The door opened onto the ornate main hall, laden with imagery showing Jannan's time in Orphicca. Niches housed the busts of his acolytes, whose names Eigenea had forgotten. All throughout the space, monks knelt, heads down.

"What do they pray for?" Karrid asked.

"In the end, nothing," Zinthia replied. "It's not our prayers that matter."

"That's odd for a monastery."

"Not at all. We live here to ponder the mystery Jannan left us. He said the one rule of the order was that each monk pray only for all fellow monks who do not pray for themselves."

"That sounds logical."

"It isn't. If the monks pray for themselves, by the rule, they *cannot* pray for themselves. If they don't, then they *must*."

Karrid processed the sentence. "That's impossible."

"No, it's a paradox. This, in the end, is what occupies our time. It serves as a more intimate bond to Ouranos than mere prayer. Come, I will show you."

"*Please* don't convert her today," Eigenea said. "I need her."

As they neared the end of the hall, Eigenea saw the corridor that led to the entrance to Sebastyn's prison. "I'm going below."

Karrid's hand rested on her saber hilt. "I should go with you."

"I'd rather not give him the satisfaction of seeing the Elite involved."

"He does love attention," Zinthia said.

"Show her the monastery grounds. When I'm done, I want to look in on my hawks."

She had forgotten how many stairs there were.

As she descended, Eigenea felt the precarious weight of the hill poised above her. At the bottom, a torch-lined corridor led to a heavy oaken door crossed with thick iron bands. The sentinel icons etched in the metal glowed faintly at Eigenea's approach, and the door swung open.

The tiled dome chamber was forty feet wide. Twelve concentric circles of glyphs and runes ringed its circumference: binding spells in a hundred different languages. The space in the middle was occupied by three full bookshelves, a bed, a wardrobe, a couple of tables, and a formidable liquor cabinet, all arranged around the plush chair that Sebastyn occupied.

He lifted his bald head from the book he was reading. Silver-framed lenses magnified his pale blue eyes. A meticulously trimmed black beard cupped his chin, though he still had the look of a hungry mongrel.

"A visit from the grand Archmage!" he said, smiling. "Such exalted company. Oh, these precious, priceless instants are too few."

Eigenea stepped over the glyphs. "Still here, are you?"

His gaze, as always, was unfocused, as if he was blind and looking only at the direction her voice was coming from. "My dear Miss Mauer, had I the means to indemnify your disesteem I would do so doubly over. I sense Patheus on you. How is the angel? Still well versed in para-logic? Still rationalizing the arcane into measured statistics? Still desiring oblivion? I could help him with that last one. You should have him visit me."

"You don't have the skill."

"Dispensing with angels was one of the first tricks I learned,"

"But you still haven't managed to escape. I can see six, no, seven ways out from here, and I helped build this cell."

"We could discuss the particulars of my incarceration all day, but I would not dare wear out your patience."

Eigenea crossed her arms. "How uncharacteristically direct of you."

Sebastyn set his book aside. "Our conditions are wrought by our deeds, and occasionally the more esoteric aspects of fate. I sit here entombed with my thoughts, and find frankness the best tool to employ."

"Ghosts of old, I'd forgotten how exhausting it is to listen to you. But since we're being frank, you know about the Shadowsaint."

"The city still speaks to me, Eigenea. Even here."

"I mean you know more about it than you told at your trial."

"That could be construed as a compliment. But, yes, my knowledge on the subject is broad. I know it will grow with each encounter, and that you couldn't muster enough lightning last night to incapacitate it."

"Ah, so someone's passing secrets to you."

"Secrets," he said, smiling. "Funny little things. So fragile and delicate. But in the end they're just facts benefiting from the state of being valuable to someone."

8

THE COURTYARD raged with combat.

Karrid counted forty-eight monks, all paired off and engaging each other with blades, staffs, flails, and hammers. Robes fanned through the air as the combatants leapt and flipped and pirouetted away from blows. The speed and elegance of the motions belied the savagery of the attacks.

"I was not aware the Jannanites were so schooled in martial discipline," Karrid said.

"The calling makes many demands of us," Abbess Zinthia replied. "Preparation is always prudent."

"What are you preparing for?"

"Whatever befalls us. Come, you should see the central chamber."

Zinthia led her into a passage lined with murals. One showed Orphicca being swallowed by a massive wave from the sea. The next had fiery stones falling from the sky onto the city. Another showed a colossal explosion consuming the city, scorching the land around it. Every painting portrayed a devastating fate. Karrid noted the plaques beneath each one: *Flood, Burning Sky, Immolation.*

"These are rather grim," Karrid said.

"Jannan taught us to ponder the end of things, and cherish the impermanence of our trappings."

Karrid studied the destruction depicted. “None of these portray the coming of the Gloss.”

Zinthia did not answer, instead bowing her head before passing through the door at the corridor’s end. Within, gilded columns rose a hundred feet to a great glass dome webbed with support beams. Several monks knelt in a circle at the chamber’s center. It was to these that Zinthia gestured.

Karrid inhaled sharply when she realized what floated there. It was the skeleton of an angel: skull tilted back, arm and wing bones outstretched, as if embracing the sky above.

“He was the first angel to come to Orphicca,” Zinthia said. “He said the city needed a direct link to Ouranos. So he became one. His bones accumulate our prayers of paradox. Focus them like a signal lamp. This city may be forsaken, but Ouranos hears us all the same.”

Karrid felt faint vibration in the air, like the buzzing of a swarm of bees. She stepped closer to the chamber’s center, and the buzz increased.

“This is...remarkable,” she whispered, stunned to reverence by the sight.

“I’m glad you think so. Not everyone does.”

Karrid looked at Zinthia. “How could they not?”

The Abbess led her out of the chamber. “Some thought a beacon to Ouranos unwise. When Voskus Mauer became the first Archmage, he theorized Jannan’s link might attract something hostile.”

Karrid’s attention was drawn to the nearest mural. It showed Orphicca besieged by armies. A fleet of ships sat in the sea, hurling projectiles. Catapults and siege engines advanced on the city. In several spots, the walls were collapsing. The image made her feel negligent. Here she was, sightseeing at a monastery when she should be working against the Bahl-Maqrea. All because of the Unctions.

She quietly damned the Shadowsaint.

"Others are less metaphysical in their condemnation," Zinthia said.

"Like who?" Karrid asked.

"Sebastyn and his followers. They merely think we are heretics."

9

"THE GODS are not from this world, Eigenea. Neither is the Gloss. They are unconstrained by the natural strictures that bind us. We are cyclical beings, existing in ringed patterns of fate and destiny. Orphicca is an affront to that truth."

"Back to condemning progress, are we?"

"Simply challenging your conventions."

"By praising dried-up traditions and the wisdom of ancestry? I'm certain our hunter-gatherer forefathers appreciate that. Except they can't, because according to your thinking their constant struggle for survival was pre-ordained. A poorly expressed truth is indistinguishable from a falsehood. Cyclical nature did not stop the founding of Orphicca. And all the assaults of the world's armies have not torn it down."

"And now we're all trapped in it."

"Yes, with the Shadowsaint stalking our streets."

Sebastyn smiled again. "You think in such simplistic terms for an Archmage. Let me disabuse you of that with some unencumbered clarity. The Shadowsaint doesn't just see us as a source of dimension. It watches us with something other than eyes."

Eigenea smiled back. "Now that's interesting. Because last night it was so close to me I could have leaned in and kissed it."

Sebastyn's gaze intensified.

"Oh, that got your attention, didn't it? Yes, I was face to face with it. It could have killed me handily if it wanted to, but it didn't. I think it was studying me, and I suspect you know why."

"It isn't studying you, it's *judging* you. The Gloss was a test from Ouranos, one we failed. The Shadowsaint is our punishment for that failure. It is the will of the old gods, and will remain with us until we turn our prayers to them. I was always good at prayer. It's just another form of communication. Even your ancestor Voskus knew that."

Eigenea leaned forward. "You just said it saw us with something other than eyes. You wouldn't know that unless you'd gotten a good look at it in Rampart Square. It studied *you*, didn't it?"

Sebastyn's smile faded. "Your recollections of that night might be tainted by anger."

"Oh, I know they are. The Shadowsaint isn't beholden to your precious cyclical laws, you *know* that. Patheus said it pooled like rainwater in the city until it could unfold itself. I've seen spells like that, embedded like traps until the right person triggers them. You're right, it doesn't see us as a source of dimension. In fact I don't think it saw us at all, until you made it aware of us."

"You've given voice to a delightful theory," Sebastyn said. "I shall have to ponder this."

"You do that, just like I've pondered how you'd know about my recollections of Rampart Square. Unless you were listening."

Sebastyn stared at her, bottom lip quivering.

"You've been tapping the wind around the manor to bring you my words," she said. "I've recognized the spell for a while. The wind is my domain, and as of now I'm telling it to ignore you."

Anger spread across Sebastyn's face. "Sanctimonious witch! You cannot evade the inevitable. The old ways cannot be shrugged off so easily. Past sins always slither behind you. You Mauers always had your sorcery handed down to you. True mages like me had to work for it. I'm defending Orphicca from relics like you."

Eigenea seized his wrist. A modest current flowed from her. Sebastyn's eyes widened, pupils dilating in his thick lenses.

"You see, Sebastyn, you still fail to comprehend, and that's why real sorcery remains impenetrable to you. Mages don't *defend* culture. We're its senses, like antennae on bees, probing the environment for change. Sorcery itself? It's nothing special, just a knowledge of how things work, and which forces can be applied to alter those workings. It's very *literal*, demanding precision from the user. But it differs from other endeavors in one vital respect: it means being acutely aware of the cost incurred by your action, and possessing a willingness to bear that burden in full." She leaned in close to his face. "That's something you never had."

She released his wrist and he slumped in the chair.

"You attach significance to your cult's obedience, make them believe it grants them access to truths beyond their meager lives, even get them to wear a gaudy little pin identifying them as one of the gullible. Ghosts of old, sometimes I think you believe the platter of shit you're feeding them."

Sebastyn lifted his head. "Your time is coming."

"Of course it is." She leaned into his face. "Time comes for all of us."

Eigenea had watched over twenty generations of hawks grow up on this ledge. The Jannanites tolerated the nest only because Eigenea had asked them to, though they did appreciate the fact that their vineyards were mostly free of mice.

The mother eyed Eigenea as she leaned from the tower window. The young nestled beneath her. One brave chick popped its head out, looked at Eigenea, and gave a squeaking call.

"And good day to *you*, young lady," Eigenea said.

"I always worry," came Zinthia's voice, "when she talks to animals."

The Abbess and Karrid reached the top of the tower.

"This view is spectacular," said Karrid.

Eigenea looked at the panorama, *her* city, spread before her. To the east was a skyline of turrets, domes, spires, and steeples. It was said Voskus Mauer taught those towering forms to speak to each other. To the south she could barely make out the harbor beyond the wall, made unusable in the wake of the Gloss. North lay the Bahl-Maqrea siege encampment.

"They've lit their forge fires," Karrid said. "They're preparing for another attack."

"Then they'd best prepare for rain," Eigenea said. She turned to Zinthia. "And so should you."

The Abbess' white eyebrow arched. "So your visit was productive?"

"Very much so. Whether it was helpful remains to be seen. I know the City Guard check in on him daily. Has he had any other visitors?"

"You know we'd never let anyone in to see him."

"Yes, I know. Thank you, Zinthia. Now Karrid and I must speak in private."

The Abbess hugged her, then looked at Karrid. "I hope you'll visit again."

"I intend to."

Zinthia descended the stairs. Eigenea looked out at the nest.

"What was that about rain?" Karrid asked.

"There's a storm about fifty miles out to sea." She pointed to the horizon, where a small saucer of cloud hung stark white. "I've convinced it to come visit us." She turned to Karrid. "I've been working on a conjuration to use against the Shadowsaint. It requires a bit more lightning than I can muster."

"And if it doesn't work?"

Eigenea thought of the Iron Garden.

The birds in the nest squawked.

Eigenea looked out towards the skyline. "There's only one thing that gets them that excited."

Patheus was a bright point visible over the city, speeding towards them on outstretched wings. In moments he was hovering outside the tower window.

"I found it!"

"Found what?" Eigenea asked.

"The flaw in the Unction! But I don't know how to reconcile it. I need you. We have to hurry."

10

AN ANGEL, Karrid learned, does not merely soar through the air on beats of its wings. It defies the pull of the world. She did not feel like a burden under his arm, but rather a weightless feather gliding alongside him.

Even more stunning was the realization that she saw, in some tantalizingly limited increment, what Patheus saw. Perspective warped. The city below became an incongruous blur as buildings left smeared traceries in their wake. Time seemed to blossom and dissolve at a pace both ponderous and shockingly swift. The sky spun into a pastel swirl.

She looked up at Patheus. To her surprise, the angel tipped his head and returned her gaze....

The city's beautiful from here, isn't it? No wonder the kingdoms of the world envied it, and decided it needed to be leveled.

Again and again, invaders came with genocidal intents. The floor of the bay is littered with corpses of a dozen sea-giants, and ten times as many wrecks, all mercilessly sunk for the crime of assaulting the city. Some of that is Eigenea's doing. She beat back many who came here to despoil this place, but it might surprise you that she talked most of them out of their plans. She's quite the diplomat when she needs to be, demonstrating the futility of conflict with Orphicca with almost unnatural ease. But then, there's a lot that's unnatural about her.

Ah. Look there, the web-like lines spreading from the city. That's the world's vitality drawing into Orphicca. The Gloss leach it from other lands. That's the cost of the Gloss' gift. The farther away, the worse it is. The Viridian Sea on the far side of the world is unnavigable because of the layer of dead fish choking the surface.

You're asking how this could happen. I'll show you. The Gloss appeared in a glistening cloud of radiance, filling the sky. It circled the world three times. I and other angels followed it, hoping to divine its nature.

It reached Orphicca, cohering into a great reflective shoal above the city. The firmament was obscured by an aerial view of our city reflected down at us. It hung there for a full day before Eigenea asked me to carry her up to it.

In her eyes it was but a glittering mass humming with energy. I saw its true form, like dust, only much smaller. Each infinitesimal grain was lit with a fragment of a spark, as if a ghost had parceled itself out to reside within a million million motes. Each coordinated with the others in a language built from numbers, forging a single unified whole, eclipsing the light of Ouranos.

Eigenea greeted it. It came as a shock to both of us when it responded. It called itself the Gloss, claimed they traveled the void in search of refuge. It sought only the most blessed of places, a location fated to be their home.

Eigenea, ever the contrarian, didn't believe in fate. She told it Orphicca was nothing special, just a city where people got on with their lives. There were no resources to plunder, few riches to procure. We do not seek the grandeur of the great empires, she said, or the glories of conquest. We are probably the least-blessed city in the world.

It is perfect, the Gloss said, as it broke into its component particles.

Eigenea summoned the wind to stop its descent. It did nothing. She tried to speak to the ward spells Voskus Mauer had cast across the city. They were silent. Below, people danced in the streets as countless flecks of light fell, soaking into the buildings and roads. The Gloss imprinted itself on the structure of the city, rendering it immutable.

The next morning, messengers were dispatched to spread the news. People on the walls watched in horror as the horses and riders turned to dust. Many demanded Eigenea pry the Gloss from the city. Within days, other effects became apparent. Those who had been on death beds now walked with newfound health. Within a month, ruined buildings stood as if remade. Within a year, farmers reported crops and livestock exceeding the needs of the city.

And then, of course, there were you Lastborn, with your dark eyes and rapid maturity. No one knew what to make of you, or why the Gloss gave you to us. It wasn't until a few weeks passed without new pregnancies that we realized how significant you were.

Some people raged. Others felt hopeless. In the end they fell back into familiar patterns, accepting the new truth:

The City of Blasphemers was now burdened with a blessing it did not want.

The communion faded, and Karrid looked down. They were descending towards the manor. It was a sprawling place from this vantage. Karrid could make out the circular garden with the iron growths.

She pondered what Patheus has just shown her. Despite the dreamlike nature of the revelations, one fact nagged at her: the manor below was resistant to the Gloss thanks to Voskus Mauer's sorcery. But he had also cast ward spells across Orphicca.

Why hadn't *they* worked?

The sight of the Unction hanging in the war room gave Karrid pause. Overhead light cast its shadow onto the table. Paper lay everywhere, full of inked scrawls and tabulations. Empty ale bottles littered the floor.

Aughan looked up from his cleaning, a chain of healing amulets hanging from his neck. "Madam, may I please spindle this? The scent has grown intolerable."

"Not yet!" Patheus cried, waving at the shape. "I've studied this all day and it doesn't make sense. These intersections are asymmetrical. The vector differentials needed to turn a person into this don't calculate."

Eigenea grabbed his shoulders. “Patheus, slow down. You know I can’t follow your logic.”

The angel closed his eyes and breathed. “Its level of manifestation informs its orientation. I’m trying to solve the equation for a hostile entity emerging from unseen angles to Unction the unwary, but only a fraction of it adds up. Something’s changed.”

“What if it wasn’t hostile?” Eigenea asked.

Patheus snapped his head to her. “How could it *not* be?”

“I saw it watching you last night, when you floated right in front of it. It didn’t attack you. In fact I don’t think it could fully perceive you.”

Karrid gestured to the Unction. “It perceived its victims easily enough.”

“It may not see them as victims, just a source of what it needs. But why rob a warm body of its dimensions if all it gains is a few moments of corporeality?”

“It’s looking for something!” Patheus said, wide-eyed. “These manifestations are exploratory! That changes everything!”

The angel sifted through the strewn papers, scribbling notes.

Karrid stepped to Aughan. “How do you feel?”

The ape paused, not expecting her question. “I am adequate. Thank you for asking.”

“And thank you for snatching me from a rather long fall.”

Aughan’s mouth tried to curl, but it was obvious he was not accustomed to smiling. “I could not let one so skilled with the saber go to waste.” He turned to Eigenea. “How was your visit?”

"Illuminating. Sebastyn's clearly getting information from somewhere."

The statement puzzled Karrid. "You said he sees what his cult sees."

"He knows the Shadowsaint is robbing victims of dimension, but Patheus just confirmed that yesterday. I told him I was cutting off his access to the wind, and he put on a good show of outrage, but he's being fed secrets from somewhere."

"You suspect the Shadowsaint," Aughan said.

"To be honest, I just don't know. If we had an inkling as to its needs and motivations I could at least make an educated guess, but we don't even have that."

"I've got it!" Patheus shouted, plucking strands of the Unction like harp strings. "Isolated divisors. Uneven polynominals. It's a compulsion. It…" The angel leaned in and sniffed the Unction. "I think it has a duty to fulfill." He looked at Eigenea. "It's never attacked any of you."

"Yes, it has." Aughan said.

"Only after you jumped on it. But it's never instigated a fight."

"The woman who first saw it," Karrid said, "claimed it leapt away from her."

"It's not trying to terrorize us, It's trying to complete a mission. The Unctions are attempts to manifest fully, but it hasn't found the way yet. It's like having one lock and a hundred keys."

"What will it be when it fully manifests?" Eigenea asked.

"I don't know, but we'd best find out. It will appear in Little Ul-Chabaad, right after sundown."

"That's less than an hour!" Karrid said.

"Ghosts of old," Eigenea muttered, "the market is still open."

"I have to get there before the Unction!" Patheus shouted. And then he was gone, the backdraft of his departure sending papers into the air.

The labyrinthine streets of Little Ul-Chabaad were narrow and dark.

Karrid saw turbaned heads turn at their approach, eyes wide at the sight of the galloping silverback with an old woman astride its back. People cleared the street before them.

They raced along the canal, crossing it at the Bridge of Virtues. Monkeys and starlings scattered from their path. Beyond lay the market, where merchants hawked wares from blue and white striped tents. Large carts hauling produce filled the street, forcing them to work their way down the crowded sidewalk,

Karrid looked up. The storm Eigenea had summoned was certainly taking its time getting here.

"I see him!" Aughan roared.

The path opened onto an intersection bracketing one corner of the market. Patheus stood at the center, glowering as he scanned his surroundings. People pressed up against the walls. Eigenea gestured for them to leave, but they stayed frozen.

"It's here," the angel said, his voice a rumbling choir. "I can sense it."

The sky above the intersection darkened with hundreds of starlings.

Patheus looked up. "I'm all right, my friends. Stay where you are."

He took another step forward, and the flock dropped and swirled around him. Several of the onlookers clapped, earning them a stern look from Eigenea. The swirl of birds nearly concealed the angel, but Karrid saw him feeling the air in front of him.

"Damned protective birds," Eigenea muttered.

Without warning, the staggering mass broke from their orbit and shot forward. Something flickered ten feet in front of Patheus, and a floating sphere of red webbing expanded into being.

"Unction!" someone cried. People broke into panicked runs, draining away from the intersection.

That was when the rain started.

Karrid peered into the downfall. Fifteen feet in front of her, she saw water cascading down the contours of something that wasn't there. The shape grew, gaining form.

Aughan dropped into a crouch. Patheus shot a hand towards him. "No! Nobody move!"

The angel spread his wings and lifted a foot into the air, slowly floating towards the shape. Lightning flashed, and the gap in the rain grew more pronounced. Karrid made out the legs, torso and head.

"I'm right here," Patheus said, growing a little brighter.

The rain-sketched head turned, water rolling down its incline.

The angel's body jerked forward. The air rippled. Water sprayed to all sides. The black shape become visible through the rain, its tendrils around Patheus like a net. It was larger than it had been last night, and its stinger had grown back.

Patheus tried to grapple with the Shadowsaint, but it twisted, lifting the angel and slamming him to the ground. The pavement cracked with the impact. The stinger punched into the road near his head with terrifying speed, sending up stone flecks.

Aughan rushed forward and tackled the Shadowsaint. They slid across the ground with a grating rasp, the snared angel dragging behind them.

Karrid drew her saber and charged.

The Shadowsaint flung Aughan off and stood upright. Eigenea raised a hand, sparks flashing off her fingers. The Shadowsaint ran, weaving like a length of black satin caught in the storm, legs skittering across the wet pavement. Karrid looked around to get her bearings, dread rising in her stomach.

"It's heading for the wall!" she shouted.

It vanished around the corner. Patheus rose and sped after it. A moment later his body flew backwards, landing hard on the intersection.

Eigenea looked at Karrid and pointed to the fallen angel. "See to him!" she shouted as Aughan lifted her up and carried her after the Shadowsaint.

Karrid rushed to the angel. He had a fist-sized hole in his chest, pulsing with silver light. She instinctively felt for a heartbeat. Patheus grabbed her wrist. His eyes opened, ablaze with radiance...

It struck me, Karrid! What an interesting sensation. Is this pain? It took something from me, something it needed. I'm not sure what. I tried to commune with it, but there's not enough thought to touch. Only part of its mind is here. But I felt something. It has to complete its function, but doesn't know how. It's lost, without context. Imagine if you lived in a cave without light or sound, and found a way out. What would you do if you ended up in this city? You wouldn't recognize anything, couldn't process the stimuli assaulting you. There would be nothing for your mind to grasp.

It's searching for something…

Something it has to destroy…

Oh my...

The communion ended abruptly. Patheus looked up at Karrid, the light of his eyes matched by the glow radiating from his skin.

"I do believe," he said in a voice like a sea of gentle kisses, "that I'm having another epiphany."

His prone body rose up. Karrid stepped back. The angel looked at her, light pouring from his eyes.

"Go after them. You need to be there."

Eigenea and Aughan stood at the end of the street, facing an open plaza. The Northern Wall rose eighty feet on the other side, slick with rain. Torches blazed at intervals along the wall, casting everything in wavering light. Eigenea turned to Karrid as she approached, gesturing her to stop.

"What is it doing?" Karrid asked.

"We have no idea."

The Shadowsaint paced along the base of the wall. In the torchlight Karrid could make out its shape. The crab-like legs touched the plaza floor on delicate points. The torso was wider than looked possible. Its tendrils twined into limbs, which it ran across the brickwork. A wedge-shaped head pivoted frantically.

Why hasn't it sunk into the ground yet?

"It's looking for a way up the wall," Aughan said.

"I don't think so," Eigenea said

It staggered, as if stepping into an unexpected hole. Karrid saw it struggle to extricate its leg, leaping a few feet to one side as it pulled free.

The head turned and looked at Karrid. She could feel its gaze like a wave of cold focusing on her like a searchlight. Beneath that was a underlying sense of recognition. The head turned again, first towards Aughan, then Eigenea.

It dropped into a crouch and charged.

Eigenea raised a hand. The angry clouds above churned. Lightning lanced down with an angry crack. A furious nimbus formed around Eigenea. She reached her other hand towards the Shadowsaint, and a white-hot arc leapt from her to the approaching thing.

A pain cut across Karrid's belly.

The Shadowsaint stopped and looked down at the blinding cascade striking its torso. Its tendrils unwound, spreading outward.

The Northern Wall lit up with dazzling hues. Shifting prismatic colors danced across the brickwork. Karrid looked to the Shadowsaint, and saw shimmering light fanning out behind it.

Like light through a prism…

The lightning stopped. The air around Eigenea was thick with steam. The Shadowsaint was motionless.

Several stones atop the wall slipped free, crumbling to rubble when they hit the plaza.

"That can't be," Eigenea muttered.

More stones darkened. Huge cracks ran along the brickwork. In moments the entire section resembled a stretch of time worn ruins.

"No!" Eigenea shouted, running towards the wall. Aughan swept her up and carried her back to the street. The three of them watched as the wall collapsed, blossoming into a vast cloud of dust.

There were shouting and screams. Karrid heard Eigenea call to her. But something else was calling as well. It wasn't a sound as much as an intuition drawing her attention. She turned in time to see the Shadowsaint's angular head sinking into the ground. As she watched, tendrils shot up, clawing at the plaza floor before slipping away.

It's being pulled in.

City Guard poured into the plaza. Karrid was aware of the rain stopping, and the thick smell of stone dust. She looked at the breach in the wall, easily a hundred feet wide. Guard scurried atop the rubble, sabers raised.

In the darkened distance, the countless torches of the Bahl-Maqrea surged forward.

11

THE SCRYING GLASS showed the scope of her failure.

The view from the Northern Wall magnified to the hills beyond the encampment, where rows of fresh reinforcements had been waiting for the signal to advance.

The bay was covered in a thick mist. The Bahl-Maqrea's four-masted ships looked like skeletal hands rising up. The sun, still low in the sky, sent long shadows reaching across the fog towards the cliffs of Orphicca. How long had this fleet been hanging just over the horizon with opportunistic intent?

The streets of Orphicca were filled with panicked people with nowhere to go. Every terrified face stung Eigenea.

Aughan led Zinthia into the parlor.

"This won't be good news," Eigenea said.

"It isn't," the Abbess replied. "The magistrates arrived at sunrise with writs of absolution. They've released Sebastyn."

"Of course they have. He knew this would happen. If he'd escaped, he'd be a fugitive. Now he has the run of the city. What about the monks?"

"They are deploying as we speak to assist the Guard."

"Good," Karrid said, stepping from the hall. "We could use the help."

Eigenea scowled. "I guarantee Sebastyn will find a way to curb their efforts."

"You're sure he's involved?" Karrid asked.

"He could've easily communicated to the Bahl-Maqrea. Summoned them. Told them he would enable them to take over the city. But right now I'm not sure of anything" – she raised her wine glass – "except this. How bad is it out there?"

"They overran much of Little Ul-Chabaad. We're holding them at the Bridge of Virtues. But their reinforcements will be here soon." She turned to Zinthia. "Even with your help we'll only last two days."

"You underestimate us," the Abbess said as the clock struck nine bells. "I'd best return."

Aughan showed her to the door. Karrid stepped up to Eigenea. "I've just come from a meeting at the Citadel. The magistrates demand you be brought into answer for the collapse of the wall."

"What did the mayor say?"

"He told them they could have you tomorrow."

Eigenea looked to the image of the fleet. "If there is one."

"How *did* the wall come down?"

Eigenea shook her head. "I'm not sure."

"Yes, you are," came Patheus' voice.

They looked up. The angel lay across the ceiling, wings spread, looking quite comfortable. "It Unctioned your strike, turned it into something the Gloss couldn't tolerate."

"That's not possible," Eigenea said.

"You think the Gloss is impermeable?"

"No, but I'm an elementalist. My sorcery can't simply be *changed*."

The angel dropped to the floor. "By anything?"

"Another Mauer could do it, but if you haven't noticed I'm the only one."

"Regardless, you all saw it happen." Patheus looked at Karrid. "And I suspect you saw more than most."

"What does that mean?" Eigenea said.

Karrid looked at her. "Last night, I felt a...connection with it."

"With what?"

"The Shadowsaint. I could sense its gaze. When your bolt struck, I felt it." She placed a hand on her stomach.

"When did this start?"

"At Cenotaph Circle. On the roof, I sensed it looking at Patheus. I thought I imagined it, until last night. Eigenea, it *called* to me."

Eigenea sat on the couch. "Explain."

"As the wall fell, I felt something begging for my attention. I saw it sinking into the road, but it was resisting. It wasn't taking refuge in the city. I think it was being pulled in."

Patheus gripped the sides of his head. "That's it! That's what it's trying to do! Escape the Gloss!"

Eigenea gripped her forehead. "Ghosts of old, what are you talking about?"

"The Shadowsaint took something from me when it struck last night, a handful of divinity. But that contact also triggered an epiphany."

"About what?"

"The Gloss. The numbers don't add up."

"*Nothing* about the Gloss makes sense," Eigenea said.

The angel paced. "Orphicca is a big city. It has a metabolism, linked systems of resources, with the good of the populace as its guiding priority. The Gloss optimized that. Our food and water supply, our sewage, our health, all maintained with peak efficiency. They took the greatest city and inflicted it with perpetual obsolescence by perfecting it. But we forget the rest of the equation, that the lands beyond are slowly dying. The Gloss is clever, channeling all the world's vitality to one location and letting the rest slowly fade away."

"How is that clever?" Karrid asked.

"The Gloss made our labors futile, along with our genius, and our hope. You've seen the malaise in this city. The thing soaked into these old stones has, by every measure imaginable, done more harm than good. So I ask you, if the other lands died off tomorrow, how would you feel?"

Karrid shook her head. "Horrible."

"Yes. Much of the population would be overcome with remorse."

"You're saying the Gloss crossed the void to riddle us with guilt?" Eigenea said.

"Exactly. Many people would find it too much to bear. They might become despondent enough to, perhaps, hurl themselves from the city walls."

Karrid's eyes widened. "And the ones who didn't…"

"Couldn't reproduce," Eigenea said.

"The Gloss isn't a blessing or a curse," Patheus said. "It's a brutally effective way of killing the world."

Eigenea stood. "Why would it want to do that?"

Karrid looked at Eigenea. "Abbess Zinthia told me Voskus Mauer thought Jannan's bridge to Orphicca might attract something hostile."

"He did," Eigenea said. "He cast warding spells on the city as a contingency."

Karrid's black eyes narrowed. "Are they still active?"

"Yes, but they proved useless against the Gloss."

"Maybe they weren't," Karrid said. She turned and strode briskly from the room.

Eigenea and Patheus followed her down the long hall to the entrance. In the front yard, Karrid stopped and stared up at the facade of the manor. Eigenea followed her gazed.

The gargoyles looked back.

Karrid pointed to them. "They're only alive as long as you tell them they are,"

"Yes," Eigenea muttered. "An old Mauer trick."

"You said Voskus told the buildings of the city what to do. What if he crafted defenses against all those scenarios in the murals at the monastery, hoping to counter whatever befell

Orphicca, and buried them deep in those hidden directions Patheus told us about?"

"He couldn't have conceived of something like the Gloss," Eigenea said.

"His hexes kept it out the manor," Patheus said. "Maybe he told the city to go one step further and birth a creature capable of protecting it. That would explain the Shadowsaint's compulsion, and the exploratory manifestations."

Eigenea stared at the gargoyles. "Why would a defensive spell turn citizens inside out?"

"Jannan's paradox," said Patheus. "Those who pray for themselves *can't* pray for themselves."

"What does that have to do with this?"

"Could Voskus have instructed the buildings to follow such a rule?"

"Of course not. Spells are literal things. They have to…"

Realization hit her.

"What is it?' asked Karrid.

Eigenea turned to her. "He cast spells to defend the city. He never said anything about the people in it."

She turned and walked into the manor. Karrid and Patheus followed.

In the war room, Aughan was picking empty bottles off the floor. He flashed Patheus a scowl.

"We need to bring the garden fully awake," Eigenea said.

Aughan's eyes widened. "Madam…"

"Don't worry. I just need to tinker with it. But I'll need bait." She pointed across the room.

Aughan looked, and gave her a disgruntled expression. As he trundled off, she turned to Patheus. "You two need to be present when it manifests."

"I don't know where it will be. I don't have an Unction to examine."

"If you're both right, you won't need one." Eigenea walked to a cabinet and pulled an item from a drawer.

"What's that?" Karrid asked.

"A mage compass." She held it between her fingers, feeling mild charge flow from her. "Right now I'm setting it to aim at any concentration of Mauer sorcery." She handed it to Patheus. "It should get you there in plenty of time."

"You're not coming?" Karrid said.

"No. With a touch of luck, it will come to me. You need to keep it occupied until it does."

Karrid squinted at her. "How are we supposed to do that?"

Eigenea looked at Patheus. "You have to give it what it needs."

The angel was studying the compass, smiling.

"We can't do this without you," Karrid said.

Eigenea placed a hand on her shoulder. "You've already shown you can."

"What if Sebastyn shows up?"

"If you need help, I strongly suspect you'll get it. Now, go to the mayor. Tell him I'm ending this tonight."

The pair left, Patheus still grinning like a drunkard.

Aughan returned, carrying the glass box containing the Shadowsaint's stinger.

12

KARRID left the Citadel, and found Patheus standing on the steps.

"Anything?" she asked.

He held up the compass. "Too early."

They climbed into her carriage. Outside the archway, injured guards were being rushed to the barracks. Karrid once again felt negligent in not joining.

"That was an exceptional bit of calculation you did at the manor," Patheus said, his wings spread leisurely across the carriage seat.

"It wouldn't have occurred to me without your communion. But I still don't understand why I felt a rapport with it."

"That's the thing about Mauer sorcery, it always recognizes its ilk. I'm actually ashamed I hadn't thought of it earlier."

"Thought of what?'

Patheus handed her the mage compass. Karrid looked at the angel, puzzled. "What's this for?"

"Look at it."

She did. The needle was pointing at her.

"Why is it doing that?"

"Because the Lastborn weren't caused by the Gloss. They're a defense mechanism too. Voskus knew the city would need a new breed to defend it. Rapidly maturing. Frighteningly intelligent. Exceptionally skilled at combat. I wouldn't be surprised if you have a few other talents you're not aware of yet."

Karrid moved the compass left and right. The needle swung to track her.

"You're saying the Lastborn are weapons?"

"Potentially, but that's true of everyone, isn't it?"

Karrid looked out at the sun, low in the sky, partially obscured by small mass of cloud.

"Did Eigenea say she was summoning another storm?"

The angel didn't answer. She looked at him. He was staring at the compass.

The needle pointed west.

The souls went silent as Eigenea entered the Tormentorium.

She placed the stinger on the shelf beside the decanter holding the Mother-of-Silence.

"You're about to have a very unique opportunity, old girl," she said, twisting the cork out. "I know you'd like to be spirited into an *eidolacra*, but I have something *much* more interesting."

Dark vapor exploded from the decanter, rising to the ceiling in an angry churn. Eigenea could feel the Mother-of-Silence's hatred towards her. She held up the stinger with both hands.

"I know you want to possess me, but have a look at this."

The vapor dropped in coils, wrapping around the stinger, flowing along its contours. Eigenea felt its curiosity grow.

"I know it's not much, but it's better than flesh. Of course, if you want to go back in the bottle…"

The vapor contracted onto the stinger like inhaled pipe smoke. It flexed in Eigenea's hands, and she felt it radiate bliss.

"Good girl," she said. She tucked the stinger under her arm and looked around at the other decanters. "Now, as for the rest of you…"

Rampart Square was deserted.

Patheus exited the carriage and flew around the fenced-in park three times. Karrid could see that his eyes never left the compass.

He landed in front of her. "It's pointing to the middle of the Square."

"Is it here?"

"Not yet, but it's coming, clawing its way out from the city."

Karrid looked around. "Has it ever *returned* to a location?"

"No, but it's never had a sip of my divinity before, either. Maybe it's remembering."

Without warning, the carriage sped away.

"Now where's he going in such a hurry?" Patheus said.

Karrid noticed mist creeping in from the edges of the Square.

"Sebastyn," she muttered.

"Very good," came a voice.

She turned to see a figure approaching through the thickening mist.

"I've heard so much about you, Lastborn," he said. "The clever Elite working with Eigenea. Not so clever to tell when you're being followed, though. Hello, Patheus."

The angel glared at the bald man. Karrid was unsure of the look in his eyes.

"Nothing to say?" Sebastyn said. "That is such a disappointment. But I'm certain we'll have plenty of time to talk later."

"What do you want?" Karrid asked.

"What we all want. The Shadowsaint. It and I shared a moment four years ago," he turned and took in the misty square. "Right here, in fact. We were fated to meet again."

"Fate," Patheus said, "is just the delusion we use to justify our choices."

Sebastyn smiled. "Is that angel wisdom? How sad. It is the will of Ouranos that I rule this city. There will have to be some changes made."

Patheus stepped forward and sniffed the air. "You summoned the Bahl-Maqrea."

"One does not *summon* such a savage tribe, but the wind was nice enough to convey my offer. I told them they could cast the populace of Orphicca from the walls, and make this city what it's meant to be: a tribute to the old ways, a living prayer to Ouranos."

"Your cult wasn't enough?" Karrid asked.

"Oh, they could have done it, but I needed them for another task."

Figures became visible in the mist. Karrid counted at least thirty. They carried weapons. A few bore the silhouette of City Guard epaulets.

"The Bahl-Maqrea are a distraction," Karrid said. "To keep the Guard occupied."

"You see, you *can* be clever if you set your mind to it. I'll have to remember that when this is over."

"The Shadowsaint won't do your bidding."

"What makes you think I want it to?"

Patheus began laughing.

"I just got it," he said. "What Eigenea told me."

"What are you cackling about?" Sebastyn demanded.

"'Give it what it needs.'"

His wings snapped open, sending the mist into swirls. One beat, and he sped towards the center of the Square.

***

"You shouldn't have sent them alone," Aughan said as he took the stinger from Eigenea.

"They'll be fine. Besides, I didn't want Patheus here while we did this."

"This...*thing* can really kill an angel?"

"It can destroy anything. That's why I conjured it in the first place."

The ape gave her a disapproving look.

She stepped to the center of the garden, looking up at the jagged shapes around her. "When the Gloss first came, we had no idea what it would do to the city, the *people*. The mayor was worried we'd all turn into ghouls or monsters. He told me he wanted a way to destroy the city and everyone in it, just in case the worst happened. Place it up there."

Aughan hoisted the stinger up to the bough she pointed to, close to the center of the garden. It squirmed as he released it.

"Are you sure you can control it?"

"No, but that's never stopped me before. The effect should be easy to moderate. And while that's the Mother-of-Silence in there, it's still part of the Shadowsaint. Now step back."

Aughan withdrew to the entrance as Eigenea pricked her thumb and let the blood fall to the soil.

Slowly, the iron shapes around her began to grow.

"Patheus," she whispered, "don't let me down."

"Patheus!" Karrid shouted, peering into the mist.

"I suspect he's quite gone," Sebastyn said.

Karrid drew her saber and held it beneath the mage's chin. He raised a brow. Karrid heard a shuffling, and saw his followers moving in.

"I think I've seen enough," came a voice.

The sound of objects whipping through the air came in a sudden, coordinated wave, followed by grunts and yelps. Karrid was aware of many more figures in the mist. The metallic sound of clashing blades rang out, followed by the dull thud of falling bodies.

Sebastyn looked around, trying to mask his panic, small tongues of fire playing across his hands. A figure stepped out from the mist behind him. Stark white hands lay upon his shoulders.

"No fire today, I think," Abbess Zinthia said, looking over the mage's shoulder and winking at Karrid.

"I need to find Patheus," Karrid said.

"Go." The Abbess jerked her head sideways.

Karrid ran in the direction Patheus had flown. The mist around her was filled with Jannanite monks in combat with Sebastyn's followers. She dodged blades as she weaved through the melee. Once clear of the battle she shouted the angel's name. He did not respond. She kept a hand outstretched before her, fearful of running into an Unction.

The sound of something dragging across the grass whispered beside her. Karrid turned, saber raised, to see one of the Shadowsaint's tendrils snaking through the mist. A massive crab-like leg jutted into the ground beside her, its joint a full six feet above her head. She ducked and rolled, coming up to see the mist before her flicker with shadow. There was a sound like a deep belch. The air around her shimmered. Karrid took a tentative step forward.

A fierce and sudden wind struck her, accompanied by the loudest roar she had ever heard. She fell back into the grass, dropping the saber and clamping her hands to her ears. The air above her cleared as a vast cavity opened in the mist like a bubble, revealing the night sky.

The Shadowsaint stood in the clearing, looming over her, easily a hundred feet tall.

Eigenea stared at the view from Rampart Square on the scrying glass. “Ghosts of old,” she muttered.

A moment later the roar reached the manor. Aughan’s ever-implacable manner seemed to slip at the sound.

“Gather your blades,” she said. “I suspect we’ll have a visitor soon.”

“I cannot do battle with *that!*” he shouted.

An involuntary laugh escaped her. “No, I’ll handle that.” She turned to the hidden passage leading to the garden. “It called. Time for us to respond.”

The Shadowsaint twitched and flailed, as if unfamiliar with its own body. The stinger tail lashed out, splintering a pair of trees.

Karrid scrambled backwards.

Its torso bent, and it looked down at her. She felt that cold gaze of recognition, a thousandfold greater than she had last night.

It turned and strode off, giant legs churning sod with each thundering step. It vanished into the mist until all that was left were the tremors.

“Karrid,” came a whisper.

She twisted her neck to see Patheus on the grass not far from her. She scrambled to hands and knees and crawled over to him. “What happened?”

"It needed dimension. I gave it some. Let it gorge on me. I've got plenty to spare."

Across his face veiny blisters throbbed. New ones blossomed, while others receded back into his perfect skin.

"You were Unctioned?" Karrid asked.

The angel looked at his hands. One finger expanded into a loop of flesh. Another split lengthwise into three writhing petals. "An odd sensation. A bit like being in Ouranos. It felt as if I was swimming in a sea of infinite directions."

"Are you all right?"

He propped himself up. "It depleted a lot of my divinity, but it still hasn't fully manifested. There's more inside it. I saw something, a strange equation I do not understand. I'm calculating it now."

Footsteps approached. Abbess Zinthia ran to them. One side of her white face was terribly burned, but she showed no sign of pain.

"What happened?" Karrid asked.

"Sebastyn escaped. Set the grass around me ablaze."

"He'll go after the Shadowsaint," Patheus said.

The sounds of collapsing stone reached them.

That was when the screams started.

Eigenea stood at the center of the garden, arms outstretched. Thin lightning snapped from her hands to the thorny shapes towering above. They glowed a faint red, reminding her of the furnaces on Kiln Row.

The Iron Garden began to sing.

***

They cleared the mist to find the neighborhood in ruins.

Several buildings lay leveled. Shop fronts were now piles of rubble. People ran from the destruction.

"At least it will be easy to follow," Patheus said.

He grabbed Karrid and Zinthia and lifted them into the air. They saw the Shadowsaint almost instantly, bringing down a four-level warehouse with a swing of its tail. Its tendrils whisked at the ground, sending sprays of debris into the air.

"It could level the city," Karrid muttered.

"It's trying to get at the Gloss," Patheus said, "but it doesn't know how."

The air filled with a bone-deep hum. Karrid's teeth ached. It reverberated like a single note held by a choir of millions. Even Patheus was affected, suddenly losing altitude. He landed at the end of a ruined street.

High above, the Shadowsaint leaned its head towards the distant sound.

"Good work, Eigenea," Patheus said.

"What is that?" Karrid asked.

"Her garden, it's awake."

The Shadowsaint twisted its body and surged forward, each step threatening to knock Karrid off her feet.

Zinthia looked at the wreckage. "My monks will tend to the injured."

"We need to get to the manor," Karrid said, holding her arms out.

Patheus looked at her. "I can't carry you with that noise in the air."

"Fine," she said, scabbarding her saber. "We run."

***

The gargoyles flew out, flitting about the Shadowsaint's head. They led it on a route that would minimize damage to the city.

Animals fled as it dredged up the glade with its tapered legs, each step scarring the land that Mauers had tended for years.

Tendrils, now two feet thick, swept forward, striking the gate wall with such force that stones hit the facade as if catapulted.

One leg drove into the front yard.

The Shadowsaint stopped.

Eigenea stepped around the chunks of fallen masonry around the entrance and looked up at the towering figure.

"That's right," she said. "There's no Gloss here."

The torso bowed down so quickly Eigenea could hear the wind in its wake. The Shadowsaint's head dropped until it loomed over her. In the faint moonlight it reminded her of a ship's prow carved in slick black marble. Hooked mandibles hung beneath, and tapered flanges rose from each side like donkey ears. Eigenea saw parts of the head shift and blur, as if it was still putting itself together.

"This is Mauer territory. You recognize that. Nothing gets into this manor uninvited."

Tendrils reached down and probed the front lawn. One waved slowly in the air before Eigenea.

"*You* are invited. You will find answers here."

There was a creak like straining wood as the Shadowsaint began diminishing in size. It shifted its legs, swinging one at a time over the wall.

Eigenea turned and entered the manor. Aughan stood at the end of the hall, blades in both hands. His expression at the sight of the Shadowsaint ducking to follow her through the door made her smile.

“I can handle this,” she said. “Go see to the Tormentorium.”

With an angry growl, he turned away.

Eigenea waved a hand and the wall slid aside, revealing the passage to the garden. She frowned. “No need for subterfuge today.” With a creaking rumble, the passage contracted until the garden stood just beyond the door.

The sky above the garden churned. Clouds gathered above the tops of the structures, contracting into a swirl.

Eigenea raised a hand, and the garden ceased its song.

The Shadowsaint’s head pivoted down at her.

“Don’t worry,” she said. “Just a little demonstration. This is the Iron Garden. Look up there. You see that? It’s your old stinger. It's the reason you can understand me. I granted it a little life, placed it here, gave it a jolt, and it sang to you. The garden sent that song all across the city.”

A tendril snaked through the air, reaching up to where the stinger writhed in its bough. The head looked at her, tilting slightly.

“You’re wondering why I’m doing this. A few reasons. I can’t abide any more Unctions in my city. I’m a Mauer. It’s my duty, and like you, I have yet to carry it out. The Gloss was my failing. I couldn’t stop it descending. Sixteen years and I still don’t know what it is or why it came here. Frankly I know longer care. Voskus crafted you to protect us, so we’re going to see this through, tonight.”

***

Karrid climbed the mountain of ruins blocking the street.

"I've lost sight of it," Patheus said, scampering behind her.

"I thought I saw the gargoyles," she called back. "I wish I knew what Eigenea was planning."

The sound of the garden suddenly stopped.

Instantly, Patheus scooped her up and took to the air. The wreckage below warped and blurred. Her ears still buzzed from the sound. As they rose she saw the trail of ruins cut through the district. Patheus followed it. She reached for the hilt of her saber. In moments, the roof of the manor was visible above the trees.

Patheus reached one arm forward and took her hand.

Zero is never really zero, Karrid. I've sought oblivion, but I know now that doesn't exist. The light of Ouranos reaches everywhere. See? Raw nothing coheres into immensities of causality and consequence. Worlds are born. Some have sorcery. But look there. Some have machination-driven systems devoid of gods. Others rise from webs of instrumentality where thought manifests action. A few are just a homogeneous fog of cold probability conducting souls like lightning. Existence dwells in a panoply of states, as if the light of Ouranos was passed through a prism.

I think I know what I saw inside the Shadowsaint. It's been bound down in the stones of Orphicca with the Gloss. It's seen it. Heard it. Knows its purpose. And more.

There is not one Gloss, but many. They slip between those states of being, riding the light of Ouranos to obscured expanses. They seek out worlds that show potential, gauge if they're stuck in cyclical patterns of stagnation, unable to perceive the future. Those they ignore. But if a world strives to break its ancestral chains, they are judged a threat. The Gloss sees such ambition as arrogance. Could not a culture with such drive someday become something more? Something that could ply the same light as the Gloss?

Something that could surpass them?

The Gloss would have passed over this world, but it sensed the prayers beaming from Jannan, bridging the distance to Ouranos. It saw Orphicca was different from the rest of the world. This city sought to be something greater, but it was alone in that endeavor. Then I carried Eigenea up to it. Its million million motes all focused on her, sensed her power, the pervasive force of her sorcery, and the lengths that she would go to. A world that could produce such a creature could indeed threaten them.

Karrid, the Gloss descended because it was terrified of Eigenea.

"You're like an *eidolacra*, a vessel for housing Voskus' ward spells, cobbled together from stone dust and dead skin. The detritus of the city hidden away in unseen directions. We thought you would return in six years. We never considered that you returned only when you had the *ability* to. Your brief jaunts among us take considerable effort, especially with the Gloss constantly pulling at your heels. But the Gloss has been draining the world's essence into Orphicca, and that includes its *sorcerous* energies. I'm guessing it has no use for that, but *you* do. Voskus always was good at utilizing whatever resources he could access. That's why this place is full of artifacts."

The Shadowsaint looked up at the structures of the garden. A few tendrils wrapped around the nearest trunks.

"Do you admire my work? It's called an Immolation Engine. It's a fairly ancient technique for leveling a city. The Jannanites have a painting depicting its effect. It takes any force, like sorcery or divinity, and amplifies it, resonating like a tuning fork. It could turn my lightning into an all-engulfing fireball. Orphicca would be incinerated in moments, though, I must admit, I doubt it would do much to the Gloss."

There was a rumble from the clouds above.

"But you're not just a spell. Patheus said you could unfold into a shape we cannot perceive. You absconded with dimensions trying to become something the Gloss couldn't get its hands on, but you weren't able to really manifest until Patheus got to you."

Eigenea stepped closer to the Shadowsaint. Parts of its body continued to blur.

"There's a lot more to you, isn't there? Folded up inside. Enough to spread across all those unseen directions and permeate every square inch of this city."

It looked down at her with something other than eyes.

"Enough to Unction the Gloss," she said.

As they approached, Karrid saw the upper limbs of the garden rising over the manor, pointing to the roiling clouds above.

"Look at that," Patheus said.

The gate wall of the manor was ruined. Whole chunks of the facade had fallen away.

"Eigenea," Karrid muttered.

They set down on the lawn and ran for the door. Just before they reached it, Sebastyn stepped from the shadows.

A torrent of fire flowed from his hands, engulfing both of them.

The Shadowsaint stood in the center of the garden, tendrils twining among the growths, weaving into the upper branches like vines. Above, the storm cloud flickered with internal light.

Eigenea withdrew her blade and poised it over her thumb.

"You can come out now," she said.

Multiple footsteps sounded behind her. Some of them were metallic.

She turned to find two Bahl-Maqrea in their gray-green armor, longswords drawn. Sebastyn stepped from between them, staring up at the garden in admiration.

"Oh, Eigenea, I knew you were working on something here, but I never expected *this*. You *really* believe destroying the city would be preferable to returning to the old ways?"

"This never had anything to do with the old ways," Eigenea said. "You just want the city for yourself."

"I'll have so much more than that. I'll have your sorcery. I'll have your manor," he stepped forward. "Now step away so I don't have to incinerate this place. I'd hate to damage *my* new Immolation Engine."

"If the Gloss lets you keep it."

Sebastyn turned to her. "Why wouldn't it?"

"I suspect it's keeping you on a tight leash."

His eyes narrowed in those thick lenses. "You'll display respect to me, witch."

"Ha! That'll be the day. When did the Gloss first recruit you? I'm guessing after the very first Unction. It must have realized what the Shadowsaint *really* was, probably even worked out its connection to me through Voskus. That must have come as a shock: a trap that didn't spring until years after they it arrived. It needed someone to be its eyes and ears so it could get control of the situation, and who better than a mage able to communicate with *anything*. You had the magistrates send me after a fictitious warlock just to keep me off the trail."

"Civic leaders will clutch at any hope they're given," Sebastyn said.

"Most people will." Eigenea stepped forward. "That's why it was easy for you to gather a cult so you'd have eyes everywhere. But you didn't count on Patheus being able to find the Shadowsaint. And when Aughan's attack caused it to become corporeal, the Gloss realized it had a problem." She looked at the Shadowsaint. "You weren't praying to it at Rampart Square, you were showing the Gloss where it *was*, taking its full measure so the Gloss could pull it back into the city. Trying to have me killed was just a bonus."

"You underestimate yourself. You were a threat to them. The Gloss told me this manor was resistant to their influence, and you would not heal as others under their blessing would."

"I don't need its blessing to heal. Remember what I told you in your cell: sorcery is a willingness to bear the cost in full. I'd wager the Gloss taught you that lesson while you were imprisoned. Did it hurt? Please tell me it hurt. That thought makes me happy." She pointed at the two Bahl-Maqrea. "You got back in their good graces by coming up with the idea of displacing the citizens and repopulating the city with true believers. A fresh start. No more doubters. No more sorcerers.

Except you. Is that why you did it? What am I saying? Of *course* that's why you did it."

Anger spread across Sebastyn's face. Fire licked from his clenched fists.

"Madam," came Aughan's voice, "may I now kill these two?"

Sebastyn turned in time to see the ape drop from atop the wall onto one of the Bahl-Maqrea with a dull crunch. The other brought his sword around with impressive speed, but Aughan caught it with crossed blades.

Sebastyn raised his hands, both ablaze. He did not see the tendril that wrapped around his midsection, lifting him up and bringing it face to face with the Shadowsaint.

"You should know," Eigenea said, "that it heard every word."

Panicked, Sebastyn gripped the tendril with both hands. Flames flared, and the Shadowsaint released him. He ran up the incline of the garden, past Aughan and the Bahl-Maqrea delivering punishing blows to each other.

In the parlor, he looked back; Eigenea waved to him. He turned to run, but instead found a livid gray cloud of smoke blocking his path. He opened his mouth to scream, and the souls of the Tormentorium rushed into him.

Eigenea looked at the Shadowsaint, then to the clouds above. She nodded, and the lightning came down.

13

SPECTRAL BRILLIANCE poured from the manor. It spread across the city, reaching each district and borough, illuminating every enclosed space.

In the Citadel, the mayor and his staff looked up as the walls of the office pulsed with luminescence.

In Little Ul-Chabaad, the Bahl-Maqrea heard a sound like a great exhalation. Every surface oozed glints of light. They rose like a swarm of star-flies, a golden blizzard in reverse.

In the war room, the air grew cold, and Unction above the table flexed. The light fractured the space it occupied into facets. Bones tumbled into place. Knots of sinew slipped loose. Flesh unfurled. The dream tabernacle cracked open, spilling spindled Unctions across the floor. Their filaments spun into the air in a frenzied dance of remaking.

Eigenea shielded her eyes against the blinding glare of the lightning. The garden was a white-hot jumble of barbs and angles. At the center, the Shadowsaint's form unfolded into concentric polyhedrons of radiance. Maddening vistas abruptly opened around her, like multiple views from a scrying glass all at once. Reflections compounded each other into perspectiveless depths until the garden appeared infinitely wide.

Focusing on the Shadowsaint, she found only a void. Lightning bristled around the absence, contracting it into a rarified keyhole view of stars and darkness. Just before the void collapsed, she felt gazes fall upon her. Impossibly ancient, they viewed her across eternal distances.

She averted her eyes. She'd had enough of the infinite today.

The lightning stopped. The garden glowed around her. She saw Aughan against the doorframe, breathing heavily. Bits of armored plating lay scattered on the ground. The entrails of the Bahl-Maqrea were strung across the branches, smoking in the heat. She ran to the ape. He waved off her assistance with a dismissive grunt, and gestured inside.

Sebastyn stumbled across the parlor towards the hallway, coughing uncontrollably, limbs twitching like one possessed. He turned to her, blood-red eyes magnified in his lenses, wisps of gray vapor leaking from his mouth.

"Your tormented ghosts c-can't stop me," he sputtered. A faint golden nimbus pulsated around him. His fists ignited into torches. "The Gloss is in m-me now, and it's very angry."

Eigenea tried to muster a charge, but she was spent. She pulled her small blade.

There was a blur of motion, and a shape appeared in the hallway. Its blackened flesh smoked. The brittle remains of ruined wings spread.

"Patheus," Eigenea muttered.

"Guess what we've learned tonight?" he said.

Sebastyn turned. He moved to step toward the angel, but couldn't. He looked down at his chest, where two feet of saber protruded.

Karrid's face appeared over his shoulder, black eyes reflecting the flame sputtering from his hands. "We Lastborn are fireproof."

Sebastyn's corpse slid from Karrid's saber onto the parlor floor. The golden nimbus flickered and extinguished.

"No no no," Patheus said, limping towards the garden.

Karrid followed. Above, she saw an aerial view of the manor reflected back.

"The Gloss is leaving!" Patheus cried.

"Good riddance," Eigenea muttered.

The angel spun on her, black bits of flesh flying from his cheeks. "If we let it go it will do it again to some other world!"

"That's not my concern."

"No, it's mine. Eigenea, every path I've chosen, each calculation I've made, every instant of my very long and wasted life has brought me here."

He leaned down to Karrid, and placed his blistered lips against hers. In a voice resonant with pure divine love he said, "Goodbye, my Lastborn."

The angel hurled himself down the slope of the garden. At the bottom he leapt, skeletal wings out as if trying to fly. He snagged two branches, still pulsing an infernal crimson, flesh hissing on contact. Silver light leaked from his scarred body.

Karrid lunged forward. Eigenea's arm blocked her. She looked in the Archmage's eyes. They were sad and triumphant at the same time.

Everything turned white.

A blast wave slapped her to the ground. She felt bones shift on impact.

Intense brightness rose from the garden, narrowing like a focused beam. Karrid clamped her eyes shut. She heard an almost metallic crackling from above, and the pained roar of something impossibly old.

As the light diminished she forced her eyelids open. The sky shone with countless stars. There was no sign of the Gloss.

Eigenea lay beside her, face red from the heat, looking at her with a stunned expression.

"What is it?" she asked.

The Archmage smiled. "Your eyes are blue."

14

ZINTHIA sipped from her wine glass. "I'm not happy keeping Sebastyn's corpse beneath my monastery."

Eigenea laughed, sending a pain through her ribcage. "I'll burn it as soon as I know it's no longer a threat. How many were injured?"

"Many hundred. They recovered a great deal during the night"—she touched her scarred cheek—"though the process halted at daybreak."

"Looks like the healers will back in business."

She looked at the scrying glass. It showed the Citadel. A line of magistrates in Sebastyn's service were being led away in chains. The mayor stood at the top of the stairs and watched them go.

Aughan entered the parlor. "I have escorted the victims to their homes."

"How much do they remember?" Eigenea asked.

"Very little, though they all claimed to have dreamed of Ouranos."

Zinthia turned at her, eyebrow raised. "It's said Jannan works in mysterious ways."

Eigenea waved a hand dismissively. "Don't you have monks to *not* pray for?"

"I suspect she's about to get more," Karrid said as she came in, arm in a sling. "Most of the Bahl-Maqrea retreated, but a few hundred just fell to their knees and began praying."

"Why?" Eigenea asked.

Karrid shrugged. "Take your pick. The sight of the Shadowsaint's rampage, ghostly light spreading across the city, the Gloss rising, the brilliant beam that burned it from the sky. Whatever the reason, they now think Orphicca is a blessed place."

Eigenea gripped her forehead. "It never ends."

"On the other hand, the first travelers left the city this morning. Caravans are preparing to depart in the next few days, and the harbor's being reopened. The mayor's happy that Orphicca might become a trading city again."

"It'll be full of visitors, all anxious to see the City of Blasphemers." She downed her wine. "Ghosts of old, it will be *exhausting.*"

Karrid didn't answer. She crossed the room and stood in the charred doorway to the garden. Eigenea and Zinthia joined her.

The iron structures had vanished. The only thing the garden contained were the bones of Patheus, floating serenely at its center, skull tilted back, arms outstretched as if embracing the sky.

"I noticed on my way here," Zinthia said, "that there was no birdsong."

"They're mourning him," Karrid said. "Just like us."

"Oh, he's not dead." Eigenea said. "But then he was never truly alive, not as we understand it. He's a creature of unseen spaces. Jannan became a bridge to Ouranos. I suspect Patheus achieved something more."

"Best be careful," Zinthia said. "Your manor might become another monastery."

Eigenea looked at the remains of her friend, and followed the gaze of his empty eye sockets up to the sky above.

15

This sequence never reaches an end. Few do. The consequences of our actions reflect off moments too acute to avoid, or splinter into a spectrum of new significances. Here, in the unreckoned spaces beyond the world, they embark on trajectories too swift to follow.

Wisps seep into hidden realms and birth gods. Base intents magnify into world-snuffing malignancies. Angels immolate themselves on iron spikes and become...

Well, that's the question, isn't it?

Epiphanies reveal truths outside the scope of mere experience. They can come from Ouranos, conveying divine insight, or from convoluted equations aligning into flawless solutions. Or perhaps they are the cunning strategies of long-dead sorcerers...

The Shadowsaint imbued me with what it knew of the Gloss. Now I propagate that knowledge. I listen for prayers of souls looking up to find perfect mirror images reflected back at them. I ride the light of Ouranos across a topography of eons and bestow comprehension where it's needed. I have become an epiphany. It is a bliss indistinguishable from oblivion.

Gaze at this immensity in the gaps between moments.
Worlds are born. Worlds die. Worlds live again.
The prayers for those who do not pray for

themselves shine like a beacon into
the void. Follow it to its source
and it becomes clear that
all sequences collapse
down to
zero.

THE MISTS OF LU-SHAN

DONNA ROYSTON

MY SERVANTS were not happy. They all filed out of their small room and looked reproachful while Chang Min came forward (I think they had drawn lots) and addressed me, saying that their quarters were cramped and had mice. I comforted them, saying that at some moment in life we all have to brush mouse droppings from our pillows, and that they should try to harmonize their personal will with the natural Way. This did not appear to mollify them. I added, then, that it was only for two nights and that the memory of even such a fleeting holiday would be greatly treasured by their overworked master when he had returned to the Imperial City. At this, their expressions brightened and their eyes shone, because it pleased them when I had to wheedle for the service that they should give eagerly and without complaint. They consulted briefly, and Chang Min conceded that perhaps it would not do too much harm to their well-being to stay in a country inn for two nights and that they fervently wished good health and long life (the liars!) to their most beneficent employer—as long as it was only two nights. And so the crisis was averted, both sides saving face.

The landlord, a friendly and obliging man giving the utmost of his simple amenities, bowed many times, apologizing while he explained that he had to seat me with his sole other guest, unless I preferred to wait until the other was finished eating, for he had only one table. One must expect less formality at a rural inn, so I said that I had no objection to dining with his other guest, and I hoped my presence would not disturb him; I added that if this person had any objection, I was content to wait—but I did not place unnecessary emphasis on this. And when I followed the landlord to the next room, I saw the guest, seated at the table. He was dressed plainly, in the style of a minor official; he sat with an erect posture, an unyielding bulwark of a man with dark complexion and thick hair, and his eyes met mine coldly.

And I recognized him at once. General Ko Hung was the idol of the land since his great victories during the previous summer. I had stood as a spectator among the cheering throng that had lined the road for his victory procession, and this man was unmistakably him.

After the obligatory courtesies and introductions had gone back and forth, our host being the intermediary (Ko Hung gave a false name), I was seated at the table: a very rustic affair, unpainted, and not even covered with a cloth. I realized that the innkeeper was not in on the secret—that is, he was not obliging Ko Hung by keeping his identity confidential, but truly did not know that his guest was the famous general. Strangely, too, Ko Hung appeared to be unattended by his staff. My own body servant, Fei Lien, had come with me into the room and stood in the background. A quick glimpse in his direction told me that his eyes were fastened on Ko Hung in amazement.

Meanwhile, the general continued with his meal, his black brow lowered, and he gave me no further acknowledgment as I sat opposite him. The innkeeper, who had left us alone, reappeared long enough to set a dish of noodles with vegetables before me, and then bustled away again.

I found myself ruminating over what I had heard about the general. I did not know him personally, but we were not, after all, far separated by common acquaintance, both of us being employed by the emperor's court. So I had some (what I believed to be) reliable information. And there was no one in the entire land who was more gossiped about than Ko Hung.

For he was not only great in military accomplishments, but learned as a scholar; he had taken the civil service exam at age sixteen and received the highest score that anyone had attained in over fifty years. And yet, neither victories nor erudition fully accounted for the adulation with which the public regarded him. He had *majesty*, some said. Others, less entranced, said he had a vast self-regard. Some men said, in lowered voices, that Ko Hung was a man with a destiny; and others, hearing this, shook their heads in alarm and were silent.

All this passed through my mind. But I could not sit with him in silence for the entire meal. A light subject of conversation was needed, I thought.

"And have you come to see the dragon?" I asked.

"Dragon?" he repeated.

"There are, I think, no less than three pools of Lu-shan that are supposed to have resident dragons."

"I did not come for a dragon," he said.

"There is generally a hermit or two living here, as well," I added. "You are aware, are you not, that the recluse Kuang Su, who was summoned in vain by the emperor to supply him with wisdom, lived here a century ago before ascending into Heaven to become an immortal?"

"I was not aware of that," he said.

"The mountain is a lodestone for seekers," I said. "Perhaps because it is so easy to get lost in it."

"A paradox?" he said. For the first time in our one-sided conversation, his expression had sharpened from boredom into interest.

"One who seeks is very often also one who is pursued," I said. "When you lose yourself you must turn your gaze away from what is behind you and look at where you are going."

"To be lost," he said, with heavy irony, "seems to me a less profitable state than you describe. It is confusion."

"There is much to find that can only be perceived by not looking and understood by not thinking."

"I see you have studied the Way," he said, "to have mastered such riddling language. Are you, then—seeing that you are here—pursued?"

"By a pack of hungry servants and remorseless duties," I replied. "I am making a short pause here, to find a poem or two on Lu-shan."

"A poet," he grunted, dismissively.

I saw that I had become irrelevant.

I also perceived that the general, however exemplary he was in military and scholarly spheres, failed in the social graces. I was tempted, since he did not want to talk of amusing trifles, to see if he could be needled by letting him know that he had been recognized. "Allow me to congratulate you on your wonderful victories on the western frontier, General," I said. "You have served your land and emperor far beyond the abilities of your peers. You must feel singularly blessed."

"Thank you," he said. Again his manner communicated boredom. But for a moment, I saw alarm flicker in his eyes, and I now knew the posture for a sham.

Neither of us spoke for the remainder of our meals. But after he had finished his noodles and drained his cup, he looked at me and said, as though explanation were necessary, "I have come to meet the hermit who lives on the mountain. He is said to have wisdom." And then he rose and bowed and wished me to find good poetry, and retired to his room.

How very strange—that I had provoked the great general into a lie.

In the morning I was up early, but Ko Hung was earlier still. I saw him, as I looked out the window, disappearing into the mist, on foot and unaccompanied. It is an uncanny sight to see a man become gray and insubstantial-looking and utterly dissolve.

Fei Lien brought me, as I had requested, clothes that were suitable for mountain climbing: a red shen-i embroidered with gold dragons, and a red cap.

"Make sure not to omit anything from the supplies," I told him. "I do not want to reach the top of Dragon Head Peak, sit down to compose, and then find that there is no ink."

"Rest assured, esteemed master," he said serenely. "Your writing materials will all be present and ready to serve you."

With that, we went outside to join the others, assembled on the path. They now knew about our famous fellow-guest, and were disappointed to learn that he had already left the inn. By "disappointed," I mean they were excessively, even offensively, downcast, as though I had personally done them an injury, and they could talk of nothing else.

I turned my mind to the reason I had come. This was my holiday, and I was going to enjoy it, if by dint of determination I could. I felt the awesome presence of the mountain all around me, in spite of the mist that prevented me from actually seeing it.

Lu-shan rises vertically toward Heaven, a thing too great to be expressed by the word "mountain," for it is not one peak but nearly a hundred. The sheer sides of these peaks are mostly worn and fissured granite, but where there are outcrops and ledges, or any purchase in a crevice, pine trees cling. The trees are ancient, yet they are so dwarfed by the size of the mountain itself that they are like moss on a boulder. When there is no mist in the valley, the observer who gazes upward sees ragged, jagged rock shoulders and long waterfalls. These cataracts strike the rocky walls and throw out a fine spray which dazzles the eye and joins with the sea of cloud that flows around the mountain, sometimes hanging motionless around the peaks, sometimes wreathing sinuously around its sides, sometimes (as today) rolling through the peaceful valleys, a silent, slow-moving flood too circumspect to touch anything with a heavy hand. Clothed in its ever-moving mists, the mountain, it is said, never looks the same twice.

I had seen Lu-shan's worn cliffs, its waterfalls, many times as I passed it in my travels. This morning, standing outside an inn at the foot of Dragon Head Peak, submerged in the cloud-sea, I "saw" the mountain only as I conjured it in my imagination. At the edge of vastness, the world had become very small.

We set out, I heading our small procession. Fei Lien, as the chief of my servants, followed me, carrying my satchel with pens, brushes, ink, and paper. After him followed Chang Min, carrying a red and gold folding chair. Chuan Hsu and Hsiao Kang brought food and drink, supplied by the innkeeper. Teng Ai carried the food serving implements, and Kai Huan carried my umbrella. Kan Pao carried scrolls of classical literature. I must point out, lest you think I encumber my servants unnecessarily, that these were for his own use. He is hoping to enter the civil service, and in his unoccupied moments he studies for the examinations. I encourage him in this effort because the sooner he passes his exams and procures a gainful position with the government, the sooner he will leave my own employment. And I benefit from his studies in another way: when he is not preparing for his exams, he writes poems of his own and asks me what I think of them. Thus, it is much better that he study.

"I have devised a plan," I told Fei Lien, who moved up to walk beside me for ease of hearing my instructions. "I will divide the journey up the mountain into stages, and I will write a poem for each stage. For instance, here we are at the base of the mountain, at the start of our journey. We should pause in a picturesque spot that will be conducive to my poetic imagination, and there I will write my first poem."

Fei Lien nodded gravely. "I will assist in selecting a suitable spot."

We walked on for several moments. The mist was, as I have already mentioned, thick, so there was no grand vista looking upward at the mountain peaks this morning. To my left appeared a rocky boulder that was attractively fringed with ferns and overhung by a graceful cryptomeria tree. I started to gesture toward it, but Fei Lien frowned and shook his head.

Perhaps he was right. I did not press it. We continued, and shortly came to a grove of small trees with deep green, glossy leaves and sinuous trunks. I paused to consider the possibilities here.

"Not suitable," said Fei Lien.

"Why not?" I asked.

"Noble lord, the scene has no suggestiveness, nor harmonic resonance with the beginning of a journey," said Fei Lien.

I could not think of an argument against this, so I resumed walking. Behind me, the procession also started forward again. I thought I heard a sigh, but when I glanced back I could only see duteous and keen faces.

Our path, going ever upward, turned this way and that. There were markers, I saw, ones that looked very old and worn, and I wondered who had placed them there. But I was grateful for them, for I saw they would keep us on the path.

"Fei Lien," I said, "perhaps I should not seek a perfect spot. After all, the work of a poet is inward. I can compose a poem on the start of a journey without the benefit of a striking view or a symbolic setting."

"There should be no compromise in the creation of art, respected master," he said.

"In an ideal situation, perhaps, but we are progressing upward, and soon we will no longer be at the beginning of the journey."

"It is a great, dizzying height, lord, that will require exhausting toil and all our strength to climb. We are merely strolling on the mountain's little toe."

"Here is where I will write, Fei Lien," I said. "Chang Min, place my chair."

Chang Min came forward and set the chair down carefully and unfolded it, making sure, by moving some stones, that it sat level and secure. I sat down. Fei Lien placed paper before me, handed me a brush, and stood by, holding the ink pot.

I pondered.

At times during an uneventful journey, I entertain myself by composing literary works in my head. Usually this is poetry, but not always. At this moment, for some reason, my mind began to pursue not ideas for poems, but the beginning of a treatise on the subject of hiring servants for one's best advantage. I observe that many officials fail miserably at this. To wit:

The Art of Hiring, Supervising, and Rewarding Servants for Your Best Advantage and Personal Safety

There are a number of reasons to have servants, in spite of all their trouble and expense. First, of course, they are a necessity for a man of certain position and responsibility. This fact cannot be denied. A man in a high position in the Emperor's court cannot take care of his own laundry, cook his own meals, light his own fires, do his own shopping. You must find people who can do these things for you, competently.

The man who would hire a servant usually commits one (or more) of several errors. The first of these errors...

"Uncle Ch'o?" said Kan Pao.

I turned to look at him. He was sitting at the side of the path, bent over a scroll. "Yes?"

He looked up, his face wearing a dissatisfied expression. "This story about Confucius and the fisherman, it doesn't make sense."

"What is it in particular that disturbs you?"

"It's just ...strange. I mean, the fisherman tells a story about a man who's afraid of his shadow and his own footsteps, and he runs faster and faster to escape, until he falls down dead—that's kind of funny, I like that. And I see that's supposed to be Confucius, making rules and making things busier and busier, instead of stopping and making things simpler and being still. So when he hears the story, Confucius sees how wise the fisherman is and bows to him and asks to be his pupil. And the old man says *no*, because..."

> *The first of these errors is, he hires a young relative who is in need of a job but ill qualified in every other respect. It is a virtue to take care of one's family and advance them when possible, but you should seek another and better way to accomplish this. Think of what happens to a relative in a paid position. He will see you in your nightclothes, and eating meals. He will see you spill soup on your robe. He will know that you suffer from digestive ailments or a sluggish colon. Seeing you every day in your own household, and being encouraged by your other servants to recount family lore consisting of stories of your childhood and early mistakes and indiscretions (which he, being younger than you,*

should not even know, except that they have been retailed to him by your aunts), what can possibly happen but that he will find common ground with his fellow servants instead of you? Disharmony comes to your home, where all should be tranquil repose and quiet time for thought. This sad end is best avoided altogether: do not hire a relative, no matter how much his mother pleads, with tears running down her face, that her son desperately needs a chance to...

Suddenly I realized that Kan Pao had stopped talking. I had the impression that he had finally stated his point, or asked a question. I almost made the mistake of asking him to repeat what he had last said. Then I recollected myself.

"Nephew," I said, "there are two kinds of understanding with which to approach this story. The first understanding is of the civil service examiner, who tests one or two thousand young men each year, and who will not care about the subtleties of the story's meaning or your grasp of it. He will ask you to write it out verbatim, and if you pass to the next level, he will perhaps question you about whether it was a rice farmer, rat catcher, or fisherman who explained the Way to the Master, but he will not ask you what you learned about the proper cultivation of your person, guarding of your truth, or avoidance of what is external to you. The second understanding is that the sacred writings do not reveal themselves easily or quickly; they will give you years of contemplation, and as you get older you will marvel that you see different ideas in them which you had not noticed when you were younger. So ponder them, but do not ask me for their meaning. If I tell you what the story means, it will cut short your process of understanding. It is only through your own striving that you will understand."

"But somebody must have figured out by now what it means," Kan Pao protested.

"Indeed so, I agree completely," I said. "But can he tell you what he has learned?"

Kan Pao made a vexed sound and rolled his eyes up to the sky. It is hard on a young person, when the sages do not have his convenience foremost in their thoughts.

Kan Pao returned to his scroll. After a further distraction of picturing Kan Pao in a conversation with Confucius and imagining what each would say to the other, I came back to myself and realized that the paper was still before me, and Fei Lien was still standing by with the ink. Where was I? Oh, yes. The beginning of a journey.

"Fei Lien?" I said.

"Yes, noble lord?"

"Our fellow guest at the inn, General Ko Hung. Do you not find it odd that he came to Lu-shan unaccompanied by any servants or companions and went out this morning onto the mountain by himself?"

"Perhaps," Fei Lien conceded. "But it is a humble pilgrimage..."

"Yes, last night he said he came to seek out a hermit who lives here. He suggested that he was in search of wisdom."

"And is there a reason to doubt this, esteemed master?"

"I had the impression from talking to him that he had no interest in pondering the Way. Why, then, seek wisdom from a recluse? This strikes me as contradictory."

"Perhaps the matter that concerns him is too near to his heart to discuss."

"Perhaps," I said. "Perhaps that is it."

But I did not believe it. The man had at first disdained the suggestion of seeking a hermit, even when made lightly, and only a short while later had thrown it to me in the manner of one tossing a scrap to a dog.

I reflected a bit longer on this puzzle, and once again realized that I was avoiding the task of writing a poem. Now, being stern with myself, I focused on what needed to be done. Beginnings.

The path rises before me, ascending step by step;
In swirling mists, the goal cannot be seen.
Would not an archer be helpless in such obscurity?
Would not two armies fall to confusion?
But a walker keeps to the path without thought
Reaching the destination with ease.

I wrote the poem on the paper, and then read it aloud to everyone. There were some nods of approval, and some pursed lips. I was not satisfied with it, myself. Not every poem is a success, but I would revisit it later to try to determine exactly what was wrong and fix it, if possible. Now it was time to move on. Fei Lien put the writing materials away, and we resumed our journey.

***

There came to our hearing, as we walked the path upward, a sound of falling water, and soon we came to a rushing stream and crossed over it. The sound still grew louder, however, and I saw that we were coming to one of the many waterfalls that tumble over the mountainsides. Here we paused and I wrote another poem, this one about the power and effortlessness of water. This poem, although there was nothing technically wrong with it, did not particularly interest me. My spirits sank a little as I contemplated the poem. While I knew that I should keep a detached attitude, and I should not worry about two poems that I did not think were as good as one might wish, I couldn't help thinking that my artistic abilities were sinking into mediocrity, at best.

I sighed.

Then we continued on, climbing upward. To my disappointment, the mist continued unbroken, although we had been ascending for hours and the air had become much cooler.

I am not used to mountain walking, and as I paused to breathe, I realized that my legs were feeling weary and my knees weak.

"Let us stop here for a while," I said. "I think it's a good time for something to eat."

Kan Pao blew out his breath with relief.

"Are you tired?" I asked my nephew, a little smug that I was hardy enough to tire him.

"Hungry," he said.

Chang Min set up my chair and I placed myself in it, a little heavier than usual. My back creaked.

"The vegetation has changed here," I commented. "The cryptomerias have given way to pines. To one experienced on the mountain, the change is probably a sign of a certain height. It is unfortunate that we do not know what that height may be, and how close to the top of the mountain we are. I wish we could get a scenic view through the mist."

"Would you like your brush and paper, lord?" said Fei Lien.

"Yes."

As soon as he handed me the brush, I wrote:

The mountain speaks its own language
Which I cannot comprehend
Trees, ferns, and mosses are its words
Its breath a moving fog.

I read it out loud, decided (with relief) that it pleased me, and gave paper and brush back to Fei Lien. As I did so, my glance moved to the trees behind Fei Lien and I was startled to see that, without having made a sound in his approach, a stranger had materialized from out of the mist: an old man in a monk's robe, with a satchel slung across his shoulder. He was wrinkled and weathered-looking (somewhat like the mountain, I thought); bald on top, he made up for it with a long gray beard and hair that flowed from the back of his head and over his ears to fall loose on his shoulders. His eyes had a strange quality—of wildness—and the thought crossed my mind that he might be one of those hermits who become crazed from isolation and too many austerities.

I stood, joined my hands, and bowed to him.

He smiled in return and inclined his head.

"The blessing of Heaven on you, sir," I said. "My name is Sun Ch'o, and I would be most honored if you would partake of our hospitality, humble though it be."

"The mercy of Heaven for all," he replied. "I am Szu-ma Yu, servant of the Way and disciple of the Buddha. I make my small home here. I thank you for your offer and accept it with gratitude."

I introduced him to my servants, who all made a respectful greeting, and we sat down. While Teng Ai prepared the food and Hsiao Kang assisted him by lighting charcoal in the brazier, Szu-ma Yu said, "I have seen visitors come to Lu-shan before, but never an expedition such as yours. If I am not too bold in my curiosity, Sun Ch'o, may I ask what you seek?"

"A most precious thing, master recluse," I replied mysteriously.

He did not respond to this as I expected, with a question as to what the precious thing could possibly be—indeed, he did not respond at all—so I tried to smooth over the awkward silence that followed. "You see, I must periodically audit the finances and governmental actions of Lu-shan District. For years, in my comings and goings, I have imagined climbing the mountain instead of viewing it in passing. I have pictured myself wandering its paths, enjoying the scenery, and writing poetry. Yesterday, I decided that it was time to finally do it. So I came here after finishing my business with the governor, and I have made myself a day of leisure to write poetry and see the views from the mountain. The views, I'm afraid, have all been of mist, but the poems may pierce obscurity to see Lu-shan itself."

Now he smiled and responded with approval. "I am happy for your good resolve. Would you be pleased to share more of your poems?"

"That is a dangerous question," I warned him, "for I am indeed very pleased to share my poetry. Please stop me if I share for too long." And I recited some for him—my best, not the ones I had written today. I explained my idea of writing a sequence of poems to correspond with the stages of climbing the mountain, and added the one I had just written, in case he had not heard it as he had approached. Szu-ma Yu did not seem to weary of poetry, and he clapped his hands with child-like delight at the one written about Lu-shan. His enthusiasm was heady stuff for me and I cannot remember any other reading so pleasurable for me and my listeners, or perhaps I should say, one listener.

We passed from there into a discussion of the pleasures of poetry in general, and the benefits it bestows on mankind, while Fei Lien and Teng Ai served the food and drink. In the midst of this pleasant conversation, I heard footsteps; I turned my head and saw my fellow guest from the inn, Ko Hung, striding up the path. He stared at me and snorted. "Sun Ch'o the poet," he said. "I have climbed three peaks today, and how many have you climbed?"

"Only this," I said. "But I am having an enjoyable day. Have you found what you were seeking?"

"No."

"Then allow me to assist. I have by good fortune happened on Szu-ma Yu, venerable hermit of this mountain, whom I believe is the one that you seek."

Ko Hung gazed at Szu-ma Yu with an incredulous expression, then looked back at me. "I am not looking for him!"

"Then I apologize for the misunderstanding. What, or who, do you seek?"

He paced several times on the path and ground his teeth in anger.

"I had exact instructions on where to find what I sought. Or so I thought. Mist and clouds! As soon as I ascended, I found myself in the wrong place! A second time, a third time! Hermit, is this the peak called the Dragon's Head?"

"It is."

"And is there a cave on it?"

"There are many caves to be found all over Lu-shan."

"I asked if there is a cave on *this* peak."

"There is, above us."

"Show it to me."

Szu-ma Yu scratched himself indecorously, looking thoughtful, and then belched.

"Is there a treasure that you hope to find hidden on Dragon Head Peak?" he said mildly.

"You know of it!" Ko Hung exclaimed.

"There are treasure hunters from time to time," said Szu-ma Yu. "No one has found it, however."

"Found what?" I asked.

"The sword of Huang-ti," said Ko Hung.

"Or perhaps the South-Pointing Chariot. Or the Book of Pai Tse," Szu-ma Yu added. "At the Yellow Emperor's death, it is said that he was carried by the Responding Dragon away to the West, and one of his three precious treasures was hidden on each great mountain that he flew over. Some say that Lu-shan was one of those mountains."

"I seek the sword," said Ko Hung.

"It would be a marvelous treasure to find," I said. "But this is only legend. Where did you get the exact instructions that you mentioned?"

"Scholars have their uses. Old scrolls in the imperial palace, written with ancient symbols. In fact, not even scrolls. Rolls of bark, I was told."

"Really," I said. "But suppose it's the Book of Pai Tse that was left here?"

"I will know after I look in the cave," said Ko Hung.

"Assuming that what you seek is here, don't you think it is better to leave the relic undisturbed?" said Szu-ma Yu. "It was hidden for a reason, I am sure. The other seekers, after I have talked with them for a while, have always decided that it was best to end their search."

"When I make a resolve," said Ko Hung, "I carry it out."

"But why would you want such a thing?" asked Szu-ma Yu.

"Why?" Ko Hung repeated, as though amazed. "Old man, even if the thing concealed on this mountain was naught but the button from Huang-ti's cap, what matters—all that matters—is that it is the relic of Huang-ti. Any mortal man bearing his relic would be acknowledged to possess the Mandate of Heaven."

"You think that it will make you emperor, then?" I said, shocked. "But we have an Emperor—who shows no sign of having lost the Mandate of Heaven."

"The Mandate of Heaven has been withdrawn before, when the time needed another man who was more fit. It will pass to me, who has the strength to use it."

"This is not wisdom," said Szu-ma Yu.

"What would you know of wisdom, charlatan? All I require of you is to show me to the cave where the relic is hidden."

"The cave lies above, at the top of the peak," said Szu-ma Yu. "Humbly, I regret that I may not go with you; I have work that I must get done today." He held open his satchel, with an apologetic air, and I saw that it contained some herbs that he had gathered.

Ko Hung seemed, for a moment, taken aback. Then, "I have been delayed enough!" he said. "Enough searching— Why should I seek and waste my time when you know where it is?" He strode forward and seized Szu-ma Yu by the arm. "Show me where it is, old man, and do not make me lose my temper. I could pick you up and throw you like a child's toy. And on this mountain I cannot say when you would reach the ground."

"Ko Hung!" I said. "Take your hand off him!"

Kai Huan and Chang Min—they are my bodyguards—had readied themselves, hands on sword hilts, and awaited my command. But, although their response was quick and correct, I suspected they would be ultimately, and fatally, reluctant to fight the nation's hero. I cast about in my mind for an alternative, if there was one.

Ko Hung released Szu-ma Yu and drew his own sword. He held it lowered, but with the menace of one who did not expect refusal, ever, from anyone, and his expression was grim now. "Think carefully, Sun Ch'o," he said. "I will be generous if it goes no further. But do not stand in my way. The child-emperor will be swept aside, and I will be He whom you must please, and to whom you will perform the nine prostrations."

"You would create a civil war."

"Not I. The people will know me for their lawful ruler. Should there be war, it is the puppet and his kinsmen who would be responsible for bloodshed."

"Put up your sword, Ko Hung," said Szu-ma Yu. "I will not have violence, either to threaten me or defend me. If you wish to be shown the place, I will take you. I ask only that Sun Ch'o accompany us, to witness the Mandate of Heaven being bestowed upon its new possessor. Such a glorious event should have witnesses, lest there be doubters."

There was a pause, while Ko Hung turned this over in his mind. His eyes were narrowed as he looked at me, and then at Szu-ma Yu. Whatever his suspicions were, he seemed to overcome them.

He smiled, then, all at once in a good humor. "I do not need to believe your reasons in order to agree, old man. You fear for your safety; I have no reason to harm you if you keep faith. So let us go together! A pleasure excursion. And Sun Ch'o will have an opportunity for making more poetry."

I was, of course, in accord with going, for the reason of assuring Szu-ma Yu's safety, and avoiding violence—but also, it need not be said, for the reason of intense curiosity. We therefore set out, all of us together, with Szu-ma Yu leading the way, Ko Hung after him, and I and my retinue following them.

As we climbed the mountain, I pondered what I had learned of the general. The revelation of his motive was a hard problem to reconcile to his character. Why, I asked myself, would a man of so great honor and accomplishment, a man who required loyalty in his own subordinates, and who would, I was sure, be outraged by a personal betrayal, pursue such a path? Why would this man, who, I pointed out to myself, scorned both the fanciful and the philosophical, listen to tales of an ancient, dragon-transported sword, and then determine to search it out? If he thought it useful as a tool for legitimizing, in the eyes of the common people, a seizure of ultimate power, then any ancient sword could be produced and called the sword of Huang-ti.

Ah, I replied to myself, maybe he needs to convince himself most of all. And of course the spurious does not confer authenticity. Maybe fanciful dragon legends of today offend his deep need for an ancient and very powerful dragon who honored the empire's founder.

I could not believe that Ko Hung was a man without honor. I wondered if he felt some distaste for the task he had set himself. Maybe he is a man, I thought, who must keep busy. Not with any kind of work, but that which is difficult and which requires his full effort. When there is nowhere else for ambition to go, what then? Men must have an ambition to work for—something not yet attained—in order to live. Most of us have modest goals. But a few must have a great goal. They thrive on struggle, on problems, on adversity; and without that struggle, without purpose, without new frontiers, their minds go astray. They turn from emptiness, which is unbearable, and if there is no struggle to occupy them, they create one.

...Along these lines I speculated. How accurately, others must judge. Still the path ascended, and the climb began to seem interminable. I reached a point where all I could focus my thoughts on was no longer the question of the general's character but taking the next step upward. Keeping my feet on a treacherous path was my own challenge: it was all rocky mountainside, uneven and jagged, on which one had to test and judge where to place each step so that the foot did not slip: a rock that seemed to be part of the solid bones of the mountain could turn out to be but loosely held by the thin soil. I even saw Ko Hung stumble. Only Szu-ma Yu went as lightly as one on level ground, stepping easily from rock to rock, and occasionally calling out to take care in a dangerous spot. I saw Ko Hung as a gray figure, and Szu-ma Yu as one who moved in and out of existence, gaining substance if he paused on an outcrop to look behind as I moved forward, dissolving again as he continued ahead. Muffled voices behind me were passing warnings back, and they were the only way I could tell my servants were still following.

Sunlight, unexpectedly, broke upon us. We had emerged above the level of the cloud-sea, and we now found ourselves on a bare rocky ledge at the summit of the mountain. The peak had its name because from a distance the protruding rock suggested, to an imaginative person, a dragon's head. We stood on the dragon's snout.

I was captivated by the wondrous sight of the cloud-sea, as it flowed in slow streams and created its own ever-changing shapes. The rock on which we stood seemed to float on the mists, and one could almost think it would be possible to step down off the mountain and walk away into the distance. Across the gulf could be seen another peak of Lu-shan rising above the clouds, thinly clothed with pines, ghostly pale, like a distant island. But in spite of the unearthly illusion, I couldn't quite forget that we were elevated over an unseen gulf of empty space and far below, hidden by the cloud-sea, was the valley floor. Distant sounds of the waterfalls rose upward; closer, I heard the quiet disembodied *cronk* of a raven in flight through the clouds below. Other than this, however, as far as could be seen, there was only the cloud-sea, rolling slowly between the two peaks.

"Where is it?" Ko Hung demanded, rudely interrupting my appreciation of the view that I had gained with so much toil. "Where is the cave?"

"The cave is under this ledge," said Szu-ma Yu.

"What? Where? How can anyone reach it?" Ko Hung asked in rapid succession, as he comprehended.

Szu-ma Yu indicated the rock face that went perpendicularly down the side of the outthrust ledge. "There are handholds in the rock. You climb down, and to your left is the opening to the cave."

A feeling of admiration swept over me for Szu-ma Yu's gentle cunning. Indeed, why resist Ko Hung's threats? Only show him the impossible place that he could not reach, and the crisis was over—for today, at least. Perhaps he would return with men and ropes and ladders, but that would require time and planning. And then I thought: surely the hermit had not climbed down there! Handholds! There was nothing but weathered rock and a fall to the death when your hand slipped. Who climbs around on bare cliffs—under ledges, where you can't even see before climbing over the abyss—looking for what might be there? There was no cave; it was a fiction.

Ko Hung looked long at the rock, thinking, I would guess, what I was thinking. But I had underestimated his resolve, and his desire. At last he went to the edge of the precipice and began to lower himself over it. Not at the tip of the forward-jutting ledge—the dragon's nose, you might say—but rather under a cheek to reach his chin. I heard his boots carefully searching the rock for purchase, saw him test his foothold, reach with one arm, let himself down slowly, then reach downward with his other arm. He gave one look at Szu-ma Yu that I could only describe as dangerous—as if to say, *If you have lied to me, you will pay.*

"This is not necessary," I could not resist telling him. "Come back later with rope..."

I glanced at Szu-ma Yu, who was watching Ko Hung impassively. "He has chosen. He will carry out his resolve."

Ko Hung's head disappeared over the edge, his expression implacable. He did not bother to speak. He was concentrating solely on what he was doing.

For myself, the height was too giddy to even stand close to the edge. I visualized Ko Hung's downward climb in my imagination, and strained with him, but I could not watch. I imagined his hands grasping difficult holds, groping for a hold he could not find, a foot reaching into emptiness. Each moment I expected to hear the sound of crumbling rock and a despairing cry.

We waited.

"I see no cave," came Ko Hung's voice, harsh and strained, from below.

"It is there," said Szu-ma Yu, calmly.

There was a silence that stretched out into an ever-lengthening time in which I listened for Ko Hung's voice again, but it did not come.

"He has found it," said Szu-ma Yu.

There followed an interval in which we waited, and heard nothing. I looked out across the strange cloud-sea, its endless expanse like a meadow of gray-white cobwebbed grass covered with a predawn dew. No—I changed my mind, and it was a ghostly ocean, dreamed by a blind man. And then it was something else: another world altogether, where dead ancestors might at any moment be seen, the vaporous ground supporting their unweighty bodies, strolling without actually having to move their legs.

This thought made me shudder and momentarily wish that I was Kan Pao, seventeen years old and still without memories of dead friends and family members. And then I realized that I was warding off the merely fearful with the dreadful, and I recovered some tranquility of mind.

Seventeen years old again? No—mercifully—whatever else might happen, I did not have to fear *that.*

But I knew why I was thinking of the dead, instead of composing my final poem in this place of ethereal beauty. It was the thought of Ko Hung's desire for the throne. I did not doubt his ability to take it, sword or no sword. Should he actually climb back up to the ledge holding a sword, it was possible that he really would call on me to testify to the authenticity of his claim—something I did not wish or intend to do. And if he didn't…

Upon this thought, I heard a scuff of boot on rock and grunts of exertion: Ko Hung was climbing back up. I could not but be moved by his courage and impressed by his strength. Szu-ma Yu moved close to the edge of the precipice, looked down, and, bracing himself with left arm enwrapping a pine, reached over with his right hand and helped drag Ko Hung up onto our ledge, where he rested for several moments on his knees, panting. Szu-ma Yu bowed and stepped backward, retreating without a word to the edge of our little group.

Ko Hung's head came up slowly. He had a long bundle slung across his back, securely tied, and an expression of triumph on his face.

He took off the bundle and laid it across his knees, and began to tug at the wrapping. Layers of rotten leather, silk, and cotton padding fell away. And there, revealed, lay an ancient scabbard and hilt.

"It is fitting," Ko Hung breathed. "Of course it would be difficult to find and reach, so that only one who would risk his life could obtain it. And I have."

He stood, and withdrew the sword slowly. It was dark—black with age, I think, although it seemed not to have corroded.

Ko Hung held it up, enraptured, tip pointing to the sky. "Look, Sun Ch'o! The Mandate of H—"

His gaze had traveled down the blade to look at me, but was arrested. I thought he was looking at Szu-ma Yu and I turned my head to see what had so affected him.

It was not Szu-ma Yu. Moving in the mist on the path below us was a shape, indistinct ... but large... I saw golden shining eyes ... dread seized me, for it could only be a tiger, of enormous size, following us, his easy prey. This was only an instant's thought; then the face solidified around the eyes, as the creature came closer, and a body. A sinuous serpent shape—

A dragon!

It walked unhurriedly, even languidly. Its footfalls were silent, until I heard one claw faintly rasp against a stone, the only sound it made.

It paused to examine Teng Ai, youngest but for Kan Pao. He stood perfectly still, waiting for what was to come; fear was in his eyes. For a moment, no one moved, man and dragon looking into the other's eyes. Finally, the creature broke its gaze and turned to look at Chuan Hsu. After another long moment, it shifted its regard away from him, to Kai Huan. Not one of us moved or spoke, paralyzed with fear in its presence, while it considered us, one by one. It came to me, and looked into my eyes with its own strange amber-colored eyes, deep as the fathomless Lake of Immortals. A sensation came over me, as though I were falling asleep. Then it turned, and took a step closer to Ko Hung. Its golden gleaming skin brushed against me for a moment, powdery smooth and cool.

I watched as Ko Hung endured the creature's gaze, and the terror in his eyes was painful to see. The sword, still slackly grasped in his hand, now rested its tip on the ground.

With the quickness of an eyeblink, the dragon snatched him up. One moment, both were still, and the next, Ko Hung was being held in the dragon's mouth. He did not cry out. The dragon shook him gently, and the sword fell to the ground.

Then the dragon spread its wings, which had been so tightly folded against its back that I had not even realized they were there, and lifted itself into the air. The movement was as light and effortless as a deer's spring—with the difference that it did not return to earth but caught the wind and mounted into the sky. Briefly it was lost to sight in a billow of mist, but then it reappeared, circling higher. The terror of its presence gone from among us, I heard groans, and a quick look around me showed faces pale with horror, Teng Ai sinking to the ground as though he felt faint, Kan Pao hugging himself to quell his trembling.

I looked up again. The dragon had soared to such a height that he was tiny—he looked like a bird unless an onlooker's keen eyes could discern his sinuous shape and long tail. And then, as we watched, something separated from the soaring creature, and was falling—it had dropped Ko Hung.

We all cried out as he tumbled.

Teng Ai, sitting on the ground and looking upward, covered his eyes.

"That is the end," Chang Min whispered.

"He must be dead already," said Kai Huan.

And then I saw the dragon dive, hurtling downward, angling toward Ko Hung, and both disappeared into the flowing sea of clouds. Several moments later—and we were all waiting, holding our breath—we saw the dragon again, flying upward, carrying a body. Around the peaks of Lu-shan, over the cloud-sea he flew, swooping and soaring, at times tossing Ko Hung's unresisting and limp body up into the air and catching him again, playing joyfully. At one moment it seemed cruel and the next, to my mind, innocent, as though it were sharing its beautiful playground with a dull companion. I went from pity for Ko Hung to admiration for the wondrous creature over and again.

And we watched, unable to look away, so rapt that I cannot say how long this went on. Then, to our sudden alarm, the dragon, flying lower, turned straight for our peak. We scrambled as he came hurtling toward us. At the last moment, with a slight twitch of the wings, he lifted over our heads and dropped Ko Hung on the ground—and was gone.

I went to Ko Hung's body and knelt beside him. He lay unmoving, but he was unconscious, not dead. I could find no outward injury; I patted his face, called his name, and had Fei Lien sprinkle water on him. He awoke slowly and looked at us as though he found himself among strangers. Then his gaze shifted to the sky and remained there. Perhaps, mentally, he had not yet descended to earth and was still soaring and tumbling in the heavens. Whatever was going through his mind, he had received a great shock and was as helpless as a blade of mown grass.

"Put him in the chair," I said. "We will carry him down to the inn and get a doctor to care for him." Chuan Hsu and Hsiao Kang obeyed, and fitted in the handles that would allow the chair to be used for carrying.

"It is less than an hour to nightfall," said Szu-ma Yu. So quiet had he been, and so riveting the dragon's appearance, that indeed I had forgotten him. "Please take my advice and shelter at my hut this evening; it will be dangerous to try to descend in the dark."

I opened my mouth, wanting to ask a question, but some thought or feeling stopped me and I remedied my hesitation by saying, "Thank you for your kind offer; we accept."

As Ko Hung was settled into the chair, he lifted one hand and gestured at the sword. "Bring it," he croaked.

My nephew went and stood looking down at the sword. Then he knelt down, sliding his palms under the blade with great care.

"No," I told him. "Leave it there. The guardian will take it back. It does not belong to any mortal now."

Kan Pao looked confused momentarily, then stood up and backed away from the sword.

I felt Ko Hung's glare and pointedly did not give it my attention.

So we started on our way, following Szu-ma Yu downward on the path. As darkness enfolded the mountainside, we took a short side-way and came to his hut. It was very small, but sufficient to shelter all of us for the night.

We helped Ko Hung lie down on Szu-ma Yu's sleeping mat. He would not speak, but he did drink a little broth that was prepared for him.

We sat, our backs to the hut's wall, and ate a modest meal. Everyone was quiet, still affected by the awe we had felt at the miraculous event we had witnessed. One by one, each went to sleep until only I was still awake.

I found myself trying to remember if I had seen Szu-ma Yu during the dragon's flight. Where had he been, exactly? Somewhere to my right and behind me. Or so I had thought…

And then, out of nowhere, my final poem of the day came to me, vivid and powerful. Quickly, lest the poem evaporate as suddenly as it had come, I pulled a piece of charcoal from the brazier, and wrote in quick strokes on a piece of paper that lay near me, then dropped the coal and sucked on my fingers to cool them. For a time I sat and looked at the poem, marveling. It captured the beauty and power of the heavenly apparition in language to move and astound all who heard it. I had written a poem that would make me celebrated among the literary greats of history.

Then, because even great poets need to rest, I lay down and slept soundly.

In the morning I was awakened by the sound of my nephew's voice.

"...the fisherman says he's really hard to teach, and Confucius asks if he can be the fisherman's pupil and learn from him..."

I opened my eyes, and turned my head. Ko Hung was sitting up on his mat, awake, patiently listening to Kan Pao setting forth his problem, his dark eyes fixed as intently on my nephew as if Kan Pao were a lieutenant giving a report from the battlefield. Around him were ranged my servants in attitudes of respect or fascination. I suppressed the urge to groan. Well, Ko Hung had been a scholar of renown. He could cope with my nephew.

"...and the fisherman jumps in his boat as if he's scared and says 'I am leaving you now! I am leaving now!' And he does..."

The door to the hut was open, letting in gentle light and birdsong. I could not see any mist. I arose, feeling stiff, and was trying to steal out quietly when I heard Ko Hung say, "Kan Pao, allow me to consider your question for a short while. Ask your master to sit by me that I may speak with him."

All heads turned to look at me—since I had heard, I didn't see any reason to wait for the request to be relayed to me. I went and joined the others.

"May I be of assistance to you this morning?" I asked him. "We can carry you down in the chair to the village, where a doctor can be summoned—"

He silenced me with an imperious gesture, frowning. "Sun Ch'o, I do not leave enemies behind me."

"Am I your enemy?"

"Your report to His Imperial Majesty can destroy me."

"I have been pondering that. On one hand, it is my duty to do my part in preserving the realm."

"What is on the other hand?"

"That my truthful report will not preserve the secrecy of the sword's hiding place, and it seems to me that Heaven's wish is clear on that point."

"Are you saying that I can return to my army and you will say nothing of what happened here?"

There was a silence.

"No, General," I said at last. "If you return to your army, I will have to speak."

"Then I will make sure you do not reach the Imperial City."

I heard an intake of breath and everyone around me became still, tense.

I was struck, momentarily, by the thought of a treatise-never-written, imaginatively titled "How to Keep Yourself from Making Enemies at Court, and Stay Alive." There are two reasons why I have never written it. First, I hesitate to offer such advice lest it be, after the work's completion, rendered grimly humorous by my own fall from favor. It's better to remain silent on the subject for that reason alone.

But the stronger argument against it was that it felt disrespectful to the memories of honorable men who were exiled or met death, by implying that the failure was on their part. I have been at court long enough to know that better men than I have been undone by schemers, enemies, and rivals. It is never far from an official's thoughts that he could be next.

What would have been my advice to myself, had I actually set down in writing my imagined treatise?

I had no idea.

"If I may make a suggestion…or rather, ask a question…why return to your army?"

He barked a laugh, but it sounded uncertain.

"If you are weary of fighting…" I said.

"I am not weary!"

I tried a different tack. "You have seen something wondrous, but you have not been given the Mandate of Heaven."

He lowered his gaze. For the first time, he looked defeated. "Like the fisherman, it appeared to me, and then it withdrew. Not the Mandate of Heaven, but something more…"

"But it is not gone."

"What do you mean?"

"Is a teaching something that you grasp in an instant, like a piece of fruit? Or is it something that you glimpse through the mists and pursue with great dedication?"

He looked up at me. There was a long silence.

Finally: "Give me paper and ink," he said.

I motioned to Fei Lien to bring my writing supplies.

He took the brush and wrote, then handed the paper to me, still wet. "It is my resignation," he said. "You may give it to His Majesty."

I bowed.

"Now, scholar," said Ko Hung, turning to my nephew calmly, as if he had not just been threatening my life, "I will interpret your story."

At that moment, as I fanned the paper dry, rolled it up, and tucked it in my sleeve, I suddenly remembered my poem of the night before. How could I have forgotten? I had to look on it again—and, indeed, copy it in more permanent form and store it safely. I returned to the corner where I had spent the night.

I could not find it. Where had I laid it, in that moment when I drifted to sleep? I remembered clearly my certainty of its greatness, my belief that it expressed a great insight in words of surpassing artistry...and yet, incredibly, I could not remember a word of it. In my need I did not hesitate to call for assistance. "A piece of paper, Fei Lien! It must be found!"

"Master, what—?"

"I wrote a poem last night. I cannot find it! Search everywhere!"

It does not take long to search a small, one-room hut. I left him still futilely turning around and opening our few pieces of baggage, and, in desperation, went outside to search the ground around the hut. Szu-ma Yu was standing and gazing outward, looking peaceful.

"I have lost a piece of paper..." I began.

"Yes?" he said.

"I had written a poem on it last night..."

"A thousand pardons," he said, turning to me. "I used a piece of paper to start the fire this morning. I save scraps for that purpose. Even in the summer, it gets cold here."

The breeze lifted tendrils of his hair and whiskers so that they stirred and floated about his face, and the early sun threw flickers of gold over him. I noticed again the strange quality of his eyes—wild, I had thought yesterday. Today they seemed deep and ancient. Under that gaze, instead of uttering a stricken cry and tearing my hair, I found myself strangely calm. After a moment, an idea raised a faint glimmer of hope. "Did you read it?"

"I did not notice the writing on it until it was in the fire," he said, regretfully. "Something about a dragon. You do not remember what you wrote?"

"No," I said. "No. Not a word. Strange..."

"I am very sorry," he said. "But you do have your other wonderful poem written about Lu-shan."

"Yes," I said, resigned. "I have that." I imagined releasing the poem into a wind and watching it be carried away. "Very likely it would have struck me as trite and embarrassing when

I reread it in the light of day. This has mercifully spared me from such a deflation."

We stood for a moment in silence, looking across the peaceful valley.

"The general may be in search of a teacher, to guide him to wisdom, Venerable One," I said.

"It was in my thought to have him stay with me for a while," said Szu-ma Yu.

"I almost envy him."

"Almost?"

"My daily affairs cause me considerable frustrations.... Treacherous court politics, too much travel, not enough quiet."

"And yet?" said Szu-ma Yu.

"I like to think that my work is of some benefit to others."

"By adding up numbers?"

"What I actually do is keep corruption in check."

"Ah," he said.

A short while later, as we prepared to leave, Szu-ma Yu bade farewell to my servants each in turn, giving some words of parting that were apt for each one. My nephew he encouraged in his studies. To Hsiao Kang, who rarely speaks, he said, "Good fortune to you, peaceful one! 'The man without anger and without violence, him should you befriend, for he is noble.'" Hsiao Kang bowed deeply.

He thanked Teng Ai for his skillful cooking, told Chuan Hsu a joke, and gave Kai Huan a bag of herbs with instructions for mixing a poultice for treating neck pain. He smiled and told Fei Lien to stay in practice and keep his body agile, but his tongue circumspect. Fei Lien had formerly been a popular entertainer who had been famous for his flawless impersonations of public figures, but his career had been cut short by an unfortunate misjudgment in the nobleman he had chosen to caricature. Apparently Fei Lien must have told him his story—and somehow I had slept through the conversation. Szu-ma Yu accompanied each parting with a long, direct gaze before the other bowed and moved to take his station, which lent the occasion great solemnity.

He spoke to me last of all, and only said, "I hope you will return to Lu-shan."

And I bowed and said, "I hope that, as well."

"Do you wish to write a final poem, for the departure from the mountain?" Fei Lien asked me.

"Ah! Oh. Yes. I do, certainly."

Fei Lien produced my brush, ink, and paper, and I looked outward and thought, but no words came.

I looked at the rest of my servants, as they waited, and I realized that they were all talking together and laughing, or, in the case of Hsiao Kang, simply looking peaceful and contented, and no one was complaining or bickering. Even Kan Pao was ignoring his scrolls and was listening with respect to Teng Ai, who was telling a story.

"What do you see, Fei Lien?" I asked, at a loss.

"Rocks, trees, waterfalls, a little morning mist...the view is very rewarding."

I pondered.

Finally, I wrote:

Where may be found
the things that slip from our grasp?
—In the mists of Lu-Shan.

I hung it on a tree near Szu-ma Yu's hut, and we began our descent.

THE ROOFTOP GAME

DAVID KEENER

Part I. Opening Moves

i. Now

In the opening, achieving positional advantage is paramount.

— Karkomir, Grand Master, from Salasia

LYDIO MALIK lay on his back on the sloped roof of the highest tower of Paksenaral, the ancestral fortress of the Burgundar line. He tried to relax, to take advantage of this brief respite in the fighting and rest his tired, aching muscles. He crossed his hands behind his neck and looked up at the sky. A few puffy white clouds glided gently across the vault of blue, guided inexorably by the autumn winds toward the Cragenrath Mountains, violet and robbed of detail in the distance. The sky seemed so peaceful, so at odds with everything going on below.

Lowering his gaze, Malik saw smoke billowing up from the numerous fires that were consuming Lantille, the wind bending the smoke towards the mountains like a dark and ragged banner. The city's Gladis Market was a raging inferno; the blocks of wooden merchant stands, livestock holding facilities, and tenements were all burning. There were fires down by the river, as well. The docks, a few ships and a number of nearby warehouses were ablaze. Other ships had cast free, and were fleeing the fires and the fighting.

The most worrisome fires to Malik, though, were the ones on the far periphery of the small city that marked the headquarters, support buildings and barracks of Lantille's militia. He didn't think there'd be any help coming from that direction, at least not anytime soon.

In Malik's estimation, the attack had been a meticulously planned "smash-and-kill" raid utilizing a limited number of Kashmal rebels, probably no more than a few hundred men, and carefully timed to take advantage of King Salzari's excursion to the north. The enemy's undetected infiltration into Lantille, and into the fortress, strongly implied insider help. Given the widespread mayhem, he concluded that the effort had almost certainly been supported by at least one combat mage.

If the Kashmal had possessed mages, they'd have used them in the failed rebellion of two years ago. So, the mage represented foreign aid to the rebels. Malik could almost sense unseen forces moving pieces on a chessboard and aligning them against King Salzari, and against Salasia.

He found his fingers toying with the makeshift rope that was his lifeline. The rope was made of strips cut from sheets and tied together. One end of the rope was tied around his waist and the other looped around the spire of the tower. He had a certain amount of play in the rope, so he could move around the circular roof with its rippled, orange tiles, even stand, without having to worry about tumbling nine stories to his death.

Come to think of it, falling was probably the least of his worries.

He could hear the sounds of fighting somewhere in the fortress below, the clashing of swords, a few shouts and screams, and every once in a while, an explosion. The rebels hadn't taken the fortress yet, but it wouldn't be long.

When the sounds of fighting were done, he suspected the Queen would be dead. They'd be coming for him next.

Malik sat up and drew his sword out of its sheath. There was a thin strip of cloth tied to the pommel; the other end was tied to his right wrist. He couldn't afford to drop the sword and have it slide off the roof. There was undoubtedly more edgework in the offing.

Unless an enemy mage turned up and roasted him. Still, you could only plan for the things you could control. If a mage showed up, then the game was over, and that was it.

He eyed his blade critically. It was clearly showing some serious wear. There were numerous nicks in the blade and, although he'd wiped it off, there were still traces of blood around some of the nicks. Well, he didn't think he was going to live long enough to worry about the blade rusting.

He tested the edge with his thumb. Dull.

It had been sharp earlier this morning.

Malik reached into a pocket, took out a file and began sharpening the blade.

Time was the only thing on Malik's side. The enemy hadn't brought enough forces to hold the fortress for any significant time, especially if they wanted to escape the storm that would be coming their way. Even now, any remaining militiamen were probably rallying. Calls were likely going out to nearby towns for armed help. The garrison at Evanscap wasn't that far away either. If he had to guess, the King was going to hear about this mess by evening. And he had mages.

A soft gurgle came from above him. He raised his head and watched as Princess Analisa, all of seven months old and heir to the throne of Salasia, shifted sleepily in her basket. The royal basket, as he liked to think of it, was suspended above him on the roof, where the slope increased dramatically. Like him, the basket was attached to the spire by a makeshift rope. Additional cloth strips were tied around the princess' basket to ensure that she didn't fall out.

It was too bad escape hadn't been an option. He'd just have to hold out as long as he could.

Lydio Malik, Royal Bodyguard for Princess Analisa, resumed sharpening his sword and waited for the enemy's next move.

ii. Four Months Ago

I feel as if I were a piece in a game of chess, when my opponent says of it: That piece cannot be moved.

— Soren the Mad, Grand Master, from Zembelis

SALZARI RUKITAR, the King of Salasia, walked the labyrinthine halls of his family's ancestral fortress, flanked by his bodyguards and trailed, as always, by his secretary and a gaggle of advisors. Still vigorous at forty-seven, he walked quickly, the less fit among his retinue scurrying to keep up.

He was a little irked at the interruption in his routine that his next appointment had caused. Tradition required his presence, but he was a busy man and had many calls upon his time. There was a reason he delegated whenever he could. Despite the ubiquitous government bureaucracy, the kingdom didn't exactly run itself. Somebody had to make the difficult decisions, like what to do about the unsettled situation in the north.

Two years since their failed rebellion, and the Kashmal tribes were still making trouble. Oh, they'd been soundly defeated in battle, and he'd been suitably harsh with the terms and penalties in the aftermath, but he'd stopped well short of the butchery that other rulers might have engaged in.

He wrenched his thoughts away from the Kashmal situation to focus on his next appointment. As he walked, he said, "Winton, you've read the particulars. What do you think of them?"

His secretary, struggling to keep up, puffed beside him. "Sire, they're excellent as always. Interestingly, there are six candidates this time instead of the usual five. There was a tie for fifth in the competition."

"A tie, you say? That hasn't happened in years. Since I was a child, in fact."

Old Napotan, his father's favorite guardsman, had retired, opening up a slot in the elite Phoenix Guard. Capped at only two hundred members, the competition for the open position had been fierce. For the first time, he'd understood that the royal guardsmen he'd always taken for granted were truly the best of the best. Some of them served as personal bodyguards for the royal family. Others functioned as royal investigators, the eyes and ears of the King.

"The best fighter is the Yallon fellow," Winton said, his glasses sliding partway down his nose. "He's a beast, a real giant of a man, and the overall leader in points. But a little thick, I think. The Neferian is interesting. Lydio Malik…"

Kanlo Mudelsen, a trade advisor, interjected, "Certainly not the Neferian. He's lucky he even got this far." Kanlo shook his head, his long gray hair whipping from side to side seemingly adding emphasis to his comment. "Quite frankly, he's not even in the same class as the others."

"That doesn't even make sense, Kanlo," the mousy-looking secretary responded. "He's here because he tied for fifth in points. All earned fairly, I might add."

"I agree with him, though," said Pavel Gundarsen, Salzari's political strategist. "The Neferian would send the wrong political message. We're already getting inundated by thousands of refugees from their vicious little war. They're coming across the straits in anything that floats. Appointing a

Neferian would simply encourage more refugees to come here. Not to mention, they're losing. Badly. Do we want to send a message to the winners that we support the Neferians?"

Salzari said, "We do believe in the Neferian cause." There was silence for a moment.

Winton said, "Pavel, the Neferian is actually a fourth generation Salasian. He's served in the army, where he distinguished himself in battle. Mustered out, joined the City Guard and has a sterling reputation as a crime investigator."

A servant rushed ahead of the group to open a wide, ornately carved wooden door. Salzari and his retinue walked through the door into bright sunshine and made their way through the south gardens to the Phoenix Compound, which included their headquarters building, barracks and stables.

Captain Perin Davani, the gray-haired leader of the Phoenix Guard, greeted Salzari and his retinue as they arrived at the training area, a grass field adjacent to the barracks building and outlined by a three-bar wooden fence. About fifteen guardsmen were sitting on the fence, waiting to observe the selection. The six candidates were standing at attention in the training area, ranked in order of points. Salzari noticed that they'd placed the Malik fellow, notable because of his darker skin, almost like a permanently dark tan, at the very end on the right. Yallon was obviously the huge man on the left, head and shoulders taller than the others, none of whom would have normally been described as small.

Salzari asked Captain Davani, "Who do you favor?"

"Sire, I'd recommend Kelson. Second in points, but sharp as a new nail. The leader, Yallon, well, he's a good fighter, but that's all he is."

Salzari turned to Denzi Trufar, his military advisor and the only one who hadn't yet weighed in on the choices. "And you, Denzi. You've been quiet so far. Your recommendation?"

"I like Malik, Sire. He's not the best of the fighters out there, but he learns the fastest."

Salzari approached the candidates to examine them more closely. Saying nothing, he walked slowly down the line. The men stayed at attention, staring straight forward.

The king strode back to Captain Davani. "I'd like to see Yallon and Malik fight," he said loudly for the benefit of the audience. "Unarmed."

Davani barked a few orders. The other candidates assumed positions on the fence, looking a little disconcerted at seeing their own chances vanishing. Salzari glanced at his timepiece to note the time as Yallon and Malik faced off in the grass.

Yallon made the first move, a powerful roundhouse punch that missed badly. Malik counter-punched him with a quick flurry of strikes to Yallon's torso that didn't seem to hurt him too much. After a few minutes, Salzari noticed that Malik was controlling the pace of the fight, moving around, trying to tire Yallon and, most importantly, to stay out of Yallon's reach. The fight could easily be lost if Yallon was able to turn it into a wrestling match where his size and strength could be used to maximum advantage.

Five minutes into the bout, Yallon managed to land a vicious uppercut to Malik's jaw that stunned him for a moment. Yallon pressed his advantage and pounded his torso unmercifully while he held his arms up to protect his head. The powerful blows knocked Malik off his feet. Yallon stepped forward, preparing to jump on him. Malik kicked him in the knee that he'd just put all of his weight on. Malik rolled to the side as Yallon yelled in pain and fell full-length onto the ground.

Malik got to his feet, holding one arm across his damaged ribs, and landed a few hard kicks on Yallon before the giant, grimacing in obvious agony, climbed to his feet.

After ten minutes of continuous fighting, which Salzari verified by checking his timepiece, both fighters were a sweating, bloody mess. Malik was circling the less mobile giant, hunched over to protect his ribs, and striking whenever he saw an opening.

Malik lunged in with a flurry of jabs. Yallon absorbed the punches, then pounded his way through Malik's defenses before the smaller man could back away. Yallon delivered a powerful blow to Malik's ribs, eliciting an agonized scream of pain. The giant head-butted Malik in the face, breaking the smaller man's nose, grabbed his shoulders to hold him in place, and followed up by driving a knee into the Malik's stomach. While Yallon was momentarily supported only by the leg with the knee he'd hurt earlier, Malik kicked it again and it promptly collapsed. Yallon fell on top of the Neferian.

Raising his upper body with his left hand, Yallon began pounding Malik in the head with his right fist. When he was satisfied with the result, he finally rolled off the smaller fighter. With his damaged knee, it took him a while to laboriously get back to his feet. He faced the King and his companions, raised his arms in triumph and seemed surprised when nobody cheered.

He looked behind him. Somehow, Malik was on his feet again. Wobbly, yes, but definitely standing. Hunched over in pain, his face almost obscured by blood, the smaller warrior made a "come hither" gesture with his hands when he saw Yallon looking at him.

Salzari said in a voice loud enough to be heard across the field, "Enough." Both men were already so badly battered that he'd have to engage the Royal Healer to heal them properly. And he'd seen everything he needed to see.

Turning to Captain Davani, Salzari said, "I've made my decision." He pointed at the candidate he'd chosen. "That one. No, not the big one. The other one. Malik. I like him. He doesn't give up."

iii. Now

Chess is ruthless; you've got to be prepared to kill people.

— Nunzio Cragenrath, Grand Master, from Cragenrath

MALIK looked on with curiosity as a hand holding a silk handkerchief trimmed in lace rose above the edge of the roof. The hand waved the handkerchief back and forth a few times, as if to make sure that it had caught his attention. The hand and the makeshift flag withdrew below the roofline and a moment later a man's head appeared in the same place.

Malik raised his eyebrows when he recognized Tulis Razmar, Lantille's Chief of Trade. His presence confirmed Malik's conjecture that the attackers had benefited from insider help. Thanks to Razmar's betrayal, he was reasonably sure that the man's direct liege lord and, supposedly, close personal friend, Callum Burgundar, was already dead, and most likely the Queen, too. So much for oaths.

"Good morning, Lydio," Razmar said with an easy, friendly smile, acting as if there was nothing unusual about meeting on a rooftop. "Do you mind if I climb up so we can talk?"

"You can sit on the edge. The first five rows of tile. Try anything…I'll gut you like a fish."

Razmar climbed very carefully onto the roof. He was a tall man, in his forties but still fit; clean-shaven, with close-cropped hair liberally infused with gray. He wore fancy leggings and what looked like a bright-colored tunic, now mostly covered by the leather armor he'd added to his ensemble.

"Infernally good view up here, my friend," Razmar said.

"Yes, we can see most of your handiwork from up here," Malik replied, making a sweeping gesture with his left hand, his non-sword hand, to encompass the fires that were raging throughout the city. He stood, one leg higher than the other on the slanted roof, holding his makeshift rope with his left hand for balance and leaving his right hand free for swordplay if necessary. He could feel blood trickling slowly down the back of his leg.

Razmar shrugged. "Sometimes it's necessary to take actions we regret in order to pursue a greater good."

"That being what?"

"Karsh, the whole Kashmal region, Lantille, we're going to form our own kingdom."

"I doubt it." Malik looked at him levelly. "For what you've done today, I think King Salzari is going to crush you like a grape under a blacksmith's hammer."

Razmar laughed. "He can try. We've got serious backing."

Interesting. Malik was sure the King would love to know about these mysterious backers. Meanwhile, Malik was willing to talk for as long as Razmar wanted. The more time the traitor wasted, the better for him, and for Princess Analisa.

As if reading his mind, the older man glanced up at the baby's wicker basket lying behind Malik and further up the slope of the roof. "How's the princess doing, Malik?"

"She's quite well, actually. She's taking her morning nap. Thank you for inquiring about her health." Malik was silent for a moment. "You know, it's so peaceful, I might just have to kill anybody who interrupts her nap." *Because she'll want to be fed,* he thought, *and she'll cry, and I don't have anything for her.*

"You're a good man, Malik. It would be a shame if we had to kill you."

"You can try. You may recall that I left a bunch of your men on the stairway as we retreated up here."

"I know. I was appalled." Razmar chuckled ruefully. "Impressed, but still appalled. Still, here you are now. Injured. Wearing damaged leather armor. Making your heroic last stand on a hot tile roof. How long do you think you can last?"

"Long enough."

"You know you can only delay the inevitable. The princess is going to die no matter what. The only real question is whether you die, too."

"At least I won't be a traitor," Malik replied.

"Oh, that hurts. I prefer to think of myself as a patriot for a grand new kingdom." Razmar laughed easily.

"Just out of curiosity, why do you want to kill the princess?" Malik asked politely. "I would have thought you'd want her as a hostage. Better chance of negotiation with the King that way."

Razmar paused for a moment, as if thinking about whether he should answer the question. He shrugged. "It's a condition from our backers. They want the King's line ended."

"Ah. So what happens if your backers get what they want? How long do you think they'll keep supporting a bunch of lost-cause, would-be kingdom builders?"

Razmar laughed. "Let's just say that our mutual interests are well aligned. You should worry more about your situation than ours." To emphasize his point, the older man looked around the roof. "One last time, will you give us the princess?"

"No."

"Well, we're going to have to kill you then."

Malik shrugged. "Bring it on."

Razmar shook his head in mock regret. Malik watched impassively as the older man climbed slowly and gingerly down from the roof.

Two of his borrowed Kashmal fighters helped Razmar back through the window. He was sweating from the exertion of climbing. Growing up in the shadow of the Cragenrath Mountains, he'd done some rock climbing when he was a younger man, but facing that sheer, nine-story drop on the way back had been more daunting than any climb he'd ever done. Going up was easier than coming back down, though not by much.

He straightened his clothing self-consciously, then looked around. There were ten Kashmal warriors with him in a fancy bedroom, including his second-in-command, Pandomar, a stocky, red-haired warrior. One thing for sure, Pandomar wasn't going to be doing any climbing; he'd lost most of his left arm at the Battle of Antigon two years before.

A pair of warriors were guarding Melly Scarp, the royal nanny, who managed to look both defiant and scared at the same time.

"You," he said, pointing at one of the warriors. "Get up there and kill him. He's injured. He's got so much blood pouring down his right leg, it's a wonder he can even stand."

The fighter looked at Pandomar, who nodded slightly. The man moved obediently towards the window.

"You're not going to beat Malik that easily," Melly interjected from across the room.

Razmar laughed. "Perhaps not." He turned to Pandomar. "Let's put some archers in the south tower."

"Ser, we didn't bring any archers."

Razmar sighed. "An oversight. I'm sure that the Burgundars have some bows here somewhere. Find them. Find someone who knows how to shoot them. Put them in the south tower." The Kashmal were useful, but sometimes they had no imagination.

Pandomar gestured to one of the younger warriors. "Nakanti, handle it."

"Yes, father," the youth said. He turned and strode from the room.

The Kashmal fighter heaved himself over the edge of the roof, lunged to a standing position, drew his sword and took a step towards Malik.

The fighter's forward boot slipped on the wet tile where Malik had urinated only a few moments before. He fell forward, audibly cracking his chin as he landed face first on the orange roof tiles. Stunned, he dropped his sword, which slid off the roof, followed almost immediately by the screaming rebel warrior.

A few seconds later, there was a thud and clatter as the fighter hit the ground below.

Malik couldn't help grinning. All of his fights should be that easy.

Danteel the silversmith had closed up his small shop hours ago. He'd carried in his display tables, pulled down the shutters and latched them securely. He'd even taken down the shop sign. There was a battle going on in the city and, even though he didn't know what was going on or who was fighting, it was best to make sure his shop didn't look like it would be worth looting.

Danteel was a prudent man. A cautious man.

His shop was fairly typical, a three-story wooden building with a high, peaked roof. What was most important, though, was its location, which was close to Paksenaral, the fortress that dominated the city of Lantille, and, by extension, its residents, most of whom could afford his prices. He and his family lived on the upstairs floors, with the downstairs serving as a common room at night, and his shop during the day.

Danteel didn't like not knowing what was going on. Prudent men didn't like surprises.

What really worried him right now, though, was his thirteen-year-old son. Chanama had bargained with Danteel for some time off that morning so he could visit the Gladis

Market with some of his friends. He was still out there somewhere.

Whatever was going on, it was bad. The streets were deserted; people were huddling indoors for safety. The smell of smoke was everywhere.

iv. Two Months Ago

No chess game is ever over if the mage piece is still in play.

— Anonymous

IN ONE CORNER of the Phoenix Guard's grass-covered training field, Lydio Malik ran through his practice routines by himself, as always. Thrust, parry an imaginary foe's counterstrike, sweep left with the heavy, steel practice blade, twice the weight of his issued sword, then dart right, pivot, and begin a new sequence of moves, as if he were surrounded by deadly, invisible enemies.

Which wasn't far from the truth, sadly.

Malik practiced in full gear, despite the summer heat, with the heaviest, and dullest, practice sword he could convince a blacksmith to make for him. Full gear included studded leather armor over a padded tunic, his sword, durable black leggings and an assortment of knives tucked away in different places. He was more lightly armored than most of the other guardsmen, and certainly less well dressed than many of them, but he preferred to be as unencumbered as possible. He figured speed was his biggest advantage against foes in most fights he could imagine being involved in as a guardsman.

Pivoting, he did another sweep with the blade, which was when he spotted Gaston Hundersen standing a safe, carefully calculated distance away. Malik stopped, breathing heavily from the exertion, lowered his sword and said, "What do you want, Gaston?" His fellow guardsman was not a friend, although, in fairness, he didn't routinely belittle Malik for his Neferian heritage as most of the others did.

Malik glanced around, noticing that all of the other guardsmen around had stopped what they were doing, and were watching them from a distance. Not a good sign.

"Captain Davani wants to see you in his office." Gaston spat on the ground. "I don't think it's good news. I was you, I'd pack my bags afore you go see him." He looked at Malik disdainfully. "And maybe wash up, too."

Without a word, Malik nodded at Gaston, sheathed his practice sword and walked off the field. As he passed a few of the other guardsmen, one of them said, "Bye, bye, Malik." There was widespread laughter, then another piped up. "Hey, Lydio, I hear they're looking for a bouncer at the Drunken Otter."

He ignored them, just as he ignored all of their petty little harassments, racial epithets and the myriad other ways that they expressed their prejudices. He was the first Neferian to ever be selected to the Phoenix Guard and, no matter what happened next, he'd represent his kind with steadfast poise.

Malik headed directly for Davani's office, refusing to cater to the man by washing up first. Let the order's leader see, and smell, what a hard-working guardsman looked like.

That was probably a little unfair to the other guardsmen. Despite their attitude toward him, they were all good, no doubt about that, and they certainly practiced regularly. But it felt to him that most of the men were, at best, simply maintaining their level, content with the skills they'd brought to the Phoenix Guard and unwilling to push harder. Malik blamed Davani for that.

He strode past the barracks and entered the low, stone building beyond it that served as the order's headquarters. Moments later, Davani's administrative adjunct, Delma Sturgsen, a matronly woman who'd grown up in Mozanya where Neferians were increasingly common, looked at him with sympathy in her eyes and ushered him into Captain Davani's utilitarian office.

Malik stopped in front of Davani's desk and stood at attention.

Davani ignored him for a moment, his head down as he continued writing on a sheet of paper. Malik recognized petty game playing when he came across it and ignored the intentional snub.

Finally, Davani pushed the sheet of paper aside, looked up and said, "At ease."

Malik remained at attention, deliberately, albeit slightly, provoking Davani.

"I'll come straight to the point, Malik," Davani growled. "You're not working out. We're an elite unit and you, quite simply, don't fit in." The gray-haired officer rose to his feet. "The most important thing for our order is teamwork. We work together to serve the royal line. Together." He put his hands down on the desk, leaned over it and glared at Malik. "Nobody wants to work with you." He opened a drawer, pulled out an official looking document and set it on the desk facing Malik. "I want your resignation. Now."

"Permission to speak freely, sir?"

Davani looked at him for a moment, his jaw clenching and unclenching in anger. There were forms that even a commanding officer had to follow. Grudgingly, he said, "Granted."

"I'm not resigning. If you want me gone, then you're going to have to bring charges against me." Malik fixed a level gaze on Davani's face. "I'm prepared to defend myself against any proceeding you may choose to bring."

Davani's face turned red and he slammed his hands down on the desk in anger. He looked as if he was about to shout at Malik, but what came out instead was a much more restrained "Sire," in a surprised voice as the door opened behind Malik and King Salzari strode in, trailed as always by his diminutive secretary, Winton. The King's two bodyguards took up positions outside the door.

"Ah, just the people I was looking for," Salzari said cheerfully. "An opening popped up in my schedule this morning so I decided to check up on our latest recruit." The King turned towards Malik and smiled. Malik noticed his penetrating blue eyes. "Good morning, Lydio Malik. How are you adapting to life as a guardsman?"

"It's been… interesting, Sire."

"Quite. Well, I'm hearing good things about you." Turning back to Davani, he said, "I noticed from your reports that you haven't given Malik an official assignment yet. I rather think he'd be perfectly suited to be Princess Analisa's bodyguard. Her primary, I think."

"But Sire…"

"Make it so," the King said firmly. Without looking again at Malik, he said, "Malik, please find Horatious, my household

Chief of Staff, for the particulars of your assignment. You are dismissed."

"Sire," Malik said. He did an about-face and walked past Winton as he exited the office. The mousy-looking secretary fixed his bulging eyes on Malik's face, the left side of his lips quirked upward in an almost imperceptible smile.

Most people dismissed Winton as inconsequential, a servant undeserving of their consideration. Malik suspected that Winton enjoyed being underestimated. He couldn't help but wonder what hand the secretary had played in the King's unexpected visit.

Part II. The Middle Game

v. One Month Ago

Chess is not for timid souls.

— Naryan Svenkali, the Scourge of the North,
Grand Master, from Neferia

MALIK walked through the Hall of Ancestors on his way to begin his shift protecting Princess Analisa. Disappointed that Malik hadn't been dismissed from the order, his fellow guardsmen had begun referring to his assignment as Diaper Duty, though never in the hearing of anybody in authority, and calling him the Nursemaid.

He glanced up at the portraits of twenty-seven generations of ruling Rukitars, ensconced in their ornate and gilded frames, as he traversed the dark-paneled length of the hallway. Five of them had been assassinated. He liked to think that their spirits sometimes looked out through their portraits, as if they were windows between the spirit realm and the material world, and that they approved of him as a bodyguard. He took his duties seriously. Those five Rukitars who'd died by violence demonstrated that real threats existed. Nothing was ever going to happen to the princess on his watch, not if he could help it.

Near the end of the hallway, he opened a discreetly unobtrusive servant's door and made his way to the quarters of his royal charge through the maze of plainly decorated servant passages. He'd made it his business during the past month to learn his way around the palace.

Not just how to get between a few key duty areas, but to learn the palace's halls, passages and exits like the back of his hand. He'd even sought out the palace mechaneers for further details on the building's layout. With an assignment like his, you never knew when that sort of information might become important.

Malik opened a door from a servant's passage and walked out into the main hallway of the Royal Wing. A moment later he knocked on the ornately carved door of the chamber of his royal ward. It opened immediately, revealing Ronston Hardasi, a fellow guardsman. Beyond him, he saw Queen Andu tar Kadafi Rukitar hand her baby, Princess Analisa, to the nursemaid. The queen was conversing with Tulis Razmar, an envoy from the Burgundars, who were allies and close personal friends from Lantille in the north.

Malik made a point of trying to know as much as possible about the people allowed into close proximity to members of the royal family. He'd recognized Razmar from a reception the night before, where he'd quickly come to the impression that the impeccably dressed envoy had an exaggerated sense of his own importance.

Focusing his attention back on Hardasi, Malik couldn't help but notice that the guardsman was holding the door open with his sword hand. He said mildly, "You know, if I'd been an assassin, you'd be dead already." He didn't think guardsmen should even open doors; they should hang back to deal with any threat that might come through a door.

Still in conversation, the queen turned and headed for the exit, Razmar falling a pace behind as dictated by court protocol. Hardasi and Malik stepped out of the way to let the queen and her guest pass between them.

Razmar stopped to look at Malik. "Seriously, assassins?" Shaking his head, he said, "We're in the middle of the royal palace. How would an assassin even get to us here?" Apparently, Razmar had excellent hearing; Malik hadn't intended his comment for anybody but his fellow guardsman.

The queen turned back toward them, laughing, her raven tresses shaking with her merriment. Smiling, the young queen said, "I confess, Malik may be a little paranoid, but I suspect there's no better guardian for my baby." There was an edge to her statement that shut Razmar up.

Hardasi waited until the queen and her guest had progressed some distance down the corridor before he stepped out of the way to let Malik enter the room. "Good news, by the way," he said conspiratorially. "I think you're just in time for her majesty's diaper change." Without any further word, Hardasi left the room.

Melly Scarp, the nursemaid on duty, turned to him. "Hi, Malik," she said cheerfully. "You want to help me change her?"

"Melly, I'm a trained killer. My job is to kill anybody who might try to harm our little princess, not to change diapers."

"Well, you might as well watch and see how it's done. You never know when what you learn might come in handy."

Malik went over and looked down at the princess, all of four months old and fussing because of her messy diaper. Melly undid the baby's diaper, just as she decided to discharge a fresh flow of urine. Malik neatly stepped back as the unexpected flow dribbled over the edge of the changing table.

"Nice reflexes."

"We train for situations like this."

"I bet." The maid snorted, laughing heartily. "Why don't you stand over here and distract her while I take care of things."

Malik stepped around Melly so the, ahem, dangerous end was no longer pointing in his direction. Princess Analisa was undeniably cute. She had bright blue eyes, just like her father. She smiled at Malik and made gurgling noises as she saw the guardsman leaning over her.

Melly finished wiping and powdering, then folded on a new cloth diaper. She pinned one side of the diaper, then said, "Drat!"

"What?" Malik turned his head to look at the nursemaid.

"Lost the other pin. I guess I'll just have to tie it."

Melly twisted the two corners that needed to be attached and nimbly tied them together. The effortless way she did it reminded Malik of sailors he'd seen; he realized that she had more than a passing facility with nautical knots.

When the princess made another gurgling noise, he held a finger in front of her face. She grabbed it with both hands. Her tiny, stubby little fingers were a brilliant white against his much darker skin. Still smiling, she pulled his finger towards her mouth.

Malik didn't realize it until later, but that moment when little Analisa had grabbed his finger was when she became his princess. Not just a shape in swaddling clothes, not just a baby needing a diaper change, but his princess.

His.

vi. Now

You win chess by taking away your opponent's choices, so that he can only do what you want.

— Lydio Malik, Phoenix Guard, Unranked Player, from Intus, Salasia

MALIK had just finished changing the Princess Analisa's diaper, using up his one and only replacement, and had his back turned, when he heard the next fighter climb onto the edge of the roof. He calmly turned and threw the exceedingly full diaper that he'd just removed at the man, who cursed when it stuck to his armored chest with a wet thud.

The royal bodyguard stood and charged downward at the fighter who, thinking he was a safe distance from Malik, was prying the diaper off with one hand; his other hand wasn't holding his sword in an adequate defensive position, which was always a mistake around someone of Malik's skill level.

The fighter screamed as Malik ran him through, eyes wide in disbelief at how quickly he'd taken a mortal wound. The man dropped his sword to the roof tiles with a clatter and it promptly slid over the edge.

Holding on to his makeshift rope, Malik kicked the fighter in the chest to dislodge his sword from the man's torso. There was a sucking sound and the sword withdrew about a hands-width from the dead warrior's chest.

Malik gritted his teeth. He hated it when his sword got stuck. He kicked the body three more times before his blade came free. Propelled by the last kick, the rebel's body flew backwards off the tower, turning a few uncontrolled somersaults before it landed in the courtyard below.

vii. Two Weeks Ago

> *I am convinced, the way one plays chess reflects the player's personality. If something defines his character, then it will also define his way of playing.*
>
> — Vladimar Kramner, Grand Master, from Rusitania

IT WAS THE MIDDLE OF THE NIGHT, just after his shift had ended, when Malik walked into the royal kitchen looking for a cold dinner. He'd been on shift in Princess Analisa's quarters through the dinner hour, and his fellow guardsmen hadn't seen fit to make sure that a meal was delivered to him. Just another of the petty ways in which they constantly slighted him.

He found the cook, a chubby, bald man named Rinaldo Sigursen, sitting at the kitchen table looking morosely at a chess set.

"Problems?" Malik asked, gesturing at the board game.

"I've got a bet with Chently, the Queen's butler, that I can beat him in a chess game. He got called away, so we agreed to finish the game in the morning."

Malik scanned the board intently. "How much is the bet?"

"Well, it's only a crown," Rinaldo replied. "But it's the principle of the matter! Chently's insufferable. He's always lording it over the rest of us. I just wanted to take him down a peg." He groaned and put his head in his hands. "I didn't realize he was such a great player."

"You're playing white, I assume?"

"Yes."

"You're down in pieces, but you've got checkmate in seven moves if you execute properly."

"What!" The cook looked up in surprise.

"You win chess by taking away your opponent's choices, so that he can only do what you want." Malik reached down and moved the mage piece. "See, the queen is now in danger. He's got no choice but to protect her, because all of his other choices are worse."

Malik showed Rinaldo the rest of the key moves, as well as Chently's possible responses.

The cook shook his head disbelievingly, studying the changed board. "It seems so simple, now, but I just couldn't see that." He looked up at Malik. "You know, you're all right." He got up from the table. "Let me warm up something for you."

The cook began bustling around the kitchen. Over his shoulder, he said, "I'll get you a good meal, then you're going to have just enough time to pack when you get back to your quarters."

"Come again?"

"Nobody's told you?" Rinaldo turned and looked at Malik in surprise. "You're leaving for Lantille in the morning. The queen and the princess are going to stay in Lantille with the Burgundars, who are old friends of hers. The king is going to stay for a week, then he's taking a bunch of troops and going further north to show the flag around Karsh."

viii. Now

In life, as in chess, forethought wins.

— Cho Sumari, Grand Master, from Hestria

MELLY sat on an ornate wooden chair, under the watchful eyes of her two guards, and observed the preparations for the next assault on Malik with a certain amount of fear, as well as curiosity and, perhaps, just a bit of anticipation. So far as she could tell, the royal bodyguard was still ahead in points in this dance of death that Razmar had put in motion. Malik had predicted and prepared for every move made so far by the traitor.

It had taken quite a while for Razmar to cajole two more fighters into agreeing to assault Malik, and neither had been willing to do so without some sort of lifeline. It had taken even more time to track down some ropes.

She thought it was interesting that Pandomar, who seemed to be the leader, or at least the most senior, of the Kashmal fighters, hadn't really helped. *An uneasy alliance*, she thought. She didn't think Pandomar had much respect for Razmar, who came across as something of a manipulative bastard.

The two reluctant volunteers, one tall and lanky and the other stocky but tough-looking, had ropes tied to their waists and attached to a bed post of a heavy wooden bed that had been pushed up next to the window.

Malik was sitting down on the tiles just below the royal basket, conserving his energy. When the next fighter climbed to the roof, the man was head and shoulders taller than him, with a scruffy brown beard and shaggy hair. Malik hadn't heard the climber because the Princess kept crying insistently. She was undoubtedly hungry by now.

He noted that the man had a rope tied around his waist. He'd imagined, or at least hoped, that it was getting harder for Razmar to convince his men to climb up and challenge him.

It amused Malik that the rebel fighters were worried enough now that they wanted a safety line in case they fell. From a numbers perspective, given the vicious fight up the stairs of the tower and now on the roof, they should be considerably more worried about him than any potential fall. Malik assumed the rope was tied to the bed in the room below. It was the only piece of furniture that was built solidly enough to serve as an effective anchor.

He rubbed his eyes tiredly and stood up, his joints creaking in protest. He was a body length and half away from his fresh assailant, who drew a long, narrow sword. Grinning at Malik with crooked yellow teeth, he stepped to the side and another fighter, shorter, wider and more heavily muscled climbed laboriously onto the orange tiles. A rope was tied around his waist as well.

Left hand on his lifeline, Malik drew his sword and descended down the slope to dispatch his newest challengers.

As he approached, he exchanged a few quick parries with the lanky fighter, who showed some dueling experience. The stocky fighter drew a shortsword and moved up the slope, trying to circle around Malik so that he and his partner could both attack at the same time. A dangerous combination.

Malik dropped to the tiles on his back, sliding downward, which put him into the position he wanted. He kicked the lanky fighter in the kneecap. The fighter yelled in pain, lost his balance and tumbled backward off the roof.

The stocky fighter charged forward and thrust his sword at Malik in an attempt to run him through.

The blow never landed.

There was an audible thud as the falling fighter hit the end of the rope, then a loud cracking sound from the room below as the bed broke apart where Malik and Melly had weakened it during their siege preparations. The pieces of the broken bed joined the first fighter in his uncontrolled plummet. The combined weight suddenly hit the remaining fighter as he was trying to step forward, slamming him face-first into the tiles and then yanking him off the roof before he even realized what had happened.

Malik smiled as he heard cursing from the room below. *You take away your enemy's choices so he does what you want*, he thought.

As he stood up, something slammed into the side of his head, slicing from his forehead just above his right eye and all the way to his ear. He realized almost instantly that he'd just been hit with a glancing arrow shot. He threw himself back down on the tiles and tried to roll out of range of the south tower, the only tower the enemy could have used to target him. He almost made it to safety, but couldn't help screaming in agony as an arrow lodged solidly in his arm.

His sword arm.

While Razmar cursed uncontrollably, Melly watched as Pandomar stared for a long moment at the remains of the shattered bed lying beneath the window. He turned his head, fixed his gaze on Melly, and said, "You knew?"

"Of course," Melly replied, smiling brightly. "Who do you think sawed the bed in pieces?"

The fighters in the room glared at her now with tangible animosity. Melly felt her own survival balanced on a knife-edge. Even Razmar stopped cursing to pay attention to them.

"The sawdust went out the window, I assume?"

"Yes."

"And cutting the sheets into strips and making ropes of them?"

"My father was a sailor on the River Gahtani. He taught me knots."

Melly was so focused on Pandomar that she was surprised when Razmar started laughing. She could tell that Pandomar and his Kashmal warriors, however, were not amused as they withdrew their attention from her and glowered at him.

"Clever, my dear. Very clever." Razmar turned towards the warriors. "Let that be a lesson to you, men, she doesn't even have any weapons, and she's still managed to kill two of you. Face it, you've been beaten by the nanny." He shook his head, still laughing.

"Well," Pandomar said, "we'd be gone by now if you hadn't gotten your mage killed."

Razmar shrugged. "I had no way of knowing that the Queen's butler was a mage. At least he's dead, too." He smiled at Pandomar, but there was nothing friendly about it. "Meanwhile, the vaunted Kashmal warriors, the terror of the mountains, the scourge of the valleys, can't even manage to finish off a single injured man."

That was news to Melly. She'd had no idea Chently was a mage, either, and she'd known him for years.

Pandomar scowled and stepped forward. "We'll get him."

"I hope so," Razmar said glibly. "There must be some reason for us to be allied with your tribes. Right now, I'm having trouble figuring out what it is." He turned towards Melly. "Do you have any more surprises for us?"

"Um, no. I'm done," she said.

Well, that was only sort of true, Melly thought. It was a dangerous game Malik was playing up there on the roof. But she didn't think Razmar knew that the game had a well-defined time limit. It wasn't common knowledge, but she knew that the Queen used some sort of magical artifact to communicate with the King every morning and every evening. She didn't think that Razmar knew this, so it had just been dumb luck that his attack had occurred after the morning communication. Missing the evening contact, though, was going to be noticed.

If Malik could just stay alive until sunset, well, then they might all have a chance to survive. By her estimation, it was perhaps an hour past the noon hour. Malik needed to survive about another four hours.

She studied Pandomar thoughtfully, still unsure why he hadn't killed her yet. He was stoic as Razmar berated the tribal fighters, finally demanding that two men be sent downstairs to retrieve the ropes.

Danteel sat in a wooden chair next to one of his shop's shuttered windows, periodically peeking out through an observation hole at the empty streets. He was wearing his sword for the first time since his brief stint in the militia fifteen years before. A prudent man carried a sword in times of trouble, no matter how out of practice he might be with it. Still, once trained, always trained, as one of his long-ago weapon instructors had said.

His wife had fixed him a cold lunch, which now rested like an uncomfortable lump in his stomach. She was upstairs with the younger children, while he waited for either Chanama to return or for some enterprising soul to take advantage of the situation to rob his store.

He heard footsteps on the wooden walkway outside, which he'd built so that his more genteel customers didn't have to worry about mud and other sundry substances when they alighted from their fancy carriages.

He stood up, hand on sword, then relaxed as he recognized the familiar pattern of the family knock on the door.

Danteel strode to the door, unlatched it and peered through the gap. Chanama stood outside, tall and gangly like a colt.

"Pa—"

"Get inside, boy." He quickly ushered his son inside and latched the door again. "Thought you'd hunker down for the duration."

His son stared at the sheathed sword hanging at Danteel's belt, something he'd never seen him wearing before.

"I did," the boy said. "But the Market's on fire…most of the waterfront's on fire. I had to move when it starting coming my way."

"All right." Danteel nodded. "When trouble comes, you make the best decisions you can. You did well. Good to see you safe and sound."

"I saw something weird on the way, Pa. I think some-body's fighting on the roof of the north tower."

ix. Five Days Ago

Chess is a waste of time, an outmoded hobby from a past era, of interest only to imbeciles, the elderly and other useless layabouts.

— Tulis Razmar, Revolutionary, from Lantille, Salasia

MALIK strode up to the group of ten servants surrounding Angston Malde, the Burgundar's liaison with the Queen's security forces. Malde was a thin, balding man in his late fifties who looked dapper in what Malik recognized as the latest in court styles. The liaison glanced up at him, but continued to pass out instructions to the servants. All of his orders seemed to address minutiae associated with court etiquette and precedence.

Malik waited patiently for Malde to finish. After listening for a few minutes, he came to three conclusions. First, Malde liked to lord it over the other servants. Second, he was ignoring Malik. And finally, he didn't seem to have the same grasp of court precedence as Malik.

"Excuse me," Malik said. "I have a few questions…"

Malde said sharply, "I've already spoken to your senior officers. All necessary security arrangements have been made."

"Well, I still have some things I need to know."

"Sir," Malde said haughtily, "that is not my problem." He turned away from Malik to speak to another servant.

Malik reached out with both hands and gently pushed the two closest servants aside as he stepped forward between them. He dropped his hand heavily on the liaison's shoulder and spun him around. The functionary's mouth opened wide with surprise. Malik grabbed him by the throat with his right hand and lifted him into the air. He took four more steps to the left and slammed Malde's back into the wall, his feet dangling two feet off the floor. He held the man at arms-length with no visible strain.

In a soft, calm voice, he said, "I am the primary bodyguard for the princess. If I have questions about her safety, there is nothing more important in your life. Do you understand me?"

Malde moved his head up and down ever so slightly, which was about all the mobility that he had left with Malik holding him up by his throat. The bodyguard let him go; the functionary fell to the floor and slid to a sitting position. Holding his throat, he gasped for breath.

Malik turned to the servants. "Leave us."

The servants obediently scurried away.

Malik squatted next to the liaison. "I don't care what you've discussed with the rest of the Queen's security forces. I do things my way.

"So, I want to understand the layout of this entire castle. If you have plans or drawings, I need to see them. I want to know about any nooks, crannies, hidden features and possible escape routes. I want to see the towers. I want to see the lowest levels. I want to see the private areas. By the end of the day, I will know this castle like the back of my own hand, or I will pitch your worthless carcass from the highest window of the tallest tower."

x. Now

It is not a move, even the best move that you must seek, but a realizable plan.

— Yevgen Borovsky, Grand Master, from Rusitania

MALIK sat on the roof just below the princess's basket, safely out of sight of the archers in the south tower, and waited for the next development. He'd achieved an almost meditative state, ignoring the pain of his various wounds, impending exhaustion and thirst. His sword arm, now bandaged with a strip of cloth cut from the princess's blanket, was all but useless; he couldn't hold his sword in his right hand anymore.

He'd trained left-handed for just this type of eventuality, but no master swordsman was ever equally proficient with both hands. Never in his wildest dreams had he ever expected to really have to fight any adversaries with his off hand.

Now his life, and the life of his princess, depended on it.

He'd moved his sword's sheath to his right side so he could draw his sword cross-body with his left hand. He held his favorite dagger in his left hand. It had been a gift from the legion when he'd left the service. His men had told him that he'd clearly need something to cut his meat with when he left, especially since he was getting "a little long in the tooth." Then they'd handed him an excellent Sarakanth blade, razor sharp and perfectly balanced for throwing.

Malik heard sounds from the other side of the roof, the dangerous side that was under the watchful eye of the enemy archers in the south tower. He recognized the sounds of someone climbing onto the roof. After a moment, he was able to determine that multiple men had just climbed onto the roof.

They would probably split up—send one around the spire to take him from behind.

He stood up slowly. It was time for some more edgework.

He turned around to wrap a little bit more of his knotted lifeline around his waist. When the makeshift rope was suitably taut, he charged forward, the rope drawing him into a circular path around the roof's spire.

As he rounded the roof, he saw three fighters arrayed in front of him, all with ropes tied around their waists. He threw his dagger at the second fighter and saw it sink with a meaty thunk into the man's throat. Still running at full speed, he drew his sword in a flashing arc that parried the closest fighter's blade and knocked it to the side. He slammed his shoulder into the man and knocked him backwards off the roof.

The third man tried to run him through, but misjudged his strike as Malik's anchoring rope turned his running path into an arc. With the fighter's sword out of any realistic defensive position, Malik cut his throat as he sprinted by, blood spraying into the afternoon air.

Malik continued running and managed to circumnavigate the entire roof so quickly that he was able to get back to the relative safety of his side before the shocked archers managed to get off a shot. Hidden from their view, they never saw how his injured leg finally buckled underneath him, throwing him heavily to the tiles on top of his damaged right arm. They never saw how stunned he was by the impact, how helpless he was for the next five minutes or how he was barely able to stand once he finally managed to get to his feet again.

xi. Four Hours Ago

In master-level chess, you have to drive your advantage home unmercifully.

— Fisher Kozen, Grand Master, from Malawi

MELLY clutched Princess Analisa's basket to her chest and ran as fast she could in the wake of Ronston Hardasi, the bodyguard on duty when the attack started. He led them down a narrow, marble-lined hallway in a seldom-used section of the fortress, desperately looking for an escape route that wasn't blocked by enemy forces. His bloody sword was out; he'd already had to cut his way past a few attackers. She couldn't help wishing Malik was here; he'd know what to do.

Hardasi stopped suddenly as six enemy fighters rounded the corner up ahead. To Melly's eyes, they looked like Kashmal tribal warriors, which wasn't much of a surprise. They were at the bottom of most of the unrest in the north. The surprise, of course, was that they were here right now in what King Salzari had considered a safe bastion for his family.

There was a momentary tableau as the two sides considered each other. Melly saw smiles appear on the faces of the fighters as they realized the import of the basket that Melly was carrying. She surmised that there were probably bonuses, or at least bragging rights, for any fighter that actually managed to kill the queen or the princess. She wondered if they realized the kind of wrath Salzari would unleash upon the north after today.

The warriors charged and Hardasi met them with a whirling storm of steel, one expert swordsman against six seasoned and well armored opponents.

Melly could see that it wasn't going to be enough. Hardasi was good, but he was far too outnumbered. She put down the basket and grabbed an unlit torch from a wall sconce. It was the best weapon she could improvise.

To his credit, Hardasi managed to kill two of them and injure two more before they finally got him. He fell to his knees, impaled by a sword, the point sticking wetly out of his back. He dropped his sword on the stone floor with a metallic clatter.

A bearded warrior planted his boot on Hardasi's chest and pushed until his sword came out with a sickening squelch. As Hardasi's body fell to the side, the four remaining warriors advanced, grinning mercilessly.

Somewhere behind them, Melly heard a door open and she saw three of the warriors turn to face the other direction. Suddenly Malik was there, like some magical demigod of death and mayhem. It was as if the warriors were standing still. His sword licked out, bypassing parries and finding weak points in armor. He slaughtered them in under five seconds, the first still falling to the floor as he thrust his sword through the throat of the last.

"All of the planned escape routes are blocked," Malik said, casually wiping his sword on the fur coat of one of the warriors.

"What are we going to do, then?" Melly asked, strangely calm despite all the bloodshed.

"We're going to the north tower. If they want us, they're going to have to pay the price in blood." Malik grinned, and added, "More blood than they ever expected."

xii. Now

Never underestimate the power of a pawn.

– Karkomir, Grand Master, from Salasia

MALIK lay on the tiles next to the princess. Smiling, he sang her a lullaby in a rough, untrained voice, the rhythmic banging from below providing the beat for the melody. The princess began fussing again, albeit weakly. Malik was happy to see that she was still all right.

He'd pulled himself up to her level because he wanted to see her face one more time before he died. Survival had always been a long shot, but now he could sense even the possibility receding. Between his injuries, the blood loss, his almost unbearable thirst and the sheer exhaustion settling in from the day's extreme exertions, he just didn't have much left. He couldn't even feel his right arm anymore. Every other part of his body ached, and he was still losing blood slowly from some of his wounds.

Beneath him, his enemies were trying to dismantle the roof so they could get at them more easily. He'd been told the roof and supporting structure were ironwood, though, which explained why the tower could have such a flat slope for so much of the roof, even in the north where snow was so prevalent.

The princess turned her head toward him, whimpering despite his tune. Her blue eyes glittered in the afternoon sun. She was beautiful.

His princess.

His.

Part III. The Endgame

xiii. Now

You have to have the fighting spirit. You have to force moves and take chances.

— Fisher Kozen, Grand Master, from Malawi

MELLY had decided that the only reason she was still alive was because Razmar was a show-off. He enjoyed demonstrating his power in front of others, and she was the only available audience. Plus, under the pretense of talking to her, he could say disparaging words about his Kashmal partners. She could see that Pandomar was seething with anger, as were his men. She suspected it was only Pandomar's oath to his clan leader that kept him from killing Razmar himself, and, in turn, he was all that kept his warriors in check.

However, Razmar wasn't unintelligent. His superior attitude and constant needling were carefully calculated. He knew there was a limit to how far he could go, but he enjoyed testing that limit.

Surprisingly, while it was true that Razmar would never be liked or respected as a leader, his tactics were extremely effective at spurring his Kashmal compatriots in their labors. She suspected he was a highly proficient merchant.

He should have stuck to business. Salzari was going to kill him when he caught the traitor. Slowly and painfully.

There was a loud `clunk` as a hammer fell to the floor from the hole that Pandomar's men had ripped into the ceiling. Melly was just thankful that the banging had finally stopped.

A stocky man stuck his head out of the hole and looked down at them. He had a wrinkled face surrounded by a halo comprised almost equally of long dark hair and a bushy beard shot through with gray. "Sorry about that, it slipped." he called out. "It don't matter, though. It's all ironwood. Every single strut and every single roof board. Can't even imagine how much this gods-be-damned tower must've cost."

"What about the nails?" Pandomar asked.

"It's mage-built. Every single damned nail's been driven at least a half-inch deep, and then covered with filler. You'd have to find each nail, so's we'd need more light up here. Then you'd have to chisel down to the head of each nail afore you could even try getting it out. I'd estimate an hour per nail, eight nails to a roof board.

"You'd need to take out two roof boards afore you'd get a man through them, and then that devil Malik would just be there with his sword."

"How about if we had men working in parallel?" Razmar said.

"Para what?" The man looked doubtful.

Razmar scowled. "If we had multiple men working on nails at the same time."

The man looked up and away from the watchers below, clearly studying the construction and the web of struts supporting the roof. Looking down again he said, "Four men at once, perched on the supports, two on each board. So you're looking at maybe four hours to make a man-size opening."

Pandomar and Razmar both cursed at the same time, then eyed each other sheepishly.

Razmar called up, " How about burning the roof?"

"Hellfire, man, you ever tried to burn ironwood?" The man chuckled.

"No."

"It burns, but you gots to get it ferociously hot afore it catches. And even then, it takes hours and hours to burn through. You're better off prying out nails than trying to burn ironwood."

Razmar thought a moment. Then he grinned evilly. "I have an idea," he said. "Two ideas, actually."

The warriors in the room stared at him balefully. They'd already learned to be leery of his ideas.

Lydio Malik clutched his father's hand as they walked down the...well, he wasn't sure what the street was really called, so he just called it the Street With All the Statues. Intus was like nothing Lydio had ever seen, and he was almost six years old. There were so many people, dressed in so many different ways, and speaking languages he'd never heard before. Everything was so much larger than the farming village where he lived with his family.

Some soldiers in polished armor came along, shouting, "Make way, make way!" All of the people shuffled to the sides of the road. His father lifted him onto his shoulders so he could see better.

A group of soldiers marched past them, the beat of their boots echoing off the buildings. Lydio thought they looked really dangerous, like nobody would ever mess with them, not like the other boys in the village who picked on him because of his dark skin. There was a gap and then another group of soldiers marched by, and Lydio thought they looked way more dangerous than the first ones. They were wearing black armor with gold trim.

"Look at the sojers, Daddy," Lydio exclaimed. "How come they have black armor?"

"Those are the Phoenix Guards, boy. Must be royalty coming down the street."

"Are they really, really dangerous?"

"Son, they're the toughest fighters around," his father said. "They're elite, so elite that there's only ever two hundred of them."

"I wanna be a Phoenix Guard!"

His father laughed. "You can't, son, they'll never take a Neferian, no matter how good he is." It was years before he understood the bitterness behind his father's laughter.

The Phoenix Guards moved past but the banging sound of their boots didn't go away. Then he realized he was dreaming, lost in a childhood memory, but the banging was real. He wondered what his enemies had been up to while he'd been lost in a stupor.

His thoughts were muddled, fuzzy from fatigue, but he nevertheless tried to reason out what their next move could be. Dismantling the roof wasn't going to work for them, not in the timeframe they needed. He had the sense that the banging had stopped for a while, and then restarted while he was dreaming. Why had it stopped?

Because they'd realized they couldn't get through the roof easily.

Why start up again?

A distraction?

Had he been in their place, he'd up the ante. Hit him with multiple attacks at the same time.

If he were going to do that, some sort of distraction would be useful. A distraction…like the continued banging from underneath the roof.

He sighed. Letting the knotted rope slide through his left hand, he started to lower himself down the relatively steep slope of the roof, where he'd been resting next to the princess. As he did so, he caught sight of something — a jug of some kind — arcing through the air. It shattered on the tiles just below him and a clear liquid splashed out.

He had a feeling it wasn't water. Probably oil.

Malik desperately scrabbled with his feet, first to avoid sliding down into the oil. And second, to get back up to the princess before his assailants pitched the next oil-filled container at them.

And there it was…another ceramic jug. Malik reached up and batted it aside. It landed with a crash on the lower part of the roof.

Another one sailed overhead, aimed in a high arc at the spire above the princess, but the thrower's aim was bad. It sailed over Malik and the princess and landed with a crash in almost the same spot as the one Malik had diverted.

A fourth jug sailed through the air on an almost perfect trajectory for the princess. Malik lunged upward, got his hand on it and reeled it in to his chest, unbroken.

He quickly tucked it into the foot of the princess's basket; anything you had that the enemy didn't know you had was a potential advantage.

He heard more ceramic breaking from the other side of the roof. The banging was still continuing from below, so it was hard to be sure what he was hearing from the other side, but he was pretty sure the jug throwers were abandoning their position on the roof. He was certain he knew what was going to happen next.

The princess cried weakly, disturbed by all the noise. He wrapped the knotted rope around his left arm and then, with the limited mobility available to him in his precariously angled position, he pulled Princess Analisa's dainty, frilly little blouse up to cover her nose and mouth. He took her blanket and wrapped it around the bottom portion of his own face.

He heard the sound of something striking the other side of the roof, a flaming arrow most likely. There's was a whooshing sound as the oil on the other side of the roof caught fire. Then tendrils of flame raced across to their side. Larger fires started where the oil jugs had broken on the tiles. Gray smoke billowed into the air and enveloped them.

Danteel had an advantage over his neighbors. Most of the other buildings around his shop were only two stories tall, so the windows on his building's third floor gave him a good view of the city. In fact, only the Teradawn clan, with their ancient, upgraded four-story tenement, possessed a better vantage. Of course, that was mostly because they were even closer to Paksenaral, which gave them more elevation.

Danteel and his hulking friend, Orlik, were discussing the Situation, while Chanama took a turn looking out the third-floor window at the north tower with a sleek-looking farlooker, a mechanical device that enhanced vision. It was an awkward device, but exceedingly useful.

The silversmith had ventured out and found Orlik, a fellow shopkeeper, with whom he'd served in the militia. As a fourth-generation weapon smith, Orlik had always been fascinated by gadgets. Living up to his military reputation as a scrounger, he'd "liberated" a farlooker when he and Danteel had mustered out.

So far, they'd ascertained that Chanama had been right about fighting happening on the roof of the north tower. There was indeed a man on the roof, and he was defending what looked like a baby basket that was somehow tied to the roof's spire. And he was wearing colors that Danteel and Orlik both recognized as belonging to the Phoenix Guard. He could only think of one baby that the Phoenix Guard would be trying so desperately to protect.

Now they were trying to burn that lone guardsman out.

"It has to be the Princess Analisa," Danteel said.

"Yeah."

"It's got to be a small force," Danteel mused. "There's no army roaming the streets, pillaging."

Orlik grunted. "So they smashed the militia by surprise, caused havoc by burning everything in sight…"

"Then punched out the fortress garrison."

"Pa," Chanama interjected. "There's some men coming out the front gate."

"Let me see," Danteel responded. His son handed him the farlooker.

Danteel leaned over the boy and focused on the front gate. A team of eight men, attired like Kashmal warriors, was moving quickly through the streets. Two of them carried bows.

He handed the farlooker to Orlik, who grunted.

"I won't stand for it," Danteel said, standing up tall. "Once trained, always trained."

"I'm in," Orlik said.

xiv. Now

It's always better to sacrifice your opponent's men.

— Samiel Tartak, Grand Master, from Antellum

THE FIRES had died out and a mild afternoon breeze was gradually clearing the smoke away, but Malik couldn't stop coughing. The blanket had helped, but he'd nevertheless inhaled a lot of smoke.

Still, there really wasn't anything to burn on the roof, except the oil itself. Now that the flames were gone, he expected the next attack at any moment.

He was right about the imminent attack, but not its direction of approach. Still coughing, and spitting phlegm out of his mouth, he just barely caught a glimpse of something flashing through the air. An arrow struck the tile next to the royal basket and ricocheted away. He tried to backtrack its trajectory from the brief glimpse he'd gotten and realized that his enemies had placed an archer outside the castle. Probably in that tall building that the Burgundars should never have allowed so close to the fortress.

He tried to judge the arrow shot critically. The four-story building was downhill from the fortress. The distance was long and the elevation difference was extreme. It took an excellent archer, a seriously powerful archer, to get an arrow up here. But it took time, precious time, for an arrow to traverse that kind of distance. At least two whole seconds in flight, with an extreme arc to get it on target.

Malik quickly struggled to his feet, standing outward at an angle supported only by his lifeline, and positioned himself between the archer and the princess.

He spotted another arrow arcing in their direction and managed to knock it aside with his sword. He suddenly doubled over, coughing uncontrollably, and missed the next one. He and the princess lucked out, as it flew harmlessly past. He managed to divert two more arrows, but then one came in too low for him to effectively reach. Or maybe he was slowing down.

He screamed as it drove into his lower right leg and lodged solidly into bone. His leg buckled underneath him, but he managed to assume a kneeling position that still kept his body between the princess and the archer.

The arrows stopped. Despite his fatigue, Malik was still alert enough to recognize this as yet another bad sign. A moment later, a single fighter, rope tied to his waist, stepped carefully into view, careful of his balance and avoiding the still smoldering pools where the oil had burned. His sword was held quite properly in a guard position.

"Hoy, Malik!" he called. "Having a bit of trouble, eh?" The man had an erect, confident carriage. He wore a fine set of half-

and-half armor, heavy leather with a chain mail insert covering his torso—less than half the weight and better mobility than chain mail, but more protection than leather in most fighting situations. He moved easily, gracefully. Malik decided that he was the most dangerous opponent they'd sent up yet. If he was alone, it was because he didn't want any interference.

"You got a name?" Malik said, using his one good leg to lift himself into a standing position. His arrow-shot leg, the arrow still protruding, protested every movement.

The fighter looked up at Malik, ten feet away and perhaps eight feet higher, and laughed. "Nakanti, son of Pandomar, hero of Antigon, and, soon enough, the slayer of the Royal Bodyguard."

"Well, that hero thing is kind of dubious, seeing as how your side not only lost but got horsewhipped all the way back to your caves in the mountains." Malik saw the man's face flush with anger; he'd all but called Nakanti a savage, an uncouth cave dweller. "And the slayer part, I think I object to that."

"Well, come on down and let us do the dance of steel, that we may decide the issue."

Malik reached into the princess's basket, ignoring the protests from his bad leg, lifted the jug of oil and smashed it on the tiles a few feet in front of Nakanti, splashing him with oil.

Nakanti jumped to the side, landing in a spot untouched by oil from this or any of the previous jugs. Oil from the new jug ignited when several narrow streams reached still smoldering patches. Unfortunately, Nakanti was untouched.

"Tricky," the fighter said. "But your tricks won't save you now."

Orlik led the way down a narrow alley, massive war axe in hand, followed by Danteel. Orlik's oldest son, Miska, already the biggest man among all of them at nineteen, carrying a heavy-weight bow, came next, and eight other locals that Danteel had quickly recruited. They made a motley procession, but they all shared a determination to do something about the Situation. None of them could stand by and let the princess be slaughtered. Maybe they couldn't take back the fortress, but they could damn well take out the archers their enemies had sent out to get a new angle on the lone rooftop defender.

They were all armed with weapons from Orlik's shop. The bulky weapon smith hadn't hesitated for a moment at arming his fellow volunteers. Most of them even had some experience using them, thanks to mandatory militia service during previous conflicts with the Kashmal.

As they reached the final corner, Danteel called a halt. Then he peeked around the corner at the Teradawn tenement.

He turned and said quietly to the men, "Door's been smashed open. If these buggers have any brains, they'll have left at least one guard in the foyer."

Orlik rumbled, "You've been here before, I take it?"

"Yeah. There's a stairway on the left. If a guard gets up the stairs, our job gets harder. Much harder."

"All right," Orlik said. "We go in fast, two on each side of the entrance, Miska down the center with the bow. Two on the left, enter and then wait to see what has to happen, 'cause Miska's going to cover the stairs with his bow, and you ain't getting in his way if you know what's good for you."

Orlik picked three men to join him and Miska on the initial assault, leaving Danteel to lead the remaining men in behind them. One of the volunteers who hadn't been chosen for the initial strike complained, "Hey, I want to fight, too."

Danteel chuckled. He pointed at Orlik's little team as they assembled at the corner. "They're Shock. The rest of us, we're Awe."

"What's that mean?" the volunteer asked.

"They see Orlik and company, they're shocked," Danteel said.

Orlik turned and added, "They see the rest of you guys, they go—'Awww…we're so screwed.'"

The men chuckled. A moment later, Orlik led his assault team around the corner.

xv. Now

> *The winner of the game is the one who makes the next-to-last mistake.*
>
> — Samiel Tartak, Grand Master, from Antellum

MALIK was surprised that Nakanti waited patiently for him to a come down to a fighting position lower on the roof. He thought about leaping from above and various other stratagems, but decided that Nakanti was too good a swordsman for such maneuvers to work. So he descended laboriously, unwrapping the lifeline from his arm and half-hopping on his one good leg. He tried to fake being worse off than he really was, but there wasn't much room to fake being worse off.

The Kashmal warrior waited until Malik caught his breath from the laborious climb down, then inquired politely, "Are you ready now? I can give you a little more time if you'd like."

Malik raised an eyebrow. "You worried about my health?"

"You have fought valiantly. I can't help but regret the passing of such a mighty warrior." He paused. "But rejoice to know that your name will forever take pride of place in the songs they shall sing of my accomplishments."

Malik gave him an incredulous look, then shook his head tiredly. "Let's get it over with."

Their swords clanged and slid against each other in an intricate series of strikes as they tested each other's skills. They were both hampered a little, Malik by his immobility and Nakanti by his desire to avoid some of the still-burning patches and rivulets of oil. Malik would have been by far the better swordsman under normal circumstances. As it was, Nakanti clearly had the edge—younger, faster, fresher and uninjured.

Nakanti suddenly darted up the slope, higher than Malik could reach with his sword, but instead of going after the princess, the younger fighter wheeled, drew his sword along Malik's taut lifeline and cut it asunder.

Malik figured out what Nakanti was doing just barely in time to brace himself, so he staggered but didn't fall. He could feel his legs shaking with strain.

Nakanti laughed and, still keeping a safe distance from Malik, pretended to saunter casually as he descended the slope back to Malik's level.

Malik said, "Well, you've cut my rope. If you're going to play fair, you should get rid of your rope, too."

"You're welcome to try to cut it yourself." Nakanti grinned, showing off his white, slightly uneven teeth. "If you can."

The warrior circled around Malik, testing the bodyguard's defenses, carefully aware of his footwork to avoid tripping on the edges of the tiles or stepping in any of the oil. His moves gradually got more aggressive as he pressed Malik harder. Worn down as he was, Malik was having an increasingly difficult time parrying his thrusts.

Malik had realized one thing, though. Nakanti had probably never fought anybody of Malik's caliber before. He didn't realize that there was a slight predictability to his moves. Malik waited for Nakanti to make the right move.

The bodyguard recognized the minute stance change that heralded Nakanti's next thrust. Instead of blocking it, he deliberately stepped forward and drove his right shoulder into Nakanti's blade, trapping it in his own flesh. Malik roared with the pain, but still managed a descending swing that took out the younger man's throat in a wash of blood.

His sword clanged down to the tiles and wedged there as Nakanti fell on top of it. Then Malik slipped and fell on top of him. There was a snapping sound as Malik's sword shattered; he saw the middle piece of it arcing through the air.

Then he and Nakanti were tumbling. He dropped what remained of his sword and scrabbled against the tiles, breaking his fingernails, to try to keep himself from going over the edge. Somewhere in that mad rolling, Nakanti's blade came out of his shoulder, adding a whole new dimension of pain to Malik's experience. He just managed to slow himself in time as the fighter and his blade both went sailing into the abyss. When he stopped, both of his legs from thigh down were hanging in the open air.

Malik carefully shimmied his way fully back onto the roof. The pommel of his sword was still attached to his left wrist, along with eight inches of the shattered blade.

Melly saw the rope go taut as Nakanti fell off the roof and knew that Malik had managed to kill yet another attacker. Only one person so far had been knocked off the roof and lived, and he had steadfastly refused to go back up and face the "demon" again. She suspected that Nakanti was the best fighter they'd sent up so far, too good to be shouldered over the edge like the one survivor.

She felt a brief twinge of sorrow. Nakanti had been kind to her. Under other circumstances, she could have even liked him. This was tempered by her elation at knowing that Malik, and the princess, were both still alive.

She heard Razmar by the window cursing and making disparaging remarks about the tribal warriors. She looked up a Pandomar, who was standing near her, and saw his face tighten as he realized that his son was gone. His face flushed with anger at Razmar's comments, but he visibly controlled himself.

"I'm sorry for your loss," Melly said.

Pandomar fixed his penetrating gaze on her face. He grunted, then nodded almost imperceptibly as he realized she was serious. He turned to watch as three of his men grabbed the rope and began the laborious task of hauling Nakanti's body up to the window.

One of the men suddenly screamed and fell backward, clutching an arrow that had sprouted from his chest. The other two men dropped the rope and leapt away from the window.

Melly took this as a good omen. Someone was trying to help them. She struggled not to smile, since antagonizing her captors wasn't really in her best interests.

"Ser Razmar," Pandomar said drily. "I believe we have a new player in your little game."

"We're not leaving until the princess is dead." Razmar looked around haughtily. "If your paper warriors could just do their job, we'd already be out of here."

The Karshmen in the room glared angrily at Razmar, except for Pandomar who was completely still. Melly wondered if Razmar knew how close Pandomar was to just killing him and leaving.

After a long moment, Pandomar pointed to one of his men. "Tell the archers in the south tower to kill whoever's shooting at us." The man started walking to the door. "Run!" Pandomar roared, spurring the fighter to sprint out of the room.

Time dragged by as the opposing archers fought their slow-paced, long-range duel. While the struggle continued, Pandomar's men managed to raise Nakanti's body without exposing themselves to arrow fire. Pandomar had his son's body placed on what remained of the bed, now pushed up against the far wall. Nakanti looked almost like he was resting in state.

From what Melly overheard during the struggle, it was clear that the opposing archer was part of a group that had forcibly replaced the team Razmar had placed outside the fortress. The archer was also acting strategically, suppressing the capability for the rebels to get to the roof rather than trying to inflict damage. Melly suspected that her unlikely ally might also be conserving arrows.

Razmar pushed for another team to be sent to take out their opposition, but Pandomar summarily rejected the suggestion. By then, someone had organized the locals and there were hundreds of hostile citizens in the streets, many of them armed with makeshift weapons, all focused on the drama of the north tower stand-off. Instead, Pandomar pre-staged three fighters with ropes, so that they could go on the attack as soon as it was safe again.

Melly heard someone running up the stairs, then one of the younger warriors burst into the room and shouted, "They got him! They got him!"

She felt a pang of sorrow for the unknown archer. Still, by her estimate, whoever it was had cost Razmar and Pandomar more than an hour, maybe even an hour and a half, of precious time.

xvi. Now

Tactics means doing what you can with what you have.

— Alina Skye, Mercenary Commander

MALIK was lying down and resting. Well, actually, he wasn't completely sure he could stand up again. He was feeling very light-headed and he wasn't tracking well. Still, he was aware that there'd been a significant delay in the struggle, although he wasn't sure why. Maybe his enemies were fighting amongst themselves. That would be good.

He wasn't sure how long the delay had been. He thought he might have been, at best, semi-conscious for a good while after the last fight. If his enemies had had their act together, they could have killed him easily.

Malik heard the scrabbling that presaged another fighter climbing to the roof. He struggled to a sitting position and almost fainted from the pain of his crippled right arm. He used his left arm to painfully lever himself up onto one knee. Through strength of will alone, he made it to a standing position, his severed lifeline hanging behind him.

He hadn't been able to tie it back together with just one hand.

When the three warriors made their way to his side of the roof, they beheld Malik standing, swaying, yes, but still on his feet. His face was stained with soot and splattered with blood, which also darkened his entire right side and pooled around his feet. His hair was half burnt off and he looked like some maniacal demon silhouetted against the blue sky.

He threatened the three warriors with the eight inches of his broken sword in his left hand and roared, "Who wants to die first?"

His attackers spread out and deliberately started towards him. Then he saw them pause and look to their right with surprise. A second later, there was a painfully loud crack as lightning enveloped all three attackers and propelled them off the roof in a greasy cloud of disintegrating body parts.

Malik looked to his left and saw the King's secretary, Winton Marshfel, floating in midair.

An arrow flashed towards the diminutive secretary, but slowed and stopped an arm's length away. Winton looked at the south tower with an expression of annoyance. He gestured and a fireball materialized and sped toward the tower. There was an explosion outside of Malik's view.

"What in the seven hells is going on here?" Winton demanded. Then he spotted the basket. "Is that the princess?"

Malik fell backwards, unable to stand any longer.

"Yes," he said. "That's the princess."

"The Queen?"

"Dead. Everybody's dead, except maybe Melly if they didn't cut her throat right away. They had inside help. Kashmal rebels, led by a local man named Razmar. You really, really want to talk to him, if you can find him."

"Yes," said Winton, pursing his lips. "I think we have much to discuss."

He floated over the roof to the princess. Her basket lifted into the air to meet Winton. He waved diffidently and her basket's lifeline obediently untied itself. He grabbed her basket and turned back to face Malik.

"Lydio, you rest for a few minutes. I'll be back for you."

With that, Winton and the princess disappeared with a pop.

Melly saw Pandomar look up sharply at what sounded like thunder outside. He turned to Razmar and said, "I believe we have overstayed our welcome."

"What?" Razmar looked at him disdainfully. "What do you mean?"

"You've not been to war, have you?"

"What's that have to do with—"

Pandomar said softly, "You'd know the sounds you hear when the mages show up and all hope is lost."

Melly kept her face impassive, but, inside, she exulted. The princess was safe! She could only hope that Malik was safe, too. She was much less sure of her own safety, though.

The tension in the room was thick, but she could sense a change in the dynamic between Pandomar and Razmar. In some indefinable way, she could feel the mantle of leadership settling around Pandomar.

Pandomar turned away from Razmar and walked over to the prone form of his son. He reached out and cupped his son's cheek tenderly with one hand.

Without looking at Razmar, Pandomar said, "Kill him."

"Wait, you can't—"

Two of his warriors stepped up to Razmar and immobilized his arms. While the traitor struggled ineffectively, a third fighter stepped up behind him and cut his throat with a broad knife. Blood spurted into the air and the two warriors holding him let his body drop unceremoniously to the floor.

Pandomar walked over and stood in front of Melly. She was tied to the chair and could do nothing but look up at him defiantly.

"He knew too much to be left alive," he said. "And you…this was all a waiting game, wasn't it?"

"Yes," she answered, looking up at him and refusing to show how afraid she was.

"Well played."

Pandomar bowed slightly, then he and his men exited the room and ran for their lives.

Miska lay on the floor, fortunately unconscious for the proceedings. The healer, a wizened grandmother in a maroon robe, had finally managed to get the arrow out of the red ruin of his eye socket.

Looking up at Danteel, Orlik and the other six surviving volunteer fighters that were standing around them, she said, "He's lucky he turned when he did. The arrow ruined his nose bridge and the eye's a total loss, but it smashed the eye socket apart and exited rather than going into his brain."

Danteel saw Orlik breathe a sigh of relief. His son was going to live.

"The biggest problem," the healer continued, "is going to be infection." She paused, looking around. "I'm not too worried about that, though. When it comes to healing, I'm just a minor Talent. When the King finds out what you've done, I'm sure he'll make his Royal Healer available. She's got the power to fix all of this."

"All right, I've got you, Lydio. Stay with me."

Malik was dimly aware of his surroundings. Strangely, he felt like he was floating, which was odd. He felt cold and a shiver shook his frame, which hurt and reminded him that he was still maybe slightly alive even if his head was full of cobwebs.

Now he was moving through a crowd of Salasian soldiers and a few Phoenix Guardsmen who parted in front of him. For some reason, they were all saluting with their right fists clinched over their heart. He wondered who they were saluting. He was still wondering when he lost consciousness.

xvii. Later

One doesn't have to play well, it's enough to play better than your opponent.

— Sigbart Forester, Chess Scholar, from Tarrasch

"SIRE," Winton said. "I have the final tally for you."

King Salzari nodded, his visage devoid of emotion. Winton had known his liege lord for more than thirty years and recognized the pain that his friend was feeling, even if he was covering it up as much as possible. Soldiers, guardsmen, various functionaries and advisors surrounded them.

Now that Winton's secret was out of the bag, the oh-so-carefully hidden secret that he was a powerful, unregistered combat mage, the secret that he and King Salzari had hidden for so many years, people were looking at him much differently. He'd gone from being a funny-looking fop to a major threat in just a single day. Nobody was quite sure how to treat him anymore.

"There were one-hundred and fifty-four raiders," Winton said. "Two of them were captured by local volunteers."

"We will want to meet the volunteers and see that they are rewarded for their service."

"Indeed, sire, they also played a critical role in saving the princess."

Salzari raised an eyebrow, then nodded.

"Fourteen were captured during the final pursuit, after I brought a cohort through." A cohort was about five hundred men, a tenth of a legion. Bad enough that he'd had to reveal that he was a mage. Opening and sustaining a portal revealed to anybody with any knowledge of magic that he was at least a Beta, the second highest ranking of a mage's power. "The rest are dead, except for their leader, a warrior named Pandomar, who appears to have escaped."

Salzari went still, which those close to him knew was never a good sign. "How?"

"He was apparently a shifter." Winton paused. "I'm sorry, sire." Salzari waved his hand, his signal for moving on. "He presents as a black and tan mountain panther, with three legs. There were sightings, but we didn't put it together until it was too late. He escaped through the city and disappeared into the wilderness."

Looking around, Salzari said, "We want him dead. Put a price on his head that will make him the most wanted man in the Thousand Kingdoms."

"They were accompanied by a combat mage," Winton said. "A Gamma, based on my evaluation of his performance. He was killed during the takeover of Paksenaral."

Salzari nodded.

The King had already been briefed on Chently's heroic actions, but there was no need to make Chently's name, or the fact that he'd been a mage, known to the court. There were already people wondering how many other hidden mages Salzari had.

In actuality, Chently had gotten lucky and taken out a more powerful, but less fresh, mage by surprise, though he hadn't survived.

Looking around, Winton continued. "I think it's common knowledge by now, the Kashmal attackers had inside help, orchestrated by Tulis Razmar. We have truth scryers checking to see if anybody else was involved, though that's not my area of responsibility. I'm just a secretary."

There were a few titters from the audience, quickly subdued.

Salzari stood up. Addressing the crowd, he said, "We will return home to arrange the Queen's funeral. When we return, we will settle the Kashmal problem."

He turned and strode from the room.

Some time later, Malik awakened in a soft, comfortable bed. He didn't feel any pain anymore. He tried moving his arms and legs in turn and was pleased to see that they all seemed to respond.

"Malik?"

He heard Melly's voice and turned towards her. She was sitting in a chair next to the bed.

"The princess?" he croaked.

"She's fine," Melly said.

His princess was fine.

His.

He nodded and fell asleep again.

A GUN FOR SHALLA

DAVID A. TATUM

I.

KUSK sat on his bench, looking out the open porthole of His Majesty's Ship of the Line Elephant watching the becalmed sea return to stillness following the practice drill's final broadside. Lying immobile for several hours would disturb most sailors, but their anxiety had been relieved by the weather wizards' prediction of a front approaching from the south. It would be upon them within an hour, allowing them to resume their voyage.

Yet they were still ordered to battle stations. The Captain called for endless full-powered drills whenever possible, but with nothing to target, Kusk wasn't interested. He'd never had a problem producing fireballs, though his preferred magical focus made it a trifle difficult aiming them. He lost himself in balancing the two-foot-long sawed-off fire-staff in the palm of his hand, before juggling it with a number of elaborate flips and spins. He was so caught up in his idle entertainment that he didn't notice when his fellow fire mages launched a salvo.

"KUSK!" Gunner's Mate Petrecki bellowed, his feet pounding the oaken deck as he stormed into the asbestos-lined stall. Startled, Kusk missed his staff, which then spun its way into a tangle of his dirty, waist-length hair before it fell to the floor. "Have you gone deaf? Why haven't you fired your practice shot yet?"

"And how do you know I didn't?" Kusk asked, wincing as he tried to pull the end of his staff back out of his hair. How the heck did it get that tightly lodged in there so quickly? "That was a pretty impressive wall of fire we put out there."

"This is a seventy-four gun ship of the line," Petrecki said. "That means thirty-seven wizards are supposed to send out a fireball per side...yet for some reason, that last salvo only had thirty-six fireballs go out. And there's only one wizard's fireproof stall that wasn't warmed by the back-fire you'd expect from a wizard sending off a fireball—yours."

"Actually, while this ship is called a seventy-four, the hull is pierced for and crewed with eighty fire wizards," Kusk said absently, still fussing with his hair. "So if only thirty-six fireballs went out, that means four people failed to take a shot."

"I didn't actually count them!" Petrecki snapped. "Look, you didn't take the shot and we both know it. What I want to know is if you have some explanation, or if I should recommend a hearing before the Captain's mast to judge you for dereliction of duty?"

That drew Kusk's attention. If he was going to be accused of dereliction of duty, he wanted the luxury of actually being derelict. Abandoning his fire-staff for later extraction, he turned to his superior and took a formal stance. "I didn't hear the order."

Petrecki snorted. "Yeah, I've heard the other wizards mention the asbestos is a bit too thick in this stall. But they all know to cast fireball if all the other wizards on your side cast fireball, so why didn't you?"

"I suppose I just wasn't paying enough attention," Kusk said.

Petrecki's mouth worked for a bit, a variety of emotions flashing on his face. In the end he just sighed, not deigning to get into an argument with Kusk right then. "Whatever. Consider this an official reprimand. But you'd better fire in coordination with the other wizards from now on or I really will put you before the Captain's mast."

"Yes, gunny!" Kusk replied, saluting.

"Now…come with me. The Captain has an assignment for you."

Munck, Captain of the Elephant, read his orders for the sixth time. He didn't like these orders; the plan—what little he knew of it—seemed far too risky, with too small a reward for success. Worse, the man who would be representing his crew was a screw-up. He wished he could send more people along, but his orders said the liaison insisted he only send one person ashore, and there was only one person in all of the squadron's command who had the necessary talent.

Not that he knew this Kusk all that well. It was almost impossible to live for long on a ship without meeting all of your fellow crewmen at least a few times, but Kusk was little more than a "ship's gun." They were barely part of the crew at all, usually spending most of their time in asbestos-lined isolation, even sleeping and eating there. Munck had a hard time even remembering what Kusk looked like. He had the impression of a younger man with impossibly long, tangled hair and that was it.

That impression proved accurate when his best petty officer led Kusk into the room. Outside of the hair, though, he didn't look much like the stereotypical "gun." Most of the fire wizards drafted into the navy grew to become fat and flabby from their sedentary lives, and ashes typically stained their skin and clothing from their constant fireballs. Kusk was skinny as a rail, and while there were streaks of dark ash in his hair he had been able to keep his clothes and skin relatively clean. Most of them also had full-length fire staffs, as well, but it looked like Kusk had made some modifications of dubious legality to his own.

"Thank you, Mr. Petrecki," Munck said. "You can go."

"Yes, sir," Petrecki said. Shooting Kusk an indecipherable look, he stepped out of the room and closed the door behind him.

Munck took a closer look at Kusk's face. Still no visible ash. It was a puzzle how the man managed his duties as a ship's gun and not get ash on his face, but that was something to work out another time. He had a special assignment for this man, and the less he looked like a typical gun the better.

He must have spent too long watching the young man, because he'd started fidgeting hesitantly. "You asked to see me, sir?"

"I went through our records and found out something interesting about you, Kusk," Munck said, hoping he was pronouncing the young man's name right. He found that crewmen responded better to officers who remembered their names. "You are the only man in our crew who has a particular talent. Care to guess what that talent is?"

Kusk frowned. "Well, I'd guess it was some form of magic. When the press gang caught me, the only thing they cared about was that I was an expert in fire magic—they didn't bother to learn that I spent most of my days brewing beer, nor did they care that I owned my own inn to sell it from. Nor did they even ask if I knew how to sew or if I could cook, or any number of other skills I possessed."

"Beer? Did you brew stouts and porters or lagers and ales?" Munck began, then shook himself. "No, never mind—that's unimportant. The other skills you mentioned aren't exactly uncommon in the navy, though. Most sailors learn sewing pretty quickly, as we all must mend our own clothes, for example. You are right, however, that the talent I'm referring to is a form of magic." He paused. "You are the only 'light-light' wizard in the squadron."

Kusk winced. The phrase "light-light wizard" was a bad pun referring to a certain combination of magical affinities. Light magic focused on healing, restoring, and repairing damage to the target. Dark magic focused on wounding, damaging, and destroying the target. Over hundreds of years, though, wizards learned that this model had been too simplistic—and it led to a very discriminatory philosophy that "only good wizards use light magic and only evil wizards use dark magic." In truth, wizards had "elemental affinities," and these elements could be used in applications that would be considered both "light" and "dark" without any alteration of the spells involved.

For a while, wizards had claimed only four affinities: fire, water, air, and earth. Ironically, "light" (as in the manipulation of brightness and color, as opposed to the ability to heal) turned out to be an affinity as well, the fifth of the affinities to be accepted as its own branch of magic by most academic wizards.

About one in three wizards had two affinities, and one in a hundred had as many as three. New magical specializations developed as wizards learned to combine their effects—wizards with affinities for air and water (the most common pairing, according to the last magical census) were able to become weather wizards, for example. The triple affinity combinations sometimes gave abilities that even the double-affinity wizards lacked. Another form of magic only available with a particular triple affinity combination was colloquially called "light-light" magic. Tangible illusions could be created by combining light, fire (the basis for the second "light" of that appellation), and air magic. Its practitioners—Kusk included—felt that an undignified name, however.

"Yes, sir. I'm quite skilled in illuminated magic," Kusk replied. "What does that have to do with anything?"

"Tensions between our kingdom and the Skorran Empire have gotten worse than the government is letting on," Munck said. "Two months ago, our consulate in the city of Ankerst was destroyed in a riot. We believed there were no survivors, but last week we learned that was untrue—at least one member of the former consul's staff is secretly being held prisoner."

"I remember hearing about that riot," Kusk said. "It sounded…bloody. There was something about food being stolen from their mouths. We were being blamed for crippling their fishing industry, as I recall."

"Hogwash. The Skorran government is fomenting these sentiments as a precursor to war," Munck explained. "We know this, and are doing what we can in the political and diplomatic fields to calm things down, but we aren't likely to succeed. We are hopeful, however, that we can slow things down. We aren't ready for this war. Unless we can hold back the call for war for a few more months, giving us time to position our forces and recruit the next wave of soldiers, the Skorrran army will run right over our borders like they weren't even there. We must be careful not to do anything to further provoke them in the meantime.

"And yet we are being tasked with rescuing the survivor from Ankerst. Apparently, this person is related to someone high up there in our own government, though I don't know who or how. We have made contact with a group in Skorra who say they can rescue them for us, but they need help. Specifically, they need the help of a wizard who can manage some form of illusory magic. We'd prefer to send more people, but they won't agree to a meeting if we do. So, we're sending the only wizard skilled in illusory in a week's sailing distance."

"I was starting to wonder where I came in," Kusk said.

"I don't know the whole plan," Munck said. "But I do know our part in it. After night falls, we shall arrive close enough to the fishing village of Kohorn that you can take one of our small boats to shore. You are to meet with an old war hero, rebel leader, and spymaster who will be traveling under the name of Bowyer. He will give you more specific instructions about the rescue itself, and then later you are to help crew a ship, probably a fishing vessel of some kind, that we will rendezvous with outside of Ankherst. Any questions?"

"Yeah—what will you do for a 'gun' while I'm gone?"

"So what if we're down a single gun for a few days? It is no great loss to us," Munck replied. "Don't worry—you won't be missed."

"I wouldn't expect to be," Kusk said. "Few people notice they're missing a gun until they try to use them."

II.

GETTING ASHORE at night was difficult in the best of circumstances. With the need to remain silent while navigating unknown waters, few harbor lights, a heavy rainfall, and Kusk's own hopelessness as a navigator, it would have been impossible. It was only through the skills of a trained coxswain that he arrived on shore at all, but then that coxswain had to leave, taking the boat (and Kusk's only protection, as he'd had to leave his staff behind) with him.

Kusk had, after hearing about this mission, thought briefly about desertion. He hated being in the Navy. Well, it wasn't so much being in the Navy as much as it was being a gun. Before he was press-ganged, he had felt useful. He had been trained as a wizard from a very young age, but after his father died he left a successful job as a court mage to take over the old pub that had been in his family for over ten generations.

Keeping that pub was the only reason he hadn't deserted. The press gangs didn't discriminate between wizard or mundane, and neither did the laws for desertion—anyone who deserted would have their property seized, be outlawed, if captured would be sentenced to death, and any surviving family would be fined considerably for the crime. Fire wizards like Kusk had it worse—even without deserting, they were stuck in asbestos boxes for the next six years, rarely allowed out, while they served as a gun. The only thing keeping the fire wizards from rebelling at the treatment was that they were far outnumbered by other types of wizards, and it was those other wizards who enforced the "sentenced to death" part. Wizards could be particularly creative when it came to administering capital punishment.

Kusk was now alone, unsupervised, and on "dry" land which allowed him the first real chance to desert since he was press-ganged, but he wasn't feeling well enough to appreciate that fact. That he was seasick—a condition that hadn't plagued him since his first week on board the Elephant, but always returned on smaller boats—was no real surprise. That he was wet and cold, as well, just added to his misery. Worse, there were no spaces at the local travelers' inn to rest.

Tired, ill, and soaked to the bone from the rough seas, Kusk was getting desperate. He was even having trouble walking, as the long, thick wizard's beard he usually took such pride in was damp enough with water to be uncomfortable.

"Look, I'll sleep on the floor, if I need to. Just give me somewhere to rest my head!"

The innkeeper shrugged sympathetically. "Sorry, mate—I can find you a table near the fire and a hot meal, but not a bed. Ask around, though—I'll turn a blind eye if one of our other patrons is willing to share a room."

Figuring he wouldn't get a better offer, Kusk staggered over to the bench the innkeeper had pointed at. A roaring fire was being maintained on a hearth that backed into a stone wall, but the rest of the building was built of logs and had many draft-producing gaps in the structure. The fire helped immediately, but he knew before too long he would be overheating on one side and still wet and miserable on the other.

He was seated at an otherwise full table, and the boisterous discussion of other travelers passing through town was loud, overlapping, and consequently incomprehensible. Kohorn may have been a small town, but Kusk learned this inn was a popular stop among merchants shipping their goods between coastal cities. While there was a lot of laughter in the crowd, there were a lot of merchants and drayage drivers who were travel worn and surly as well. As tired and desperate as he was, Kusk wasn't about to try and talk someone from this crowd into loaning him a bed.

He didn't even know how he was supposed to make contact with the spy who was supposed to explain the rest of the mission to him, other than he should listen for the word "rabbit." It was far too loud to make out anything anyone was saying. This mission was not off to an auspicious start.

A half hour later, his prediction was true—his beard still dripped while his back roasted from the fire. He wanted to turn around, but the design of the bench wouldn't let him. At least things had quieted down, as his tablemates were starting to make their way out the door or up the stairs for the night.

Kusk didn't have a private table for very long. Only a minute or two after the group he'd been sitting with had broken up, a fresh face sat down next to him.

"You look miserable," the newcomer said. It was hard to make out what the man looked like—the hood of his traveling cloak was drawn up, hiding his face—but the few bits of hair to escape concealment looked clean, if otherwise poorly maintained.

"I was nearly drowned on my…uh, fishing boat, on the way into port," Kusk said, shrugging.

"Fishing boat? You don't exactly look like a fisherman." When Kusk didn't say anything after a moment, the stranger continued. "You look more like a drowned rat. Or perhaps a drowned rabbit."

Kusk stiffened. This was it—he either pretended to ignore the code word and live out his life on the run in Skorran lands, or he went on the mission. Some small feeling that maybe he could actually be useful and not just another gun, for once, inspired him to give the correct counter-sign. "I'm not, usually. We all have to do what we can, sometimes, to make ends meet."

"Hah!" the stranger said, slapping the table happily. "Thought so. Call me Bowyer, Mr. Fish. Knowing how crowded things are around here, I'm guessing you need a change of clothes and a place to sleep. Come with me and I'll take care of that."

Bowyer's choice of refuge was not as comfortable as sleeping on the floor at the inn would have been. It was a small hut, just down the road, but the roof had gaping holes in it, allowing the rain to pour in, and there was nothing warming the place up when they arrived. Kusk was quick to help with the little bit of fire magic he could manage without a staff after Bowyer set up some kindling in the cold hearth.

"Well, that answers my question about what type of wizard you are," Bowyer said, a little startled by the sudden flames. He lowered the hood. Kusk thought he looked exactly like he pictured the "war hero" and "former rebel" he'd been told to meet. Bowyer's hair was graying slightly, and there were a number of worry lines around his lips. He had a bit of a roguish glint in his eyes, though, and he held his head high like an aristocrat. "Now, get out of those wet clothes, Mr. Fish. We set a few supplies aside in this abandoned hovel in anticipation of your arrival, so we need to get you kitted out. I'll get you something dry…and hopefully a little less conspicuous. Skorran fashion runs more towards cotton or woolen shirts and leather pants rather than linen robes. And you should probably do something about that beard—most people don't wear long beards, here, until well after their hair has gone grey. Not even among the wizard set, and you won't find many wizards on Skorran streets—it's illegal for them to enter most cities."

Kusk frowned, watching Bowyer disappear into what must have been the only other room in the building. That beard meant a lot of things to him. For one thing, as a wizard, beards were a status symbol. He was rightfully proud of having the longest beard of his fellow fire wizards. It also said something about the status of a "gun" in the Navy—most sailors were required to shave their beards, but no one had ever complained about Kusk's. In a way, he kept it almost as much in defiance of the press gang that captured him as he did for aesthetics.

But having a beard, especially one of that length, made him stand out in Skorran lands, which probably wasn't a good idea on this type of mission. At least he'd learned to speak and understand several foreign tongues as part of his magical training, Skorran included; were he less educated, he would have been even more out of his element than he was now.

"I'm not complaining, mind you," Bowyer called from his room. "We'll take any volunteers around here."

I didn't exactly volunteer, Kusk mused. But then when does anyone ever care what I want to do in this racket?

"So, what exactly am I supposed to be doing?" he said aloud, absently untying the belt that held his robes closed. It was wet, and his fingers were still numb from the cold, which made things difficult.

"How much do you already know?" Bowyer asked.

"Not much. There's a member of the old consular staff that needs rescuing, we can't afford to be implicated in the rescue effort or else it might spark a war, and when the job is done we're to proceed by boat out of the harbor, where we'll reunite with the Elephant."

Bowyer returned to the room with an armload of clothing, shaking his head. "They didn't tell you much, did they?" He pointed to a pile of debris in the corner of the room. "There's a privacy screen over there you can set up, if you're modest, but I really must insist you change."

Kusk took the set of clothes and headed over to the debris pile, where there indeed was a rickety old folding stand he was able to set up and get dressed behind.

"The person we need to rescue is the daughter of the late consul," Bowyer began. "Who we believe also happens to be the fiancée to the colonial viceroy of Fernham."

"It would have to be someone pretty important," Kusk snorted. He doubted anyone would be rescuing him if things went pear-shaped. "No one's going to sanction this kind of mission to rescue the daughter of a scullery maid."

"The Skorran government hasn't tried to make any demands for her release, or even interrogated her, as far as we can determine. We have to be careful. They won't admit that anyone from the consulate survived the riot, so they would have no compunction against killing her if it suits their purpose. On the other hand, if we can get her out safely and without doing anything else to cause an incident there shouldn't be any further repercussions from her escape—they can't complain that we freed a prisoner they didn't admit to having."

"Makes sense."

"But they might complain if the collateral damage becomes noticeable. So, no killing anyone, no injuring anyone, no damaging distractions, nothing like that. Fortunately, I have a plan and a team of disaffected locals who have most of the skills I lack, but none of my companions are wizards, nor can any of them manage the type of disguise we need for one critical step."

"And that's why you asked for me," Kusk said.

"Exactly."

"So...what, exactly, is this plan?"

"Well..."

III.

AFTER A FEW DAYS of, quite frankly, boring travel disguised as a merchant, Kusk found himself in another ramshackle hut on the outskirts of Ankherst City. He had thought there would be even more excitement just to get this far, but his illusions must have been convincing enough that everyone believed them to just be the traders they pretended to be.

Everywhere he went in the Skorran Empire felt horribly cold, to him, but the clothes dictated by local fashion helped considerably; a cotton shirt and leather pants were all he was permitted indoors, but outdoors he was allowed to wear a heavy cloak made of boiled wool.

Seeing how easy it was to conceal things in the cloak's folds, he wondered why he'd had to leave his fire staff on the Elephant. At the moment, he was working on creating a replacement using a bit of alderwood he'd picked up on the road. He could do minor magics without one, but Bowyer and his people were expecting some rather powerful magics from him, and he wasn't sure he could deliver without some sort of focus. He wished he was better at carving—this alternate staff might not be as stable as he'd like.

Kusk barely rated any sort of introduction to the other participants in Bowyer's plan, most of whom had been waiting when he'd arrived. Kusk was just "Mr. Fish," not asked for his opinion on anything and not an expert at prison breaks. He wondered if being a fish was any better than being a gun.

When he first met the other people involved in the plan, he tried to get more details, trying to get more involved. For most of them it was like talking to a wall. They didn't seem to want him to know about them, and didn't care to know about him. "Don't ask questions," he had been told. "Bowyer knows what he's doing better than any of us, and he also knows exactly the right amount of information to give you to get the job done. Just do what he tells you and we'll all get out of this with great success. We might even live through it, too."

After that, being left alone by the others suited him just fine.

It seemed to suit his companions just fine, as well. Bowyer explained that none of these people would be going by their right names, for secrecy's sake, but all of these people were experts in their respective fields, whose names would be respected if known.

There was Mr. Wax, a locksmith and metalworker; he was less clean-shaven than most Skorrans, from what Kusk had been led to believe, but the week-old growth of beard hair did a good job of hiding burn scars from his trade.

Mr. Twine was the youngest man on the team. He had the calluses Kusk recognized from ropemakers and riggers on the Elephant, and the odor of a local fisherman.

Even after having sat with him for a few hours, Kusk couldn't have given a useful description of Mr. Hands, the pickpocket. He was of average height and average build, with a plain face and a fairly basic hairstyle. Kusk decided the man must have spent quite a bit of time practicing to appear so ordinary.

And then there was Ms. Honeytrap, a rather buxom young woman wearing far too much makeup and who normally worked in a profession Kusk would not speak of in polite society—and he had yet to let the Navy life wash the polite society upbringing out of him.

He wasn't the only one meeting these people for the first time, though they all seemed to know Bowyer. Mr. Wax and Mr. Twine seemed to know each other very well, and were the most familiar with Bowyer himself. Kusk guessed that they were also members of Bowyer's rebellion. The others didn't know each other or anyone else in the room, as much strangers as Kusk himself.

This was the cast of characters who would get the consul's daughter out of the prison undetected, with Kusk's help. Mr. Bowyer and Mr. Twine would then be joining the escape out of the city. And everything was on hold, waiting for Kusk to get himself ready.

"How long until that stick of yours is done?" Ms. Honeytrap asked, gesturing to his staff. "My time is money, and you lot aren't paying me enough to forget about money."

Kusk glanced over his work. It was rough, but he was used to buying his staff from a proper craftsman and then tweaking it instead of carving one himself from scratch. He was rather happy that it looked like it might work at all. "Well…I could probably cast a spell or two with it."

Bowyer stepped through the front door, shooting Ms. Honeytrap a dark look. "Probably a good thing, since we need to move on this today. Mr. Fish, why do you still have that beard?"

In truth, Kusk just couldn't bring himself to shave it off, but he figured he needed some excuse. "Well, I've got to test this thing out on something," he said.

Channeling a little focused magic through his new staff, Kusk tapped his beard and it appeared to shrink down until there was just a light fuzz over his face. Another tap, and the beard re-appeared. A third tap, down it went again.

"Good enough?" he asked, looking over at Bowyer.

"It'll do," was his reply. "Lady and gents, it's time to begin the rescue operation."

IV.

ALL IN ALL, Kusk felt it was one of the smoother, better run operations he'd ever witnessed. Things were going exactly as

Bowyer planned them, with precision timing that his compatriots in the navy could only dream of.

> *"The first step," Bowyer had told him, "involves getting the key to the prison away from the guards. To do that, we need to get a guard with the key isolated where we can snatch it. We know a girl who will be perfect for that part of the plan…"*

There was only one entrance to the prison, at the end of a dead-end alleyway lined on either side with windowless stonework buildings. The other end of the alley opened up into a well-trafficked market street, and it wasn't uncommon for people doing their shopping to stop in the shade of the alley for a rest. Nor was it uncommon to see the odd prostitute trying to earn a little cash during those "rests." And the guards were not above…indulging, if the girl looked fresh enough. Ms. Honeytrap's approach was somewhat anticipated, once the guards saw her attempting to ply her trade to the market goers.

Kusk, lying hidden on the roof of one of the alleyway's buildings, couldn't make out what she said, but whatever it was seemed quite effective. Both of the door's guards seemed interested, and one of the few complete sentences he heard was a laughing "One at a time, boys!"

Negotiations finished, she led one of the guards down to the marketplace, and then zigged out of sight into a nearby building. Along the way, a nondescript man brushed past the guard. That was Mr. Hands, picking the keys out of the guard's pockets. Mr. Hands passed the key off to Mr. Wax, who true to his moniker took a wax impression of it before handing the key back to Mr. Hands. A few minutes later, a disheveled guard—armor slightly askew—stepped back into sight, where Mr. Hands again bumped into him to return the key to his belt. Evidently, the first guard enjoyed his time, as he had a brief word with the second guard, who in turn went around to enjoy Ms. Honeytrap's attentions.

After that, it was a waiting game for Kusk. Mr. Wax had assured them he could finish forging a duplicate of the key in a couple hours, but in the meantime they had to be sure that nothing happened to put the guards back on alert.

> *"When we get the key made," Bowyer explained. "That'll be the time for Mr. Twine and me to begin our job. Ms. Honeytrap can get to them one at a time, but we'll need both of them off the door for the next step. Fortunately, there's a reward out for my capture, and the guards will be more concerned with my capture than with guarding a door that has a supposedly unpickable lock…"*

Whatever Ms. Honeytrap had done with the guards, they weren't quite as sharp as they had been before their encounter with her. Both of them were quite disheveled, and hardly seemed able to keep their eyes open much less remain as alert as guards should be. Bowyer's appearance changed all that.

"What ho, lads!" he called down the alleyway, doffing a cap to the two guardsmen. There was a moment of confused recognition, but at first they didn't react.

A panicked scream—sounding remarkably like Ms. Honeytrap (which, Kusk knew from the plan, it was)—prompted the guards to abandon their post. One went off in pursuit of Bowyer, and the other in the direction of Ms. Honeytrap. They ran off, leaving the door unprotected save by a lock. It was Mr. Twine's job to ensure Bowyer escaped, which left Kusk to go into the jail and perform the actual rescue. Kusk had not been privy as to how, but he'd been assured that the guards would be left alive and unharmed in the end.

He slipped down a rope ladder that Mr. Twine had prepared earlier, dropping to the ground unnoticed. It was surprisingly well-made, resembling some of the better work Kusk remembered from the riggers on board the Elephant. He wasn't sure where Bowyer had found these people, but they sure seemed skilled at their jobs. Probably better than he was at illusions.

Kusk turned to the door, watching the crowd in the marketplace down the alley to be certain he hadn't drawn too much attention, and inserted the new copy of its key (or rather, the first key—Mr. Wax had delivered three to him, but the other two were for indoors. Somehow, Wax knew which key belonged to which lock and had labeled them). He didn't turn it right away, however.

> *"There are three people whose presence won't be questioned no matter where you are in the prison," Bowyer had explained. "The Warden, Ankerst's Captain of the Guard, and the Mayor of Ankerst. You need to use your magic to disguise yourself as one of those three people before you go in there."*
>
> *"How am I supposed to do that? I may be able to cloak myself in an illusion to make me look like someone else, but only if I know what those other people look like, and I've never seen any of them, before. And even if I did know them, another mage would spot me without even trying."*

"There shouldn't be any mages in the prison—like I said earlier, it's forbidden. As far as your disguises go…" Bowyer pulled out a modest-sized portrait. "I can't get them to model for you, but I was able to sketch out a few reasonably accurate pictures of them. Ms. Honeytrap knows all three of them, uh, intimately. She'll work with you to make them look right. It'll be accurate enough—you only need to be able to fool a few people as you walk past them, and those people should only have a passing familiarity with these gentlemen at best. It's not as if you need to fool their families or anything like that."

This was the part of the plan Kusk was least thrilled by. They could have at least made arrangements for him to see one of these people in person. It was very hard to try and impersonate someone based on someone else's recollection of them.

Still, he grabbed his new staff and focused his magic, changing his features to match the portrait of the Captain of the Guard for Ankerst as best as he could. There were no mirrors to check his reflection in, so he could only hope he looked like a human being, at least. A turn of the key and he was in the prison.

The first guard he saw was a big test, but he was able to pass by them without raising any sort of alarm. The same held true for the next three or four guards. Much to Kusk's surprise, the disguise he was wearing was actually working. Maybe this crazy plan wouldn't get him killed, after all.

Bowyer had shown him a map of the inside of the prison he'd obtained from a "Mr. Mole." These maps seemed accurate, so Kusk had a general idea of where to go and how to get there, but they weren't perfect. She wasn't being kept in a normal prison cell—they had that much decency, at least—but rather down the hallway, up a tower, down another hallway, and to a secure office on the right. Kusk got turned around a couple times, but finally found the room he knew the prisoner was supposed to be in. That was when everything fell apart.

> *"So, what does this consul's daughter look like?" Kusk had asked.*
>
> *"Well," Bowyer said. "I've never seen her, nor do I have any pictures. The consul and his wife had a few traits I would expect their child to have—both had unruly brown hair, hazel eyes, and aquiline noses, and both were reasonably fit. Given their ages, I'd expect any daughter of theirs to be in their twenties or thirties…"*

Unruly brown hair? Check.

Hazel eyes? Yep, them too.

Aquiline nose? Yeah, even that.

Reasonably fit? Um…hard to tell.

Twenties or thirties? Not even close.

This girl had to have been seven, maybe eight years old at the most. Admittedly, there were probably a lot of girls and women in this city who would match the rest of the description, but how many of them would be in the right cell from the exact part of the prison that the Consul's daughter was supposed to be in?

"Um…who are you, milady?" Kusk asked.

The child turned those two hazel eyes on him, giving him a glassy stare. It was not a look one would expect on a seven-year-old girl, but barring some sort of magical illusion to cover her real expression, that's what she was giving him.

"Shalla," she whispered. "Who are you? You're trying to look like the Captain of the Guard, but I can tell you aren't. I can see the real you underneath the Glow."

Well, one thing about this girl Kusk learned right off—she was sensitive to magic; only someone sensitive to magic would see a "glow" around him while he was in disguise. That probably meant she would be able to perform magic, too, with a little training. And no, she wasn't also an illusory wizard in disguise—Kusk would see that kind of "glow," himself.

"If you're who I think you are, I'm the person sent to rescue you," Kusk said.

She blinked up at him. "Who do you think I am?"

"I think you're the daughter of the old consul, who was killed just a few short months ago."

She smiled. "Then…then you are here to rescue me! But why?"

"Well, to begin with, we thought you were a lot older," Kusk said. The distant sound of footprints down the hall reminded him of the precariousness of their position. "But the why can wait. Do you need anything? We need to go, and soon."

The girl grabbed a doll, shaking her head. "No…I have everything I want. Everything I can take with me, that is. Unless you can bring back my parents? You're a wizard, right? That means you know how to do things like raise the dead, right?"

Kusk flinched. Necromancy might really exist, but all he really knew of it was that the International College of Wizards had declared it anathema and forbade its practice. But even if it was permitted, Kusk didn't know how to do it, nor even what magical affinities were required to do the kind of thing this little girl was asking of him.

"I'm not that kind of wizard," Kusk said sadly. "All I can do is help you get out of here, so you can grow up and become a woman they would be proud of."

V.

GETTING OUT of the building was harder than Kusk had thought. The original plan called for him to use another illusion to disguise the prisoner and lead her out of the building. It was straining Kusk's magical talents to do that much, but that had been assuming the girl he was rescuing was an adult woman who would be close to the size of one of the shorter guards, at least. The amount of magical energy required to make a seven-year-old girl look like an adult male while also maintaining a disguise around himself was significantly higher.

He needed to disguise Shalla as something that a warden, a mayor, or a guard captain might have with him as he walked through the halls of a prison, but which was Shalla-sized. Shalla was about three feet tall, about forty pounds, and very much alive. This presented a problem.

The easiest thing he could think of was a sack of laundry, or something similar. It was simple enough to take Shalla's bedding and turn it into a makeshift bag to carry her in, but he couldn't hide it if she started moving around in the bag. That would raise questions.

Unfortunately, he couldn't think of anything that might move which he would be taking through a prison hallway.

There were several animals he might be able to disguise her as, such as an especially large dog, a pig, or something else like that, but no animal form would work here. The Skorrans didn't even think much of guard dogs, so it would be strange to see one walking along these prison corridors. So a sack it was, with Shalla promising to do her very best not to squirm.

Also, it was unlikely that the Captain of the Guard, a warden, or a mayor would be carrying his own sack of goods, anyway. Kusk ditched that disguise and, much to Shalla's amusement, changed his face so that he vaguely resembled some of the other guards he'd seen walking around the building. He wouldn't look like any one of them, specifically, but he'd be familiar enough that no one would question his presence.

Bowyer's plan called for him to leave the same way he came in, so it was merely a matter of retracing his steps. After making sure none of the guards were looking, Kusk (using his staff as a pole to help carry his bag with, in a fashion he'd seen some of the local townsfolk doing on his way to the prison) stepped out of the locked office. A brief journey up the hall went fine. The trip down the tower stairs went without significant incident (though he nearly gave the game away when he bumped Shalla's bag against a passing guard. Fortunately, he didn't even seem to notice, and ignored Kusk's muttered apology as he just kept walking).

Breathing a sigh of relief, Kusk got to the ground floor. Just one hallway with no turns to go, and then he was out of the prison, free and clear. The next leg of their escape—to the rendezvous with Bowyer and his team—would be a cinch after that.

Of course, that was when he was stopped.

"What do you have in that bag, soldier, and where do you think you're going with it?"

While Kusk obviously didn't recognize the voice, that tone seemed universal in every service for every nation. It just shrieked "petty officer trying to reinforce his authority by berating a lowly recruit." Kusk didn't think his disguise indicated he was a "lowly recruit," but he wasn't all that familiar with Skorran's uniform system.

"It's laundry day, sir," he said, hoping to leave the rest unsaid.

"It is not!" the petty officer snapped. "The barrack's laundry service isn't scheduled for another three days."

Kusk had to think fast. "Not taking it to the barrack's laundry. I'm taking it to my wife. She gets things cleaner than we do…or so she claims."

The petty officer snorted. "Right, your wife wants to do it all. That's a laugh. That's also a lot of laundry."

"It's been a while since I took a batch home with me," Kusk replied, shifting uncomfortably. Why was this guy asking so many questions? Had he caught on or something?

"You look nervous," the petty officer said. "Why are you nervous?"

It took a few seconds for Kusk to think of an answer, and all the while the petty officer looked more and more suspicious. If he really was a guard, why would he be nervous? Why would someone be nervous about their laundry? Or rather, about someone else seeing their laundry.

Well, that's an idea, Kusk thought. He set the bag down, grasping his staff. He had to be careful not to do anything that this overly-curious petty officer might see, but he could still create a few illusions.

"I'm just worried you're going to make me dump this bag where everyone can see," he said, untying the bag and reaching in. Shalla squirmed, but thankfully said nothing when he grabbed what had been her teddy bear. Now, it was a bit of sheer cloth cut to show off certain feminine assets—the sort of thing that Ms. Honeytrap might wear to entice her clients. "This sort of thing is kind of hard to explain."

The petty officer relaxed and started laughing. "Oh, put that away. Take ten demerits for non-regulation underwear, and my congrats on a good catch. Are you really getting your wife to launder that?"

"Who do you think wore it?" Kusk said, laughing along with him but still feeling a little tense.

"Go on," the officer said, walking away with a jaunty wave. Breathing a sigh of relief, Kusk started down the hallway. Kusk got about half-way to the exit when, marching out of an adjoining corridor, another petty officer stepped up into his face.

"What do you have in that bag, soldier?" the petty officer asked, stepping into his face.

Kusk froze. Seriously, did these people have nothing better to do than demand that their soldiers explain what was in a laundry bag?

"Oh, to hell with it," Kusk muttered, then decked the man unceremoniously.

VI.

He may have gone unchallenged from then on, but Kusk knew that it wouldn't be long before the man he had dropped to the ground with one punch regained consciousness and rang the alarm. The discovery of Shalla's absence would probably have been a long time coming, but now they'd be looking for him that much sooner.

There was a contingency plan that Bowyer had set up for the off chance he had been discovered. It involving a long run through the streets he probably wasn't in shape for, Mr. Twine's rigging of a trap, and Bowyer doubling back from leading his guardsman on a wild goose chase in time to help out, but that plan seemed overly complicated in Kusk's mind so he was glad it wasn't needed. The real trick would be escaping town—there was no way for them to get to sea before the alarm sounded, now.

A quick stop to change disguises in one of a nearby building's more secluded rooms (the same one Ms. Honeytrap had been using earlier) and they were back out into the market, resuming his normal (but beardless) appearance and doing the bare minimum to disguise Shalla as his daughter. If he looked a little frenzied, well, there was only so much magic could do to disguise a person.

Bowyer had established a safe house near Ankerst's docks—a tavern that Ms. Honeytrap used to work in, vaguely reminding Kusk of his old pub back home—which was relatively safe. They could wait for the heat to die down a bit and plan their next step.

"Mr. Fish," Bowyer called, waving him over to one of the inn's tables. That caught the innkeeper's attention. At first, this worried Kusk, but a brief nod between Bowyer and the innkeeper convinced him that the two knew each other, and that the inn would help cover them if it could.

Bowyer wasn't alone. Kusk recognized Mr. Twine and Mr. Wax as well. Mr. Hands and Ms. Honeytrap were nowhere to be seen; he wondered why they weren't there, but wasn't overly concerned.

Guiding Shalla with him, Kusk joined Bowyer and the rest of the team. "Gentlemen," he said, nodding in greeting.

Bowyer raised an eyebrow at Shalla. "Interesting choice of disguise for your consulate's daughter."

Kusk winced. "It's not much of a disguise. I would like to introduce the seven-year-old daughter of our late consul."

"I'm eight!" Shalla protested.

Faces fell around the table. "Really?" Mr. Twine said. "She is the fiancé of the viceroy of Fernham? He likes them young, doesn't he?"

"Who?" Shalla asked, eyes widening.

"I think there's been a mix-up," Kusk said. "She's definitely the daughter of the old consul, but the betrothal part must have been a rumor. Girls this young don't get into arranged marriages where I'm from."

Bowyer shook his head. "This…isn't good."

"Why?" Kusk asked. "She's still the person we were sent to rescue."

"She's just a child!" Mr. Twine snapped. "Probably some scullery maid's daughter. No one pays good money for some maid's brat."

Kusk stiffened, shifting in his chair to better defend Shalla from his tablemates. "Money? You were planning to…sell her?" This was not what he signed up for.

"Doesn't matter, now, does it?" Mr. Twine said, getting up and storming out of the building. Kusk thought to follow and find out just what that meant, but he couldn't risk stepping outside.

Mr. Wax stood up, bowing slightly. "My apologies for our friend. He doesn't mean to be rude, but he is upset. This was supposed to be our new start, and…well, anyway, I'll go see if I can calm him down."

Bowyer sighed, watching Wax follow Twine out the door. "No, Mr. Fish, we weren't planning to sell her. Not exactly."

That did nothing to convince Kusk to let his guard down. "What do you mean, 'not exactly?'"

"Mr. Wax, Mr. Twine, and I are all that's left of a popular rebellion that had been based in the Vahlwood Forest," Bowyer explained. "Well, it used to be a popular rebellion, anyway. The people were being starved and forced into indentured servitude by ridiculous taxes, raised only so that the local nobles wouldn't have to spend their own small fortunes on behalf of the Skorran Empire. A decade ago, when the Imperial throne was still in dispute and we were supporting the rightful heir, we even enjoyed some support among the other nobles who weren't happy with some mentally unstable upstart taking over while our rightful Emperor was out fighting in the wars overseas.

"After the succession was handled, however, our support disappeared. The taxes remained a problem, but any sympathetic nobles were systematically removed and replaced by toadies to the Emperor. We continued to fight, but in the end we just ran out of time, money, and resources. There is no one we can legitimately put on the throne to replace the current tyrant, and any new nobles will be succeeded by his toadies. There is no path to victory, and we had so many losses the people became afraid that joining us would just make their situation worse. So, we had a choice: Keep fighting pointless battles for an increasingly unappreciative bunch of serfs, or leave.

"Then we discovered that this young lady, here, had survived the riots in Ankerst. The rumors were that she was someone vitally important; heir of a noble line, the fiancé of the viceroy, and a powerful young woman in her own right. We knew we could rescue her for your people with minimal outside help. It appeared to be the perfect opportunity: one last strike against Skorran injustice as our retirement. Wax, Twine, and I figured that we could win refuge with your people in exchange for her. If she really were the heir of a noble line and the fiancé of a viceroy, that would be true. For some little girl, though?" Bowyer shook his head. "No government would stick their neck out for us, not for her."

Kusk frowned. He wasn't all that connected with his own government's politics, but surely they would appreciate the rescue of one of its children? "Even so, there is no reason to blame Shalla for that."

Bowyer's eyes flashed, and Kusk immediately realized his faux pas—no true names when discussing business. Shalla wasn't so uncommon a name that it should draw red flags, but he still broke one of the Rules. Still, attaching a name to a little girl wouldn't be too bad…right?

"Perhaps not," Bowyer said. "I suppose it doesn't matter to you or to her. However, it does matter to us. We can't afford to stick our necks out for no reward. From this point, you're on your own. You should be fine—you're free, so it should be no problem to steal a small fishing boat and get out to your ship on your own. We're just not coming with you."

Kusk tensed. "Um…that won't work. I don't know how to sail a boat."

Bowyer raised an eyebrow. "It was my understanding you were a Navy man."

"I am. But I'm a gun."

That threw Bowyer for a loop. "Oh. My apologies."

Shalla, who had been watching the back and forth intensely, focused on Kusk at this comment. "What's a gun? Is it a bad thing?"

"Yes," Kusk grumbled.

"Not really," Bowyer said at the same time. Then he looked at Kusk in surprise. "Yes, you say? What's wrong with being a gun?"

Kusk sighed and turned to address Shalla. "Until a couple hundred years ago, we wizards didn't know much about magic, other than that it existed and that some people could control it. There was no in-depth study of how magic worked and no schools to learn from; it was up to each wizard to learn everything they needed to know by themselves. In that time, most wars were fought using weapons fueled by gunpowder—the same material that makes fireworks fly—to send iron or lead balls across the field at great speed. These weapons were dangerous, but heavy, inaccurate, and slow to fire. They were called guns, the largest of which were called cannons, some of which could throw iron balls weighing as much as sixty-eight pounds each.

"But then magical affinities were discovered. Wizards learned standard spells based on affinity, such as how to cast a fireball that would cause damage at the same range of these cannons, and at a much faster rate. Armies continued using smaller guns like muskets and rifles, because it was very hard to find skilled wizards in enough numbers to replace a large army that might number in the hundreds of thousands of soldiers, but the navy only needed a fraction of that number. The navy recognized it was possible to replace these heavy weapons with wizards like me for even the largest of navies. As a joke, we were called 'guns,' just as the old cannons were. The name stuck."

He turned to Bowyer. "But we don't get treated nearly as well as the cannons of old. The cannons were regularly treated to prevent rust, and had teams of six to twenty-four people to take care of them. We wizard-guns are yanked off the streets with little explanation and then tossed into a stall, with barely any pay to cover the losses to our businesses back home. We are frequently ostracized by anyone who isn't another gun. Our problems are ignored…unless they prevent us from doing our job, and then we're blamed for it. And if they need a fire wizard to do some other job—such as rescuing a little girl from a jail—we're tossed ashore with no ability to protest, few instructions, no time to prepare, and no regard for our ability to do the job."

Bowyer winced. "Exactly the sort of injustice I started a rebellion to stop."

Kusk shrugged. "People don't think enough of us to do that kind of thing. After all, I'm just a gun."

Shalla glanced up at Kusk. "I don't think you're just a gun. You wouldn't have helped me like you did if you were."

Kusk laughed slightly. "Thank you, Shalla. It would be nice if other people remembered I was more than just a gun, sometimes."

Bowyer sighed. "I can't say you would be treated any better if you stayed here. The Skorran Empire doesn't like wizards or magic all that much. We have fire wizards in our navy, too, but from what I understand they're chained up when not in use, and treated even worse than you were."

Kusk nodded. That explained how his illusions would hold up as a disguise—in the Skorran Empire, wizards and sorceresses were separated from "normal" people early on and forced to live in carefully monitored, isolated communities of other wizards. They didn't even use wizard guards to look for people like him, from what Bowyer had said. He knew the Skorran Navy used fire wizards and weather wizards, just like every other navy in the world, but that seemed to be the limit of their interaction with mundanes. That meant there probably wasn't anyone in town who was magic-sensitive enough to see through his illusions. Well, no one except Shalla, it seemed.

"I have a home to go to. Even as a press-ganged gun, I'm only required to give three more years of service before my tour of duty is up, so I should be able to return to my inn and my brewery in time; those will be lost if I desert. No, staying here wouldn't make much sense for me." He glanced at Shalla. "Plus, I made a promise to this little girl, so I need to get her home, too."

Bowyer grimaced, glancing at Shalla. The little girl looked up at him as innocently as a girl her age could. "Well, it doesn't sound like you can fulfill that promise on your own. Let me go talk to Mr. Twine—we have a job to finish."

VII.

IT HAD TAKEN BOWYER AND MR. WAX almost an hour to talk Mr. Twine down, bringing him back to the inn for a final discussion. Kusk spent the intervening time looking after Shalla while eavesdropping on a conversation between two local brewers—one of rum, the other of mead—on the merits of sugar versus honey. As a once and future beer brewer, himself, he had to hold himself back from getting involved and discussing the benefits of malt over either substance.

Mr. Twine was in an even worse mood when, just as he was returning to the tavern, he was doused by a pitcher of cider that one of the tavern wenches had tossed at the two brewers after their argument nearly broke out in fisticuffs. The argument between rum and mead was abruptly ended when Mr. Twine smashed bottles of the arguers' favorite drinks over their heads, knocking both men out. The tavern keeper looked at him in askance, but the glare on Twine's face was enough to make him carry the drunken sots out back without comment.

"All right," Mr. Twine began. "I understand that, despite having been in the navy, you can't sail a boat. You need us, and I still have enough respect for Mr. Bowyer to be a part of this even if I no longer see any point to this mission. We have a problem, however."

"And that problem is?"

Mr. Twine blew out a frustrated breath. "I've seen on the map where you're supposed to meet your ship. It would be foolish to try and get there in an open boat, rowed by oars, so we'll need something bigger. We were planning on that anyway, but if we're going to travel by sail the winds are wrong; we can't even leave port without rowing our way out. Unless you're a weather wizard in addition to being a light-light wizard, I'm afraid we're stuck here until the winds change. Given the time of year, that might not be for weeks."

"It's illuminated wizard, and…oh, never mind," Kusk said. "No, I'm not a weather wizard."

"What's a weather wizard?" Shalla asked.

With a frustrated sigh, Kusk indulged the girl's curiosity. "A weather wizard is someone with affinities for both air and water magic."

"Oh! But aren't you a wizard?"

"I am. And so are you, but it doesn't help us unless we have the right affinities. And I don't have those," Kusk said.

"She's a wizard?" Bowyer asked incredulously.

"With everything else we got wrong about this girl, that surprises you?" Kusk laughed. "Or rather, since she's a girl, she would be called a sorceress. So she does happen to have some value, despite what Mr. Twine may think."

"I can see when people Glow," Shalla said. "Papa said that meant I had magic."

"But she's completely untrained," Kusk continued. "I might be able to teach her, if she has the right affinities, but that's very unlikely."

"How long would it take you to teach her?" Mr. Twine asked. "The guards already cut off all land-based exits from the city. We're fine holding up here while they still do the street sweeps, but in a few hours they'll begin house-to-house searches. We have a day or two, tops, before they'll find us, and it'll take longer than that for the wind to change direction naturally."

"To teach her one spell?" Kusk asked. "A few hours, at most, if I had access to the right tools and materials. But as I've said three times, now—it won't do any good unless she has the right affinities."

"Then we're stuck here," Mr. Twine said, shaking his head. "And they'll eventually capture us. Bowyer and I will be hung as traitors, and you'll probably be executed as a spy, if you aren't disappeared, studied, and dissected in the government's efforts to figure out how wizards tick. And the best this…girl, here, can hope for is that they will be put right back where she was."

"You mean I have to go back?" Shalla asked. "But…but I thought I'd be able to go home. That's why you got me out, right?"

"I want to get you home," Kusk said softly, putting a comforting hand on her shoulder. "And I want to go home, myself. I'll take being a gun over being a specimen, any day. But if we can't figure out some way out of the city, we're stuck here."

"No!" Shalla shouted. "I won't go back to the prison! They're mean, there. They never let me get enough to eat, and they're always talking about how they killed my parents. I hate it there. Hate it, hate it, hate it!"

"We're not going to send you back," Kusk said, trying desperately to calm her down. "But—"

"No!" Shalla said, jumping off the bench and running for the door.

"Stop her!" Bowyer said. "The guards will recognize her, and—"

"I know," Kusk said, already running after her. He caught her just before she could make it out the door, pulling her back. "Shh, shh, shh. Sorry, Shalla, we want to take you home, but—"

"No! I don't want to go back! I'd rather die!" This pronouncement, restricted as she was by Kusk's arms, was punctuated by a stamping of her feet…and a powerful blast of icy wind.

Kusk froze—were he not a fire wizard, that might have been a literal statement, but the grin growing on his face proved that Shalla's little outburst hadn't hurt him.

"Well…it seems we have a way out of here, after all," he said. "But we'll need supplies."

Bowyer, who had run over to help Kusk with the girl, nodded. "All right. Mr. Twine, Mr. Wax, if you please? You're the only two, here, that the guard won't arrest on sight."

"And what is it that you need?" Mr. Wax asked.

"I need you to find me a few pieces of wood. Cherry, ash, or yew would be acceptable—there are a few other woods that might work, but I won't bother mentioning because you won't find them around here. One has to be about…" He double-checked Shalla with a smile. "Oh, about three or four feet long. The others should be even longer—six feet or so. Less than two inches thick for each of them."

"What do you need all that for?" Mr. Wax asked.

"Well, I'm going to want a weapon, and this little lady needs a staff, too. It turns out we have a weather wizard, after all."

VIII.

SITTING ON THE BED in their room at the inn, Shalla watched as Kusk sped through the process of carving a complex set of runes into the first scrap of ash that Mr. Wax had been able to find for them. He must have shaken the rust off when he carved that first alderwood staff right before the rescue mission—this carving was cleaner and he was making faster progress than he ever remembered managing, before.

"What are you doing?" Shalla asked.

"I'm making you your first staff, so we can get out of here," he said.

"I know that," she replied, rolling her eyes the way only a child her age could pull off. "But what are you doing to make that stick into a staff?"

"First of all, I made sure we got the right kind of stick," Kusk explained, showing her the wood. They were in a hurry, but he had a few moments to give the young girl her first lesson in magic. "Not all sticks are the same. Sticks you get from yew trees, ash, teak, or even alder bushes if you can find a piece wide enough and long enough, work with magic—whatever affinity you have, they will contain any magic you 'push' into them. Some other woods work well with some specific affinities, but not others. Cherry contains fire magic very nicely, which would be good for me but not for you—but other affinities don't work with it at all. Some woods don't work with magic at all—you can't make a working staff out of oak or pine, for example."

"What about rosewood? I loved the rosewood dulcimer that a musician played for us in the consulate, once," Shalla said.

"Rosewood isn't a very common wood, but if you can find a good piece of it you could make an excellent staff for people with air affinities. But a good wizard's staff is more than just a piece of wood. For a wizard to use it as a staff, you need to carve runes into it." He set the staff he was carving down and picked up the alder wood staff he'd used for the rescue. "Runes are a whole language of writing, and if you go to a wizard's school you'll need to learn them. Even non-wizards can learn runes, and there are several books written with runes, but we wizards can use them to enchant objects so that our magic can work with them.

"Now, a trained wizard can accomplish many simple magical spells without a staff, but more complex magic requires a staff for concentrating and focusing your magic. You only need five runes to create a basic staff, but some staffs are created to assist in the casting of specific spells, or a specific class of spells. All of us guns are issued a fire-staff that is crafted specifically to cast fireballs, and it has the runes for that spell carved into it—I can only use it to cast that particular version of the fireball spell. This staff that I already have carved is only useful for spells with the proper blend of magic to create illusions. The one I am carving for you will be designed to help you cast the spell we need to make the wind direction change and nothing else, while the new one I am carving for myself will be something I can use for any spell."

Shalla pouted. "So my staff won't let me do any other magic?"

Kusk shook his head. "I'm sorry, but no. For this spell to work for you, I need to do everything I can to boost its strength. If I changed the rune patterns to allow you to do anything else with this staff, it would weaken it, and the spell would fail. We don't have time to teach you any other spells, anyway."

"Could I borrow your staff to try other spells, then?" Shalla asked. "The one that will let you cast any spells, I mean."

"My staff will be very dangerous to work with when I'm done with it," Kusk said regretfully. "We need to get away from here as fast as we can, before we're caught, but I might have enough wood for another staff. If we are stuck waiting for a ship long enough to give me the time, I'll see if I can make you an apprentice's staff that will work with any affinity, but would be safe for you to practice spells with."

"Are you sure I can't use your staff? If all you're worried about is keeping me from casting dangerous spells, I promise I'll only use spells you tell me I can use."

Kusk shook his head, holding out the one complete staff he had with him. "No, my staff is going to be dangerous for another reason. You see, on my illuminated staff, this rune here? This 'end' rune is actually the last rune in this sequence you need to make the staff work as a staff. All of the runes past it are there to make it easier to aim and make your spells safer, more stable, and more accurate. All useful things on an illuminated staff, and if you aren't fully trained they are critically important, but the runes consume power themselves, taking it away from your spells. Once I finish my new staff and finish testing it, I won't need those safety runes any more and will be cutting it off at this rune, making a 'sawed off' staff. A sawed-off staff can be double or triple the strength of a normal staff, but is immensely harder to handle and far more difficult to aim. It wouldn't be suitable for learning on. In contrast, an apprentice staff has even more safety runes added after this sequence to keep you safe when casting a spell."

"It increases the staff's power? Then…are you going to 'saw off' my weather staff?" Shalla asked. She seemed a little nervous at the prospect.

"No, the safety runes wouldn't be needed there in the first place. A weather staff doesn't require you to aim the spell that precisely, so it has different runes," Kusk said. "Don't worry, little one, your staff will be perfectly safe while still powerful enough for this one spell. Mine, on the other hand…well, like I said, we'll see what I have time to do for you."

IX.

SHALLA'S WEATHER STAFF was finished when Bowyer and Mr. Twine returned to the inn with news, and Kusk was starting on another. Kusk hadn't left the inn much since they arrived—just one time, heading to the local bookstore to pick up a book he wanted to give Shalla as a gift—and was looking forward to news.

"I hope you'll be done with that soon," Bowyer said. "Because we've found our ship, and we'll need you to get that girl ready to cast her spell. Once we're done loading enough supplies on board, we need to get going—they've already begun searching house by house, and at the rate they're going they'll be here by sundown. I think they've also brought out a few mages from the naval barracks to help them look, so your illusions won't keep us hidden for long."

"No, my illusions would stand out like a sore thumb in this magic-dry city," Kusk said. "Her weather staff is complete and I've already taught her the spell, so give the word and we'll be ready. This was just a side project I started to kill time while we waited for your return."

Shalla was napping in the bed at the time, but it wasn't hard to wake her up. She was thrilled to hear that her first staff was ready, but less thrilled to hear her apprentice staff wasn't. Still, they bundled her up to try and disguise her without magic and they were ready to go.

Unable to safely use his magic, it took a great deal of effort to avoid the guards for the walk to the ship. He couldn't even maintain the illusion hiding his beard, but a little hair powder to hide the color and tucking the beard in his shirt to hide its length managed to save him from having to shave it off. He did get a few odd looks, though, when he stopped at a bookseller's stand on the way and bought a book, trying to avoid showing his face to a rather bored-looking market guard who seemed to ignore anyone once they made a purchase. The book itself might have raised a few eyebrows in Ankherst, as well, but it would be very useful should he try teaching Shalla other magic.

He might as well not have done anything. In fact, considering the guard was "on high alert," things seemed far too calm—not a single member of the town guard was seen on the walk from the inn to the dock. Even places where there were usually at least three soldiers posted on the street at any one time—like the port admiral's office— were abandoned. Kusk didn't think this was a good thing, but didn't feel like voicing his suspicions anywhere where Shalla could hear. Bowyer didn't seem to be concerned about it, so his own fears would probably be dismissed out-of-hand.

While he had never learned any real seamanship, Kusk hadn't spent the last two and a half years in the navy without picking up some things. He recognized that the boat Mr. Twine had purchased for them was a small ketch, with the appellation Otter adorning the stern in relief. It didn't look to be in ideal trim, but it was seaworthy enough to get them where they were going. It might even be adequate for naval service as a dispatch vessel, with a little work. It was a far better ship than he'd expected.

"How did you arrange to buy a ship like this?" he asked Bowyer, glancing around as some last-minute supplies were loaded on board.

Bowyer shrugged. "Just luck—I ran into a local merchant who was desperately selling everything he had to avoid debtor's prison. I was planning on buying that coble, over there, but this ship was a much better deal for the same price."

Kusk glanced over at the old fishing boat that they were originally planning to purchase. It had visible spots of dry rot, and while it might have gotten them to the rendezvous that would likely have been its final voyage. "The same price? That seems…strange."

"Like I said, we got lucky."

"We seem to be a little too lucky, today," Kusk said, glancing at the shore. "You said the guard had been alerted to our escape, but I haven't seen a single one of them on the streets, even at their usual stations. And—"

"We're probably already caught in a trap," Bowyer said, sighing. "I know, I just didn't want to say anything yet. I would bet they're going to let us get to sea, and then send someone after us when we're out of sight and they don't have to admit why they're chasing this eight-year-old girl. I'm not sure why they allowed us to buy this ketch—maybe it really was just luck—but I've gone through it and she seems solid enough, so I'll take her."

Kusk shook his head. So they were walking into a trap and they knew it, but Bowyer didn't feel the need to let him know. One minute on board a ship and he already felt like people were treating him as a gun, again.

"Forget about the rest of the supplies—we aren't going that far— while I talk our little weather wizard into getting the wind going our way. If we move faster than they expect us to, we may be able to get past whatever they're setting up before they're completely ready."

Bowyer grinned. "Well, now—that isn't a bad plan at all."

Kusk walked up to Shalla, who was looking out over the stern of the ship. She seemed fascinated by everything she saw, her childish excitement endearing. Kusk hoped the early departure would be enough. They had originally planned to take a month's supplies with them, in case storms made the rendezvous impossible, but as it became clear the guards would catch them if they took the day they needed to source and load all of those supplies, they were only taking on the ballast and a couple days worth of food and water. It would speed things up, but they were losing their margin of error.

He held her weather wizard staff out to Shalla, trying not to think about that...or at least not to let it show on his face and worry her. "So...are you ready to cast your first real spell?"

"Already?" Shalla said. "But they aren't done loading the boat, yet!"

"I know. It takes a long time to load cargo into a ship, but the magic you're going to be summoning can take an hour to work and they'll be done by then. So...are you ready?"

She gulped audibly. "I...I think so."

"Then let's try, shall we?" He handed her the staff. "You don't have to say the words aloud as long as you focus on them. Ready? Now—cast!"

There wasn't anything visible if you couldn't see the 'glow' of her magic. It would alert any wizards who might be looking in their direction, however, so Kusk did his best to keep her from being seen. She was squinting with concentration, her lips puckered up as she held her breath. All of that effort was unnecessary, and in fact probably hurt her magic, but it didn't matter. Impressively, she cast the spell right the first time.

"All right, that's enough," he said, breaking her concentration.

"It is? But…I didn't do anything, did I?" Shalla asked.

"You did plenty," Kusk said. "The magic worked, but it'll take an hour or two before the wind you summoned gets here. In the meantime, why don't we go below decks? Then I'll show you where I'm at with your next staff, and explain what all the runes mean."

X.

KUSK'S ESTIMATE proved pessimistic, as it was only about twenty minutes before the first of the winds Shalla had summoned arrived. They'd barely had time to stow away the cargo before the wind was ready to carry them out of the harbor.

"Wow," Shalla said, feeling the increasingly strong breeze on her face as she stepped back above deck for their departure. "Did I really do that?"

"Yes, you did," Kusk said, looking a little nervous as he followed her out of the small cabin (normally belonging to the ship's captain) that had been designated hers. After a few minutes showing her what he'd done so far on her apprentice staff, he'd suggested they go back outside and see how things were going. He could hear the wind from inside the cabin, and it was already reaching the full strength he was expecting from the girl's summons. If it was this strong already, it would wind up much heavier than he thought possible, leaving him to wonder if Shalla hadn't overdone it.

Kusk was a little surprised to see Mr. Hands and a half-dozen other men he didn't recognize now on board, helping Mr. Twine and Mr. Wax set the sails. Still no sign of Ms. Honeytrap—probably a good thing, as he wasn't sure how he would explain the older woman to Shalla—but it no longer seemed it would just be Bowyer and his two fellow former rebels trying to crew the ship alone. Probably a good thing—Kusk had never been good with the mechanics of sailing, and wasn't looking forward to the inevitable moment he was asked to help with the rigging. The one time he'd tried, the Elephant's bosun had berated him for his sloppy knotwork.

Mr. Twine, coordinating the crew, paused while running across deck to bow slightly to Shalla. "Not bad, little lady. This wind should get us all the way to the rendezvous, no problem."

Shalla smiled up at him. "Thank you! I like being able to help."

With a nod, Mr. Twine resumed his trek across, where he snapped a few orders to one of the crewmen because a lanyard holding down one of their lanterns had gotten loose.

They were moving, Kusk realized. They were still in the harbor, but they were hopefully away from the dock and the city of Ankerst for good. But they were in a moving ship, much smaller than the Elephant, and his seasickness didn't even seem to be threatening him. Odd, that.

He kept an eye on Shalla as she looked out over the starboard side of the ship, watching the other ships in the harbor. You could see activity on several of them as the first favorable wind in a while was allowing them to leave the harbor.

Mr. Twine ducked below decks briefly, returning a few minutes later reading something off a piece of paper.

"Helm! Set course. West-northwest a quarter west."

"Uh…sir?" the person on the wheel replied, looking confused.

Mr. Twine sighed, stepping over to him and pointing at the nearby binnacle. "Turn the wheel right until that compass shows that our bow is pointed in that direction. Got it?"

"Yes, sir!" the crewman said. Evidently, the crew wasn't all that skilled in seamanship, themselves. Kusk mentally shrugged—his job was to mind Shalla, not (thankfully) crew the ship. He was just as lost as that crewman.

"Heh. Mr. Twine seems to be forgetting his concerns now that he's on a ship, again," Bowyer said, stepping over to Kusk. "I should have let him get back to sea a long time ago. Not that he'd have left while I still needed him."

Kusk gestured to one of the crewmen he didn't recognize. "More former members of your little rebellion?"

"Family of. The ones in most danger of reprisals for their family's service to me. As I said, Mr. Twine and Mr. Wax were the only remaining survivors," Bowyer said, grimacing.

Kusk nodded sympathetically. He continued watching Shalla, now near the bow so she could look out over the sea. He'd intervene if she got in anyone's way, but for the moment she seemed fine. Her not being in earshot gave him another opportunity to address some concerns, however.

"And Miss Honeytrap?" Kusk asked. "Why is she the only member of your team who isn't here? Is it safe to leave her behind?"

"Ms. Honeytrap is a very mercenary young woman. So mercenary I never let her know the whole plan," Bowyer said.

"She's not here because she didn't care to leave. She was just in it for the money. That said, her reputation suggests the one moral she does have is that she keeps her clients' confidence no matter what. I don't think she betrayed us."

"But you don't know for sure. She'd better not have—it would make protecting Shalla that much harder."

"I used the possibility of her turning traitor to convince Mr. Twine to carry out the plan despite our...disappointing bargaining chip. He and Mr. Wax may not have had their faces plastered over wanted posters like I once did, but she could point them out to the guards as her conspirators. I figured Mr. Twine and Mr. Wax would be far less likely to give up on us that way."

"Did you investigate alternate routes out of town?" Kusk asked. "If we couldn't buy a boat in Ankerst, what would the plan have been?"

"Quite frankly? If we couldn't have bought a boat, we'd have stolen one. There was no land route that would have been safe. But I think I get what you're saying. They figured we would escape by ship, and wanted us to use this particular ship. But there's nothing wrong with the boat—Mr. Twine and I went through it with a fine-toothed comb."

"We'll find out soon," Kusk said, glancing over to see how far away they were from the dock. It wouldn't take long before they were out of sight of the harbor. "I don't suppose this ship has any weapons?"

"I have a bow and a set of arrows," Bowyer said, grinning ruefully.

Hardly a fire staff, but it was something. In fact, with a little creativity (and a bit of risk) it could be a better anti-ship weapon than the usual rifle or musket that the marines carried on board the Elephant. Those were good for targeting enemy crew, but not so much for sinking the opposing ship. An arrow, however, could be used to do more than just kill a man. "Start prepping some fire arrows, then. We're going to need to fight our way out before this is all over, and while I might be a 'gun' there's only one of me."

XI.

KUSK felt a growing sense of unease the further away from Ankerst they got. Something was going to happen. He didn't know what the Skorrans' plan was, but he was fairly certain that despite his earlier suggestion, they did not evade the trap by leaving early. He just didn't know what the trap was.

His first hint came from a frown on Mr. Twine's face as he studied some charts.

"Something wrong?" Kusk asked. Shalla was taking a nap in her cabin, and Bowyer had gone to set up a mess, having volunteered to act as cook for the two or three meals they would need to have on the trip.

"The ship's charts and my own don't agree on something," Mr. Twine said, pointing to some lines on the two maps that—as far as Kusk was concerned—were just one wiggly line versus another. "You were a gun. Do you understand what I mean by a 'shallow draught' vessel?"

Kusk didn't quite, but he knew the gist of it. The "draught" referred, as he understood it, to how deep below the waterline the keel of your boat sat. A "shallow draught" would mean your keel could operate in shallower waters.

"More or less."

"The coble we originally planned to purchase was a shallow-draught fishing boat," he explained. "By the chart, this would allow us to head to your rendezvous point as straight as the wind allowed...which, with a weather wizard on board, can be plenty straight. The problem is that this ketch, despite being a pretty small coastal trading vessel, wasn't designed as a shallow-draught vessel." He pointed to one of the lines on his chart. "My old map says there's a sand bar that the Otter can't cross over. This chart says it isn't there. Now, sand bars do shift, so it's possible it isn't there any more, but I find it difficult to believe that a sand bar as large as the one my old map says should be there would disappear without any hint of ever existing."

"We need someone to do some soundings, then," Kusk suggested, happy that he knew enough about sailing to offer that suggestion, at least. "Prove to ourselves that the sandbar is gone."

"We don't have anyone here trained for that kind of thing. Not unless you..."

Kusk's eyes widened. "Me? No. I wasn't given any training—you're lucky you don't need me to tie down any of the lines; the bosun on my old ship said none of the knots I tied were acceptable the one time I tried. I certainly never learned anything complex like running a sounding line. A few of the weather wizards were taught those sorts of things, using their water affinities to help them, but there's no point in asking Shalla, either. I don't know the spell."

"I'll have to come up with something. Damn. I'm starting to wish we'd taken the coble, after all—even if it did smell of rotten fish."

Kusk shared a small laugh, but felt his unease grow. So there was, indeed, a reason they were suckered in to buying this ketch. But why? What did the Skorrans hope to accomplish, here?

Not for the first time, Kusk wished his country had treated him as something other than a gun, and had given him a little training. He might be better equipped to predict the Skorran's moves if they had.

Thanks to Mr. Twine's old charts, the Otter managed to avoid running aground on the sandbar. They would have to go around it, but at least they weren't stuck. However, a few minutes after they began a more northerly detour, they sighted another ship.

"Sail sighted, Mr. Twine!" one of the crewmen called. Kusk held Shalla back from running over to go see, a sinking feeling developing in his gut. "Looks like a revenue cutter, sir."

"Shallow draught, too, I'd wager," Mr. Twine grumbled, stepping over to see better.

Kusk risked a glance. Yep, there they were. "Mr. Twine, another one coming up from the south," he called.

Cutters weren't very big—sometimes they were simple open boats, though revenue cutters were usually larger. Designed to be fast ships with the crew and arms needed to force a smuggler into surrender, they were about the smallest warships you might find. They were more than adequate to take on either a coble or a ketch, however, even if the later were fully crewed and as heavily armed as they were rated for. Two of them against the Otter would be overwhelming odds.

"And the trap is sprung," Kusk muttered to himself.

"Mr. Twine, can we avoid these ships?" Bowyer asked.

"Not with that sandbar in the way," Mr. Twine said. "We managed to avoid running aground, so at least we can maneuver to fight one at a time, but we can't evade them both for long."

Kusk looked at Bowyer. "I'll get my staff," he said.

"And I'll get my bow. I've got a hundred arrows ready—that's all we have on board. Hope it's enough."

"Come on, Shalla," Kusk said, grabbing the young girl by the hand. "We need to get you somewhere safe. Things are about to get a little hot around here."

XII.

THEY WERE BELOW DECKS, in the cockpit—what would have been the surgeon's bay if they'd had a surgeon. The safest place in a ship during a battle, supposedly—at least, that's what Kusk had always been told. Now for the hard part: convincing Shalla to stay there.

"All right, Shalla. Things are about to get…loud, and maybe a little scary," he said. "But you should be safe here."

"I will? Then why don't you stay here?" she asked, pouting. "I want you to stay here with me. I want you to be safe."

This was going to be harder than he thought. "I can't. This ship is about to go into a battle and needs weapons to fight it. I'm a gun, so I'm the only weapon we've got."

Oh, dear—there were the tears in her eyes. Yes, it was going to be much harder than he thought. "You've been helping me learn so much! You're a great friend, a good teacher, almost my fa—uh, you're just…you can't go! You have to stay safe! You aren't just a gun! You're so much more…"

Kusk's heart was breaking. He didn't want to leave her behind, but he certainly couldn't let her on deck. "Maybe I am," he said. "But right now we need a gun, and so I'll be one. I need to be, to keep you safe. So please…stay here, okay?" When she didn't say anything after a moment, he remembered the book he had bought her in Ankerst. He found her still unfinished apprentice staff and handed it to her, then pulled out the book he had bought. It was a book on translating runes, and while not entirely focused on what runic characters meant in the practice of magic it did have a bit on that in its appendices. It was the perfect primer for a young magic-adept girl her age. "Here. I've almost finished your staff, and drawn all the runes I haven't finished carving onto the wood. While I go be a gun again, why don't you take the time to study these runes? You'll want to be very familiar with the runes on your staff before you start casting serious magic."

Shalla sniffed, rubbing one of her eyes with the back of her hand. "All right. But only if you promise to be safe. And to remember you aren't just a gun!"

"I'll remember," Kusk said. With great care, he gave her a kiss on the forehead before taking his goodbyes. He left the cockpit, closing the door behind him. He missed the wonder on Shalla's face as she touched the spot where he'd kissed her.

Kusk returned to the deck just as Bowyer had finished setting up a lone battle lantern off the mainmast. It was daytime, so they didn't need the light, but he did need something they could light fire arrows from.

"They're still out of my range," Bowyer said, not even glancing up at Kusk while he continued his preparations. "What about yours?"

Kusk glanced over the side to judge the distance. They were outrunning the cutter coming up from the south, but the other one was well positioned to intercept them. It wasn't close enough to engage yet, however. At least, not close enough for Kusk—there might be some wizards who would try it, with the right staff. He wondered if his choice of a sawed off staff was the right option this time.

"Not yet. At the rate they're closing, though, I might be able to get a lucky shot off in a few minutes."

"They probably don't expect us to have any 'guns' at all," Bowyer said. "The element of surprise is a tool we can't risk losing. Don't fire until you can't miss."

"Aim for their sails and rigging," Mr. Twine said, coming updeck to join the conversation. "And do your best to protect ours. Our best chance is to strike fast and then run for it. We've got no chance in a boarding action."

"Understood," Kusk said, focusing magic into his staff. Up to a point, the more magic he could concentrate into it the more powerful his fireballs would be. Unfortunately, he had made this a more general staff rather than a fire staff, and that limited how quickly he could make a fireball, but that first shot would be strong enough. He just had to be sure not to overdo things—focus too much magic into a staff and it could break. Or shatter. Or even explode…catastrophically.

"Almost in range," Bowyer said grimly. "It would be pushing it to go after the rigging, though."

"Go ahead and start firing," Mr. Twine said. "Maybe they won't realize your real target if you send a few elsewhere at first."

Closer and closer the cutter came. The southern cutter had almost disappeared over the horizon, but this one could not be avoided. Fortunately, they hadn't started sending their own fireballs at the Otter.

"Hmph," Bowyer grunted as he sighted another shot. He'd been very conservative with his fire arrows, not letting more than three or four go in a minute despite being capable of firing much faster.

"Something wrong?" Kusk asked.

"Not really. I just noticed their flag, though—they aren't using a Skorran flag."

"What are they using, then?"

"It's a black flag. Pirate colors." He paused. "There won't be any point in surrendering, if it comes to that. The black flag suggests they intend to kill us all, just so they can disavow ever having captured that girl."

"That's probably why they wanted us to escape by boat," Kusk said, gauging the distance. He should be able to take an accurate shot soon. "This way we're in international waters, and even if one of us survives we'd never be able to prove that it was the Skorran Empire who killed that little girl." His hands tensed around his staff. "Well, the Skorran Empire won't be killing her. I'm not going to let that happen."

Angrily, he thrust his staff out, taking careful aim. A sawed-off staff was not the most accurate, but with a fireball it didn't need to be.

Boom.

It was, perhaps, the most powerful fireball Kusk had ever cast. It went perfectly on track, striking the cutter's mainsail. A large hole burned through the sail…but then the fire immediately went out.

"You got them," Bowyer said, impressed. "Since they haven't started firing on us, I figured we were still out of your range."

Kusk grimaced slightly. "The advantage of not being on a warship, I suppose. If they keep to modern naval policy, their fire wizards won't be able to cast any spells until their cutter is broadside-on to the Otter. Meanwhile, I can fire from any angle, so I can fire even though our bow is facing them."

"Advantage us, then…but you don't look happy."

"My fireball went out far too soon," Kusk said. "They have an extremely powerful water-affinity wizard, over there, who can douse my fireballs before they do much damage. I can still take out their sails and rigging, but it'll take dozens of accurate shots whereas without him it would only take a half-dozen at most."

Bowyer glanced at his fire arrows. "If they can do that, will my little arrows even matter?"

"It takes energy to do that, and they could exhaust themselves very easily trying to put out a dozen small fires, so yes, your arrows do matter…but we'll need to start firing faster. You'll run out of arrows quickly, I'm afraid."

"Then we'll have to make it count," Bowyer said. "I don't suppose you can extinguish fires, yourself?"

"Well…sort of," Kusk said. "I can deflect fireballs with some effort, but if we get hit I can't put that kind of a fire out. And I can't do it and send out my own fireball at the same time."

"Then let's burn out their sails before they can bring their guns to bear," Bowyer said.

XIII.

KUSK had managed to hit the cutter with several fireballs, but he hadn't completely disabled its sails. Worse, the enemy crew was well-trained and responded to his fireballs swiftly. One ruined sail had already been replaced and they could see the cutter's crew preparing to replace a second. Worse, because of the sandbar, the Skorrans were still able to pin the Otter into a position where they could fire upon them. They only had minutes until they were in range.

"This is getting us nowhere," Kusk lamented, firing off one more fireball. Again, it slightly damaged the sails, but otherwise did nothing.

"We've been firing on the wrong targets," Bowyer said. He had yet to resume his arrow strikes, wanting to wait until he could accurately target the sails himself.

"What do you mean?" Kusk asked, beginning the process of concentrating magic in his staff again. It was starting to overheat.

"They can repair their sails," Bowyer said. "But they can't replace their dead. We need to take out their weather wizard!"

Kusk frowned. "But which of them is their weather wizard?"

Bowyer took one of his arrows, lighting it in the battle lantern. "Well, if you don't know, we'll have to kill them all."

An arrow flew. Its fire was extinguished before it finished crossing the distance to the cutter…but it continued on, and struck dead one of the crewmen who was trying to set a fresh sail.

"Changing targets," Kusk said, aiming at the bunch of crewmen with his fireball. Several were killed, and the replacement sail was destroyed, but it wasn't long before another sail was pulled up from below decks.

Kusk had no idea how much damage he was doing to the enemy ship after a while. Smoke was making his eyes tear up, and he'd been singed a time or two when enemy fire came a bit too close. And the true battle hadn't even begun, yet—this was still the maneuvering phase.

The Otter and the cutter continued creeping toward one another, and finally the inevitable happened. A broadside of fireballs came at Kusk, forcing him to deflect them all and ending his own ability to fire at them. Bowyer continued trying to snipe as many of the cutter's deckhands as he could, but nothing diminished that rate of fire. Now the battle was truly engaged.

For one man against the eight fire wizards aboard the cutter, Kusk was holding his own surprisingly well. The Otter continued onward, and he managed to deflect every fireball sent their way. Kusk was reminded that they didn't necessarily need to sink the cutter or kill all of its people—they just needed to avoid their fire long enough to swoop around them and slip away. If the cutter followed...well, the Elephant was out there, somewhere. Not even a large fleet of cutters would survive a battle with her. Amazingly, it seemed, the battle was fairly even.

Until a line of people started emerging from the decks below, all in the distinctive uniform of a Skorran gun. They lined up along the side of the cutter, and pulled out their staffs. The cutter had just effectively doubled its firepower.

"I can't stop them all," Kusk said desperately.

"Do your best!" Bowyer called, sending an arrow out at one of the guns. Before it hit, a wave of sixteen fireballs came flying at the Otter.

Kusk followed Bowyer's instruction and did his best. To his surprise, he was able to stop all sixteen oncoming fireballs…but he suffered for it. Concentrating that much magic into his staff was heating it up, and burning his hand where it touched.

Bowyer was now shooting at the enemy guns, and two of them were killed before the next salvo. Again, Kusk did his best and stopped the fireballs. His staff started charring around some of its concentration runes, and blisters started to appear on his hands.

The third salvo only had eleven fireballs. It was easier to handle, by far, and within Kusk's normal ability to handle it…but on top of the previous two salvos it was just too much. Kusk halted the salvo, but at the cost of his staff. The concentrated magic exploded, sending him flying. He blacked out before he hit the deck.

Shalla was trying to ignore the explosions going on over her head, but it was hard for her. The book on runes helped, but she was worried for her friend and rescuer. If only she could help.

Well, if she had a staff, maybe she could? She looked at her unfinished staff, and the runes still uncarved on it. She glanced at the book on runes, translating them. Only one of the seven remaining runes were needed to make it work…and she had a carving knife somewhere on her, didn't she?

Focusing on her carving—she had to be very, very careful, as she didn't want to ruin her staff—she was able to ignore the sounds of the fight for a time. She consulted the book carefully, and noticed a slight change she could make to the runes to make the staff more powerful. Perhaps the change was because this was intended as an apprentice staff, but otherwise the real difference between an apprentice staff and a normal staff were the six remaining uncarved runes, all of which were to limit its power and make it safer. This other change didn't seem to have any other effect, from what she could tell.

Mulishly, she decided that she would make the change now and apologize later. Perhaps, when she was done with her apprentice work, she could make this into a "sawed off" staff so she could keep using it; she wasn't sure she would ever want to give it up.

She had just finished with the final detail when the loudest explosion of the battle sounded above her…and she instantly knew that her friend was in trouble.

XIV.

KUSK didn't think he was out long. If it had been too long, he feared they would have sunk. As it was, there were flames all across the deck, with crewmen running around with buckets of water trying to extinguish them.

He slowly sat up, and the world spun around him. He watched as another salvo headed there way, only seven shots strong. Bowyer was having some success, at least.

The fireballs hit the Otter before he could react. Not that he could necessarily do anything—without a staff, could he even block one? One of the fireballs struck one of the crewmen, killing him instantly. The others hit the hull, igniting more fires. The bucket brigades redoubled their work.

"Mr. Fish!" Bowyer called. Kusk turned to look at him, startled. An elbow gestured up the deck, where little Shalla was coming on deck. Just then, another salvo—six fireballs strong—was on its way. They were aiming at the rigging, but she was about to walk right into it.

"No!" Kusk cried. He jumped over a cargo hatch, tucking and rolling. He was going to be too late. A fireball was heading right her way. Desperately, he thrust out his air magic, hoping against hope.

Boom.

The fireball exploded and Shalla was knocked to the ground…but there Kusk was, standing over her. He couldn't stop it, but he did detonate it prematurely, saving her life.

"I…are you all right?" he asked Shalla.

She didn't seem to hear him. "Your staff is missing…was that explosion your staff?"

"Are you okay?" he demanded, shaking her slightly to get her attention.

"I'm fine! But you're bleeding. Your hand—"

"Mr. Hands!" he cried, drawing the pickpocket's attention. "Take Shalla back down to the cockpit and keep her there!"

"Yes, sir!" Mr. Hands said, saluting. He wasn't sure it was sufficient.

"Wait," Shalla said, standing, pulling away from Mr. Hands before he could grab her. "If your staff is broken, you need a new one." She reached down and picked something up.

"Here—I finished the one you were making for me. Only it isn't an apprentice staff."

Kusk stared in wonder, seeing that end rune, now carved into the wood, waved in his face. He took the staff and stared at it in wonder. "How…"

"I finished it for you," Shalla said. "I hope you like it."

Kusk took the staff, noticing the end rune carved into it, and better than he could manage himself. It was the more powerful form of end rune, inappropriate for an apprentice staff, but still remarkable. He wondered how an eight-year-old girl could manage it.

His inattention was costly, however. A final salvo, five fireballs strong, was inbound…and headed directly for Shalla.

"No!" he cried. It was probably a coincidence. They were probably targeting the crewmen fighting the fire, or the more vulnerable areas of the ship, but that wasn't what ran through his head in that instant. At that moment, all he could think of was that they were targeting Shalla. They were targeting an eight-year-old girl whose only crime was thinking he was something other than a simple gun.

They would pay.

His magic shunted itself into the new staff, flowing faster than he could ever remember before. The burns in his hand were meaningless. The fires around them were ignored. Only the girl was important. Keep the girl safe—that was all that mattered.

Five fireballs froze in mid-air, then shot back in the direction they came from. Five fire wizards found that they were vulnerable to their own magics as they were engulfed in flames. A series of additional fireballs, launched rapid-fire from the staff of an angry Kusk, followed them up, ensuring the fire wizards were dead. A moment later, more fireballs hit the cutter, slamming in from stem to stern.

No weather wizard could douse that many fires. The cutter was dead in the water, and her crew would be lucky to save it. The sails were in flames, and there didn't appear to be anyone running to replace them this time. Smoke obscured the deck, but the lack of return fire proved the last of the enemy guns was, indeed, killed by Kusk's furious attack. The Otter, meanwhile, sailed on by, resuming its course for the Elephant.

As they passed the cutter, the men on board desperately fighting for their lives, Bowyer shook his head. "Remind me never to piss off one of His Majesty's guns."

Kusk discovered one unforeseen casualty of his exploding staff: His source of pride, his knee-length beard, had been singed. Cutting it back to intact hair left it only an inch or two long at most.

Somehow, he couldn't bring himself to care.

The second cutter never caught up, but dogged the Otter's tail all the way to the rendezvous. When the Elephant came into sight, though, they ran back in the direction of Ankerst.

It didn't take long for the Otter to send the appropriate signals and interpret the appropriate counter signal needed to verify each ship's identity. A launch from the ship of the line was lowered over the side, with a crew of men in their best uniforms to escort Shalla back to the ship.

Bowyer laughed, seeing the escort. "They'll be surprised."

"So...what are you going to do now?" Kusk asked, a comforting arm returning Shalla's hug as they waited. He'd kept what was supposed to be her apprentice staff, but he'd found another piece of suitable wood and together they'd worked out a set of runes for her to have a new apprentice staff of equal utility. She was holding that in the arm that wasn't hugging him, and had promised she wouldn't alter this one without a master wizard's permission.

"I don't know," Bowyer said. "My plan was to use our reward for this rescue operation and spread it amongst the crew. Mr. Twine is especially looking forward to retirement, and I think I'd like to join him. A decade of fighting the good fight and losing has me tired. But I can't see much reward coming for an eight-year-old girl's rescue, no matter how much she needed that rescue, so I'm not sure that's in the cards for us."

"If you need a reward, I could always talk to my grandfather," Shalla said.

"Oh? Who's your grandfather?"

Shalla blushed. "Well, I'm not supposed to say—it's a secret! He wasn't married to my grandmother when she gave birth to my momma. But I suppose you'll have to know, won't you? He's just my grandpa, but momma always said most people would know him as Cerus IV."

Kusk's eyes widened. "Wait, Cerus IV? You don't mean—"

"The King?" Bowyer said incredulously. "You're the granddaughter of the King?" He started laughing. "Oh, boy."

A bosun's whistle signaled that the escort from the Elephant arrived, and before Kusk had time to say anything more, he was taken aboard the launch. Twenty minutes later, Shalla having been taken on board separately with all the ceremony that could be mustered on board a ship, he found himself meeting Captain Munck again.

"So…good work, Mr…um…gun? Now, return to your post."

Kusk wasn't sure if he should laugh or not. Back to the grind, where his captain didn't know his name, stuck in a small asbestos box. Back to being nothing more than a gun.

He looked at his navy-issue fire staff (somehow, his sawed-off version had disappeared during his absence), comparing it to the new battle-tested general staff he wielded.

"Well…maybe not just a gun, after all."

XV.

IT HAD BEEN A WEEK. Kusk had barely seen Shalla in all that time, as he'd been stuck in his asbestos box the whole time. They had arrived in port and were re-supplying. As a gun, of course, he was forbidden from going ashore while they were in port.

"KUSK!" Gunner's mate Petrecki cried, storming into his asbestos box. "Explain to me just how it is you rate a summons from the King, himself, and a transfer into the Royal Guard?"

Kusk laughed, reaching for his favorite new staff. "Well, now, that'll take a while," he said, heading to the door. "What say I tell you as we head for the launch? But I think the bottom line is, that little girl we took aboard ship decided that she needed a gun.

ONCE DAMNED

MARTIN WILSEY

1. BLOOD IN THE SNOW

WHEN ALL WAS QUIET AGAIN, Thorn realized the blood dripping from his chin wasn't his.

The blood looked black in the moonlight on the knee-deep snow. The light made it bright enough for him to watch the remaining two men ride off at a gallop, taking with them the horses of the six people that lay dead at his feet.

The next sound was always the same. A creak of leather as he squeezed the grips of his swords. They had saved his life again. Blades like no other. They were perfectly matched staghorn grips, wrapped in fine leather.

The snow was thick on the tall pines that covered the region. The hush in the air consumed the sounds of the fleeing horses.

With a well-practiced motion, Thorn wiped the blood on his red sash and sheathed first one sword and then the other. He was careful of the crossbow bolt protruding from his chest, just below his left collarbone. He reached up and broke it off, leaving a few inches protruding.

"It was a good ambush, gentlemen," he said out loud to the dead.

Thorn thought, *Waiting here at the Elder Bridge was the perfect place. I had to cross here. The trees provided perfect cover on the western side of the bridge. No footprints in the snow anywhere. Perfect. The Queen must be getting tired of losing so many men.*

He looked over the edge of the thousand-year-old bridge as he leaned briefly on the stone wall. *Assigning one of you to shoot the horse out from under me and then the rest to shoot at me as I fell was an inspired plan.*

He began searching the dead, collecting coin purses, which he stashed in his black tunic. As he moved, he adjusted the curved swords in his belt. The staghorn made his elegant curved swords look like the tools of a simple farmer.

You should have left me where I fell in the snow for a few hours before approaching. Then filled me with more arrows before getting close. If you knew who I used to be, you should have been more careful.

As he took the last purse, he noticed this man had a flask on his belt. That's when he also saw the bolt that was in his leg. The fletching was all the way through his thigh. Thorn felt around the back, and the wicked blades of the arrow had cut all the way through. He broke off the fletching and then without hesitation he pulled the arrow all the way through his leg. Blood flowed freely, and steam rose from the wound. Once again, he wondered where all the blood and magic that made it came from.

He took a long pull from the flask he had taken from the body. It was a strong liquor that tasted faintly of apples. Thorn moved along and took his saddlebags from the dead horse and carefully draped them over his right shoulder.

These wounds would not close quickly out here in the cold wind.

He began to walk.

The eight horses had plowed a path for him down the middle of the road. As he walked, he could feel the magic sustaining him. It was like heat from within. The stars and moon were bright on the snow. The pines that lined the road were undisturbed.

He moved. The magic burned. His breath made no clouds in the cold. Anyone that was sensitive to magic would see him. They would feel him coming. There was no more hiding on this journey. Thorn thought he could see the distant light of the Keep on the horizon.

2. Peck's Halfway

The tracks didn't divert from the road, and just after midnight, he rounded the corner to the familiar sight of a large, multi-story inn made of stone, Peck's Halfway. He paused at the open gate and looked north into the darkness to see the distant fire in the Keep's watchtower.

From here, it was a day's ride to Bullard down into the valley in one direction and Rockriver in the other back over the Elder Bridge.

He followed the tracks in the fresh snow through the massive stone arch into the courtyard where they led to the stables. No one else was traveling on a night like this. Thorn was backlit by the waist-high flames in the raised fire pit in the center of the large, walled, courtyard when the stable boy noticed him. He was young and frightened but approached anyway. The boy's breath came out in great gouts of mist.

Thorn stood motionless, seeming not to breathe at all.

"Good evening, mmm, my Lord. Can I be of service?" The boy said in a well-practiced manner. His voice only trembled a little.

"How long ago did those horses arrive? How many men were with them?" Thorn asked in a quiet growl, trying not to frighten the boy.

"Eight horses and two men. About four hours ago." The boy glanced down at the pool of blood forming at Thorn's feet, reflected in the firelight.

"Is Peck at the bar?"

"Yesss, sir," he stammered.

"Take extra good care of those horses, lad. And throw ten more logs on this fire for me." Thorn flipped the boy a coin. Its gold glistened in the firelight as he caught it. "I'll be back out in a few minutes." When the boy looked up from the coin, Thorn was already moving toward the main door of the inn.

Blood trailed behind.

Thorn could see that no one noticed the inn door open or close.

There was an outer entry that kept out the wind and maintained the heat. The drop in temperature within the room is what made people finally look up and notice the man standing in the entryway. The cold was not from the snow.

The common room was large and crowded with about sixty men and women, plus a few children. Travelers, going both east and west, stopped at Peck's Halfway. It was always busy. Peck had many suites, rooms, and bunks of all kinds and costs for them. As Thorn scanned the room, the conversations fell silent.

Thorn heard a ten-year-old boy mutter, "Papa, that man is bleeding." He pointed at the puddle growing at his feet.

A woman whispered, "It's him."

Another quietly uttered, "Magic," and averted her gaze.

Thorn's eyes locked on two men in the back of the room who were bent over mugs of ale. After a minute, he turned his back to them to face the bar.

Peck himself was there. He was fat with a bush of curly hair on his head. Peck was clean shaven and missing a couple of teeth on one side of his mouth. He wore a white apron, stained with food. Peck was close enough to see the broken stem of the bolt sticking out of Thorn's chest.

"For the love of stone." Peck quietly cursed, "Please, Thorn. Don't destroy my inn again."

"Whiskey." Thorn requested, his back still to the people. The murmurs began behind him.

Peck was terrified. He was trembling as he set a large pewter mug, meant for ale, in front of Thorn and poured a half a bottle of strong brown liquor into it. He left the bottle on the bar and stepped back.

Thorn studied Peck's face as he watched two, tall, hard looking, well-armed, men walk up behind Thorn as he drank deeply.

"Please, Thorn. Not again," Peck begged quietly.

They stood a pace behind Thorn. One of the men was looking at the floor. "You're bleeding," he growled.

Thorn knew Peck had a small touch of talent. He could see the magic rising from Thorn as if his blood was made of molten iron.

He emptied his mug and dropped a fat purse on the bar. To Peck, he said, "For the mess."

Peck had backed up until he was pressed against the shelves behind him. "No, please. Not in here, not again," Peck whispered.

Thorn turned slowly to face the men.

"Peck would rather I die outside, if you don't mind." He turned and limped to the door he had just come in, leaving the two men looking at each other for a moment.

When they exited, Thorn was standing in the courtyard with his back to the roaring fire pit. The fire was taller than Thorn, half again as high above his head now.

The two men slowly approached, separating a bit as they came closer. Their stances spoke of experience and formal training. Royal Army training.

Thorn reached up and released the clasp on his soaked, thick, wool cloak. It fell off his shoulders to the ground into the blood that was already collecting there. He stepped forward a pace and waited. His hands were relaxed at his sides. His mind drained to empty.

Faces were crowding the windows, and those that were brave enough to come to the door could see his leg and the left side of his body were slick with blood. They could see the remains of the shaft in his chest.

Thorn didn't move as the two men drew their swords. They stalked closer and closer to him. Their breath was creating clouds.

The closer they got, the more Thorn seemed to grow still. His breath made no cloud.

When they were only two paces away, both of the men quickly raised their swords to strike at the same time.

Then Thorn moved.

Thorn drew his sword and struck in the same motion as he suddenly crossed the distance. The man on the left was cut in half diagonally by an upward cut, from ribs to opposite shoulder; the man on the right was suddenly headless--both dead with one strike while he drew the sword.

Thorn was frozen again like a statue at the end of the single stroke. He waited until the bodies fell in slow motion. His sword swirled again in a lightning-fast arc, the blood painting a line in the snow as it flew away.

Then he stood at ease and clasped the red sash that was tucked into his simple leather belt. In a smooth motion, he cleaned the blade and sheathed it.

When he began to walk back to the inn, people fled from his path as if he was on fire.

Peck was pouring the remains of the bottle into his mug as he returned to the bar.

After he had taken a long pull, he asked, “Do you still have decent whores, Peck?”

He nodded, but didn’t speak.

“Can any of them sew?” He emptied his mug. “I need a room with a hearth, lots of firewood, and your best wound wench.”

Peck called out, “Thomas! Please, take Master Thorn to suite number four and then get Cass.” A wide-eyed boy came up to Thorn's elbow, looking at all the blood on the floor. Peck set another full bottle on the bar. Thorn took it along with his mug and followed the boy.

"Lead the way, lad, before I fall down and embarrass myself," Thorn said and then drained the mug.

Thorn waited in one of Peck's best suites, thinking about the Queen.

The door opened, and a woman entered, carrying a tray of medical supplies. Her long brown hair was pulled back and tied with a leather thong at the nape of her neck. She wore a simple brown tunic with a thick rope belt.

She closed the door and turned to see Thorn standing in front of a roaring fire, leaning on the mantle. His shirt had been torn off and was hanging about his waist by his belt. She had never seen muscles like this before. His body had no fat. His skin was so thin she could see the textures of the twisting strands of individual muscles. Thorn sensed by her reaction that she could also see the heat of the magic rising off of his entire body.

"Good. You're here." Thorn said as he raised his left hand to grasp the mantle and lean into it, steeling himself. He drank the remaining contents of the heavy mug.

In a sudden flash of movement, he pounded the bottom of his massive pewter mug onto the bolt's shaft, and the cruel arrow blades burst from the back of his shoulder. His knees nearly buckled from the pain.

Cass almost dropped the tray.

Thorn took in a ragged breath and said with exaggerated politeness, "Would you mind pulling that the rest of the way out? Soonest?"

She set the tray down on the table, and, instead of going to him, she opened the door and called out for Thomas. "Bring food. Bring bread, cheese, soup, and eggs, stew and fried potatoes for six. Quickly, boy."

Thorn was still leaning on the mantle, with both hands now. He looked at her over his right shoulder. His chin rested on his right forearm.

Cass quickly walked over and added two more logs to the already tall blaze. She worked around where Thorn stood.

Standing, and without warning, she pulled the shaft out of his shoulder and threw it into the fire. "My name is Cass," she said.

He took in a shuddering breath. "Thank you, Cass," he whispered. "My name is Jacob Thorn. I'm…"

"I know who you are. You're the bastard who lived." She spat the words like an insult. She had produced a small, razor-sharp knife from somewhere. She began cutting off his clothes. He remained leaning on the mantle with both hands. Blood and magic were flowing anew. Despite the fire, the room was cooling, the very warmth being drawn out of the room by the magic that sustained him.

She removed his belt and set it with his swords on top of a large chest. She paused for only a moment and looked at them.

The rags of his shirt and pants went onto the blazing fire and were quickly consumed.

He stood there naked, covered in blood as she washed him from a large pitcher and basin.

"You are a fool," she said. "People don't hate you enough already? So you wander the countryside murdering people? And letting them see magic burning from you?"

There was a knock at the door. Thomas was there with a large tray piled high with food.

Cass took the tray and dismissed the boy. She walked over and set the tray on the same trunk as the swords. She lifted a pitcher of milk and added some to a hot bowl of soup. She took the soup and handed it to Thorn. "Drink this, all of it. Now. Before you freeze the inn solid."

He took his hands off the mantle and took the bowl. She added more wood. "You've done this before?" he asked. "You know how the magic works."

"Fools!" She started ripping up a loaf of bread into another bowl and poured more milk over it and then handed the entire milk pitcher to him. "Drink this. If you want these wounds to heal proper without freezing us out of this room."

He handed the empty soup bowl back to her as she brought him a wooden chair so he could sit in front of the fire. After he had emptied the jug, she took it to the door and called Thomas again. "Another pitcher of milk, more hot water, and clean rags, please, Thomas." He was off at a run.

Cass handed him the bowl of soggy bread with a spoon. "Now this." She dragged a table over from the wall and placed on it her sewing materials and medical supplies.

Thorn looked at the tray as he ate mechanically and noticed her face for the first time. She had scars there. Slave scars. Deep X's had been carved in each cheek. She must have once been a disgraced noblewoman: her posture and manner were not that of a slave. She must have been marked and sold into slavery.

She took the empty bowl from him and added another log to the fire. "That's enough for now." The room was still cold. "I will close this one first," she said, turning his shoulders to the light.

She quickly threaded a curved needle with a long fine black thread. Without hesitation or apology, she closed the X-shaped wound. "What was that in the courtyard? I have seen men die by the sword many times. I have never seen that before."

"It's called Masidill. The art of the draw." He paused, thinking. "It is a war art that is the beginning and also the end of a duel. Draw and Strike, powerfully, all in one. I may be the last of its masters."

She had finished his back and was starting on the chest when Thomas knocked. "Come," she called out. "Good. Thomas, I want you to help me. Wet a clean rag and gently wash his back where I have finished." Thomas did so without a word of complaint. Thorn was stoic and watchful as Cass applied medicines directly into the wound before sewing it closed.

More scars for his own collection.

As she worked, he examined her skin closely. Whipping scars peeked out from the collar of her tunic. Rope burn scars on her neck. Small wound scars here and there told a story of pain.

She finished sewing the front wound under his collar bone, and Thomas repeated his cleaning there. The boy was not afraid and not squeamish at all. He was firm and gentle at the same time.

Thorn had a gash in his ribs that he didn't remember feeling until now.

"I have never seen swords like those. But I have heard the legend of rune-marked blades like them. Made by a country blacksmith. Somewhere. No one knows."

It took almost fifty stitches to close that one. The white of his rib bones was exposed. "The story is true," Thorn said. "A country blacksmith and more. He told me this was the seventh set he had made. His best yet." Thorn winced for the first time. It was obvious he kept talking to distract himself from the pain. "After… I wandered for years, thinking I would never hold a blade again. Until I met him."

Thorn watched Cass kneel before him to close the wound on the front of his thigh. His nakedness was apparently not off-putting to Cass at all. Not even noticed. Thorn's genitals were covered in blood, and Cass washed even there with clinical indifference.

"Thomas, draw the blankets down on the bed. I will need him lying face down to work on his leg." She helped Thorn up from the chair. His skin was clammy and cold even though he was so close to the fire. He slowly moved to the bed and lowered himself onto it.

This wound was ragged. Cass had to remove some torn flesh with her knife before she could sew him up.

He never made a sound.

When he was all clean and bandaged, Cass propped him up in bed and fed him stew, hot spiced apple sauce, eggs, bacon and fried potatoes with onions while Thomas mopped up all the blood from the floor and stoked the fire.

"Why did you come here? Who were those two men?" Cass asked as she fed him.

"There were eight men."

Cass froze as the fork was halfway to his mouth.

"No more will come. The other six did this to me, at the Elder Bridge. Had that arrow found my heart or I had lost my head, all the magic in the Kingdom would not have saved me."

Cass remained motionless as he spoke. Finally, she fed him the last of the eggs. She half-filled his mug with water and then upended a paper tube of white powder into it and then stirred it with her knife.

"Now drink this." She held it out to him. "It will help you sleep."

Thorn took the mug and paused a long time. He was looking into her eyes when he said, "Thank you, Cass."

He drank it all.

3. Warm Again

THORN WOKE IN DARKNESS and realized he was finally warm. He was on his side facing the hearth. His wounds ached, but the medicines she had given him in the wounds and in his food had dulled the pain.

The fire had burned down to a deep bed of red coals. Thorn could feel the heat of them from across the room. He would live. Again.

He felt her move.

He was suddenly acutely aware of her. She was naked. His back was to her front. Their legs were tangled, and her hand rested on his hip. She snored quietly. The thick mountain of quilts held in their warmth. He was no longer drawing energy from the air around him to fuel the magic.

With a deep sigh, he fell back asleep.

When next he woke it was because of the sound of more wood being added to the fire. He looked, and he could see Cass in the growing firelight. The silhouette of her naked body was beautiful. She stood and arranged the fire with the poker, and as it flared, he saw more scars. Whip scars covered her torso. As she added and arranged wood she turned, and he could see burn scars on her breasts and cruel rope scars on her neck and wrists. Thorn had rarely seen a body with more scars than his own.

He had closed his eyes before she saw him awake. She walked around and slid back into bed, and slowly her fire-warmed body was all along his. Gently, she laid her hand on his forehead to check his temperature.

He opened his eyes.

"Fever?" he asked.

"No. The magic's chill is over," she whispered. "You are done drawing energy from the world around you. The magic is done with you. For now."

He raised his right arm so she could rest her head on his chest. "Rest now," he said.

He felt her fall asleep in small twitches. Holding her seemed to push out all other thoughts and pain as if it was a healing magic all its own. He quickly followed her in sleep.

The light in the window woke him the next day. He had lost track of time.

Thorn knew that Peck's Halfway was in a mountain pass and had steep cliffs on almost all sides. If the light was shining down here, the morning must be almost gone.

Cass had her back to him now. The quilts remained heavy on them, and he was in no rush to arise. She stirred, sensing him waking.

"I can tell you're feeling better," Cass murmured as she hugged his arm that was wrapped around her.

Thorn realized that his erection was pressed against her. Instantly embarrassed he turned from her. "Forgive me. It's just…"

"It's just that you're feeling better." She hugged his back. "I have not slept that well in ages. Thank you, Jacob. May I call you Jacob?"

Thorn had a flash in his mind of an ordinary life. Waking on a winter morning with a woman he loved. Lingering in a warm bed as long as possible. Then reality rushed back in. There would be no love for the damned.

"What's wrong?" Cass was more sensitive than he had realized.

"Nothing. Don't worry. I won't hurt you. I promise."

"I know you won't hurt me. No one will hurt me ever again. I have already had my lifetime's worth."

"I saw you. In the firelight." He rolled onto his back, and she once again placed her head on his chest. His right hand traced the scars on her back. Some were raised and coarse. Some were divots or trenches in her skin.

"Peck got me for a bargain," she frowned. "Is that what you mean?"

Thorn considered what to say before speaking.

"I think I am going to sleep every night, in this bed, for the rest of my life," Thorn said. "With you."

"Ha!" she barked. "You plan on buying me from Peck?"

"I think I will." He was suddenly serious. "I have more than enough gold I won't need. It will only be one more night. Then I will go off to my well-deserved death."

"You are not considering going up to the Keep? They know who you are. They will already know you are here." She sat up and looked into his eyes. "Those men… were probably from there."

"Cass, I was the King's Guardian. I swore an oath, a magic oath, on penalty of curse, of doom, to protect the throne or die trying."

There was a long pause.

"I lived."

"So you've been trying to die honorably ever since?" she said, as if it was all folly.

"The Gods have not made it easy. Once damned, they enjoy drawing it out, it seems," he said and looked at the fire.

"Gods be puke. Just go," she pleaded with him. "Find a quiet life somewhere. Don't be Royal Guardian, anymore. Walk away."

He petted her hair. Finally, he just sighed and said nothing.

"Please, Jacob. Just live. What good would vengeance serve? Please. I just finished putting you back together." She was about to cry.

"I was serious, you know," he said quietly. "I'll buy you from Peck. You are already free. Whether I go to the Keep or not. You will be free." He looked into her eyes, trying to discover why she would care. "I can at least do one final kindness for the world."

"Jacob, please don't go up there. They have great power. Magic, science. The Queen may even be there. The least of their weakest girls can read and brew a poison that could kill us all. The greatest of them, the High Vestal, they say, was the hand behind the death of the King."

"I know. It is why I must go." There was sadness in his voice.

"You have no honor any longer. You're truly damned already. What do you owe the world? Don't be a fool." She climbed out of bed and angrily began to dress. "I cannot send someone to his death unhealed or hungry, damn you."

She was flushed, angry. "I will bring food and check your wounds. And…"

"Wait," he said and reached out a hand to her. It was like gravity. She took it. "Let me tell you what happened. One person at least should know the truth of my oath breaking."

She sat fully dressed at the edge of the bed.

"How much of the story do you know?"

"It was the funeral of Prince Gareth. It is rumored he was poisoned. Not simply drunk and choking on food. The King attended with his six personal guards, including you, and the entire Prince's Honor Guard was there." She swallowed. "Once inside the Cathedral the doors were locked from the inside. And only you survived the day. Sworn to give your life before his. The King was killed, and you walked away in disgrace." She paused, looking at their hands. "Loyalists have been challenging you to duels ever since."

"It was sixty against six." He closed his eyes, seeing it repeat as in his dreams every night. "They had crossbowmen in the balcony. They didn't know that we six could strike bolts from the air. They didn't know we had been spell cast, giving us enhanced physical speed, perception and the ability to survive massive, even lethal wounds for a while."

Thorn opened his eyes and met hers.

"I lived. I should have fallen on my sword for that sin alone."

He stared into the distance, still holding her hand. Cass waited.

"Their leader was named Ramos. He was Captain of the Prince's Royal Guard. I thought I knew him. I thought he was my friend." The despair in Thorn's voice was clear.

Cass began crying quietly. Sobbing.

"After… I dropped my royal swords and armor, and when the doors were opened, I walked away. No one stopped me."

He was staring at her hand in his. He was caressing it as if he was trying to memorize it.

"I sold my estate. Always expecting Queen Aleena to send someone to execute me. They never came." He looked up. "I took the gold and found the wife and parents of Ramos. I told them he died with honor and had made arrangements for their welfare. They never knew who I was. Years passed, and the rumors blamed the High Vestal in the great Keep for the plot."

He looked to the window then.

"I was lost. Wandering. I think it's been fifteen years. Leaving death and chaos in my wake wherever I went."

Cass cleared her throat. "Years before the King died, I lived in the capital. I was married to a lesser noble and became lost in the decadence of court life." One of her tears fell on the back of Thorn's hand. "I caught my husband raping a small boy. He gave me these." She gestured to her cheeks. He sold me to the foulest slaver he could find." She hesitated. "I was never… obedient enough."

Thorn reached up and traced his thumb on her cheek.

"Go find Peck. I need to speak to him."

4. Buying Cass

PECK LIMPED INTO THORN'S ROOM and went straight to the fire and added a log. "Bloody gout," he said.

"Peck, see that black pouch on the mantle? Take it," Thorn said from the bed.

Peck picked it up and looked inside. "Expecting to stay a few years, are we?"

"I am buying Cass from you," Thorn stated. Making clear it was not a request.

Peck froze. Turned his head slowly and looked at him. "You're what?"

"Cass. She's a talented healer; is it enough?"

"Because you terrify me only slightly more than she does, I should tell you… I feel I should tell you," he stammered just as she walked in with another large tray of food.

After a moment, Peck said, as if deciding something, "Cass, you are free to go as you please. Both of you." He looked at Thorn for a long moment, "For what it's worth, I always thought the King was a bloody bastard and got what he deserved. Thanks again for not burning the inn down, Thorn." He limped out, tossing the pouch of gold in the air and catching it.

"What did he say?" Cass looked at the closing door.

"You are no longer a slave. You're free." Thorn said as she brought him another bowl of soup.

"Free? What does that mean?" she questioned. "Where would I go? Peck tricked you. Now he has me and your gold.

I think he freed me long ago. It's why he bought me." Thorn heard her first lie, "To stop my… suffering."

"Why didn't you leave?"

"I did." She brought him a plate of hard boiled eggs, cheese, bread and an apple. "I went to the Keep to join the order. Become a novice. I managed the thousand steps, but for complicated reasons, I couldn't stay. So I ended up here."

"You've been to the Keep?"

"Yes. And you should not go there." She was somber. "Please, Thorn. The guards are many, and they are cruel. They will never open the Main Gate for you. Never even acknowledge you with anything but arrows."

"You will guide me." He tore off a piece of bread. "To the Novice Gate of a Thousand Steps."

Cass found Thorn out of bed sometime after midnight. The fire had been stoked, and he stood naked before the hearth.

He had her small knife.

She watched him quietly for a few minutes. As she watched, she realized what he was doing.

She slid out of bed and approached in a way to make sure she didn't startle him.

"Give me that, you fool, before you gut yourself." She took the knife from him and began removing the stitches from his chest.

Thorn was amazed at her comfort in her nakedness. He considered who she was.

She was careful and systematic in the removal of the stitches. Chest first, then ribs, and as she knelt before him to remove the stitches in the front of his thigh, he forced himself to think about the killing of the King. He didn't want to embarrass himself with another reaction.

"What's wrong?" she whispered, as she moved to the back of his thigh.

"Nothing," he said, as he looked at the beams above.

"Your magic flared. I can see it, you know." She continued removing the stitches in the back of his leg and then finally stood to reposition him so she could have better light from the fire to finish his back.

When she was done, she soaked a clean rag in alcohol and cleaned each wound. Magic burned in him again, and by the time she came back around to his shoulder, all the stitchings were healed-over scars.

"Please don't go." She leaned her forehead on the nape of his neck. It was the most intimate moment he had ever experienced. His whole life had been violence and pain and death.

This hurt more than all of it.

"I must go. It is my final task. Live or die. The High Vestal must know the truth. I cannot do otherwise. I am finished hiding from the Queen. I am finished hiding from the truth, only to discover death hides from me."

"They will try to stop you."

"They will try."

She lifted her head from his nape, and he turned to her. They were the same height. Their faces were only inches apart.

His right hand traced the scars on her face. His fingers drifted to the ones on her neck, her collarbone, her sternum.

He recognized this kind of torture. Strips of skin removed, coarse salt or hot irons then applied. He clearly saw now that one of her nipples was missing.

She was watching his eyes.

"What are you thinking? Your eyes… are smiling," she asked.

"Forgive me." He looked into her face. "I believe… You're beautiful. Your strength is etched into your flesh. And still, you remain kind. Gentle. I could never be that strong."

"I am anything but beautiful." She choked out the words.

"Beauty seen is in he who sees it," Thorn whispered. "Let us sleep. Tomorrow will be a long day."

Cass wept as he held her. Thorn began to understand why.

Peck was in a joyous mood the next day as the stable boy prepared two of the best horses for their departure. Peck got to keep the other six and all their tack in payment. The horses had no ownership brands, and the tack had no identifying marks, either.

Those men had sought to remain anonymous.

Peck was surprised that Cass was to travel with Thorn. He was also surprised that Thorn would take her. He supplied heavy woolen cloaks as well as clean clothes for the trip. It was only a single day's ride north of the pass to the Novice Gate. North and away from the great East-West Road.

Peck came out to see them off. He stood near the fire at the center of the courtyard. He spoke to Cass first. "I own the stables at the Novice Gate. They will care for your horses. My advice to you is part ways with Thorn at your first chance." He looked at Thorn, "No offense." Back to Cass: "You're always welcome here."

"Thorn. Trust no one. You are swimming in a river of lies and shit. You're not smart enough to keep your mouth shut or to tell the difference. You'll probably be dead this time tomorrow so I'd just like to say goodbye. It's always been interesting."

Thorn reached around and lifted off his personal saddlebags and tossed them heavily to Peck's feet. "If I manage to live, hold this for me. If I'm dead this time, tomorrow give it to Cass."

Cass looked at the bags knowing what they contained. Her hood covered her face as it crumbled in guilt in an effort to hold off tears.

Peck picked the saddlebags up. They were heavy.

Cass whispered to Peck, barely audible as she leaned in the saddle toward him and kissed his head, "Bless you, Kevin." With that, she turned her horse and left the inn to the north on the path behind the stables. Thorn followed close behind.

Thorn looked up to where the Keep should be. Low clouds obscured the mountains. The narrow track led up toward the tree line. He could see traffic from woodcutters that had emerged from the trees before they reached it. The path was clear, and the horses were sure-footed.

5. The Path to the Keep

THEIR ROUTE took them constantly up and north. Paths followed the curve of the peaks and were designed to be traveled in all seasons. There were shelters with unfrozen water along the way, for the horses.

There was little conversation as they finally traveled into the clouds.

It was nearly dusk when saw large braziers burning to light a bridge that crossed a ravine to a small tower.

There were no guards and the tower entrance stood open and the road led directly into the mountain through the open Novice Gate.

Cass didn't speak, and Thorn followed her lead. They had to leave the horses in Peck's extensive stable near the mouth of the entry.

They could already hear the murmuring of haunting, chanting, songs from deeper in the mountain.

Thorn breathed it in. Deeply.

There was magic here.

"Do you want to rest or ascend tonight?" Cass asked. "The Keep is only a thousand steps above this place."

"I want to press on." She saw him adjust his swords. The entry tunnel was a natural cave except for the level floor, which was paved in polished flagstone. It meandered about until opening out into a space where they could no longer see the ceiling.

The cavern they were in was huge, with no obvious pillars for support. Clusters of lamps hanging on poles created pools of light that allowed them to navigate. The singing got louder as they drew closer to a large, multi-story stone building.

"The novice candidates are housed here," Cass said, as they looked into the main hall where dinner preparations were being performed by an army of young girls.

"The order only accepts girls?" Thorn asked.

"Yes, for the steps. And women. But not all. Many never even make it to the first step. Some stay and hope they are selected. I was twenty-two when I took the steps, long ago."

Thorn looked at her again closely, beyond the scars and her bright eyes. He wondered how old she was.

"There are usually about three hundred girls waiting. Only one is allowed on the steps each day. Boys enter by the Main Gate. They follow a different path."

"Show me these steps."

Thorn followed Cass around a dimly lit path as the singing got louder. Thorn heard an odd sort of harmony. Some phrases were repeating on different cycles than others. Words blended, preventing him from understanding any but feeling all. There was magic in them.

Before the base of the stairs came into view, a pool of water bordered on the right. It was held in by a thick, head-height wall, so they didn't even see it until they had reached the base of the stairs. It was smooth as glass and reflected the braziers that lined to the path so perfectly it looked like a whole other world inverted.

Every step had a novice standing upon it. Over every novice was a lamp and this lamp illuminated words carved on the wall. They were the words to the song they sang.

Thorn could not read these words or understand the songs.

"The song changes for them after three steps. The two novices above teach the new song to the novice below," Cass said as they watched. "The songs are lessons. It makes them easier to remember."

As the novices sang, each dipped a small pitcher into a basin that was carved into the stone wall and poured the water into the next basin up. Water flowed up into the mountain with the songs.

"Each day they advance a step. It takes almost three years to reach the top," Cass said, as she took off her cloak and an outer layer. There were hundreds of pegs there, but not many cloaks. "We won't need these."

Thorn thought she would be right. With all the people in the stairwell, it would be warm. Add the exertion of climbing the steps for an hour, and they would be sweating before long.

"Why are there no guards?" Thorn asked looking about.

"The guards are up there. These girls represent no threat." She pointed into the stairwell. "Are you sure your wounds are ready for this?" Cass looked concerned again.

"I'm fine." He looked up the stairs tunnel far as he could see before it wound around. There was six feet of space for them behind the novice's backs.

"The first guard will be found with an acolyte in the Chamber of Questions at the top. He will see your weapons… and…" She faded off. "Past that I can show you the way to the High Vestal's chambers. But I do not know how you will pass."

"Leave that to me." He looked at the carved words and listened to the songs. "They will learn these lessons and remember them as songs?" He started up the stairs. "Someone will write a new song about this night."

Cass was hard pressed to keep up with Thorn. He seemed to drift up the stairs. His wide pant legs hid his feet and gave the illusions of floating. Long straight steps gave way to stretches of spiral stairs and sections of almost raw cave with knee-high steps.

None of the novices gave them so much as a glance. In about twenty minutes, Thorn reached a wide landing where a cavern opened to the side.

Cass got to the landing and caught her breath before speaking. "At the end of the day, the novices from below will rest here."

The stepping basins below fed into a broad pool here, and it fed the next set of novices.

Thorn cocked his head to each side, and his neck cracked, audible above the singing.

He turned and began the next set of steps.

Thorn waited longer for Cass on the next landing. She leaned over and rested her hands on her knees.

"Did you know that one of the magics instilled in me as a King's protector was the ability to read a person's intent?"

She shook her head no, still out of breath.

"There is evil intent above. I can already feel it." He looked in her eyes. "Peck said to trust no one." He moved closer, as if floating. Cass was unable to see his feet. "He knew it was already a foundation belief of mine... I think he was talking about you. Yet you have never really lied to me. But I cannot measure omission."

He didn't wait for a reply. He headed up.

As Cass struggled up the final curve in the steps, Thorn was not in sight. She passed the final novice, went past the last of the dorms and entered an ancient door, the same one the next novice expected to pass through at midnight in a few hours.

A long hallway lined with candle lanterns led to a round high-domed room. The floor was a vast iron grate with intricate mosaic patterns of two-inch square holes with darkness below.

Thorn was there. At his feet was the guard and the female acolyte, both headless. The blood was a stark contrast against her formal vestments.

When Cass was about to speak, Thorn held up a hand and stopped her.

"Tell me only where I need to go."

"Through that door and down a long hall. You will see a large room with two wide staircases, and either one will take you to the vast library down the corridor. The spiral staircase in the great library will take you to the High Vestal's chambers."

"You have done enough. Go back now while you can. They know I'm coming."

With that, Thorn was moving. It was unnerving to watch. The motion he made with his sword sent an arc of blood in a circle, and the sash at his belt wiped the rest as he sheathed his sword. As he walked, his feet could not be seen in his formal black robes. The wide legs of the pants were silent.

He looked as if he was being drawn across ice by an invisible rope around his waist.

Like a ghost, in black, he faded around the next corner. Cass followed, and when she entered the high foyer, only seconds later, she found four more dead guards. One still stood without a head and fell backward slowly like a great tree.

She saw Thorn ascending the staircase on the left. He was so calm and expressionless. She watched the ten guards gather at the mouth of the centered hallway at the intersection.

He stopped and bowed formally to the soldiers.

And he waited.

Most of them were nervous and already had their swords drawn. A single soldier, wearing the uniform of the Captain of the guard, stepped forward to face Thorn.

For a long moment, they stood facing each other, three paces apart.

Cass watched carefully.

With lightning speed, the Captain drew his sword, but never got to use it because his torso was bisected diagonally. His sword arm was severed at the shoulder, and his head flew over the railing.

She missed it in the blink of an eye. The heat of the strike's magic rose above his sword now.

Thorn was now standing frozen in a peaceful pose with his sword extended to the right. Blood dripped from its tip. It had all happened in less than an instant.

The other nine men were well trained. In formation, they rushed him.

Thorn danced into the center of them, never stopping at any single point. Heads were dropping to the floor as he went. Cass didn't hear blades cross once.

Only one remained standing. He was six paces behind Thorn. Thorn swirled his sword, and Cass saw the blood arc away again. He slowly turned toward the last remaining guard.

Thorn said something to him, but Cass could not hear his words or the guard's reply. The guard bent over and picked up the sword of one of his fallen comrades.

With a sword in each hand, he advanced quickly. The swords were moving in circles so fast they were invisible, whistling vortexes of death.

Thorn stepped aside, and the guard's leg was severed just below the knee. Before he could fall, Thorn was behind him. A two-handed blow bisected the man's head, neck, and torso all the way to his navel.

He fell forward off Thorn's blade, still in one piece.

By the time she had reached the top of the stairs, Thorn was gone again.

Cass paused over Captain Rankin's body for a moment. She was incredulous.

She gingerly walked around. The pool of blood was spreading. A waterfall of blood was beginning to slide off the balcony under the rails to the room below.

The long hall was empty. The doors at the end of the corridor to the library were open. There were ten crossbow bolts stuck into the wooden floor in the opening. Cass was at the door in time to see Thorn running at the wall and leap up. His feet lightly touched book shelves until he easily reached the balcony above and swung himself over the rail.

The guards there were gathered around the single ornate, black iron, spiral staircase. The guard on that end desperately tried to reload his crossbow. He was run through the heart and was carried along by Thorn, impaled on the sword, around the corner of the balcony and toward the other soldiers.

The dead soldier was bristling with crossbow bolts before they reached the other soldiers that were gathered at the base of the spiral stairs. This group was a mix of spearmen and swordsmen. Some wore heavy armor and some light chain mail. She saw all the spearheads fly off and then men began to drop.

They were all dead moments later.

As Thorn started up the spiral stairs to the next level, he paused and looked down at Cass.

His face momentarily shifted from blank to a veil of sadness. He nodded and moved on.

When Cass reached the top of the stairs, she could see the two guards outside the High Vestal door were dead and the beautifully carved doors were broken open.

Beyond the doors she could see Thorn in profile, standing at rest, as if he had just strolled up to the office. Both his swords were sheathed, and his arms were crossed over his chest.

He looked to his right. Directly at Cass.

He was waiting for her.

Out of breath, she slowly entered the room. Looking carefully around the corner, Cass saw a silver-haired woman at the far end of the room, standing behind a grand desk covered with maps and open volumes of all sizes. She was dressed in the formal habit of the High Vestal.

There was a huge man standing between Thorn and the desk in the center of the massive, book shelf lined room.

The silver-haired woman spoke first.

"Cass, I am surprised to see you. When we heard he was here, we were sure you were dead or worse."

She spoke in a tone as if they were in a garden having tea.

"I hope that..." the silver-haired woman began, but her words were cut off by a rapid clash of steel on steel. The guard had attacked. His first blow had been blocked by Thorn's sword before it was even out of the scabbard. The second strike was deflected by Thorn's second sword.

Both men now had two swords drawn, and they moved in the same ghostly way, circling. Cass could not tell who initiated the next rapid clash. Steel touched steel, deflecting, whirling, the swords moving so fast they were nearly invisible.

The men froze.

They were statues, posed as if to honor the war arts. Moments went by.

"Please, forgive me." Thorn said to the man, twice his size, who moved first.

He was suddenly disassembled. One sword hand and then the other. His right leg at the thigh and then his head was cut in half diagonally between the eyes, across his face--all done before his first severed hand landed on the floor.

Thorn was not even breathing hard.

He visibly relaxed and stood upright at ease. With his swords still dripping with blood, he turned and walked to the front of the desk.

He cleaned the blood off the swords and laid both on the desk, centered on a large map of the region.

Thorn spoke to the silver-haired woman. She had a line of blood spatter on her regal habit of high office. "On this day, you, ma'am have been the bravest of all."

He smiled at her.

"You may go now," Thorn said and turned his back to her.

6. The High Vestal

THE WOMAN WITH SILVER HAIR fled the room past Cass who now stood in the center looking down at the disassembled man.

"How long have you known I was the High Vestal?" Cass asked Thorn.

"I thought I had my answer at the Elder Bridge. The High Vestal Mother had sent villains to murder me in the darkness." Thorn relaxed more. "I have known since you walked into the room with that tray in Peck's Halfway. You see, I too am well trained in the use of poisons. You had a tray full."

He stared at Cass. His face was blank.

"Why didn't you end me then? Why wait until now?" she asked him.

"End you? I didn't come here to end you. I came here with a confession for the High Vestal Mother. I did not expect to meet her at Peck's Halfway. Then I thought I'd have my absolution if you murdered me, finally finishing that massacre." He crossed his arms over his chest and leaned back on the desk. "But when you didn't, a new question remained. I could tell all the things you said were the truth. But I also know it is far easier to deceive with the truth."

Cass walked around the desk and sat in the great chair. "Ask then."

"Why did you want the King dead?"

"Because he was evil. The world is far better without him." She looked him in the eyes. "I'll not change my answer to avoid your vengeance. Even if it costs my life, the world is better."

Thorn let out a great sigh.

"Your men failed." Thorn paused. "Ramos was their best swordsman and was my equal. He killed four of my brothers. He was severely wounded. Brother Saris and I dispatched the rest and eventually restrained him before my King.

"The King said to him. 'You have fought well, my son. Tell me your name and your family so that I can send you home to them with honor.' And Ramos told him." Thorn could not meet her eyes. "And when he was done the King laughed. Instead of a quick, honorable death, the King stabbed him in the stomach, spilling his bile and his intestines. A slow death for man as strong as Ramos."

Thorn briefly closed his eyes, remembering.

"While Ramos lay slowly dying the King told him how he was going to send troops to his home to rape, torture and burn his family at the stake along with their whole village."

Cass's hand went to her mouth.

"Saris and the King began to laugh… So, I killed them. Saris first."

She stared at Thorn in shock.

"I killed the King."

There was a long pause as Thorn watched the pieces of the puzzle align in her eyes.

"I brought Ramos a merciful death after I told him that his family would be safe and cared for. He died with honor. He knew his goal had been achieved."

Cass paced the room and finally stood, the desk between them.

Thorn continued, "When you came to me at Peck's Halfway, I thought you didn't want my chaos and violence brought to the Keep. The High Vestal Mother would know what I could do. Know I could not be stopped, even wounded."

Cass was thinking, her brow heavily creased.

"When you brought me to the Keep I knew why."

"Why?" She asked.

"These were not bodyguards, they were jailers," he said. "You used me to kill them. They did not belong here. I could feel it. You were in exile a mere day's ride away." He closed his eyes again. "I never knew Peck could be so brave."

Her chin trembled. "I knew what you did for Ramos. But not why. You could not have found his parents without speaking to him," she said. "The Queen… she was…"

"When they finally broke the door of the Cathedral down I was alone. I was surrounded by the dead. I was drenched in blood. The room covered in frost." His eyes were still closed. "I kept expecting someone to stop me, to strike me down. They never did. They let me just walk away. The curse, it seemed, was to live."

She finished her circuit around the desk and now stood between Thorn and his swords. Slowly she moved closer to him.

He studied her face. The scar in her right eyebrow, the worry lines of her eyes, the flecks of gold in the brown of her iris.

She turned back to the desk and lifted the short sword. She stood face to face with Thorn, grasped his red sash, and cleaned his sword again in one slow motion. She looked at the blade and marveled at its beauty. She studied the grain of the steel, and its balance in her hand before sliding it into its sheath. He had grown still as a statue. She repeated the cleaning with the long sword.

She paused this time to study the staghorn handle, its natural polish and beauty. She slowly slid it home.

"Are you injured?"

"Not much," he said, as he began to relax finally. "Are there any others that you require I kill this day?"

"There is a garrison above with just over three hundred men, not including the boys." She looked at the man on the floor. "But there are only three more of these." She locked eyes with him again. "You've already ruined my favorite rug." A corner of her mouth rose.

"Oops." His eyes flashed his smile.

7. The Queen of Lies

"It was the new Queen all along," Thorn said, as Cass searched her library, hurrying. "I now believe she seduced King Reddick, murdered his wife, and later his only heir." He held his hand out to stop her searching for emphasis. "Then she manipulated you to use your influence to kill the King." She drew away from him as if he burned her.

"And then she stole from me all that I had," Cass fumed. "I was not in the Keep when it fell. By the time I got to Peck's they had held the Keep."

"Not for much longer," Thorn said.

Cass showed Thorn maps of the keep.

"The main hall here is several levels up from where we are." He pointed to the corridor on the same level as the upper Keep. "The barracks are here. The Main Gate is here and the officer's quarters are here."

"One of the guardians is always on duty here, in the watch tower. The top is enclosed in glass, and the fire burns there continuously. It can be seen for miles," Cass said. "The level just below is the…" she hesitated, "the portal room."

Thorn nodded. Cass was relieved she did not have to explain the significance of it to him.

"Is it a circular room with thirty-two doors? How many doors are unlocked? Do you know where they go?"

Cass brought out another map. It showed a beautifully rendered ink drawing of the Keep, including the Watchtower.

"This makes sense now. How many portals from the tower access the Keep? There are usually at least two." He was studying the map. It had the interior of the two levels of the Watchtower. One was windowless and had thirty-two doors depicted. Only six were marked.

"These two. One goes to the tower at the Main Gate, and one comes to this office." Cass pointed to a block of cells on another map. "But there is a third portal. It goes to a different circular room. It's how they got in at the beginning. That path has not been used for hundreds of years."

"The doors locked from the other side are lost to us." She shivered and looked at him. She could see her breath. "Are you all right?" She noticed a cut in his tunic.

"I'm fine." He pointed to the portal room and one of the marked doors. "Where does this one go?"

Cass sighed and straightened her spine, making a decision. She walked from behind her massive desk and over to the built-in bookcase beside the large fireplace. The shelves were covered with various relics instead of books.

She reached up and pressed a spot on the end of the mantle and pushed the shelf inward at the same time. It swung in.

"They didn't know about this one." She took a candle in with her and lit an oil lamp on a shelf.

It was more like a short hallway six yards deep and three wide. The opposite end had a simple, rectangle door frame, carved with runes in deep relief. The dark wood timbers that made the frame were a foot thick on a side. The door was the same dark wood, bound with black iron. The hinges were on the left, always on the left.

"You've seen these before?" Cass asked.

"Yes. I have used them many times. There is a bridge room, a portal room, in the capital. I have seen two others."

"I have only used this one portal. From here to the Watchtower and to the Main Gate. The ancient sorcerers that created the network of portals left us no clue how to open them." She hugged herself thinking what was on the other side. "We can't wait long. The word may spread quickly."

Thorn nodded. He was ready.

Cass reached up and retrieved a key from its hiding place on top of the carved frame. Thorn shook his head as she unlocked the door. She handed the key to Thorn and pulled on the great ring.

There was a stone wall on the other side.

Cass stared. "They locked the other side. How?"

"The Queen. Thorn pushed the door closed and looked at the frame. With his left hand, he reached inside the slit in his tunic and brought out bloody fingers. He began to paint the black relief areas around a particular rune. After a half a dozen applications the rune was completely surrounded by his blood.

It began to glow with a faint light from within the grain of the wood.

Thorn twisted the rune.

He pulled the thick iron ring and revealed another door where the wall was moments ago. "Beyond this door is another hall the same size as this?"

Cass nodded, still speechless.

"Stay here until I come back for you," Thorn said as he pushed open the other door.

Thorn disappeared into the darkness beyond the door.

She stared into the darkness and saw the far door open into the circular portal room. That door swung into the chamber as well.

Thorn moved silently to the right and disappeared from her line of sight. The far door remained open and showed the thick column in the center with the open spiral staircase that wound around it. The torches all burned between each door. Thirty-two doors. Thirty-two torches. Always burning with Earth magic that even she didn't understand.

When she saw Thorn begin to ascend the stairs around the column, she moved forward. She gently, quietly, closed the door behind her as she entered. She knew it wouldn't lock.

The room was warmer, and all she could hear was the flutter of the torch flames.

Then there were voices, calm and strong, but she could not understand what they were saying.

Cass started up the spiral stairs. The column was thick, and the stairs were narrow and went one and a half times around the stone cylinder as she approached the opening in the domed ceiling.

They were still talking.

Cass carefully looked over the edge of the floor to see both men standing in the bright light of the round chamber. Thorn was standing casually relaxed, with his swords in his sheaths. She had seen that posture before. She knew it was a trap, ready to spring.

The Guardian was naked to the waist and soaked in sweat. He had been practicing sword forms. His sweaty long black hair was dripping wet in a pony-tail. His large, double-edged, two handed broad sword was pointed at Thorn.

"Do you miss the touch of a true blade, Thorn?" He taunted, "The soft feel of it as it stands up in your hands? It's the difference between the fine daughter of nobles and a pock-faced farm girl."

In a blaze of speed, the Guardian attacked. The sword that had been pointing at Thorn an instant ago was arcing around to come down in a devastating downward cut that would have been impossible to deflect with all the power in it.

Except Thorn was no longer there.

Cass had not seen Thorn move in close and pass just to the Guardian's side. She had not seen him draw or strike.

The Guardian's sword struck the floor as his momentum made him fall forward in two bloody pieces, completely cleaved just below the ribcage.

Thorn was like a frozen statue for a heartbeat.

The Guardian tried to drag himself across the floor for a few seconds before death found him. Thorn's eyes were watching Cass, as she ascended into the room.

The room had the single column in the center that rose twenty-five feet where the flame began and rose another twenty feet above that. The wall around the room was twelve feet high. The glass dome was above that wall.

This room was hot. The cold air was being drawn up from the level below with the vented chimney effect from the massive flame.

She looked at the body. "Two down. Two to go?"

"Yes. But the others will not be so easy. I have met them. They are the Queen's Guardians. The best and most vicious of them." Thorn cleaned and sheathed his sword.

"What will we do next?" Cass asked.

"We wait here. The changing of the watch is within the hour. With luck, they will come to me one at a time, here."

8. Sharkey

THEY HAD TO WAIT JUST TEN MINUTES.

Cass had ascended the single narrow stairs. They were barely stairs, more like rocks that were mortared to protrude a foot out from the wall. She walked around the top of the wall to the other side where the guardian would see her as well as the body. They hoped the distraction would be long enough. Thorn would be behind the column as he entered.

As he appeared casually coming up the steps, he said, "Hello, Thorn." He didn't seem to notice the dead guardian or Cass at all. "Word has come up from the lower levels of your visit." The huge defender had full chain mail and heavy ornate, lobster-like, articulating plates on his chest, back, and shoulders. There was already a double bladed ax in one hand and a double-edged sword in the other.

"Hello, Sharkey." Thorn used his nickname from his youth, knowing he hated it. "Been keeping yourself busy, I hear, killing the weak, and being the Queen's whore."

Thorn could see one of those insults hit the mark.

"Did Arnor and Viktor die well?" Sharkey asked as he topped the stairs. He was still thirty feet away, not looking at Thorn.

"They have been training. I was impressed." Thorn lied. "I didn't think Viktor could get any taller, but he seems to have managed."

"Yes..." Sharkey moved with incredible speed, throwing the ax at Thorn in a deadly horizontal spinning flight, "...he has."

Thorn barely had time to draw his short sword and deflect the ax from ripping into his chest. Sharkey crossed the distance and was swinging a double hand overhead blow with blinding speed. Thorn's left hand was numb from the impact with the ax. When his automatic defense of the next death blow reacted with both swords, it was too much. While the swing was deflected, Thorn lost the grip on the short sword. It spun away toward the wall.

Neither was speaking now. The fire roared above as they circled each other. Their sword tips pointed at each other's hearts, but their swords were a foot apart. They stopped rotating with Sharkey between Thorn and his short sword.

They stood still for a few moments before Sharkey spoke. "I heard you carried farmer blades, but I had no idea they were kitchen wives fish knives."

"Fish knives for Sharkey," Thorn said and attacked. A dozen strikes were parried with the same speed they were delivered. The ringing steel was impossibly loud. Thorn retreated in an attempt to draw him away from his short sword.

It didn't work.

Sharkey never looked away from Thorn as he hooked his toe under the blade, flipped it up to his left hand and threw it at Cass where she stood on the wall. She barely dodged it, but it struck the glass point first and shattered the foot square pane of glass, passing into the darkness beyond.

"That was your only chance, Thorn." Sharkey smiled. "You don't have the reach, strength or stamina to take me now. You rely too much on your draw tricks and surprise."

Without a word, Thorn advanced and avoided Sharkey's swing instead of meeting or deflecting it. Instantly he was inside Sharkey's guard, inside his arms, spinning to face away, his back to Sharkey's front.

Thorn's sword did not slash. Its point entered Sharkey just below his chest plate and moved upward through his guts, his stomach, his heart and then protruded out just to the left of his neck.

Thorn released his sword, leaving it inside the man. All four of their hands now firmly held the grip of Sharkey's sword. Thorn need only let death take hold.

Sharkey released the sword and clamped his iron hands on Thorn's neck. Thorn dropped it and was trying to pry his fingers off.

Then Cass was there.

She had rushed down, and instead of helping Thorn pry at fingers she grabbed the handle of Thorn's sword and began to twist and wrench it savagely side to side. A great gout of blood burst from Sharkey's mouth, and he fell backward.

The sword slid out of him as he fell.

Thorn was having trouble breathing. He also had a large wound from his hip to his knee. He choked out. "Help me. Up there." He gestured with his chin to the stairs to the top of the wall. They were so narrow she could not help him up.

Standing below, holding his bloody sword she watched him reach the top and turn to the massive flame. His arms extended out, and his chin rose.

The glass behind Thorn began to frost. The great roaring jet of flame leaned toward him.

The room was becoming cold.

Thorn let out a scream of agony as he absorbed the power. It looked like his body was full of magma, glowing in his screaming mouth and the cracks of his wounds, as they began to close.

The gashes healed and the bruises disappeared as his scream faded.

The flame returned to normal. The frost on the glass melted from its heat.

Thorn collapsed to his knees.

Thorn never lost consciousness, but it was close. He was about to fall over when Cass was by his side, holding his face in both hands.

His focus returned as he exhaled a breath he did not know he was holding.

"Thorn, say something. What did you do?" Cass pleaded.

He looked into her eyes.

"I don't suppose you happen to have any food with you?" he said in a hoarse voice, as he smiled and began to stagger to his feet.

He looked down at himself. His clothes were bloody rags.

Cass handed him his sword, and he automatically cleaned it and slid it into the scabbard. He drew the short scabbard out and dropped it. He adjusted his clothes and tightened his belt.

"The last one will be Torrock," Thorn said. "Even fully healed I may not be able to overcome him. Sharkey and the others were always too proud, too certain of their prowess. Not Torrock. He is the most cautious and brutal of all."

"What will you do?" Cass was checking his flesh. Wounds that had been there were completely gone.

"When Sharkey does not return with my head, he will come here," Thorn said.

"Hello?" a voice called from the stairwell below. "My lord, Thorn… sir?" It was the voice of a boy. They proceeded down as he was emerging from below.

"I'm here, lad. Stay where you are. You don't need to see this," Thorn said, as he reached the same level.

"That is the best sight I've seen in weeks, sir." The boy was surveying the two dead bodies. "Your day's not done yet, I hate to say. Master Torrock sent me to tell you he awaits you."

"Where is he?" Cass asked.

"He is standing in the inner courtyard. Waiting."

"What's your name, son?" Thorn asked.

"My name is Penn, sir."

"Lead the way, Penn." Thorn gestured. "You don't happen to have any food do you?"

9. Torrock

THE PORTAL they took accessed a room in the guard tower at the Main Gate. It was a brilliant placement for strategic reasons. An impossible number of men could flow out of that portal to man the gate to the surprise of any intruders there.

When Thorn went from the tower to the battlements, he could see Torrock standing alone below. He was in brightly polished, full plate armor, head to toe. He held a large torch aloft as he waited. On seeing Thorn emerge, he turned and entered the keep via massive double doors.

Penn ran down the steps that went from the battlements to the courtyard and followed the receding torchlight through the open doors.

When Thorn entered the main hall, the light was receding down a corridor at the other end. They continued to follow the light as it moved through the keep, down stairs, through feast halls, armories, and eventually into a long wide corridor with cells on either side. Torrock had placed the torch on the wall in its place and waited. Two swords were drawn. They were medium length. He was still as a statue.

The helmet he wore had only a slit in front for vision.

"I remember sparring with you, Torrock. Even blindfolded." Thorn spoke low and even casually, as if they were having lunch. "You disdained armor as much as I did." Thorn entered the pool of light, his sword already drawn and raised over his head. He drifted across the floor in an eerie motion.

Torrock didn't move.

"I will allow you to divest the armor unmolested. Then we shall see what kind of swordsman you have become." Thorn paused out of range. The guttering sound of the torch was all the sound there was.

Torrock's armor bristled with sharp blades. His shoulders, forearms, biceps, elbows and knees all had fixed, shining knives as part of the bright, horrible beauty of his armor. Torrock remained silent.

"Have you become so ugly you cannot even reveal your face?" Thorn's attempts to anger him might as well have landed on deaf ears. Thorn began to slowly circle him to the right, when he could see past Torrock into the open cell beyond.

There was an open portal arch in there on the back wall.

"She wants to speak with you…" Before Torrock could finish his sentence, Thorn struck. There was a blur of strikes, counterstrikes parries and hits to armor, when suddenly, as fast as it started, Thorn's blade was shattered by opposing strikes between Torrock's swords and Thorn's left bicep was impaled on a forearm blade.

Thorn screamed but never stopped moving.

He tore his bicep clean through as he spun and stabbed the remaining twelve inches of his sword into Torrock's eye slit.

Torrock fell like an avalanche of blades. His helmet wrenched the sword handle from Thorn's grip. He used his right hand to hold his left arm together.

He turned toward Cass; Penn was still by her side. "Stay here. Penn, make sure she doesn't follow me." The corridor was getting cold.

As Thorn passed, he pulled the remains of his sword from Torrock's helm. He moved directly into the portal.

10. Once Damned

THORN PASSED THROUGH THE DOOR into another round room of closed doors. Sunlight shone down the spiral stair in the center. He ascended into a warm, opulent suite. The architecture and daylight was completely different. There was a large living area full of rich carpets, lounges, and piles of pillows. Decadent was the only word in his mind. Every wall was floor-to-ceiling windows that looked out on a tropical beach on one side and lush jungle on the other.

Trailing blood as he went, he carefully moved through a dining room, a library, and a bedroom with an enormous finely carved bed. Beyond this, he found the Queen.

Aleena was in a bath chamber. She relaxed in a pool up to her chin in water. A fire blazed in the hearth nearby.

"I don't like to be kept waiting," she pouted as Thorn stood in the doorway. He leaned on the frame so he would not fall. "Why did you bother to bring that? You won't be able to use it. Not after what you did to my poor husband."

Thorn could already feel the compulsion to drop the sword. He focused on the pain and stood straight. He stepped forward. The closer he came, the more he knew he would be unable to bring the steel to her flesh, the spell was so strong.

He began to feel something else.

Queen Aleena rose up out of the water to stand with her arms along the edge of the pool, her breasts now exposed, barely out of the water. Thorn could see runic symbols tattooed on her skin, her breasts, and the undersides of her arms.

He was becoming aroused.

"Yes. Thorn the damned. I am going to take you as you bleed. Again and again. Take sex from you as you scream. Because you will not be able to stop me. Now bring that pot of hot water here to warm my pool."

He focused on the pain. He went to the pot heating over the fire. He had paused before he upended it, extinguishing the blaze.

"I like defiance. I took the King, I took his son, I took all the Royal Guardians," she gloated.

He stepped to the edge of the pool.

"I dominated them all, just as I will you. Because it is only worth the trouble if they are lions…"

He stepped into the water, onto the first stair, ankle deep. Through gritted teeth, he spoke.

"Once Damned. Always Damned."

He drove the broken blade into his own leg, just above the knee and ripped an enormous wound straight up through his thigh to his hip. This was followed by several lightning stabs into his other thigh.

The Queen was laughing.

He carved three slashes down his chest and finally stabbed the shattered blade deep into his own heart.

The Queen laughed at his decision. "Suicide over seduction?" she laughed as the broken blade finally fell to the floor.

As Thorn's arms came up, his back arched, and his mouth opened in a scream.

The water instantly froze, trapping her. His wounds began to glow as if lava were about to spill out. Frost covered the room as he screamed the endless stream of agony and despair. The queen began to panic and tried to rise, but it was too late; she ceased moving. A light frost crept up her flesh. Her mouth was frozen open in a silent gasp. Her eyes glazed white.

Thorn was a silent statue now as well. Arms held wide as the inner glow began to fade before the wounds had closed.

Drawn by his howl, Cass burst into the room. The room was so cold, clouds of her breath instantly crystallized and fell like snow. Grasping the scene, she rushed to the fireplace. It was a block of ice. She grabbed the huge iron poker. It was so cold it burned her hands. Moving across the room at a run, she swung with both hands and shattered the queen's head into tiny pieces. Her frozen jaw remained grotesquely attached to the stump of her neck.

Cass kept moving until she reached her true goal. She swung and shattered the window.

"Quickly! Break the glass!" she yelled to Penn. Moving along the wall, she broke window after floor-to-ceiling window. Penn went the opposite way, using a bronze statue, grabbed along the way. "All of them!"

The tropical breeze flowed in from the seaside. An icy fog flowed out the other side.

Thorn was glowing inside again.

Thorn awoke, crawling back from oblivion slowly, his mind empty. His eyes fluttered open and were presented with a warm, rich scene. Dark oak beams that covered the ceiling were illuminated by a roaring fire in a beautiful hearth. The tapestries on the walls depicted a horse race over a lovely countryside of fields, rolling hills, and hedges to jump.

As he turned his head, he noticed that on each of the four walls the race traversed four seasons as well. When he turned toward the winter scenes, his gaze fell on a pale-skinned shoulder. A scarred shoulder.

He carefully moved to face her back. His left arm wrapped around her as the memories washed over him. The realization that his severed bicep was healed was his only fleeting thought of the past as he kissed the nape of her neck. The past and the future were lost in the scent of her, the warmth of her.

She started as she became aware.

She turned quickly to look into his eyes. She touched his face as if to make sure he was real. "Are you all right…" was all she could choke out before tears began to flow.

He kissed her mouth in answer. The salt of her tears was the best thing he had ever tasted.

"I took you to the Watchtower." She was having difficulty talking past the lump in her throat. "You soaked in the magic in for nine days. It was the wound to your heart that took the longest to heal." She buried her face in his neck. "I was so afraid. Then, yesterday, you sighed and seemed just to be sleeping again. We brought you to my quarters in the keep."

Over her shoulder, he could see the recovered two staghorn handles of his swords. Both blades were broken, but the handles were intact.

This made Thorn smile.

"Are the portals secure? The portal rooms?"

"Yes. Thanks to you," she said to his neck. "The Capital is in chaos, the High Houses all vying for the Throne."

"Do you happen to have any food?"

She laughed, and it was like music.

ABOUT THE AUTHORS

David Keener is an author, editor, artist and public speaker who lives in Northern Virginia. He writes science fiction, fantasy and mystery but loves the idea of mashing up his favorite genres in new and (hopefully) unexpected ways, as demonstrated in stories such as *An Unlikely Hero Road* and *The Whispering Voice*. Rumor has it that he may be work on a hard-SF zombie story.

He is the anthologist behind the *Worlds Enough* anthology series, and co-editor of the first volume, *Fantastic Defenders*. He and Donna Royston are currently producing a new anthology, *The Forever Inn*, about a magical inn that appears throughout the multiverse.

He frequently speaks at conferences and conventions. Find out more about him at his web site: http://www.davidkeener.org

On the day **Jeff Patterson** was born, the United Nations announced that the world's population had reached three billion. So he figures that was him.

Jeff's dabbled in science fiction most of his life, starting with *Space: 1999* fanfic back in the 70's, and culminating in being a regular contributor to the two-time Hugo-award-winning SF Signal website. He is also the co-host of *The Three Hoarsemen* podcast.

Jeff is the author of two books under his Bad Day Studio imprint: *Solstice Chronicles*, a collection of other-worldly holiday stories, and *Don't Tweet Where You Eat.* His far-future hard SF space opera story, "War Ghosts," appeared in *Reliquary*, an anthology of stories on the theme of relics.

Donna Royston particularly enjoys writing about people who are not quite what they seem. Her first story about Sun Ch'o was published in the *Copperfield Review* and was reprinted in *Uncommon Threads* in 2015. She is also the co-editor of *Fantastic Defenders* and is currently working with David Keener to produce a new anthology called *The Forever Inn.*

David A. Tatum was born in Ithaca, NY, the son of a librarian father and a fabric artist mother. Surrounded by books and artwork all his life, but hopeless as an artist, he decided to become an author. Now he publishes his science fiction and fantasy works through his own imprint, Fennec Fox Press, as well as his mother's books on fabric art and quilting.

Martin Wilsey is a writer, hunter, photographer, rabble rouser, father, friend, marksman, story teller, frightener of children, carnivore, engineer, fool, philosopher, cook and madman. He and his wife Brenda live in Virginia where, just to keep him off the streets, he works as a research scientist for a government funded think tank.

Martin is the author of the popular science fiction trilogy, *The Solstice 31 Saga,* as well as several short stories. He is also the editor of multiple anthologies, including *Silence of the Apoc* and *The Witness Paradox.*

www.ingramcontent.com/pod-product-compliance
Lightning Source LLC
Chambersburg PA
CBHW020600310726
48979CB00008B/1289/J
9781945994401